Julia Stagg lived in the Ariège-Pyrenees region of France for six years, where she ran a small auberge and tried to convince the French that the British can cook. Having done her bit for Anglo-Gallic gastronomic relations, she now divides her time between the Yorkshire Dales and the Pyrenees.

Julia keeps a website at www.jstagg.com

She can also be found on Twitter@juliastagg

A FÊTE TO REMEMBER

It's summertime in the French Pyrenees, and the mountain commune of Fogas is *en fête*. But Christian Dupuy has no time for the frivolity of *les vacances*. For a start he's just been struck by the arrows of *l'amour* and doesn't have a clue how to approach the woman who's stolen his heart. Then there is the not-so-small matter of local politics. With moves afoot to wipe his community from the map, Christian will have to enter the fray once more if he wishes to save the place he cherishes. In the midst of a sweltering heatwave, and with the residents of Fogas at each other's throats over their future, the lovesick and embattled deputy mayor is forced to decide if all really is fair in love and war.

Books by Julia Stagg
Published by Ulverscroft:

L'AUBERGE
THE PARISIAN'S RETURN
THE FRENCH POSTMISTRESS

JULIA STAGG

$\blacklozenge$

A
FÊTE TO
REMEMBER

Complete and Unabridged

CHARNWOOD
Leicester

First published in Great Britain in 2014 by
Hodder & Stoughton
London

First Charnwood Edition
published 2016
by arrangement with
Hodder & Stoughton
An Hachette UK company
London

A catalogue record for this book is available from the British Library.

ISBN 978–1–4448–2711–8

Published by
F. A. Thorpe (Publishing)
Anstey, Leicestershire

Set by Words & Graphics Ltd.
Anstey, Leicestershire
Printed and bound in Great Britain by
T. J. International Ltd., Padstow, Cornwall

This book is printed on acid-free paper

Pour mes soeurs, Ellen et Claire

For letting me be your shadow
and for singing me to sleep.

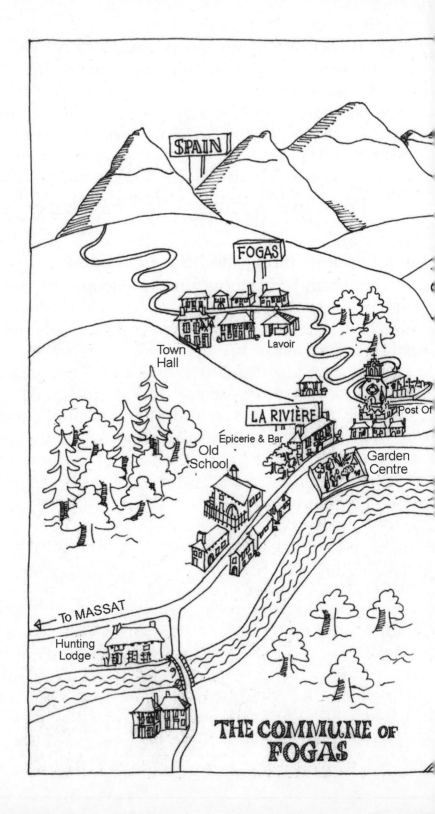

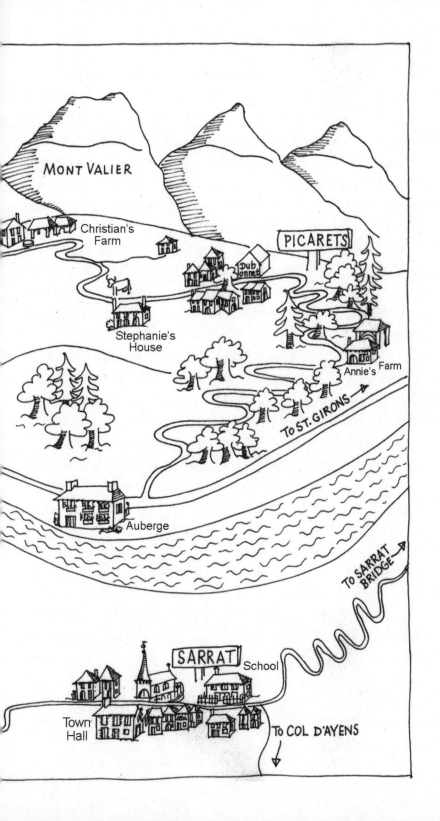

1

Christian Dupuy woke up dead. He knew he was dead because his skull was split in two, each side throbbing mercilessly, his limbs were leaden lumps of meat and his eyes were glued shut. As for his tongue, it was cleaved to the roof of his mouth by a foul-tasting layer of fur, rendering him incapable of producing anything more eloquent than a burbling death rattle.

No one could endure this and still be living. Therefore, he had to be dead.

He lay there, the sunshine spearing through the shutters stinging his eyelids and the call of the cockerel grating on his fragile nerves. Then his stomach roiled and a groan escaped his parched throat.

Alive then. But only just.

Moving cautiously, he stretched out an arm, feeling the familiar lumps of his aged mattress beneath him. So he'd made it as far as his bed. Alone. Nothing new there. And he was still dressed, his shirt twisted and tight around his massive chest like a shrunken shroud.

The cockerel crowed again and he cowered, hands moving to cover his ears. He needed to close the shutters. Or find a gun. But either option involved standing up, and right now that was out of the question.

He reached across to the bedside table, fumbling for his watch. It must be late. There was warmth already in the rays of sunlight touching his body. Peeling open an eyelid, he struggled to focus as a stab of pain seared his retina.

Seven-thirty. Time to get up.

He let the watch fall to his chest; his arm dropped to his side and his eyes closed. He was in no condition to work. Christ. How the hell had he got into this state?

They'd been celebrating. A big party for Bastille Day and the reopening of the post office all rolled into one. He remembered making a toast with champagne, could recall laughing at his fellow deputy mayor collapsed comatose next to the loudspeakers, and then bits of the meal, but not much more. Which was unlike him. He hadn't been this drunk since his sister's wedding, when he'd been woken up in the old orchard by a donkey nibbling his jacket. That had been nothing compared to this.

Through the haze of his hangover, he forced himself to concentrate until snapshots of memory came to him. René and Paul plying him with brandy in the gardens of the Auberge. Laughing as they held out yet another glass. And another. A slap on the back from Serge Papon in passing. And then, could it be right? A faltering image of dancing. Him? Under a big sheet of canvas that was slapping against its poles in the night-time breeze. The marquee. Had he been dancing in the marquee?

He groaned at the thought. What had it been? A high-tempo rhythm that had got him up on the makeshift stage doing a John Travolta. He,

2

who was as nimble as his Limousin bull on the dance floor. Almost as wide too.

Ah well. If that was the worst that had happened.

He took a deep breath, feeling queasy as soon as he did, a sense of unease rising up through his body on the crest of the nausea. There was something else about last night. They'd been trying to cheer him up. Yes, that was it. They'd been teasing him about being morose. Being a killjoy. Which was why he'd got up and danced, tired of their nagging. But what on earth had he been so depressed about?

And then it hit him. Like a sledgehammer to the solar plexus. His eyes flew open, his body jackknifed upright and a burning anguish coursed through his entire being, centring on his thumping heart and radiating out to every extremity, far worse than any hangover.

Christian Dupuy had just remembered. He was in love.

★ ★ ★

Love. There was nothing like it in the world. Even the exhilaration of an early morning bike ride up past the Dupuy farm, the Pyrenean peaks radiant in the rising sun, failed to equal the sheer thrill that Fabian Servat felt every time he looked at the woman lying in the bed before him. Red curls spilling over the pillow, her breathing soft and measured, she was beautiful. And she was his. Well, almost. If he could pick up the courage, she might be.

3

Discarding his towel on the floor, his skin still damp from his shower, he peeled back the sheet and lay down next to her. He spent every waking moment wondering at the marvel of Stephanie Morvan and the miracle that had brought them together. He tried not to think about how easy it would be for her to walk away. Tried not to think about the fact that she could do so much better than him.

She murmured as he pulled her body towards him, wrapping his angular frame around her soft curves. 'Morning,' he whispered.

'Ummm.' She turned, eyes barely open, a smile already on her lips. And then she snuggled into him.

Ask her! Now, while she was half-asleep. Ambush her before she had a chance to come to her senses and say no. Because that's what he feared most of all. That she would say no.

'Stephanie?'

'Ummm?' She gazed up at him, cheeks flushed, hair tousled, lips begging to be kissed.

'It's time to get up.'

Fabian's nerve had failed yet again. And he hated himself for it.

★　★　★

Sitting outside the bar in the morning sunshine that was flooding the valley floor, René Piquemal took a long drag on the first of the day's many Gauloises and exhaled on a sigh.

He was supposed to have quit. Again. But no matter what he did, he always seemed to end up smoking. And he was tired of it.

As if in accord, his stomach rumbled dangerously, the mixture of espresso and nicotine not a welcome one this morning. After the party last night, it was hardly surprising. A fair quantity of the brandy that had been intended to rouse a despondent Christian Dupuy had ended up being rerouted his way.

He stubbed out his cigarette, drained his coffee cup and turned his attention back to the newspaper. There was not much of interest. He'd hoped that their protest the day before over the closure of the post office might have made the front page, but that's what happened when you demonstrated on Bastille Day. All the journalists were on holiday and so nothing got reported properly.

On page six he finally found it. A good honest blockade of the Tour de France on the very day that was synonymous with revolution and it was consigned to a couple of paragraphs and a blurred photo. Ridiculous!

He threw down the paper in disgust. Which was how he noticed it. A small advertisement in the bottom right-hand corner.

'Ready to quit? Need a hand? Give us a call!'

He read it through twice, stroking his moustache in contemplation. It sounded so easy. Too easy? He reached for the packet of Gauloises. Might as well smoke the lot. Because this time he was going to give up for good.

★   ★   ★

Down the road, Lorna Webster couldn't believe her luck. She'd risen at six-thirty and started preparing the croissants and pains au chocolat, as she did every morning during the height of the tourist season. But today, a miracle had happened. For the first time since she'd fallen pregnant back in March, she hadn't felt sick. Not even when the flaky pastries had been pulled warm from the oven, the smell normally making her heave.

The sudden improvement in her condition was just as well. With every bedroom in the Auberge occupied and a fully booked lunchtime to prepare for, she was a busy woman. She glanced through the service hatch to the restaurant where breakfast was already under way, guests making the most of an early start to what was going to be another scorching summer day. Paul was discussing the best route up to the Spanish border with a couple from Toulouse who were dressed in hiking gear. He caught her eye and she grinned, giving him a thumbs up. And as she did so, she felt a fluttering in her stomach, like bubbles being blown through water.

The baby. She hadn't been sure the first time she'd experienced it. Thought it was just wind. But now she knew. Their child was moving around.

Raphaël. That was her latest suggestion. But Paul had vetoed it straight away, saying there was too much resonance with the cartoon ninja turtles of his youth. It was difficult. Choosing a name for a person who had yet to appear. And choosing one in a language that wasn't their own. For the one thing they had agreed upon was that they would opt for a French name rather than an English one. But what if they got it wrong? While their knowledge of the culture they'd been living in for nearly two years had grown immensely, they still weren't locals. What happened if they called him Sébastien and he turned out to be a Frédéric?

She flicked open the book of baby names that was never far from her reach these days.

Mathilde?

Pretty. But there was no point in looking at girls' names. Because Lorna knew without a doubt that the new life she was carrying inside her was a boy. What she didn't know was just how important his arrival would be.

★　★　★

No matter how much he desired it, Bernard Mirouze really wasn't cut out to be covert. There was the not-so-small matter of his bulky body to start with, Nature having granted him a physique more suited to sloth than stealth. Nor had he been blessed with the grace of movement so essential in all things clandestine. As he worked through his morning exercises in the copse behind his back garden, lumbering from tree to tree and then wriggling across the ground on his stomach in a grotesque parody of the man he sought to emulate, his furtive manoeuvres were accompanied by the crashing of branches, the rustle of undergrowth, and the odd curse. So it was that he proved easy to locate.

7

'Serge!' he exclaimed, a wet nose touching his cheek as he lay prone. 'How did you find me? Clever boy!'

He patted the warm back of the panting beagle and then noticed the mound of fur that had been deposited next to him on the ground.

'Another rabbit?' Bernard stood up and lifted the dead animal by the back legs, its head lolling, eyes staring blankly. 'Good dog! One more for the freezer.'

And without questioning why the beagle's offering felt cold to the touch despite its recent death, the aspiring tracker headed back to his house, his appetite whetted by thoughts of *lapin à la moutarde*. If only he had a wife to cook it for him.

* * *

As he was only a couple of houses further down the hill in the small mountain village, Pascal Souquet should have been able to hear his neighbour crashing through the trees as he practised his dark arts. But no. Even with the windows thrown wide to let in the last of the cool air before the temperature soared, the first deputy mayor couldn't discern a thing. Not the birds singing, not the whine of a distant chainsaw, not even the blaring horn of the butcher's van as it parked up opposite the disused *lavoir*. Neither could he make out what his wife was saying to him, although he could see her lips moving and presumed from the scowl on her sharp features that his sudden onset of deafness was, in this case, a blessing.

He rubbed his ears to no avail, hearing nothing but the high-pitched sound of a wet finger dragged around the rim of a glass. Knowing the cause must lie in the revels of the evening before, since he had suffered no affliction prior to that, he tried in vain to remember what had occurred. One minute he'd been raising a reluctant glass to celebrate the successful protest against La Poste, which had resulted in the reopening of the post office — a development he had no reason to rejoice in — and the next, he'd woken up on the sofa, head thick and muggy, ears not functioning. Given the mess he'd managed to get himself into over the last few months, perhaps it was no bad thing. Could they really send a man to prison if he was stone deaf?

His phone skittered across the kitchen table, the vibration telling him what his useless ears couldn't. He picked it up to study the display and his heart sank. It was *him*. The very man who had built the trap that Pascal was now enmeshed in. He stared at the screen until the caller hung up, deafness providing a reprieve. But for how long?

Well acquainted with the man concerned, Pascal Souquet knew it was immaterial. The deaf deputy mayor was in over his head and there was no way out.

*   *   *

At a mere distance of forty kilometres away to the north-east, but over such mountainous

9

terrain that rendered the journey at least an hour in good conditions and in a car more roadworthy than Christian Dupuy's old Panda 4×4, the medieval town of Foix was already astir. Capital of the department of Ariège, it was home to the *fonctionnaires*, the civil servants who were so essential to the running of the French Republic. And in a rather imposing building that clung to the rocks above the river that gave the department its name, they were at work.

Once the morning greetings and the obligatory espresso were out of the way, delivering the post was the first order of duty in the offices of the Préfecture. And in the bag today, which was lighter than normal thanks to the bank holiday the day before and the impending summer break for the month of August, lay an innocuous white envelope. Nestled among its beige padded compatriots, it gave no indication as to the impact it would have. And when a hand pulled it out of its resting place and left it on a pile of other missives that lay on the polished surface of a Louis XV desk, no one would have thought it important. It was addressed by hand. It lacked a stamp. But as the morning sunshine cut through the arched windows and burned across its surface, it was as though a fuse had been lit.

Because for the good people of the commune of Fogas, that sleepy community across the hills, which was slowly waking up from the excesses of the night before, this very letter was tantamount to a bomb about to be hurled among them.

2

You'd think it would be easy. Ten months in the place and he should really know his way around. But still he was frequently bewildered by the tangle of medieval streets and alleyways in the old town. Like today.

Having left the car at home, tempted to walk to work by the azure sky and the brilliant sunshine, he'd gone hopelessly astray. Somehow he'd ended up on Rue de la Comédie and had lost his bearings. In this part of Foix, the morning sun was of no use as a compass, hidden as it was behind the red rooftops of the four-storey houses that loomed over the narrow, cobbled streets below. He hadn't even been able to see the three towers of the castle, which sat imperiously on a rocky outcrop to the west. So when he'd glimpsed a sparkle of river down an alleyway, he'd headed for it, knowing that it would bring him safely to his destination, albeit the long way round.

Turning left as soon as he came to the banks of the Ariège, he'd followed Rue du Rival along the river until he emerged onto Place St Volusien, instantly distinguished from the many other squares in the town centre by the impressive stone abbey on its northern side. And round the corner from the abbey, he knew with some relief, were the gates of the Préfecture, where he worked. Where in fact he was the

Préfet, the State's representative for the department of the Ariège-Pyrenees, to give it its formal title. One of the youngest ever préfets in the history of the French Republic, a rising star in the ranks of the elite *fonctionnaires*, and Jérôme Ulrich couldn't even find his way to the office.

For the young man from Alsace, negotiating his way around the mountainous department for which he found himself responsible was almost as difficult, the Pyrenean valleys proving as confusing to tell apart as the twelfth-century streets that befuddled him even now. Jérôme scratched his head and stared once more at the map that covered the wall before him. Then he glanced back down at the letter he held in his hand.

Thanks to his unintentional tardiness, the cause of which had provoked much mirth among his colleagues, a pile of communications requiring his immediate attention had been waiting for him when he arrived. But this one had caught his eye. Lacking a stamp and addressed in a careful hand, the white envelope looked incongruous against the glossy walnut swirls of the ornate desk he'd inherited. It appeared spartan. Functional. Both attributes that he prized, having no fondness for the frills and fripperies that some equated with his position. As far as he was concerned, his first tenure as préfet would probably last no more than eighteen months to two years before he was moved on to something else, so he had little time for ostentatious nonsense if he intended to make his mark. Which he did. And this letter looked like the very thing that would help him do that.

With his finger, Jérôme traced the border of the place that the correspondence referred to. So small. A tiny commune hugging the border with Spain, it comprised three villages split across two valleys: Picarets and Fogas perched astride opposite mountain ridges, and La Rivière lying down below them on the valley floor. Together they made up the district of Fogas. And they were proving to be the bane of his life.

'How long would it take to drive there?'

His secretary scrunched up her face. 'About an hour?' She shrugged. 'I haven't been over there in years.'

Over there. She made it sound like it was another country. But then, looking at the terrain on the map, it was. Whereas Foix was built on limestone — all jagged crags and harsh backdrop sloping down to the Toulousain plain to the north — south-west Ariège, an area known as the Couserans, was a jumble of verdant valleys and soaring peaks. To those who lived there, it was the real Pyrenees.

'What appointments have I got this morning?'

'Nothing. It's nearly the summer break. All you have booked in is a call from the Director General of La Poste at two this afternoon. About the reopening of the post office. In Fogas.' She tipped her head at the map with a wry smile.

He grimaced. Fogas. Again. He'd spent most of yesterday, a national holiday and supposedly a day off, on the phone to various people, embroiled in the unexpected protest the commune had sprung in an effort to get their post office reopened.

The fact that they'd targeted the prestigious Tour de France meant their actions had reverberated at the highest levels. And he'd been caught up in the maelstrom. Which was perhaps why this letter held such interest for him. Not that he was the sort to extract revenge. But it had landed on his desk on a day when he wasn't naturally inclined to be benevolent towards a political district that was making so many waves. And which seemed so insignificant.

'I'll make sure I'm back for that.'

She stared at him. 'You're going to Fogas?'

'Yes, why?'

'Well, be careful,' she said, face serious. 'If you have trouble finding your way around here, goodness knows how you'll cope up in the mountains.'

He opened his mouth to reply but her next words forestalled him.

'And they have bears, you know!'

The door closed behind her and a hiss of air escaped his lips in frustration.

Of course he bloody knew they had bears! His entire term in office had been dominated by heated disputes over the government-sponsored reintroduction of the beasts in the mountains. And all of it centred in the accursed commune of Fogas.

Perhaps, he thought as he headed out into the hot sunshine, it was time to make sure that Fogas could cause no trouble ever again. Not for him. Nor for his successor.

★ ★ ★

If Jérôme Ulrich had difficulty navigating the streets of Foix, it appeared the satellite system in his car could fare no better in the wilds of the Couserans. Rather than taking him on the D117 all the way from Foix into St Girons, it had steered him across a more direct route. One that took no account of the terrain. He'd been jolted along back lanes barely a car wide and, for the last couple of kilometres, not even surfaced, and then the road had started climbing through a forest, the engine groaning at the effort as they went higher and higher. But when he reached the mountain pass known as the Col d'Ayens, suddenly the young préfet was glad his automatic map-reader had been foxed by the topography. For as he emerged from the trees into a small clearing, spread across the horizon in front of him was a long stretch of majestic peaks, their grey summits spiking into the serene sky.

He didn't think twice. He parked the car and got out. Nearly a year in the Ariège and he'd had no time to explore. He'd been rushed from meeting to meeting, liaising with police departments and fire brigades, overseeing memorial services and glad-handing local dignitaries. On top of that, he'd had to deal diplomatically with the incendiary situation caused by the presence of bears in these very forests; a situation that had literally gone up in flames despite his efforts to calm things down behind the scenes. So it was no surprise that this was the first time he'd seen anything like the vista that lay before him. It was simply stunning.

Raised in a mining community on the border with Germany, his childhood had been spent in and around the freight yards where the trains stacked high with coal lumbered past. Darting across the tracks, he would imagine his father had dug out every piece of the black rock that was on its way to support industry all over France. He'd been in the sheds the day the ground shook and Papa, along with twenty-one others, was killed in a massive explosion. Three months later, his mother had moved the family to Strasbourg to be nearer relatives and he'd become a city dweller, seduced by the cosmopolitan feel of his new home. The countryside hadn't really featured in his upbringing.

Determined to make life easier for his mother, he'd studied hard and won a scholarship to the prestigious École Nationale d'Administration, graduation from which guaranteed a fast track into the highest ranks of the civil service. He'd done well and received postings to Marseille, Lyon and the last one as sous-préfet back in Lorraine. None of this had engendered a love of the outdoors. Or an appreciation for nature. He was far too busy. But today, he was overawed by the beauty of the department he found himself in.

And the noise! In the warmth of the morning, birds were singing and cicadas tuning up in preparation for the afternoon, their soft buzz harmonising with the distant sound of cow bells, brought across on the slight breeze which was ruffling the trees and providing a welcome relief from what was already a hot day. It was the epitome of paradise. Until he remembered the letter.

Jérôme let his gaze drift down from the mountaintops to the valley below. Interspersed with lush pasture, a scattering of houses dotted the landscape, the arch of a church belfry visible over to his right, and from the valley floor came the glimmer of reflected sunlight. The river. That was the boundary.

He fetched the map from the car and opened it across the bonnet, finding his place a lot faster than he had in the office. So that was the commune of Sarrat spread out before him. It was bathed in sunshine, fields offering good grazing, the church roof newly slated.

And Fogas? Across the thin ribbon of water that separated the two districts, hidden in the depths of the valley, lay the village of La Rivière, the centre of the commune. Two gorges radiated out from it, clearly defined, but as he traced the swathes they made in the land, his eyes met nothing but trees and mountainside. Yet somewhere up there, brooding and dark, were Picarets and Fogas, the other two points on the triangle that formed this vexatious community.

He pondered his next move. Should he go down? See it first hand? He'd changed out of his suit for the drive over and, dressed as he was in three-quarter-length trousers and a short-sleeved shirt, he was suitably disguised to pass unrecognised, most people only having seen him in his uniform, which was all gold brocade and brass buttons. Besides, it seemed only fair to base his decision on his own evidence. Even though he was convinced it would make no difference.

As he folded up the map, smoothing out a stubborn crease, he knew what he was going to do. After all, if one side was already on board, surely it wouldn't be such a difficult task? And now that he was here, he could see that it made sense. It was exactly what the President had asked of his préfets. To combine resources. To cut costs. To provide for a future that was sustainable. All of which had been pointed out in the letter that had brought the préfet all this way from his desk. From first impressions, Jérôme Ulrich couldn't see anything that would lead him to disagree.

★ ★ ★

'You're wrong, I tell you!' A sturdy fist thumped the table, making the drinks arranged upon it jolt.

'Wrong? What the hell would you know?'

'A lot more than you!'

As he walked towards the small bar in La Rivière, its terrace already busy, Jérôme Ulrich pulled his baseball cap low over his forehead and cast a wary eye at the three men involved in a heated debate at the nearest table. One was short and dark and verging towards the heavier side of plump, a moustache quivering with indignation as he made his point between puffs on a Gauloise. Another was slimmer, older, his greying hair cut short around a face burning with intensity. And the third? He was clearly a drunkard. A huge slab of a man, head propped on meaty hands, blond curls hiding his face. A despairing groan emanated from him as his companions continued their raucous discussion and the préfet couldn't help checking the time.

Half past ten. And the man was already inebriated.

It was obvious they were locals. Apart from the fact that they stood out a mile from the tourists consulting guidebooks and enjoying the magnificent views as they sipped their morning drinks under a welcome canopy of wisteria, the three men spoke in the broad accent of the Ariège. It was an accent that Jérôme's ears had yet to fully acclimatise to.

'Do you think the pair of you could argue more quietly?' muttered the drunk, voice hoarse, a bloodshot eye peeping out between thick fingers.

But his companions showed no mercy.

'It's an abomination, that's what it is,' shouted the moustache, a finger pointing in the face of his adversary. 'A desecration. And I'll tell you why . . . '

Jérôme didn't wait to hear. Instead he entered the bar, the thick stone walls ensuring the interior felt cool compared to the burgeoning heat outside. Allowing his eyes to adjust to the sudden gloom, he paused at the threshold. It was a small room and although dark, despite the two long windows thrown open to let in the warmth, it was . . . homely. Surprisingly, that was the word.

19

With a scattering of tables taking up the floor, a big inglenook fireplace dominated the wall on the left, a long counter running perpendicular to it boasting a fantastic-looking coffee machine, and to his right was an archway, beyond which were racks of bread and vegetables. An épicerie. Beautifully laid out, from what little he could see.

Slightly taken aback, he decided he would have a drink before checking out the provisions on sale.

'Monsieur?' The elderly lady behind the bar was waiting for his order.

With a longing glance at the coffee machine, he decided to stay undercover and go native. 'A pastis, please.'

He leaned against the counter. The only other person choosing to drink inside on such a glorious day was an old man sitting on a stool in the corner, the greying T-shirt hanging on his sparse frame proclaiming his love for bears.

The irony of it. Here of all places, where one had been hounded to death only a month ago.

The préfet reached for his drink and added water from the jug left next to it, watching the amber liquid transform as opaque swirls settled into a cloudy mixture. It was the only thing he liked about the stuff. The way it changed. Wrong-footing you if it was your first time. He took a sip and tried not to grimace.

'Coffee please, Josette.' The drunkard was standing next to him, face grey, a hand on his stomach as though it was delicate, and a rolled-up towel tucked under his arm.

'Sounds serious,' Jérôme offered, tipping his head in the direction of the open windows, beyond which the discussion was continuing at full volume.

'Oh, it's serious all right,' came a muttered reply.

'Politics?'

The drunkard shook his head and instantly regretted it, reaching up to hold it gently.

'Religion, then?'

'No,' the man whispered, grasping the espresso and downing it in one, no care for the fact it was scalding.

'What then?' Jérôme asked, nonplussed.

But there was no need for the drunkard to reply as a chair scraped across the terrace floor and the man with the moustache leaped to his feet and provided the answer.

'I repeat, you CANNOT put tomatoes in a cassoulet!'

★   ★   ★

The tourist spluttered into his pastis, and for the first time that awful morning Christian Dupuy managed a smile.

'They're arguing over the recipe for cassoulet?' the man asked, incredulous.

'Welcome to Fogas,' quipped Josette from behind the bar. 'We take our food seriously.'

'And our heritage,' René butted in, head thrust through the open window. 'Anyone worth their salt knows that a cassoulet should be made without tomatoes.' He turned back to the

21

terrace, arms outstretched. 'Who agrees with me?'

A murmur of response came from his audience and a brave soul posed a question.

'Are you using duck confit or goose confit?'

'Duck, of course. And the finest haricots from Pamiers.'

'But you're supposed to use goose,' came another voice.

'*Goose?* Where are you from? England? Only someone who doesn't know how to cook would use goose.'

'Actually, I'm from Castelnaudary,' came the stinging retort, and within seconds there was a cacophony of voices, arguments carrying across tables and everyone shouting.

'Merde!' Christian clutched his poor head, which was pounding with every word as the tourist — for that was what he must be, dressed in a shirt and shorts, map clutched in one hand and a Paris Saint-Germain cap on his head — walked over to the door to get a better view.

'Is it always like this?' the man asked.

Josette laughed. 'Yes. Pretty much. When they start swinging punches I'll throw a bucket of water over them. Or set our second deputy mayor onto them.'

She gestured at Christian with the tea towel she was holding, and the hung-over deputy saw a flash of surprise cross the young tourist's face.

Fair enough. Christian didn't look much like a figure of authority on a good day, his farmer's gait and fashion sense tending to place him more as a man of the land than of the debating chamber. But today, he knew he presented an image of drunken excess. Still, it rankled. The way people made presumptions based on a ten-minute assessment.

He studied the young man, who had a sharp eye on the goings-on outside. He was of medium height, good-looking, strong across the shoulders and with a bearing that suggested the military. As did the cropped hair. But those hands. They were the soft hands of an office dweller. And despite his allegiance to a Parisian football club, the man's accent and demeanour suggested he was from the north-east.

A loud burst of noise from the terrace pierced Christian's ears and he winced.

'Have you taken anything?' enquired Josette, her face sympathetic.

'I know of only one hangover remedy and I'm off there now.' He tapped his towel.

'The pool?' She shivered. 'Rather you than me! It's freezing even at this time of year.'

'Never used to stop Jacques taking a dip.'

Josette's eyes flickered to the empty hearth at the mention of her deceased husband. 'You're right. He always said it was the cure for all ills. Personally, I think I'll stick to modern medicine!'

As Christian walked out of the bar, making his way through the cassoulet debate, which had settled into genial banter, he hoped his old friend Jacques Servat had been right. Because at this precise moment, the big farmer needed to be cured. And not just of an aching head.

He trudged down the road in the hot sun, not daring to glance up at the windows of the old school as he walked past. Just in case she was looking out. The last thing he wanted this morning was to come face to face with the woman who was causing him such torment.

3

Jacques Servat had been dead two years and had never felt better in all his life. If you discounted that he was still hard of hearing and his knees had seen better days. But considering he was confined to the four walls of the bar and épicerie, his after-life existence not coming equipped with a right to roam, he was doing very well, thank you. And as he watched the large figure of Christian Dupuy mope down the street, gaze steadfastly averted from the windows of the apartments which had been built in the old school, Jacques couldn't help chuckling.

The man was in love. And based on this morning's conduct, it was possible that he had finally realised the fact. Because, even allowing for an horrific hangover, the farmer had been behaving oddly.

Firstly, he'd jumped every time somebody walked into the bar, as if he was waiting for someone in particular. Then he'd been incredibly tetchy when Josette had merely enquired if he had seen the postmistress today. And finally, there was his demeanour. Beyond the bloodshot eyes. Ignoring the pallor of a deathly headache. There was a fatality about him that hadn't been there before. Not even when he'd been in danger of losing his farm and his livelihood. It was in the slope of his shoulders. The heavy lift of his legs. The weariness of his words.

He was a man in love with no hope of being loved in return.

Jacques rubbed his hands in gleeful anticipation. What sport this would bring to his days. Much as he admired the young man — saw him as a surrogate son, in fact — a ghost needed something to enliven his waking hours.

With Christian disappearing out of sight at the end of the village where the road and the river bent back on themselves, Jacques returned his attention to the bar. The debate over cassoulet had died down and René was now holding court by relaying his version of yesterday's demonstration to the tourists. Josette, Jacques' wife, was working hard, serving drinks and clearing tables while their nephew, Fabian, was behind the counter in the épicerie.

There was another man in love! But at least young Fabian had been rewarded by having that love returned. Although quite what Stephanie Morvan saw in him, Jacques couldn't understand. No disrespect to his nephew intended. In fact, the entire commune, especially the men, were still scratching their heads over the incredible fortune of the lanky Parisian who had landed in the region eighteen months ago and managed to snare the most beautiful woman the Ariège had ever seen.

Servat genes. That had to be the answer.

A clatter of glasses caught his attention as Josette came through from the terrace with a laden tray and very nearly collided with the man Christian had been talking to.

'Sorry!'

'Not at all. I'm standing in a particularly stupid place. Here, let me help.'

And just like that the man took the heavy tray from Josette and walked over to the bar.

'Thank you.'

'You're welcome. You seem busy today.'

Josette shrugged. 'It's high season. Tourists everywhere. Don't get me wrong, mind. I'm not complaining. We have to make the money when we can.'

'And the rest of the year?'

'It's quiet. Regulars like René and Alain out on the terrace. And Christian who was here earlier.'

'The deputy mayor?'

She nodded.

'Excuse me if this seems rude, but it doesn't sound enough to sustain you all year round.'

'I make do. I have my nephew helping me, now that we've extended the premises and brought it a bit more up to date. Hopefully we'll see a pickup in business over the next few years. Despite the recession.'

'And retirement?'

Josette laughed. 'Oh, that! One of these days I'll find the time to retire.'

'Josette!' a loud voice called from the terrace. 'A pastis, please.'

'Excuse me, that's the mayor,' Josette explained as she bustled out to the newly arrived customer.

Her words made the man at the counter start, and as she walked away he pulled his baseball cap lower, turning his back to the terrace to finish his drink. Which was when Jacques recognised him. The sharp nose. The haughty features. Handsome but with a touch of Teutonic arrogance.

A cold grip of fear clenched Jacques' stomach. Something wasn't right. The questions he'd asked. The intense way he'd followed René's ridiculous argument. The fact he was dressed like a tourist when he was anything but.

The man was getting ready to go when Josette came back inside.

'You off then?'

He nodded.

'Sightseeing?'

'Yes. Thought I'd visit Saint-Lizier and then perhaps Foix.'

'Oh, you must! Saint-Lizier is worth a trip just to see the Bishops' Palace. And Foix is interesting. Overrun with civil servants though!' She let the disdain colour her voice and Jacques cringed.

'I'll keep an eye out for them,' the man replied with a smile and made for the épicerie, averting his face as he passed the open door of the bar.

Josette turned to pick up his glass and noticed her husband out of the corner of her eye. He was slapping his forehead.

'What's the matter?' she hissed, making sure no one could see her talking to an empty fireplace. It wouldn't be the first time she'd been caught out and she was convinced her nephew thought she was insane. The return of her beloved husband in spectral form had been a blessing in so many ways, but it was also something of a burden. There was the fact that

28

no one else apart from her and young Chloé Morvan could see him for a start. And the fact that he couldn't speak for another. Sometimes it felt like living with Marcel Marceau. Albeit with more hair.

Right now her version of the famous mime artist was shaking his head mournfully and pointing at the back of the departing tourist she had been speaking to. Then he bent over the large table next to the fireplace, where that morning's copy of *La Dépêche* had been abandoned at the sports pages, and he started blowing. Cheeks puffed out, his transparent shape contorted with the effort as, one by one, with painstaking endeavour, the pages of the newspaper started to turn.

'Here, let me,' she whispered, moving to his side. 'Point when I hit the right page.'

She began flipping through the paper at speed and was on the obituaries section when he started frantically indicating. Bemused, she stared at the death notices, the stock sales announcements on the opposite side, and then she looked at him. But he was gesturing for her to turn back. So she did. And there he was. The tourist. In profile. The very same profile that was walking out of the épicerie. Only in the photo before her he was wearing a military-style uniform festooned with gold brocade.

Pushing her glasses up her nose, she read the caption out loud. ' ''Taking the salute at the Bastille Day military parade, Préfet Jérôme Ulrich . . . '' ' She paused, looked out of the window at the man walking down the road and then stared back at the photo. 'Merde!'

Fabian Servat, who had always thought Tante Josette was a mild-tempered woman, entered the bar just in time to witness her expletive. It was the second time in less than three months that he had heard his aunt swear and his face creased with concern.

'What's the matter now, Tante Josette?'

'I've just insulted one of the most powerful men in the Ariège!'

'What?'

Josette pointed a shaking finger at the figure getting into a car in the distance.

'Him. He's the préfet. And I've just insulted him. He let me believe he was a tourist and I made a comment about civil servants — '

'Never mind that,' growled a familiar voice from the doorway. 'What I want to know is why the Préfet of Ariège was skulking around here pretending to be a holidaymaker.'

Serge Papon, Mayor of Fogas, arms folded and bulbous forehead thrust forward, was glaring at the car as it drove past the bar, the préfet's attention fixed firmly on the road ahead.

'It's probably just his day off,' offered Fabian.

His naivety about the ways of politics in rural France earned him a scowl from both the older men present. And then Serge and Jacques turned as one to stare across the river as though they could see the troubles coming.

'Not again!' muttered Josette as she headed back to work. 'What I wouldn't give to have a bit of peace and quiet around here.'

Christian held on to the knotted roots of a tree, revelling in the serenity of his surroundings as he let his body be tugged and swayed by the water making its way past him. Already the tension in his shoulders had eased, the pounding in his head was abating and his aching heart was soothed by the beauty of the sunlight cutting through the green shade above.

Perhaps he could just stay here for the rest of his life. Although it probably wasn't feasible in winter. It had been cold enough getting in this mid-July morning, the glacial waters never still long enough to warm up the way some of the mountain tarns did.

Known locally as 'the pool', the section of river Christian was relaxing in was upstream from La Rivière at a point where the banks narrowed for a sudden bend, leaving the water deep enough to go over even the farmer's head. Normally crowded with families at the height of summer, today it was strangely deserted, no shouts of playing children audible from the baby pools around the corner where a collection of large flat rocks sheltered bathers from the river's unrelenting flow.

Feeling no need for such protection, Christian let go of the tree roots that were anchoring him and began swimming against the current. So calm at this time of year, come winter the water would be thundering past, roaring on its way down the mountain to meet up with the Salat as it emerged from the Seix valley. From there it wound through St Girons, the nearest town of any size, and then merged with the mighty Garonne, which travelled north into the heart of Toulouse and on to Bordeaux. A majestic river by this point, it cut through the coastal city and tumbled out into a broad estuary before ending its journey in the Bay of Biscay.

While René the plumber found it perplexing that the cold waters that snaked through La Rivière could travel up the map in what he perceived to be a denial of gravity, for the farmer it was fascinating. To think that tiny Fogas with its population of just over one hundred people could be connected by such an artery to the metropolis of Bordeaux! On the rare days that he felt trapped by the confines of his commune and the prying ways of village life, he found solace in the thought that the river always found a way out. So too could he, if he desired. And today, he desired it.

He eased up on his strokes and immediately started to drift backwards, the current deceptively strong. Perhaps the waters would carry him all the way to Bordeaux? Into the Gironde estuary where he could jump on a cargo ship and start a new life somewhere across the ocean. Far away from Fogas. Far away from her.

It wasn't a bad plan, Christian mused, as he stopped swimming altogether and flipped onto his back to be gently twisted and turned by the river. To leave everything behind. The idea had a certain attraction. Although he was aware of the irony inherent in his contemplating leaving just when everything was going so perfectly.

First there was the matter of his farm, which, thanks to an unexpected source, now had a viable future. With investment on the horizon, new projects to begin and the tantalising prospect of becoming less reliant on the middlemen who ate into his profits, he was excited about what lay ahead. Then there was yesterday's announcement that the post office would be reopening in Fogas. Something which as second deputy mayor he knew was vital for the sustainability of the commune. They had fought hard, and slightly underhand, to keep this necessary amenity and it had paid off, making the outlook for the three villages appear brighter than before.

Even on a personal level, things had seemed to be improving. Unmarried and still living with his parents, at the age of forty-one Christian was beginning to despair of ever finding a wife to share his life. Stuck up a mountain in a community that was dwindling and with most of his contemporaries having left the area to seek work long ago, there were few opportunities for him to meet the other sex. Then out of the blue, he'd got to know a beautiful woman. He'd even had a date with her, and she'd certainly been interested.

But Fate was a cruel mistress. She'd blinded the farmer to the attractions laid before him. Made him oblivious to the charms of the woman who was wooing him. Instead, as he'd realised in an epiphany that had come too late, he was bound to someone else. Someone he'd known since he was a boy. And someone who had no

33

feelings for him. She'd made that much clear last night as she danced cheek to cheek with a man Christian called a friend. He'd watched in agony as they'd sloped off into the darkness beyond the marquee, the man's arm around her shoulders, her body tucked into his.

Had she left with him? Agreed to accompany him to his next position of employment, wherever, as a tracker and outdoorsman, that took him? Perhaps even now, they were waking up in a tent in the mountains, preparing for an adventure that would last a lifetime. And who could blame her? What could someone like Christian offer in contrast? A life as a farmer's wife, getting up early to help with lambing, managing a household budget that was never quite enough, and out in all weathers to look for a bull that was better than Houdini at escaping.

There was no comparison. She would have gone.

The thought was colder than the waters flowing over his limbs. Gone. Was that better than if she were here to torment him on a daily basis? Would he heal more quickly if there were no reminders of the love he had allowed to slip through his fingers? Or did the perverse nature of the heart indeed mean that absence only served to heighten the pain?

Not having any degree of experience in the ways of love, Christian didn't have the answer. All he knew was that while the river had worked its usual magic on his hangover, it had failed to ease his tortured soul. So he would have to take a pragmatic approach, as he did to everything in life. He would dismiss her from his thoughts. Forget about the twist of auburn hair that fell against her cheek. Blot out the sound of her laughter, the small cross glinting on her throat as she threw back her head. And never recall the way she made him want to pull her close, enfold her in his arms and —

Banish her. Never think of her again. She was gone.

He closed his eyes in resolution and, with a resounding smack, his head clipped a rock and he was submerged. Emitting a gasp as the water surged over him, he took in a lungful of river and started to splutter. But as he struggled to surface, his long legs unexpectedly hit the bottom and he rose up, chest and shoulders suddenly exposed to the air.

Disoriented, he rubbed his bleary eyes, trying to focus on the scene around him. Where was he? He was obviously no longer in the pool. The water was too shallow. And there were more rocks, as his sore head testified. As his vision adjusted to the brightness of the sun bouncing off the river, he could just make out someone lying on a flat boulder a couple of metres away from him.

Tanned. Shapely. Auburn hair splayed over the granite. Face in repose. Eyes closed. Around her slender neck, a small silver chain decorated with a cross and next to her, a bag and a discarded bikini top.

As if to mock his pathetic attempts to thwart her, Fate had presented Christian with the very image he was trying to forget, in full, glorious, topless technicolour.

He couldn't help it. His tormented heart sent forth a cry that issued from the farmer's throat as a groan, both of desire and despair. But when the woman's eyes flashed open and she whipped round to look at him with a yelp of surprise, he somehow managed to turn it into something else.

'B-b-b-bonjour, Véronique,' he stammered, before flopping back down into the water, which failed to douse the flames on his cheeks.

★　★　★

'How long were you standing there gawping?' she demanded, a sting to her tone. 'And don't even *think* of turning around!'

Christian was taking the reprimand with his head down, standing in the river, his back to her, the swish of fabric telling him that she was frantically pulling on clothing.

'I wasn't. I just . . . I drifted . . . and then . . . '

'You drifted? All the way down here?'

He nodded and heard a snort of derision from up on the rock behind him.

'Well, you could have said something. Coughed, even. That would have been the polite thing to do.'

He stared morosely at the water eddying past. He'd embarrassed her. And made a fool of himself. She now thought he was nothing more than a voyeur. But how was he to have known she would be there? Thinking she'd eloped with the tracker the night before, he hadn't expected to bump into the village postmistress down at the river. Topless. Plenty of people sunbathed there in the nude, of course. It was a secluded spot, a small inlet on the opposite side to the path, screened from passers-by thanks to a thicket of ash and shielded by a huge rock that jutted into the water. With steep terrain rising out of it, no one could make their way here by accident. Except him.

No wonder she was sceptical. How could he have drifted all the way down the river, through the baby pools, to end up here? He scratched his damp curls in mortification, his hand coming away with a smear of red.

'You're bleeding.' Slightly less venom and a soft splash as she joined him in the river. 'Here, let me see.'

Before he could refuse, her hands were on his head, gently parting his hair.

'It's deep. How did you do that?'

'I banged it,' mumbled the farmer. 'On that.' He pointed an accusatory finger at the offending rock.

'While you were drifting?'

'Yes! I smacked my head, went underwater and then when I stood up . . . ' He turned to her and made a vague gesture to where she'd been lying, her bag and book next to her towel, and his face flared again at the memory. And at the fact that she was now wearing a bright red bikini, which pulled his attention back to her curves.

He swung round to face the opposite bank before his wandering eyes could land him in any more trouble.

'Does it hurt?' she asked.

'Not any more.' He'd said it before he thought through the implications. 'I mean . . . Christ!'

He'd had enough. His headache had returned with malevolence, thumping at his temples and pulsating behind his eyes, and the heat of what must now be a lunchtime sun was making it worse. 'Look, I'm sorry, all right? I didn't even know you were still here. You were supposed to be gone.'

He shrugged and without another word waded out of the inlet and across the shallow section of the river, intent on going home. He was stepping up onto the bank when she called to him.

'Christian! Wait, I'll come with you.'

And he had to endure the sight of her making her way through the water, limbs glistening in the sunshine, body just perfect. He made sure his eyes were fixed on the ground as he helped her onto dry land, and focused only on his bare feet as he followed her through the trees to where he'd left his clothes at the end of the path to La Rivière. Then he dressed with his back to her in the strained silence. When he turned round, he was both relieved and disappointed to see she was wearing shorts and a T-shirt. They were some way up the steep track to the road, walking in single file, before either of them spoke.

'What did you mean back there?' she asked, her voice quiet behind him. 'When you said I was supposed to be gone?'

'That's what I thought.'

'Gone where?'

'Gone. With Arnaud Petit.' Uttering the

tracker's name almost choked him.

Her silence was overlaid with the hum of cicadas and the lonesome cry of a red kite.

'No comment, then?' From some distant perspective he was aware of the rancour that tainted his voice. Up close, he could do nothing about it.

'What is there to say?' Haughty. Aloof. 'He asked me to leave with him.'

Christian felt a stab of pain but ploughed on regardless. 'And you turned him down?'

'Yes.'

Hope flooding his heart, he twisted on the narrow path to see her. She was pale, breath coming in short gasps as the hike took its toll. 'Why on earth did you do that?'

She blinked and he thought she wasn't going to reply, but then she said, 'I've just got my job back. I can't give that up.'

His laugh was cruel. Filled with the malice of a malignant hangover and the terror of an ensnared soul. 'You turned down a man like Arnaud Petit just to be postmistress of Fogas? Then you're a bigger idiot than I took you for!'

And so they emerged out of the shelter of the trees into the dusty parking space at the side of the road, the sun baking hard upon them, anger vibrating the air between them.

'Bonjour!' hailed a voice. 'Perhaps you could help me?'

Christian glanced at the occupant of the only parked car, perversely pleased to see the tourist who'd been in the bar earlier. The one who'd seemed to have trouble believing that Christian was a deputy mayor. With his baseball cap discarded on the seat next to him, he looked a lot younger. He was holding a map, and a flicker of recognition and something like wariness crossed his face as he spoke again.

'Oh, hi. I'm trying to decide which is the best way back to Foix.'

Christian leaned down to the window, the cold blast from the air conditioning doing nothing to assuage his temper. 'Sure,' he said with a fixed smile. And with a broad finger on the map he traced a route up the valley and over the mountains that lay between Fogas and the departmental capital. 'That's your best bet.'

'Not through Massat?' the man enquired with a bemused look.

'No. Over the Col de la Crouzette. Much better.'

'Thank you!' The tourist shook the farmer's hand, the grip surprisingly firm for an office dweller, and he reversed back onto the road. It was only as the car disappeared around the bend that Christian realised it had a local registration. Which was odd for a tourist.

'Why did you do that?' asked Véronique.

'What?' asked Christian, all innocence.

'Send him over the Col de la Crouzette. It's a terrible road. Especially if you're not from these parts.'

'I met him earlier and I didn't take to him,' explained Christian, aware of how petty it sounded. 'Anyway, how do you know he's not from these parts? He's got a local number plate.'

'Because,' said Véronique with exaggerated

40

patience, 'I recognised him. And he's definitely not from here. In fact, whatever has put you in such a terrible mood has just sent the Préfet of Ariège back to his office over the worst possible route. And I can't imagine that's going to help diplomatic relations in any way. But then, what would I know? I'm just the idiot postmistress.'

She set off down the road, indignation shimmering around her rigid shoulders like a mirage. And poor Christian was left in the lay-by, mouth open, head aching and with the knowledge that the day could not get any worse.

* * *

Pascal Souquet wasn't watching his phone the next time it rang. He was staring into space, contemplating a life other than the one he had ended up living. A life that involved the finer things, like foie gras and champagne, a stroll down Avenue Montaigne, a weekend break on the Ile de Ré and winter skiing in Courchevel. All of which he had once been able to afford, back when they'd lived in Paris and he'd been a man of note. Before he'd made disastrous investments and lost everything.

It was his wife who brought him back to reality, standing in front of him holding his mobile, lips pinched and eyes flinty. She threw a notepad on the kitchen table and stood, hands on hips, glowering at him.

She was angry. When he glanced at the page covered in her writing he knew why.

HE called. He said to tell you the letter has

been delivered. *WHAT letter?*

Pascal swallowed hard and for a brief second a shard of sound pierced the silence like a needle pushed through dough. But then nothing, just her finger jabbing noiselessly at the page. She was demanding an answer.

He raised his shoulders and shook his head. *Letter? What letter?*

But Fatima Souquet was no fool. She grabbed a pen and scrawled another line on the pad, chucked the phone next to it and then managed to convey with her body the sound he couldn't hear; the stamp of her footsteps across the tiles and the slamming of the door behind her. Seconds later, he saw the car being reversed out of the drive.

So, the letter had been sent, the plot was already in motion, and he was going to be dancing once more to the tune of another. But he couldn't tell his wife what it entailed. Even without his present affliction. Because when she found out what was being planned, she would leave him as she had promised. He let his gaze fall on her silent reprimand.

I TOLD you he was dangerous. You should have listened to me!

Pascal traced the words with his finger. There was nothing he could do. It was too late. He was on a path from which he couldn't turn, not without exposing himself to a possible prison sentence. He had to forge ahead and pray that everything came good. If it did, he would achieve all they had hoped for and more. If it didn't . . .

Cocooned in the unnatural hush, he felt his

42

shoulders start to heave, his chest rise and fall, moisture on his cheeks. But he was unable to hear the raw sobs that tore from his throat as he contemplated the mess he'd made.

4

'Pascal's gone deaf!' shouted a gleeful René as Christian approached the bar.

'What?'

'Precisely!' René slapped the farmer on the back, chuckling at his own joke, and they headed into the cool interior. 'Fatima was just down for some shopping. Told Josette that His Lordship has lost his hearing. She thinks it might have been something to do with the sound system last night.'

'You mean the fact that we sat him next to the loudspeakers when he passed out?'

René nodded.

'It's bad,' added Josette from behind the counter. 'He can't hear a thing.'

'No loss, living with a scold like Fatima!' muttered René. 'Two beers please, Josette.'

'Orangina for me,' revised Christian hastily.

Josette placed the drinks on the bar and turned to the farmer. 'So, how was your swim? Did it do the trick?'

Christian scowled. 'Not really.'

'Too many people?'

'Something like that.'

'Véronique was down there too, apparently. Did you see her?'

'Yes.'

'I thought she might have popped in when she got back, to discuss the new post office. Did she

44

say anything to you?'

'No.'

Josette raised an eyebrow at his terse responses and it was enough to make the sulky farmer relent.

'Sorry. It's not been a good day so far.'

'Not so great here, either,' added René. 'Our trusty mayor has gone storming back up to the town hall in a right temper.'

'Over what?'

'First of all he was harangued on his way here by the lady who drives the butcher's van — '

'Agnès Rogalle,' interrupted Josette. 'She's a distant cousin of the Rogalles up in Picarets.'

' — who was complaining again about someone stealing meat while her back is turned — '

'Seems it only happens when she's parked up around here . . . '

' — and was insisting Serge do something about it — '

'Although what he could do I'm sure I don't know. Perhaps if she spent less time leaning over the counter gossiping . . . '

' — and then it turns out the préfet was in here, snooping around — '

'How was I supposed to know who he was?'

' — so Serge has gone back to work to see if he can find out anything from his contacts — '

'Stop!' Christian held up a hand to halt the conversational ping-pong between René and Josette that was making his already sore head reel. 'The bit about the préfet. What makes you think he was snooping?'

45

René grunted. 'What else was he doing? Asking Josette all sorts of questions and pretending he was a tourist.'

'What did he ask?'

Josette fluffed up like an affronted chicken. 'He wanted to know if the business was viable.'

'And what did you say?'

'The truth. I get by. Not that it's any of his concern.'

'And then she insulted him!'

'Oh God,' groaned Christian, who was sensing that none of this boded well. 'That makes two of us.'

And he told them about the encounter in the lay-by and how he'd deliberately sent the high-ranking official back to Foix by the worst road possible.

'Merde!' said René, with the delight of the renegade. 'He's going to remember you for a long time. If he ever makes it back to the Préfecture, that is.'

The farmer let his head drop into his hands. 'Don't! If he was here on official business, I haven't helped any.'

'But it's so unlike you, Christian, to behave like that,' Josette said. 'What made you do it?'

'You wouldn't understand,' mumbled the deputy mayor.

But Jacques Servat, sitting in the fireplace, understood all too well. He'd seen love impact on many a man. And now it looked as though it could have repercussions on the commune he adored. He sighed, making the ashes in the empty hearth flutter and fall. Something told him things were about to get difficult all over again.

★ ★ ★

High above La Rivière, on a plateau just off the sinuous road that led up to Picarets, all but one set of shutters on the lone farmhouse that occupied the land were firmly closed. Pulled closed to preserve the cool air within the thick stone walls, they made the house look uninhabited. But from the open windows on the eastern side, where the shutters were held loosely on a latch to allow light into the room beyond, came the sound of voices.

'You've asked the wrrrong perrrson,' cackled Annie Estaque, her Ariégeois accent burring as she leaned back in her chair and regarded the young man opposite her. 'I don't know much about love. And what I do know doesn't seem to have got me verrry farrr!'

'But you must be able to give me some advice? I'm desperate.' Pain cracked his voice and the normally reticent Annie yielded.

'Honesty. Starrrt with that. Though I'm a fine one to talk.'

Her attention was taken by a car door slamming outside and enthusiastic barking as two dogs raced across the yard, their large bodies blurs of vivid movement across the narrow opening afforded by the shutters. Then her daughter appeared briefly in the vertical aperture, face fierce, shoulders hunched over. Neither of which suggested a good mood.

Perhaps it was just the heat. Though knowing her only child, Annie doubted it.

'Herrre's Vérrronique,' she said, glad of a chance to divert the focus from her own misshapen romantic past. 'She'd be a farrr betterrr one to ask.'

'Ask me what?' snapped Véronique as she entered the kitchen, blinking in the half-light as she bent to kiss her mother.

'How to propose to Stephanie,' replied Fabian Servat, oblivious to the temper that was crackling around the post-mistress. 'I want to put it in a way she can't refuse.'

'And you're asking me because . . . ?'

'Actually, I was asking your mother,' he corrected her with his trademark precision, consulting the screen of his phone where he'd taken accurate minutes on this inaugural meeting of the Fogas Love Society. 'And she suggested honesty.'

The snort ricocheted off the old longcase clock in the corner. 'Honesty? That's novel. Coming from someone who took thirty-six years to tell the man who made her pregnant that he was the father of her baby.'

Fabian's head snapped up at the jibe. He knew the history. Who in Fogas didn't? Having hidden the identity of the father of her child for decades, single mother Annie Estaque had only recently revealed him to be none other than Serge Papon, Mayor of Fogas. A shock for the community. An even bigger one for her daughter, Véronique.

He tried to read the atmosphere in the room, which had taken a sudden lurch. It was something he wasn't great at, human emotions were far too complex for a brain that was fine-tuned to the beautiful simplicity of mathematics. But even his skewed internal register was suggesting that things were not right with Véronique.

'So you don't agree?' he hazarded with such innocence that Véronique's wrath deflated and she sank onto a chair, taking the cold apple juice that her mother placed in front of her.

'No, Maman's right. Honesty is the best approach.'

'You mean I should come straight out and ask Stephanie?'

'Yes. No messing around. Just be upfront. It always works.'

'So, no messing . . . honesty . . . ' Fabian was tapping furiously on his phone, making sure he got every word. When he looked up, both Estaque women were staring at him with that fierce regard they shared, which, for the non-local, could stop a man at fifty paces.

'What?' he asked, no longer afraid of them after eighteen months in the community.

'Go!' said Véronique, flapping her hands to shoo him out of the house like a wayward hen. 'What are you waiting for?'

'Now?' he squeaked and the two women nodded.

He leaped from his chair in a twist of long legs, knocking the table and slopping Véronique's drink as he headed for the door.

'Yes. Now. You're right,' he muttered as he pulled on his cycling shoes and rushed to his bike.

'Let us know how it goes,' Annie called out to

49

his retreating figure.

And the Parisian took off up the steep hill which led to Picarets, his hunched form briefly visible to mother and daughter as it cycled across the gap in the shutters, already some distance up the road.

'Do you think he'll have the nerve?' asked Véronique.

'He's tougherrr than he looks. And he's besotted with Stephanie.'

Véronique sighed. 'Lucky Stephanie.'

Annie reached across and patted her daughter's hand. It was about as far as she got by way of demonstrating affection. If a pat was good enough for her dogs and cows, it was more than adequate with humans. Although she sensed that right now Véronique could do with a bit more.

'Bad morrrning?'

'You could say that. I saw Christian down at the pool. And he saw most of me.' Annie's eyebrows lifted in enquiry and her daughter gave a wry smile. 'He stumbled across me while I was sunbathing. Topless. So, added to the fact that he saw my naked backside at the hospital last year, he now has a complete set.'

The memory of the flustered farmer walking in unannounced on Véronique while she was in a state of undress made Annie smile. 'I bet he didn't know wherrre to look this time eitherrr!'

'I don't know about that. He seemed to take it all in. But then . . . ' She took a deep breath, letting her shoulders sag as she exhaled. 'We had a bit of a fight on the way home.'

'What about?'

50

'Arnaud Petit.'

Annie sat up at the mention of the tracker's name. When the big man had arrived in Fogas last autumn, she'd actually contemplated her daughter's love life, something she wasn't prone to give much thought to. And she'd wondered if this newcomer might not be the perfect man for Véronique. But her daughter had fallen for someone much closer to home. And possibly, much harder to catch.

'I thought he'd left?'

'He has. Last night. Only, he asked me to leave with him.'

Annie's jaw dropped. 'I didn't know that.'

'You were too busy dancing with Serge Papon to notice!'

A rare blush stole across Annie's weathered cheeks. 'We werrre just catching up, that's all.'

Véronique laughed softly, surprised to find herself moved by her mother's awkwardness. 'It's fine, Maman. You don't need to explain. After all, he is my father.'

'You werrre saying about Arrrnaud Petit?' came the gruff retort.

'Like I said. He asked me to leave with him. And I can't say it was an easy decision.'

'You turrrned him down?'

Véronique threw her arms out in exasperation. 'Why is everyone saying that like I will never get another chance? Like I was lucky to be asked even once?'

'It's not what I meant, love.' Annie laid a hand on her daughter's warm arm. 'So, what did you and Chrrristian fight about?'

'He was grumpy. Said he thought I had left Fogas last night. With Arnaud.'

'Was he jealous?'

Véronique snorted. 'No. Not a bit. When he heard I'd turned down the chance to be Madame Petit he said I was an idiot. Perhaps he's right.'

She turned her head and looked out at the sliver of view bordered by the shutters, pasture rustling green in the lightest of summer breezes, the mountains shimmering in the heat.

'Should I have gone, Maman?'

Annie rose from her chair and crossed to the dresser where a sun-bleached photo stood in an old frame, a younger image of herself laughing out at the camera, arms around her parents. She hadn't known it then, but she had been pregnant. What a maze of choices lay ahead of her, each one cutting off paths and opening up new avenues, not all of them an easy walk. But she'd made her way, with mistakes aplenty, to end up here, living on the farm she'd always called home, with a daughter she had finally come to understand and beginning a new friendship with the man she had wronged. None of which had made her any wiser.

She placed the photo in front of Véronique and pointed at herself with a gnarled finger.

'If I had known then what I know now, I wouldn't be who I am.'

'And that's a good thing?'

Annie shrugged. 'I don't know, child. All I know is that sometimes when you have to make a decision in the darrrk, it's easierrr than having a light shone on what awaits you arrround the corrrnerrr.' She laid a hand worn by years of farm work on her daughter's head. 'Perrrhaps you ought to take some of the advice we just gave Fabian.'

'Tell him?' Véronique's voice rose an octave. 'I can't! It's clear he doesn't care for me. Otherwise, why would he have said what he did?'

Annie held her tongue. She had no answer. But she fervently hoped that the two young people she cared about most in the world could sort things out between them. Because Christian Dupuy was about to take over her farm. And it would be so much easier if he could get on with Véronique like he used to. Especially as the girl was in love with him.

★　★　★

It was a hot ride to the village of Picarets from the Estaque farm; a long climb out in the open with the sun beating mercilessly down on him before the road dipped into the welcome shade of the forest. But Fabian didn't feel any discomfort as he toiled upwards, unaware of the sweat dripping from his chin and the energy sapping from his legs. His mind was in another place entirely.

Stephanie. She'd be home for lunch, her garden centre down in La Rivière closing for two hours in the midday heat like everywhere else, leaving shuttered-up ghost towns for unsuspecting tourists. Only Tante Josette stayed open, resolutely refusing to change the culture that her husband's family had started generations ago. Not that it brought in much business, just the odd grateful foreigner looking for a refuge from the high temperature.

Lunchtime also meant that Chloé would be back. She was supposed to be spending the morning with the Rogalle twins, Max and Nicolas, the three of them finding plenty to fill their long summer holidays. But Fabian had promised to take her swimming in the river in the afternoon, so she'd probably be home already. If she was, it wouldn't take much to persuade the budding circus star to go out in the garden and turn a few somersaults. Try out her aerial cartwheels, which she seemed to have perfected, and leave the coast clear for him.

His legs eased on the pedals as the sign for the village came into view, the road levelling out as it began to pass the handful of dwellings that constituted Picarets. But despite the easier riding conditions, Fabian's heart had started palpitating. He couldn't believe he was going to do this. He was on the verge of asking the most amazing woman on the planet to marry him. What if she said no? It could wreck their relationship. Was he rushing things?

Véronique's strident tone sounded in his head. No messing around. That's what she'd said. And she was right. If he and Stephanie were going to make a future together, they might as well make it properly. Cycling on with renewed determination, he passed the faded Dubonnet advertisement on the gable of the old Papon house — the house he was still paying rent for despite now living more or less permanently with Stephanie — and it was only when he got to the huge lime tree which cast its shadow over the small square, that Fabian realised he was missing a vital ingredient for his proposal. He didn't have a ring.

Unwilling to relinquish his mission, he patted the rear pockets of his cycling jersey, hoping to improvise. Pepper spray for random dog attacks. An energy gel in case he ran out of steam on a ride. His phone. The empty wrapper of a muesli bar. And his keys . . . his keys?

At the end of the village, he pulled up outside Stephanie's small cottage, left the bike around the back and, after a few moments of fiddling with his key ring, opened the kitchen door. He entered the house with what he hoped was an air of nonchalance. No one there. Just a half-made salad, a baguette, sliced tomatoes in olive oil and a block of mozzarella waiting to be cut.

Then he saw her. She was on the sofa on the other side of the open-plan room, long red hair curling over her shoulders in the sunshine which was streaming in through the unfettered windows. He grinned. Born and raised in the more moderate climate of Brittany, she blatantly refused to adopt the southern tradition of shutting out the sunlight during the hottest months, saying that she had no intention of living like a troglodyte and denying herself the best thing about life. She also had the windows open, a warm breeze ruffling the curtains as it snaked through the house.

'Stephanie?' He heard the tremor in his voice, felt his heart rate pick up and a quiver of panic

55

beset his limbs. 'Have you got a minute?'

She looked up and it was only as the light streaked across her face that he noticed. The frown. The paleness. The fear in her eyes.

'What's the matter?' he asked, rushing over to kneel in front of her.

She held out a letter in shaking hands. 'It's from the lawyer. My divorce proceedings have started.'

'But . . . but that's a good thing, isn't it?'

She nodded and then bit her lip, pointing to the middle paragraph. He read it and the cold hand of the past reached out to touch his neck.

'They want you to meet him for a conciliation session?' he asked. 'In the prison?'

She nodded again and then looked back down at the letter.

'When?'

'I don't know. I have to call them.'

'I'll come with you.'

'No!' She shook her head. 'It's better if you don't. You need to look after Chloé. And I don't want her knowing anything about this.'

'But you can't go on your own. Not after . . . '

She took his face in her hands and managed a smile, her green eyes still filled with apprehension. 'I have to. It's standard procedure apparently, so it's either this or not get divorced. I'll be fine.'

He doubted it. Had reason to. Because the last time Stephanie had come face to face with her estranged husband the man had tried to kill her. And Fabian. And he'd almost succeeded. That he was now in prison didn't make the thought of

56

Stephanie having to see him any easier.

'Promise me, Fabian. You'll stay here and not say a word to Chloé?'

He nodded reluctantly and she kissed his lips, her touch infused with passion and terror, binding him to her with a bribery of love.

'Ugh! Get a room!' declared a voice from the back door as Chloé entered in time to witness their embrace, something no kid of eleven appreciated. She adored her mother's boyfriend and he made the best hot chocolate in the whole of Ariège, but that didn't temper the young girl's disdain.

'Sorry, Chloé,' Fabian said, trying to sound normal. 'But she's irresistible.'

Chloé grimaced and turned to wash her hands at the sink, not noticing her mother tucking the letter into a book on the coffee table.

'Not a word,' whispered Stephanie as she rose from the sofa, her hand still on Fabian's arm.

Somehow he got through lunch. Managed to show interest in Chloé's account of her morning and wave a cheery farewell to Stephanie as he set off for the pool with the young girl in tow. His mind, however, was on other things. And for once, it wasn't about engagements and marriage proposals.

Stephanie too was preoccupied. Although as she retrieved the letter from its hiding place after they left, she did notice the silver circle of metal glinting in the sunlight by the coffee table. Picking it up, she saw that it wasn't a ring as she'd first thought. It was the hoop of a key ring. Thinking Fabian must have dropped it, she left it on the dresser to give to him later. Which, of course, given all that was happening, she forgot to do, the letter in her hand distracting her completely.

★ ★ ★

He flipped the letter between his hands like Justice playing catch between her scales. Beyond his office window he could see the slow waters of the Ariège river winding north, heading for Toulouse and then Bordeaux. Civilisation. Places where you didn't get stranded for hours on your way back to the office because someone had given you bad directions.

Jérôme Ulrich was a fair man. He could admit that the fault was partly his own. Once he'd heard the mayor was outside the bar in La Rivière, he'd been in such a rush to escape unrecognised that he'd jumped in his car and taken off up the road, realising too late that he was heading the wrong way. Instead of following the river down towards St Girons as he'd planned, he was climbing the valley to Massat.

Unwilling to turn round and drive back past the crowded terrace, he'd pulled over at a small parking area on a bend in the river to look at the map, reluctant to trust his satnav after its mistakes that morning. When he'd seen two people appear in the shade of a small path that led into the trees on the river-bank, it seemed only natural to ask them for help. It wasn't until the man strolled across to the car that Jérôme placed him. With hair wet from swimming and a

58

face flushed from exercise, the big deputy mayor had been almost unrecognisable as the person who'd been propping up the bar earlier.

Was it deliberate? Had he sent Jérôme up that awful road on purpose? The préfet liked to think the best of people but he couldn't be sure.

To be honest, he'd enjoyed the drive up the Col de la Crouzette at first, each twist presenting ever more spectacular scenery as the valleys dropped below him and the higher mountains soared into view. And being a practical person, when he'd realised he had a puncture halfway up the narrow, torturous climb, he hadn't panicked. He'd simply pulled over. Not easy on a thread of tarmac with forest rising on one side and a sheer drop into the gorge below on the other. He'd chosen the flattest section of road he could but it had still been at an incline not suitable for changing a wheel. He wasn't surprised, therefore, that as he'd proceeded to jack up the car, the jack had started groaning at the odd distribution of weight caused by the unfavourable gradient. Even with rocks wedged under the rear wheels it wasn't safe.

He'd quickly lowered the car back down and had been contemplating his next move, shirt soaked in perspiration, useless mobile phone telling him no signal was available, when a rotund man came crashing out of the bushes behind him. Face smeared with purple, he'd been followed by an affable beagle that had promptly lain next to Jérôme and offered its belly for affection. And his owner had offered the use of his jack.

It had taken a while for them to walk to the man's car and back, the man taking a short cut through the forest, explaining cryptically that he was on the hillside doing 'manoeuvres', something which, judging by the man's face, presumably involved picking and eating vast quantities of the bilberries that seemed to decorate every bush they passed on the way. But it had been worth the trip, two jacks under the car making the perilous wheel change possible.

Thanking his saviour, a man called Bernard Mirouze who had disappeared mysteriously back into the bushes as camouflaged as a hippo in a duck pond, Jérôme had resumed his journey. It was only as he'd mulled over the events that he'd felt aggrieved. But then, the whole incident served him right for asking a drunkard for advice. And then taking it. Even if the drunkard *was* a deputy mayor. Which made you wonder about the kind of community that would elect a man like that.

He'd arrived back in Foix, arms covered in scratches, clothes grubby and stained and his hands smeared with grease, to be informed by his secretary that he'd just missed the scheduled call from the Director General of La Poste. Her raised eyebrows were her only comment on his bedraggled appearance; he hadn't volunteered any explanation, happy to let her think he'd been chased by bears, as she'd predicted. Instead, he'd closed his office door, cleaned himself up as best as he could, and then phoned the head of La Poste to make a grovelling apology. Once that was done, he settled down to make his decision.

The letter.

He'd seen it for himself. Fogas was too small. Across three villages it had the sum total of a small auberge, a newly opened garden centre which, given the statistics for new businesses and the current economic climate, wasn't likely to survive, and a combined bar and épicerie run by a woman who should have retired many years ago but probably couldn't afford to. And of course the post office, which would be reopening in the épicerie, if his reports were correct. All of it situated in La Rivière.

It wasn't enough. No school. A church which had irregular services and no curé since the last one had been run out of town at the end of a rifle brandished by a jealous husband. A dwindling population. A council of only eleven members with a mayor and two deputies. And a town hall right up the mountain in the village of Fogas, which he hadn't even attempted to get to today. What a trek for all the inhabitants whenever they wanted to talk to the mayor. Which in rural France was often, given the power local officials wielded.

Added to that was the impression he'd formed of a belligerent group of locals, able to cause a fierce argument over something as innocuous as cassoulet. No wonder his short tenure as préfet had been punctuated by conflicting dramas originating in the commune. Complaints over the presence of bears. Protests over the death of a bear. And a demonstration against La Poste that had made the international news.

They were a troublesome lot.

His correspondent was right. It was time for Fogas to be subsumed by its more affluent neighbour, merged with the vibrant commune of Sarrat which lay across the river. And as préfet, Jérôme had the authority to effect such change. Whether the residents of Fogas wanted it or not. Especially when he knew he would find support in the much larger district next door.

He picked up the phone. He would set in motion a proper report so that no one could accuse him of a rash decision. But first, he would speak to the man who had taken the time to write to him and propose such a sensible idea.

'Bonjour,' he said as a deep voice answered the call. 'Henri Dedieu? Mayor of Sarrat? It's Jérôme Ulrich here. I wonder if you have time to talk about that letter you sent me?'

Jérôme glanced at the map on the wall as the man replied, and in his mind's eye he was already redrawing the boundaries, creating a new commune and erasing Fogas altogether from the history of the Pyrenees.

5

Seventy-two hours and counting. René Piquemal parked his car round the corner from the post office in St Girons, got out into the morning heat and took a deep, self-satisfied breath. He was immediately enveloped by the sweet smells of summer. The pungent aroma of lavender intertwined with the delicate fragrance of roses, all underlined by the heady notes of the nearby river in the middle of a sweltering July.

Three whole days and not a trace of nicotine had passed his lips. He'd taken the 'cure' on Saturday morning and so far it had been an astounding success, the return of his sense of smell a welcome side effect he hadn't antici-pated. Although he'd not appreciated his improved nasal faculties when his wife had served the cheese course the night before, his olfactory senses reeling at the maturing Camem-bert and his favourite Cabretou reeking a little more of goat than he remembered. But that was a price worth paying.

Feeling smug, he walked between the pale trunks of plane trees that lined Rue du Champ de Mars, keeping parallel with the Salat river as he made for the town centre. He was heading for the Sous-Préfecture, the government office positioned on a diagonal at the far corner of St Girons from where he was now. A long walk in this heat. Or anytime for the plump plumber, apart from in hunting season. But it was all part of his plan. He wanted to test himself.

First up, Café de l'Union, which overlooked the long avenue where the market took place every Saturday under the broad cover of the trees. He'd timed it perfectly. The terrace was bustling. Lots of people relaxing over a mid-morning espresso, reading a newspaper or chatting to friends. And most of them smoking.

He slowed his pace as he approached and as soon as the first swirl of cigarette smoke crossed his path, he inhaled. It was instant. A tickling at the back of his throat, no more than an itch, which morphed into a taste. A bitter flavour on his tongue. His nostrils flickering at the transient scents that twisted past him, beginning to yearn for that warm sensation of exhalation. Then the cravings, from deep within, an overwhelming need for nicotine that engulfed his consciousness. Caught in the grip of the addiction, his body responded, turning his feet towards the *tabac* at the end of the Pont Vieux where a packet of Gauloises was waiting for him. With his steps directed by an unseen force, he began to cross the square.

Feeling his willpower buckling, René knew he had to implement his cure. Following the instructions, he slowly began to rub together the thumb and forefinger of his right hand in small circles. Erase the yearning. Replace it with something else. Eyes almost closed, he concentrated on the smell. That particular smell. The one that made him think of happier things. The one that —

Something squished under his foot and he stumbled, a pained yelp cutting through his trance. He looked down to see a growling pug, lead caught around René's trousers and the old dear on the other end of it glaring at him.

'Watch where you're going, monsieur!' she spat as she scooped up the dog to inspect his paw.

'Ssshorry!' he said, his speech unexpectedly slurred.

But she didn't wait to hear, stalking off towards the Pont Vieux carrying her charge. Beyond her, the siren call of the *tabac* had faded and René was able to walk past the shop without even a sideways glance.

More confident, if a tad dizzy, he veered away from the river and up the tapering Rue du Bourg. He arrived at Place Pasteur, cutting across the square to Rue de la République, where he struck lucky. A young man was walking briskly ahead of him, lips clamped around a cigarette. Having to lengthen his short-legged stride somewhat, René tucked in behind him, letting the curls of smoke wash over his face until he felt the stirrings of desire, short, sharp pangs that grew rapidly into an all-consuming need. And at the point where it threatened to overpower him, he rubbed together his finger and thumb and thought of only one thing: his scent of salvation.

Focusing on the ground, concentrating on that smell, he didn't see the parked car. He walked straight into it and then staggered slightly as he corrected himself, leaning a hand on the bonnet of the car while he waited for his groggy senses to clear.

'Disgusting!' hissed a woman as she passed, basket over her arm. 'Drunk at this hour!'

She was gone before René could correct her. As was the urge to smoke. It was a miracle! As long as he followed the instructions he'd been given, he was able to overcome the need for a cigarette. One more test and then he would head for the Sous-Préfecture.

Aware that the hour for lunchtime closure was looming, he picked up his pace and found himself in Place Jean Jaurès, sweat prickling his shirt, his breath coming in gasps. He surveyed the square: cars parked in the centre, two busy roads wrapping around the far edges and on either side of him, a café. Which was it to be?

He glanced at the exterior of the Salon de Thé on his right. A wood-block terrace, elegant tables prepared for lunch and mostly occupied by well-dressed mademoiselles sipping English Breakfast tea. He turned ninety degrees to Café Kristal. Red plastic chairs on the pavement. A few straggling geraniums in a wooden planter. Old men leaning on tables littered with beer bottles and overflowing ashtrays. Perfect. Confident nothing could shake him, he approached.

'René!' A quavering voice hailed him.

It was Gaston, the old shepherd who'd lived his entire life up in the mountains with his sheep and now spent his retirement frequenting the bars of the Couserans, most notably that of Josette in La Rivière. Wearing a greying T-shirt with a faded image of a bear, shorts that revealed spindly legs knotted with veins, and his obligatory beret despite the temperature, he was accompanied by an ancient dog panting heavily in the heat. As René crossed towards them, he caught the odour of unwashed bodies and stale breath. Not able to decide the origin, dog or shepherd, he kept a bit of distance.

'Here.' A clawed hand was holding out a carton. Pale blue with a winged helmet decorating the front, a slim white stick was already protruding out of the top. Before he could help himself, René was reaching for it.

'Gauloises,' he murmured with awe as his fingers closed around the filter. He had it between his lips, bending over to a shaking match and had started to inhale, taste buds consumed with the unforgettable tang, when he remembered.

'Merde! I quit!' He whipped the cigarette out of his mouth, finger and thumb frantically rubbing as he tried to overcome the compulsion to take another drag. 'And so should you,' he continued with the verve of the newly converted, having regained enough control to be able to stub out the offending article. 'These things will kill you!'

But the shepherd was beyond such proselytisation, greeting René's news with a surprised look before fishing the discarded cigarette out of the ashtray and placing it back in the packet.

René wheeled away, taking rapid strides across the square to the main road, the *tricolore* that marked his destination hanging limp in the heaviness of the morning. He didn't realise he was still agitating his finger and thumb. But he did notice that he was perspiring. And that his legs seemed a bit unsteady. Thinking it was the sun, when he arrived at the ugly block of concrete that was the public access to the Sous-Préfecture, he dipped inside, glad to be out of the heat.

★ ★ ★

'Are you clear on this?' asked the man behind the desk.

The skeletal figure in front of him nodded, the long beak of his nose almost stabbing his chest in the process.

'Then we should waste no time. Start today. But be discreet!'

From an armchair by the window, Jérôme Ulrich gave his own nod of consent and the thin man backed out of the room.

'Thank you,' Jérôme said once the door had closed.

The man behind the desk shrugged. 'As you wish.'

'I sense some reluctance?'

A pause. And then a sigh. Jérôme knew that his understudy, a much older *fonctionnaire* who had occupied the position of sous-préfet in St Girons for some years and had been overlooked for promotion, was dying to lecture his young boss on the benefits of maturity in the diplomatic world.

'This place,' the man finally began, waving his hand towards the town beyond the glass. 'It's not like Foix. Wherever you go here, the mountains are constantly before you. Reminding you that this is a land ruled by Nature. And it makes the people different.'

'More feral?' commented Jérôme with a dry laugh.

The man's expression remained grave. 'More stubborn. More fixed. And more passionate about sticking up for what they love.'

'In other words, you're saying I should expect a fight?'

The man nodded.

'All the more reason why we should begin quietly, then.' The préfet rose smoothly to his feet and extended a hand. 'And we'll see how things turn out come the end of the summer.'

* * *

René didn't feel good. He stood for a few seconds inside the doorway of the Sous-Préfecture letting the cool air from a fan high on the wall wash over him. It must be the heat. Blasted summer. Hotter than it had been for years. Grass turning brown, trees suffering. There was even talk of a hosepipe ban, which was unheard of in this lush part of the Ariège, known for its mountain showers and reliable rainfall.

Mopping his brow, he turned to enter the offices beyond, paperwork clutched in his hand, but as he rounded the corner he ran head first into a bony chest, getting a lungful of stale nicotine before he was sent sprawling. Automatically rubbing his fingers to ward off the evil

69

weed, he only had time to notice a stick-thin frame and a hooked nose before the outside door swung shut.

'Ssshome people would jusssh walk right over you,' René muttered, the words sliding out in a slurred mumble. And when he went to stand, he heard a rushing sound in his ears and the world tilted on its axis.

He slumped back to the floor and sat there in the corridor, letting things settle, thinking it was to be expected. This peculiar feeling. He was going cold turkey. There were bound to be repercussions. After all, he'd been smoking for nearly forty years, taking his first inhalation at the tender age of fourteen on a cigarette stolen from Grand-père Piquemal. Two boys hiding round the back of the *lavoir* in Fogas, they'd both choked and retched and it had been enough to put his best friend off for life. Lucky him. René, aspiring to mirror the lanky sangfroid of Clint Eastwood, who wore his hat tipped low, smoke curling into narrowed eyes, stuck with it. He overcame the dizziness. Battled through the nausea. And became a very successful smoker indeed. So it was no wonder that now he was trying to quit, there was some backlash from his dependent body.

Sensing that his equilibrium had returned, René shifted onto his hands and knees and began picking up the many bits of paper that the government deemed essential for a man to register a new car. He was still scrabbling on the ground when a pair of highly polished black shoes came around the corner and into focus.

★ ★ ★

Perhaps the sous-préfet had a point. Maybe he was being rash. But even as Jérôme Ulrich considered the possibility, he dismissed it. He was doing the right thing. And by the end of the summer, his decision would be vindicated.

Heels tapping on the tiled floor as he made for the exit, he threw a nod of acknowledgement to the staff behind the glass partition who were the human face of the Ministry of the Interior. Dealing with everything from vehicle registration to identity cards, from passports to the setting up of associations, the offices of the Préfecture and the Sous-Préfecture were where the citizens of France had to jump through bureaucratic hoops dreamed up in Paris. And as Jérôme Ulrich turned the corner into the corridor, he came across one such citizen down on his hands and knees, picking up documents which had scattered across the floor.

'Can I help you?' Jérôme asked, bending down. So it was that he came eye to eye with the bleary features of the cassoulet man he'd encountered up in Fogas. The man held his gaze, clearly aware of some prior acquaintance but failing to make the connection. Not surprising. Judging by the way the man's hands were shaking, it looked as though he could be drunk.

'I know you from ssshomewhere, don't I?' the man demanded as he got to his feet, slightly unsteady.

Jérôme picked up the last of the papers and handed them over with a shake of his head. 'You

71

are mistaken, monsieur.'

'You ssshure?'

'Certain.' With a brief smile, Jérôme turned on his heel and left the building.

And that — he thought as he strode towards his car, aware that he was going to be late for lunch with his wife, who had booked a table at the amazing La Petite Maison just outside the town — is why he was right. Fogas was inhabited by a bunch of drunks. The sooner it came under the sobriety of neighbouring Sarrat the better.

★   ★   ★

'Monsieur?' *Tap tap tap.* 'Monsieur?'

'Eh?' René turned to the glass partition where a young woman was trying to get his attention. Without waiting for her to speak, he pointed at the empty space that had just been occupied by the dynamic man who had helped him collect his papers. 'That gentleman, who was he?'

'Which man, monsieur?'

'The one who just walked past. Medium height, good-looking, smart suit . . . '

'Oh!' The woman blushed and smiled. 'That was the préfet, Monsieur Jérôme Ulrich.' The name rolled off her tongue in a honeyed gush.

'Merde!' cursed René, as the haze that had been obscuring his memory cleared and he suddenly saw the man recast in shorts and a shirt, a stupid PSG baseball cap on his head. 'The lying bast — '

'MonSIEUR!' The smile was gone. 'No need for such language.'

'Sorry,' muttered the plumber, placing his thick folder on the counter and beginning to sort through the jumbled sheets. 'Anyway, I'm here to — '

Whoosh!

He was left staring at a wall of grey as a blind fell behind the glass. 'Excuse me! Mademoiselle?'

'As I was trying to tell you, monsieur,' came a curt voice from behind the grey barricade, 'we're closed. You'll have to come back after lunch.'

Not the first citizen of France to attempt to jump through a hoop only to hit a brick wall, René resisted the urge to bang his head against the window. Instead, he merely gritted his teeth like many before him, gathered up his useless dossier and, rubbing his finger and thumb frantically, stormed out of the Sous-Préfecture into the midday sun.

★ ★ ★

'So I'll lose the far end of the shop?' Josette picked up the plans from the counter and turned a half-circle, matching the drawings on the page to the collection of shelves and display cabinets that made up the épicerie. 'That's better! Now I can tell what I'm looking at.'

Having endured Josette's map-reading skills, which were on a par with her driving skills, Véronique bit her tongue.

'And the post office will need storage out back too?'

'Yes.' The postmistress resisted the inclination

73

to sigh. They'd been over the plans again and again since the idea of merging the two institutions had been broached back in November. Over eight months later, it was as though Josette was seeing the new layout for the first time.

'And how long will the work take?'

This, Véronique knew, was the real reason for Josette's lukewarm response to the builder's blueprints. Having recently endured a nightmare refit of the entire premises — Fabian, her nephew, dragging the establishment and his aunt into the modern age — Josette Servat was understandably apprehensive about the coming changes.

'They can start next Monday and it should all be done within a week.'

'Huh! I've heard that before.'

'Heard what before?' enquired Fabian as he slouched through the door.

'We're discussing the building work for the new post office,' explained Véronique with a twinkle in her eye.

He gave her a sympathetic smile and slipped an arm around his aunt's frail shoulders. 'The sooner the better, Tante Josette. Just think how lovely it will be to have Véronique helping out all the time.'

Josette fixed him with a fierce look from behind her glasses. 'Yes, it would be good to have help. Seeing as you're hardly ever here now.'

He shrugged, held up two hands ingrained with the black soil that explained where his hard work had been diverted, and smiled. 'I can't help it if I'm in demand. Stephanie has offered to do more hours at the Auberge to help out, so I'm filling in at the garden centre. I don't see things easing up much until Lorna's baby is born.'

'BABY?' Josette and Véronique chorused.

Fabian looked from one surprised face to the other, aware, despite suffering from a deficiency of perspicacity when it came to human relations, that he had just committed a blunder.

'You didn't know . . . ?' he began.

Two shakes of the head.

'Who told you?' demanded Véronique.

Fabian pulled a forgetful face, trying to negotiate the quicksands sucking at his feet. 'I heard it from . . . someone.'

'Who?' quizzed Josette.

'Stephanie,' replied Véronique. 'Has to be. Who else would tell him?'

'But how does Stephanie know?'

'Lorna must have told her. Or she guessed. You know how she is with her gypsy heritage.'

'That makes sense,' mused Josette. 'There's no way Lorna would tell her and not us.'

'So how pregnant is she?' Véronique turned back to ask the Parisian. But he hadn't lived among them for a year and a half without picking up a trick or two.

'Don't know,' he lied. 'But just think. A baby!'

It was a deflection worthy of the greatest gossip. Josette's face crumpled into a misty-eyed smile and even Véronique's dimples made an appearance.

'A baby,' whispered Josette, dropping the plans for the post office back onto the counter. 'In Fogas! How wonderful.'

'Yes,' sighed Véronique, surprised to find that her pleasure for the Englishwoman was tinged with regret. For herself.

'It'll be you next.' Josette was now tapping Fabian on the arm, a knowing look in her eye.

'Not at the rate I'm going.'

'You didn't ask her, then?' Véronique's question threw Josette back into confusion.

'Ask who what?'

'Stephanie. He wants to propose and doesn't know how.'

'You're going to ask her to marry you? Am I the last to know?'

'No. Stephanie is. Am I right, Fabian?'

'But what's the hold-up?'

Faced with the intense scrutiny of both women, Fabian accepted that no matter how long he lived here, he would never master the arcane art of intelligence extraction that the locals were inducted into at birth. Deciding it was better if he were the news, rather than the unwitting distributor of it, he offered up the necessary sacrifice and told them all about his attempt to propose, thwarted by the letter from Stephanie's lawyer about her divorce.

'It didn't seem the ideal time to ask,' he finished his explanation. 'Not when she's just found out she has to meet her violent husband in order to make their separation legal.'

Josette shuddered. 'Poor Stephanie. She really has to go and face that man?'

'It appears so. They've set a date for the beginning of September.'

'What must the judge be thinking of, insisting

76

on a meeting? When you consider what that man did . . . ' Josette grasped her nephew's arm with a frail hand, face wan as she recalled the events that had placed Stephanie, Chloé and Fabian in mortal danger.

'Yes. Well, best not dwell on that. And not a word of this to Chloé.'

The two women promised silence.

'Now, seeing as you've heard my news, perhaps you could give me some advice, Tante Josette?'

'Advice? For proposing?' She glanced towards the fireplace and a smile returned to her pale cheeks. 'Your Oncle Jacques would have been the one to ask.'

'I didn't take him for a romantic.'

'Oh, he is . . . I mean . . . was!' She watched the man in question, snoozing in the inglenook, thick eyebrows lowered over closed eyes. 'We hadn't been courting long when he handed me a hand-drawn map of La Rivière one day. With it were lots of directions, like a treasure hunt. And he gave me a spade.'

Véronique laughed, suspecting the outcome.

'Of course, I'm not the best map-reader in the world, so it took a while and I made a few mistakes. In fact, when I started digging the seventh hole, Jacques got so frustrated at my inability to follow the instructions that he took over. Said he owed it to the village to help me out before the place was riddled with holes like a Swiss cheese!'

'And what did you find?' asked an enthralled Fabian.

'A ring. This one.' His aunt held out her left hand where a thin band of gold was adorned with a small diamond. 'He'd buried it in an empty tobacco tin on the slope at the back of the shop. When we finally unearthed it, he got down on one knee and proposed. Even if I'd wanted to, I couldn't have said no after all that effort.'

'True love,' sighed Fabian, caught in the tale of fifty years ago.

'There's no such thing,' retorted a harsh voice from the door. 'Don't let them addle your brain, Fabian.'

'Bonjour, Christian,' Josette said as he bent to kiss her and then turned to give Véronique two quick pecks on the cheeks. 'You're not a believer in love, then?'

The farmer tossed his head, blond curls springing around his face, and Véronique couldn't help thinking that, if it wasn't for the sour countenance below them, they almost made him look angelic. Almost.

'No. Not at all. Men and women would fare much better if they treated relationships like they do business. It would cut down the divorce rate for a start.'

Véronique hadn't seen him since their encounter at the pool and it didn't look like his frame of mind had improved any. But still, she was an Estaque. And the one thing she was incapable of was holding her peace.

'Since when did you become an expert on romance?' she asked. 'It's not like you've had much experience!'

He flinched and she immediately regretted her

78

words. But again, being an Estaque, she was slow to admit it and so suffered the consequences. When he turned to her, his expression was hostile, his tone scathing.

'Whereas you, Véronique, are besieged with admirers and entirely suited to dispensing advice.' He shifted his focus to Josette. 'Nails. That's what I'm here for. Have you had a delivery?'

The two of them walked to the back of the shop and Véronique let out the breath she'd been holding.

'Wow. He's not in a great mood,' observed Fabian with the insight of a child.

'Seems to be a regular state of affairs.'

'You haven't asked him what's wrong?'

'Me? Why would I?'

Fabian frowned. 'Sorry. I thought . . . the two of you . . . you seem . . . '

'What?' snapped Véronique.

'Nothing!' The Parisian raised his hands in self-defence and backed out of the door, thinking that yet again he had stumbled in the mine-strewn field that represented human affairs.

But over in the fireplace, Jacques Servat — who had woken just as Josette got to the climax of her story and had been wishing he could speak so he could tell the assembled audience that the final straw had been Josette digging a hole in the graveyard of all places — had a different view. Could his nephew be right? While it was patently clear that Christian was in love with Véronique, judging by her

79

reaction just now, was it also possible that she was in love with him?

He watched as Christian placed a box on the counter and handed over a ten-euro note in complete silence while Véronique ran up the bill, neither of them making eye contact. But the tension between them spoke volumes.

It seemed as though Fabian, the person endowed with the least perception in the commune, had hit the nail entirely on the head.

★   ★   ★

Having a sixth sense was all very well in an ideal universe where people were lovely and no one wished anyone harm. In the real world, being able to discern things others couldn't wasn't always a blessing. Especially when that sixth sense wasn't always precise.

Stephanie Morvan placed the last of the geraniums back out on display and, not for the first time, contemplated the custom of closing over lunch. It meant a lot of work, pulling in the stalls she had arranged by the roadside that morning and then having to set everything out again an hour or so later. It didn't really seem practical. Still, the monotony of it took her mind off things.

She stood back and glanced at the flowers, not really seeing the glorious spill of reds and pinks and variegated greens. She had other things on her mind. The lawyers had given her a tentative date for her meeting with her estranged husband and it was only six weeks away.

A tremor of fear rippled through her. Could she do it? Sit across the table from a man who had tried to kill her, not once, but several times? She'd fled their home in Brittany with two-year-old Chloé when his violence had proved too much, and for seven years she'd hidden away in this remote part of the Pyrenees. But a year ago he'd tracked her down. And the encounter had left her with a broken arm, fractured ribs, a black eye and stitches in her head.

She'd survived though. Thanks to Fabian and the rest of the community. And now it was time to draw a line under that part of her life.

Which is where the gypsy intuition that she'd inherited from her mother came in. Despite her best efforts to persuade herself that the prison visit was just a formality and all would be fine, something was flickering at the edge of Stephanie's consciousness. And after what had happened last time, she no longer ignored such things.

Fixing her gaze on the green slopes of the Cap de Bouirex in the distance, she cleared her mind, trying to decipher what her senses were telling her. It was like being in dense fog, sound muffled, vision blurred. Through it came a tumble of movement, a flash of colour and black curls. Chloé. Then Stephanie saw her own face as clearly as if there was a mirror before her, cheeks tracked with tears. And on that scorching July day, the cold that comes only from loss wrapped itself around her.

'Madame?'

Stephanie blinked the future away and focused on the pot of basil that was being held out towards her by a hand that was more bone than flesh. Talon-like fingers grasped the plant and extended into sharp angles of wrist and elbow where, thankfully, a shirt stepped in to cover the rest of the emaciated body. Sticking out of the top, on a scrawny neck, was a face only a geometrician could love.

'How much are the herbs?'

'Three for five euros.'

He nodded, his sharp nose almost poking his chest as he did so. Then he swallowed and she was transfixed by the triangle of his Adam's apple scraping up and down beneath his sallow skin.

'Which do you recommend?'

With an effort, Stephanie tore her eyes away from the man and gestured for him to follow her into the garden centre, crossing to the far corner where the herbs were growing.

'Basil is a good choice. I'd add some thyme to it. And no garden should be without rosemary.' She pulled out two more pots and passed them to him. 'If you take some chives and coriander too, I'll give you the lot for seven euros.'

'Business must be going well,' the man replied with a slash of smile as he took the proffered plants.

'Considering this is only our second summer, then yes, I can't complain.'

'Do you run it yourself?'

'Mostly. I have a bit of help now and then.'

'No permanent staff?'

Stephanie laughed. 'Not yet. Maybe when we expand! Although given the cost of employing people . . . ' She let the statement hang and the man's nose dipped to his chest in agreement.

'Must be hard. Juggling work and family.' He pointed at Chloé's bike, which was propped against the counter.

'I manage. And people around here are fantastic.'

'Well, I wish you all the best,' he said, holding out a ten-euro note. She fished the change out of her money belt and as she held out the coins, her hand brushed his, giving both of them a static shock.

'Sorry!' he said as he pulled back his hand. 'Must be the dry air.'

He refused the offer of a bag and Stephanie watched him go, herbs clasped in the crook of his bony elbow. She kept watching him, even followed him out onto the road so she could see what car he got into. Only when he had pulled away towards St Girons did she glance at her fingers.

They still tingled, as though his flesh had burned her. Which it had. A shaft of pain had seared her arm the moment they'd made contact, followed by an overwhelming feeling of sadness. The sort that accompanies the loss of something precious. It was the very same feeling she'd had about Chloé just before he arrived.

Were the two connected? The man had asked a lot of questions for a customer. Personal questions too, now she thought about it. And he was sharp. He'd worked out she had a child, despite the lack of a wedding ring. Like he was a private investigator or something. But who would send an investigator after her?

Bruno Madec, her estranged husband.

Was he digging into her affairs because of the divorce? But why? It wasn't as if there were going to be any alimony claims. She wanted nothing more to do with him and doubted he'd expect to get anything from her. All she had was an old blue van and a load of debts after setting up the business. So what could he want?

Her gaze rested on the small bike, bear-shaped bell on the handlebars, a summer's worth of dirt on the tyres. Then she shivered, despite the heat, as trepidation seized her.

Chloé. He wanted Chloé. Was it possible that Bruno Madec was planning to seek custody, even though he knew the truth?

6

'It's an insult. To all of us. And to Napoleon most of all!'

'What's Napoleon got to do with it? Cars weren't exactly around in his time.'

René glared at Véronique over the rim of his pastis. 'It's not about cars. It's about denying us our heritage. Our patrimony. A Frenchman has a right to declare his origins and to be proud of them.'

'And a Frenchwoman?'

René ignored the passing comment from Josette, who was carrying drinks to the next table on the terrace.

'Those bureaucrats up in Paris seem to forget,' he continued, 'that this nation was built by the little people they so conveniently ignore when they concoct these schemes to make us less French than we are!'

Mayor Serge Papon, who'd only popped down to get the evening's baguette and was leaving the épicerie with it tucked under his arm, heard the discussion, saw Véronique sitting there, and couldn't resist. He ordered a pastis from Josette and pulled out a chair beside a grateful-looking postmistress.

'What's up now?' he asked her.

'René had a problem trying to register his car.' She rolled her eyes.

'I didn't have a problem. It's the *fonctionnaires*

85

down in the Sous-Préfecture that have the problem!'

'What happened?'

Véronique's head sank into her hands as René began all over again.

'First of all they closed for lunch just as I got to the counter. So I went back later but had to queue for nearly an hour. Then, when I finally got to the front they said I couldn't have the traditional number plate, even though I'm registering a second-hand car. I had to have the new type, which doesn't include the 09 for Ariège.'

'That's been the case for a while now,' explained Serge. 'Whenever a car changes ownership, the new number plate system comes into effect. And that means no departmental numbers.'

'But how is anyone supposed to know where I'm from?' demanded René.

'You can have the 09 added at the side,' offered Josette on her way back into the bar.

'In minuscule writing that no one can see!'

'Personally,' Véronique said wearily, 'I don't see why it matters. In fact, not having to change number plates every time you move department must be a real improvement for some people. And, in these straitened times, it must be cost efficient for the country.'

'Cost efficient?' The plumber nearly exploded. 'We're talking identity here. When I'm driving around I like people to know that I come from the Ariège. And I also like to be able to tell, when I'm on these roads in the summer, whether the idiot taking the turns in front of me at thirty kilometres per hour is a bloody Parisian or not.'

He took a gulp of his drink, finger and thumb of his right hand rubbing together furiously.

'Here's a man who'll agree with me. Bonsoir, Christian!' He hailed the farmer, who was extricating his long limbs from the cramped interior of his battered Panda 4×4 across the road. 'Come and have a drink with us and add some sense to this discussion.'

Christian came towards them in long strides and as René rose to greet him, Véronique finished her beer and made to leave.

'Can't you stay a bit longer?' Serge asked, his hand on her arm and his voice low so the others couldn't hear. 'I haven't seen you for days.'

She glanced at the farmer, who was ordering a beer from Josette while René recounted his tale of woe yet again, and Serge saw an uncharacteristic wariness on her face.

'I should go . . . '

'You can't even manage one more with your papa?'

A blush stole across her cheeks and he thought he'd gone too far, his paternal claim on her still relatively new and something they were both getting accustomed to. But a smile followed the colour and she settled back into her chair. 'Well, as you're my papa, I will give you the honour of paying!'

'Another beer, Josette please,' Serge called through the open window, turning back in time to see the tall farmer brushing his cheeks against Véronique's in greeting, neither of them looking comfortable.

'Bonsoir,' muttered Christian, slouching into the metal seat and stretching his long legs under the table.

'How are things at the farm?' asked Serge as Josette arrived with their beers.

'Good. Excellent in fact. I've had a letter from the Chambre d'Agriculture and my application for the grants for solar panels has met with initial approval.'

'That's fantastic!' exclaimed Véronique, her delight at his news overcoming any awkwardness. Christian smiled, causing whatever tension had been between them to dissipate.

'I won't hear for definite until after the summer, but it's looking hopeful. So you can tell Annie it's probably going to get the go-ahead. And thank her again from me, will you?'

Véronique nodded, her mother's decision to allow Christian Dupuy to have the use of her farm having had a significant impact on his life, enabling him to stay in the area when his own farm had proved unviable.

'I will. And she'll no doubt tell the pair of us to bugger off!'

'Buggerrrr off, you mean,' quipped René in an accurate imitation of the older woman's accent.

'I had another bit of news today,' continued Christian. 'I had an email from the Ariège-Pyrenees tourism department over in Foix. They want to put a webcam on Sarko's collar.'

There was a split second of silence and then everyone burst out laughing.

'You're joking?' asked Véronique. 'They want

to put a camera on your cantankerous bull?'

'That's what they've said. It's some new initiative. Something to do with promoting the region and its mountain traditions. They want to broadcast the summer pastures live on the internet.'

'And they chose Sarko?'

Christian shrugged, knowing his bull and therefore knowing why she sounded incredulous. 'Apparently he's become famous . . . '

He didn't need to explain. They'd all been there the week before when Sarko the Limousin bull had entertained the nation on live television with his usual antics, making the disruption of the Tour de France compulsive viewing. And incredibly effective.

'But what will the camera show?' asked René.

'Not a lot. Grass. Mountains. The odd fleeing backside of an unsuspecting tourist. But they're offering to pay, so who am I to object?'

'Pay?' René shook his head in despair, fingers and thumb agitating once more. 'What is the country coming to?'

'Maybe it's not so daft as it sounds,' said Véronique. 'Perhaps it will generate an interest in the area and bring more people here. God knows we could do with it.'

'Véronique's right. I was sceptical at first but now — '

'Now when you know you'll be getting paid . . . '

Serge eased back in his seat and let the conversation waft over him. It was his favourite time of the day. The ferocious heat was starting to abate, the gentle breeze coming off the river was a welcome relief, and all around him the commune was stirring. Shutters were being slapped open to welcome in the cooler air and with that came the drift of voices, the scent of cooking, a faint lilt of music, laughter. The place was coming back to life, shaking off the torpor that accompanied high temperatures, and it made Serge's heart sing.

He loved this commune, with its three disparate and discordant villages which existed in a permanent state of dispute, yet never failed to unite when an external threat materialised. Loved it so much that he'd devoted his life to it when the mines up at Salau had closed and he'd been thrown on the growing pile of the region's unemployed. Twenty-six years on, his time underground had long been eclipsed by his prowess as a politician, but his twisted hands, misshapen from years of labouring, served as a daily reminder, keeping him grounded and making him appreciate the difficulties many of his electorate faced as they tried to eke a living out of this forbidding land.

Across the river, glittering in the evening sunshine, lay Sarrat. A much bigger community. A much wealthier one. One that could afford to re-slate its church roof while Fogas still hadn't got round to replacing the statue of Jesus that had lost its head in a football incident two decades ago. But Serge wouldn't have swapped his birthright for the world.

Of course, anyone born in Fogas had an inbuilt antipathy for the commune across the water; a hatred passed on at birth and nurtured over the generations, culminating in an acrimonious division at the time of the Revolution when the leaders of Fogas seized their chance in the upheaval of a new regime to establish independence from their dominant neighbour. It was an independence they were fiercely proud of and one that Serge would fight to keep.

However, it wasn't just a genetic animosity that fuelled Serge's allegiance to this rugged region. Fogas was special. It had a bellicose personality forged from the hardship of life in the mountains. Lacking the pastureland of their affluent neighbours, many of the inhabitants had had to leave to survive and those who remained had to be adaptable. Had to be willing to take risks in order to exist. Which gave the place character.

' . . . And don't get me ssshtarted on the Ssshous-Préfecture!'

A fine example of that very character, René Piquemal was back on the subject *du jour*, face worked up, right hand fidgeting in an unusual manner. Serge couldn't help but notice that his words were beginning to slur.

'Passshtisssh, Jossshette,' the plumber said as she passed, but Christian intervened.

'I think you've had enough, René. How about I drive you home?'

'But I've only had one!'

'Well, perhaps your incident at the Sous-Préfecture has left you out of sorts. Or maybe you need a cigarette?'

'I've given up.' René folded stout arms proudly

across his chest. 'Four daysssh and counting.'

'Mon dieu!' exclaimed the farmer, raking a hand through his curls in disbelief. 'I never even noticed.'

'I know!'

'But how have you done it?' asked Véronique, remembering René's last failed attempt when he'd covered himself in so many nicotine patches he'd made himself sick.

The plumber tapped his nose. 'It'sssh a ssshecret.'

'Well, however you've done it, you don't sound fit to drive. Come on, I'll take you home.' Christian gestured for them to go, but as the shorter man stood to leave, his legs buckled and only the farmer's strong arm stopped him from falling.

'Dizzy,' muttered René. 'Ssshame thing happened in the bloody Ssshous-Préfecture. I dropped all my papersssh and the damn préfet ssshtopped to help pick them up.'

'The préfet?' Serge's voice was sharp in the softness of the evening. 'He was in St Girons?'

René nodded. 'I didn't recognissshe him at firsssht. Then when I did, he claimed never to have met me.'

'Perhaps he didn't know you without a cigarette in your mouth,' retorted Véronique as she stood to help Christian negotiate his charge to his car.

Rene's indignant response was drowned out as the Angelus began to sound, and Serge let the notes carry his gaze to the commune across the river. Something was afoot. Of that he was sure.

Not one of his contacts could tell him anything about the préfet's mysterious visit to Fogas. But even if Serge had been inclined to accept it was innocuous, news that the same man was down at the Sous-Préfecture merely days later was enough to trigger concern.

Whatever Monsieur Jérôme Ulrich was up to, all of Serge's political experience was telling him that it didn't bode well for his beloved commune. And for once, the peal of bells which he normally took great pleasure in only served to darken his mood as they tolled across the valley like a death knell for the ill-fated Fogas.

★　★　★

The chimes of the Angelus were borne by the evening breeze, up from the valley floor and over the ridges far above, uniting the geographically fractured commune with their call. To one side they floated past the disused *lavoir* and the collection of houses that huddled on the mountainside, and even reached as far as the town hall, the large building at the end of Fogas that spoke of more prosperous times. To the other, they twisted through the forest and wrapped around the huge lime tree that marked the centre of Picarets before fading into the hillside beyond, where, on a little-used track, two men stood.

For one of the men, that distant melody should have heralded rejoicing, his ability to hear the bells nothing short of miraculous after nearly a week of silence. But Pascal Souquet could take no joy in his deliverance, for his ability to hear the Angelus meant he could also hear the man standing next to him. And what that man was asking the first deputy mayor to do.

'Don't be too dramatic. Lots of small things. That's the way to go.' The man swung his gaze onto Pascal, blue eyes colder than the river in winter. 'Do you think you can cope?'

As always, contempt coloured the words. Pascal swallowed and his ears popped painfully, the only lingering reminder of his recent malady.

'What if . . . what if I get caught?' The words squeezed past his fear and the stare hardened into threat.

'Make sure you don't. I would hate to have to intervene.'

Perspiration pricked the first deputy mayor's forehead. Nothing to do with the heat as the day slumped towards night. More to do with the fact that he knew, better than anyone, what this man was capable of. He already had one murder to his name. A bear. One of a protected species, killed at his behest. A killing that tied Pascal to him in knots that were impossible to unravel. Not without Pascal going to jail.

'This is the last chance,' the man continued, switching his focus to the commune on the opposite hillside, the object of his attention and the cause of all the trouble. 'And I don't intend to fail. So do this. And do it right.'

Pascal nodded, a bead of sweat dropping onto his shirt as he did.

'Good. Start as soon as you can. We've only got until the end of the summer.'

'And then . . . ?'

'Then? Why, Pascal, then we will be done with old Papon and the meddlesome farmer and you will achieve everything you have hoped for. And all through legitimate channels.' With a mocking laugh, Henri Dedieu, mayor of Sarrat, threw his cigarette butt on the ground and crushed it under his heel before fixing Pascal with a final stare, 'Just as long as you don't let me down.'

He turned, making his way along the path to where they'd left their cars, and the first deputy mayor of Fogas measured the retreating footsteps against the far-off sound of the bells commemorating the message of the angel Gabriel. For Pascal Souquet, they had just delivered orders from the devil himself.

* * *

'It'll be fine,' said Fabian, as he ran his hands through Stephanie's hair in rhythm with the gentle chimes floating on the evening air. She was lying on the bench in the garden behind the small cottage at the far end of Picarets, head on his lap, her glorious red curls spread like fire across him. He still half-expected to burn his fingers when he touched them.

'But what if I'm right? What if that man really was snooping around?' Her voice caught in her throat. 'What if — ?'

'Shush.' He moved his caresses to her shoulders until he felt the tension in them soften, delighting in the feel of her skin, so pale against the fierce shock of her hair. From the village came a carillon of children's laughter which momentarily harmonised with the faraway bells, and he saw a flicker of a smile pass across her face as though she could pick out her daughter's voice amid the music.

'That's better. There's really no point in worrying. Especially as we won't know anything for certain until after the summer. And anyway, you've got the birth certificate.'

He glanced at the slip of paper next to him on the bench. Torn and stained, it looked fragile but spoke volumes about the strength of the woman he loved. Smoothing out the creases, he cast his eyes over it once more. The date, the time, Chloé's name written out in an ornate hand. But it was the next section that caught the attention. The part where the father's name should be. It was blank. And at the bottom, Stephanie's looping signature flowed across the page.

'How did you get away with it?' he queried, and she tensed once more under his hand.

'Chloé was born at home. The midwife knew me. Knew my situation.' Stephanie gave a bitter laugh. 'How couldn't she? I was in labour with a black eye, a sprained wrist and countless bruises. When I asked her to help, she agreed.'

'So you didn't identify Bruno as the father?'

Stephanie shook her head. 'The midwife left it blank on the certificate. When I went to the town hall to register the birth, they never questioned it.'

'So even then, you were planning your escape?'

She twisted so she could see his face. 'Does

96

that make me seem callous?'

'No. Sensible, more like. And Bruno? He never queried the fact that Chloé was officially registered in your name and without a father?'

'He didn't know. He was too busy getting drunk to ask to see the documentation.' She turned back to stare across the valley at Mont Valier, its flat top cresting the line of peaks that were shimmering in the evening sun. 'And anyway,' she continued, her voice no more than a whisper, 'I did nothing wrong. I knew she wasn't his child.'

Fabian's hand stalled. 'You knew for sure?' he asked, treading carefully in this area they had never discussed before.

'Yes. Without a doubt.'

He remained silent and she knew he was waiting for more. And that she owed him it. She sat up and took his hand in hers, stroking the long fingers as she decided what to say. How much to say.

'Bruno was at a family funeral,' she began. 'He didn't want me there because we'd had a row the night before and I was covered in bruises. He knew there would be questions, so he ordered me to stay at home . . . ' She shivered and Fabian instinctively drew her closer, his arm tight around her shoulders.

'You don't have to . . . '

'There's not much to tell, to be honest. I snuck out. Met someone. It was a fling. A rash moment. I think I did it to prove I could still control my own life. Then I found out I was pregnant. I decided to leave and Bruno came home to find me packing. He broke down in tears. Begged me to stay. Promised he'd change . . . and I believed him.' She fiddled with a strand of hair, twining it round and round her fingers. 'I still loved him. That was the problem. I thought I could make a difference.'

'And did you?'

'Chloé did. To begin with. He was besotted with her. A gurgle or a smile was all it took to turn his mood from dark to light. But then, about eighteen months after she was born, he started again.'

'Hitting you?'

She nodded. 'Only this time, he told me what he'd do if I even thought of leaving. So I planned an escape. One that would be permanent. But it wasn't, was it? And now he might be plotting to take Chloé back.'

A shaking hand went up to her mouth and Fabian's heart wrenched.

'He can't. Not with this.' He held up the birth certificate like a trump card. 'This is your proof that he's not her father.'

'Do you think it will be enough?'

'I'm sure of it. I called an old colleague up in Paris whose partner is a lawyer, and apparently it's no longer presumed that a husband is the father of a child if he isn't named on the birth certificate. Given that and the fact that he's in prison for attempted murder, there's no way any court in the land would grant Bruno Madec custody of Chloé.'

'But what if it isn't him who is seeking it? His parents would do anything for him. What if *they*'re planning to claim custody in his stead?'

'I really don't think they'd have a leg to stand on,' said Fabian, with as much confidence as he could, not having thought of that possibility.

She leaned her head against his chest. 'I hope you're right. Because otherwise it would mean a DNA test to prove Chloé's paternity and I really don't want her having to go through that.'

As the last of the Angelus bells chimed across the hills, he hoped to God he was right too.

★ ★ ★

Chloé wasn't where she should be. She was supposed to be down in the square playing with the Rogalle twins. Which to be fair, she had been. With their cousins visiting from Toulouse and swelling the numbers of their group from three to six, a robust game of rugby had commenced. For a while they were wrapped up in the sport, enjoying the freedom of the outdoors and the cooler temperatures that the early evening brought. But while Max and Nicolas were used to having a girl in their midst, their older cousins clearly weren't, and when Chloé dodged past one of them and scored a try, the trouble had started.

The taller one was the ringleader. He began to tease the twins, asking which one was her boyfriend. She'd told them to ignore him. But then his brother joined in, refusing to throw her the ball until she revealed which of the twins she wanted to go out with. She'd said neither, which had elicited a burst of laughter and she'd realised how it sounded.

Confused and annoyed, she'd told them to shut up but the taller one had begun mimicking her, his brothers copying him and taunting Max and Nicolas, who'd seemed as perplexed as she was by this behaviour, until they started making fun of her too. Then the tall cousin had made a comment about her father. Or lack of one. And he'd thrown the ball straight at her, vicious and fast.

She'd caught it easily, small hands plucking it out of the air. And on a burst of temper she'd inherited from her mother, she'd hurled it straight back at him before he had a chance to react. She knew it was a good shot before it smacked him full in the face. She was already turned and running before he collapsed to the ground in a howl of pain and a gush of blood. By the time the others managed to convince him that he wasn't dying and had simply lost a tooth, she was sneaking into the cottage and heading for her room.

What was it with boys? One minute they were friends and the next . . . Chloé had flung herself on her bed, mood dark, soul troubled. She was already in a state of turmoil as the summer days ebbed away, leaving in their wake the horrific prospect of what September held in store.

Collège. In precisely six weeks and one day's time, she would be starting at the big school in the village of Seix in the neighbouring valley. And she was dreading it.

It wasn't that she was ill-prepared for the change in an academic sense. She had long outgrown the lessons of old Madame Soum and the confines of being in a class of mixed ages and mixed abilities; she'd grown bored of all the small school up in Sarrat could offer her. Nor was she particularly worried about making new friends — given the way the Rogalle twins were behaving, right now that seemed a welcome prospect.

But there was one thing she was going to miss about her days in the tiny building perched on a plateau across the river and it was something that Seix, with its cafés and bakery and busy square, just couldn't compensate for.

Mountains.

When she stared out of her lessons from her new classroom on the valley floor, she wasn't going to be able to see the jagged line of summits that curved the horizon. She wasn't going to be able to imagine flying across the sky on a trapeze, the peaks of the Pyrenees her backdrop, while some teacher droned on about Napoleon and his stupid plane trees. Nor would she be able to watch the seasons drape the crests in their own colours, relieving her schooldays of drabness with a range of reds and greens before winter smothered everything in white.

It just wasn't fair.

She lay on the bed, railing against her future and boys in particular, the warm air in her bedroom lifted by the slightest of breezes sliding through the open window and bringing with it the chime of the bells from La Rivière. It had also conveyed the hushed conversation from the garden below, the voices of Maman and Fabian all too clear, and suddenly, Chloé's troubles were multiplied.

It wasn't her fault. She knew she wasn't meant to hear but she could hardly help it. And so she found out that she didn't have a father's name on her birth certificate. That her real father had meant nothing to her mother. But worst of all, she heard them talking about Bruno Madec, the man who had attacked her and Maman and still terrorised her dreams. From what she could hear, he was seeking to make her his child.

For young Chloé Morvan, as the final peal of the bells tolled in the distance, it seemed to be announcing that her childhood was over.

7

In any other year, for the mountain commune of Fogas the days of summer flew by in a haze of shutters opening and closing, mutterings about tourists, the soft click of pétanque balls at the lay-by and the lazy drone of conversation on honeysuckle-scented twilit terraces. But this year was different. This year the days crawled past, sweaty and slick with humidity, beaten flat of any joy by the merciless heat, the mercury hitting heights not seen in decades. The residents went about their work with sullen faces, tempers worn and patience frayed, while the children hung listlessly in the shade of trees or down at the pool, sapped of their natural ebullience. Towards the end of August, with the heatwave still persisting, the mood among the populace had become as ominous as the dark clouds that gathered in the distance but never broke.

Down at the Auberge des Deux Vallées, despite its proximity to the cooling waters of the river, things were no better. As she put the latest weekly weather forecast on the wall where the guests would be sure to see it, Lorna Webster caught herself sighing.

Sunshine. Seven squares showing bright yellow discs stretching from Saturday through to the following Friday, and all underlined with numbers ranging from thirty to thirty-five.

Who'd have thought it? She was longing for rain.

She stretched to ease the stiffness in her lower back, ran a hand over her bump that now protruded alarmingly from her stomach, and tried not to think about cooking in the heat that was already building. Wiping a tissue over her brow she turned to Stephanie, who was clearing the last of the breakfast settings.

'Tell me this weather is just an anomaly.' Lorna flicked a limp hand at the glare of sunlight bouncing off the terrace where the cat lay prostrate, watching the scurrying patter of lizards on the hot tiles with lethargic eyes.

'A-no-ma-ly?'

'Sorry! Unusual. Not normal.'

'Ah! *Anomalie* . . . ' Stephanie repeated the word in French, stressing the final syllable. When she'd started work at the Auberge she'd asked that Lorna and Paul use English as much as possible with her, and so far it hadn't proved a problem. But since becoming pregnant, Lorna found herself frequently forgetting to modify her language. Consequently, her waitress had benefited from several months of advanced lessons.

'It is not normal. You are right. Zis is definitely an an-om-al-y.' Stephanie tried to twist her tongue around the Anglo-Saxon intonation but even that couldn't entice a smile from Lorna.

Almost four weeks of unrelenting sunshine and high temperatures — which for someone born and raised in the unpredictable climate of northern England took some getting used to — had failed to break on the magical fifteenth. Pinning her hopes on old Annie Estaque's bold assertion that the Feast of the Assumption always brought the mountain rain, Lorna had circled the date on the calendar. But the fifteenth of August had passed six days ago and not a drop of moisture had fallen. Nor had the temperatures eased off, giving pregnant Lorna, her hormones already making her feel uncomfortably hot, sleepless nights and irritable days. She was suffering.

And she was getting bigger. Rapidly. In the last month her waistline had disappeared, replaced by a beach-ball stomach that got larger by the day. It was almost as though her baby felt free to grow now that the whole of Fogas knew of his impending arrival.

'Sit down and I will make you a *tisane*.'

Lorna wilted gratefully onto a chair and marvelled yet again at the ability of her waitress to read her mind.

'Were you this tired with Chloé?'

'No, I don't think so. But zen, I was not as big as you! And per'aps I was too scared to notice.' Stephanie shrugged as though casting the memories off her back. 'It was not an easy time.'

'Sorry, I didn't mean . . . '

'You English! Always apologising,' retorted Stephanie with a laugh as she placed the herbal tea before Lorna and took the remaining breakfast dishes through to the kitchen.

Five and a half months down. Three and a half to go. December had never been more longed for. Back in April, Lorna wouldn't have believed that her pregnancy would be reduced to a waiting game. An impatient ticking off of the days, a shooing out of the unbearable summer that had made her first experience of carrying a baby difficult at times. Of course, running the Auberge didn't help. While Paul did all he could to take on her share and Stephanie had been a godsend, it was high season and they couldn't afford to turn customers away. There was no avoiding extended hours and heavier workloads for the mother-to-be.

The rituals of pregnancy had also taken second place to the business. She'd been for her twenty-two week scan the week before and unlike the first one, when Paul had sat next to her, the pair of them transfixed by the fuzzy images on the screen that purported to be their child, this time, with the Auberge full and the restaurant busy, she'd had to go alone.

When she'd reached the hospital in St Girons, she was already flagging from the heat. Tired and wilting, she'd struggled to follow the rapid French of the receptionist but had managed to understand that the regular sonographer was en vacances. Instead of the capable woman who'd seen her before, she was put in the not-too-steady hands of a young man who must have been straight out of college. He got gel all over himself and the machine, turned it off mid-scan by mistake and became flustered when Lorna struggled to follow his garbled commentary. Given no chance to really look at her baby, she was in and out in record time. It was only on her way home, almost in tears at her ordeal, that she'd remembered he hadn't printed off a photo for her.

There'd been no time to get upset. She'd

arrived back at the Auberge and was plunged straight into preparation for the evening meals. Later — much later — when the dishes were done, the tables set for breakfast and the guests all in bed, Paul had consoled her, taking the view that a missed photo wasn't worth worrying about as long as the baby was in good health. Still, it would have been nice to have something to hang a name on rather than the blurred oval of nothing that was the twelve-week shot.

Lorna reached for her tea and had just got it to her lips when someone entered the restaurant. Suppressing the second sigh of the morning, she twisted to see a cadaverous figure standing in the entrance, his nose the finest example of Gallic nasal anatomy she had yet to encounter.

'Bonjour. Are you open for coffee?'

'Of course.' She gestured at the tables as she got wearily to her feet. 'Here or on the back terrace?'

As though taking pity on her fatigue, he settled himself in a seat facing the door, bony hands clasped on the table, and cast a glance around the empty room.

'You're very quiet today.'

'It's still early. We get busy about eleven.'

'I'm guessing you're not from round here?'

Lorna smiled, used to her heavily accented French giving her away, if her pale skin didn't. 'I'm English.'

'Your husband too?'

'Yes. We fell in love with the area and then this place.' She threw an affectionate glance at the solid walls of the Auberge.

A curve of thin lips came in response. 'It's easy to understand. But running an auberge? It's hard work. You must have help?'

At that moment the kitchen door swung open and Stephanie entered.

'The best help possible,' replied Lorna, with a grateful look at her waitress.

'Ah, madame, bonjour. You're having a day off from the garden centre?'

'Bonjour,' muttered Stephanie, face darkening as she acknowledged the man with an uncustomary scowl. She busied herself setting the tables for lunch, keeping over to the far side of the restaurant. Unable to fathom the tension between waitress and customer, Lorna placed an espresso before the man and watched him add sugar to it. He was on his fifth spoonful when the front door opened again, this time two policemen on the threshold.

'Bonjour, Madame Webster.' The older of the two stepped forward, removing his cap as he stretched out his hand in greeting. 'And congratulations!'

He grinned, indicating the area that used to be her waist. 'We'd heard Monsieur Webster had been busy. When is it due?'

'The second week of December.'

His eyebrows shot up as he glanced again at her swollen stomach. 'Mon dieu! I thought it was sooner. Must be those Anglo-Saxon genes.' He nudged his partner and the two of them laughed. Stephanie rolled her eyes behind them. 'Is it a boy or a girl?'

'The last ultrasound wasn't clear but Stephanie thinks — '

'Definitely male,' interjected Stephanie, and the two men, long acquainted with her capacity to divine the future, took her at her word.

'A boy? Marvellous!' enthused the older officer. 'We'll get him signed up for the rugby club at Seix. We could do with a good prop forward.'

'Prop forward?' The younger man's face was scornful. 'Pah! It's not the props that are the problem. What we need is a decent scrum half. Someone with a bit of pace to his game.'

'Are you mad? Those forwards are bone idle. If I was the coach — '

'Coffee?' Stephanie cut through their bickering, which was so ingrained it was part of their uniform.

The older officer shook his head. 'No, no coffee today. We don't have time. We've had a call from Agnès Rogalle in the butcher's van. She's had more meat stolen and wants to make a formal complaint.'

'Again? It's almost every week now.'

The policeman grimaced. 'And always in Fogas. Can't think for the life of me who it could be.'

'Old Widow Aubert?' quipped his partner with a chuckle.

'Or the Lavoir Gang?' responded the other, referring irreverently to the old men who gathered daily at the disused washbasins to put the world to rights.

'What about Pascal Souquet? Perhaps he's resorted to stuffing sausages in his ears in an attempt to regain the peace he had when he was deaf.'

'So, no coffee then,' Stephanie said pointedly, interrupting their laughter as Lorna reached out a hand to support herself on a table. 'In that case, how can we help you?'

The joking demeanour was dropped and the senior officer pulled a notebook out of his pocket. 'Actually, we've had an order from on high to inspect your licence.'

'The alcohol licence?' Lorna asked.

'Yes, if you wouldn't mind showing it to me? It's just routine, you understand.'

He gave her the stoic look of the underling carrying out nonsensical orders, but the request was enough to transform the heat that had been plaguing Lorna into a chill of concern. After the fiasco that had transpired when they first bought the Auberge, she'd been through enough French bureaucratic hoops to know that nothing was ever routine. Still, at least she had this one covered. Within minutes the relevant bit of paper was in the officer's hands.

Inspecting the document carefully, the policeman made a few notes and then handed the licence back to Lorna. 'That all seems in order. And your Alcohol Awareness Certificate?'

'Er . . . I haven't got one.'

'But you've done the course?'

'Not yet.'

The policeman froze, face troubled, and Lorna gabbled into the silence.

'It wasn't compulsory when we bought, and then . . . Mayor Papon, he allows us . . . allowed us to — ' Through a combination of worry and fatigue, her French deserted her and she glanced at Stephanie for help.

'To postpone it.'

' — to postpone it because our French is not good and we have . . . had no money for the course fees . . . and now . . . ' The frazzled *aubergiste* rubbed her baby bump with an apologetic smile.

'So, you haven't completed the course?'

She shook her head and the officers exchanged glances, the younger one sucking air between his teeth.

'You shouldn't be operating without a certificate,' he said, face grave as his colleague scribbled notes. 'We'll have to report this.'

'But Paul, my husband, he tries . . . tried to do the course,' pleaded Lorna. 'But it was full in spring, and in the summer . . . ' She gestured at the tables awaiting the lunchtime rush. 'We have no time.'

'That's no excuse, I'm afraid,' said the older officer. 'I'm sorry, Madame Webster. If one of you was enrolled on the course, then perhaps I could waive my report.'

Two years. It wasn't long enough for Lorna to have got to grips with the ways of her French neighbours when it came to officialdom, and so, with her British propensity for doing things by the book, she missed the heavy hint, the lifeline thrown out into the choppy waters of administration. Stephanie, however, didn't miss a thing.

'But Paul is enrolled on a course. For early November. How could you forget, Lorna?' Stephanie put a comradely arm around the policeman, her bracelets chiming mesmerically

111

along her pale skin, and lowered her voice. 'She forgets a lot of things lately. It's the baby.'

The man's face melted, his mask of duty replaced with a fond smile. 'Ah, yes. My wife was the same. Total birdbrain with every pregnancy.'

Stephanie shrugged a shoulder and spread her hands in supplication. 'So, everything is all right? I mean, it's only a couple of months away and in the meantime, it's not like we get a lot of underage drinkers in Fogas. Just the opposite!'

Both officers laughed and the atmosphere changed in that quicksilver way typical of a culture that lived through emotion, wrong-footing Lorna yet again.

'And after all,' continued Stephanie, still working her magic, 'seeing as they are Anglo-Saxons, you should really be insisting that they do an Alcohol *Appreciation* course instead. That way they might learn something about our fine French wines.'

'Good point! What the hell do the English know about wine? And as for that awful beer they sell — '

'I quite like the beer,' said the younger officer as they put away their notebooks, shook hands with the two women and put their hats back on.

'But it's served at room temperature! How on earth could you drink it? It must taste like dishwater.'

'Actually, it doesn't. It's rather — '

'Au revoir.' Stephanie held the door open for them.

'Au revoir!' They departed, still deep in dispute.

'I wonder who was responsible for zat?' muttered Stephanie, reverting to English as the police car drove past the window.

'They said it was just routine.'

'Pah! A sudden demand for your paperwork? *Non!* Zat is not routine.'

'Well, what then?'

'I don't know. And zat is ze problem.'

The sound of a chair squeaking on tiles made both women jump and Lorna caught sight of their forgotten customer slipping a notepad and pen into his back pocket. Throwing a handful of change on the table, he left, heading up the road in the direction of the épicerie. Stephanie shuddered as his dark shadow disappeared over the bridge.

'Do you know him?' asked Lorna.

'I 'ave met 'im once. It was enough. 'E 'as a bad aura.' She paused as if considering how much more to say and then her green gaze rested on the Englishwoman, revealing the depth of her concern. 'It sounds crazy but I think 'e might be watching me.'

'Watching you? Why?'

'Per'aps it is to do wiz ze divorce. Per'aps my 'usband will fight for Chloé?'

'He can't! No court would grant him custody.'

Stephanie sighed. 'I wish I could be so sure. But for now, you must make a call. You must make a booking for Paul on ze alcohol awareness course before ze police have time to check!'

Lorna laughed, thanked her friend for her quick thinking and decided, as she took heavy steps towards the phone, that she wouldn't mention to Stephanie that the stick-man had been taking notes. It would only worry the waitress further. Instead, she would tell Christian Dupuy when she next saw him. If Stephanie was in trouble, this time the village wouldn't let her down.

★　★　★

Two days later and still the air hung thick and heavy in the valleys. In the garden centre, Stephanie was battling to keep her wilting plants alive and in the river the bold stones of the weir were exposed as water levels dwindled. Even in the épicerie, its thick walls a natural barrier to the heat, the atypical weather was being felt.

'I've never seen the river so low.'

'Not rrright, it's not. We always get rrrain arrround the Assumption.'

Both women shook their heads, Josette gently fanning herself with a copy of the *Gazette Ariégeoise* as they sat in the dark interior of the bar, the glare of yet another sunny day whiting out everything beyond the windows.

'I hope it breaks before the fête this weekend.'

Annie snorted. 'Why? Do you think the heat will rrruin the pétanque?'

'Given the average age of the players . . . '

'Now, now, you two. No disparaging the Fogas fête. I know it's the highlight of your social calendar.' The women laughed as Christian Dupuy pulled up a chair and joined them, mopping his forehead with the back of his hand. 'I see the workmen have been busy.' He nodded

114

towards the épicerie where the back section was being remodelled to accommodate the new post office counter.

Josette glowered. 'Usual story. They kept rescheduling and then when they finally started, I was told they'd be a week. They're already into their second.'

'It'll look good when it's done though.'

'I'm not holding my breath!'

'So, arrre you all rrready forrr Saturrrday?'

Christian threw Annie a grateful glance for the distraction from Josette's disgruntlement. 'Pretty much. I take it you'll change the habit of a lifetime and attend this year?'

Annie shrugged, not having given the matter much thought, inured to three decades of self-imposed isolation as a single mother in a small community. But now that the secret of her child's paternity was common knowledge, there was no reason for her not to go to the annual fête. Apart from the fact that what passed for a fête in Fogas was a woeful spectacle indeed.

While other communes in the region battled over the best weekend slots for their summer festivities, the preferred dates being in the middle of the month-long boom in tourism that fell between Bastille Day and the Assumption, the Conseil Municipal that governed Fogas never seemed particularly bothered by the customary revels. Consequently they were always lumbered with the last weekend in August, when the region was already sated with celebration, the tourists had departed and the weather had usually turned. Combined with a programme of activities that hadn't been updated since the war, Annie didn't think she had missed much in the years of her seclusion.

'Josette!' The strong tones that rang out from the épicerie were well known and none at the table were surprised when the broad figure of Serge Papon, mayor of Fogas, appeared in the archway to the bar, perspiring heavily. 'Damn this heat! Bonjour all.'

'Can I get you a drink?' Josette was already heading for the counter.

'No, not now. I just want to know why the minutes of the last council meeting aren't up on the noticeboard outside.'

'They are.'

'No. They aren't.'

'Yes, they are.'

'I can assure you, they aren't!'

'You can't have been looking in the right place,' snapped Josette, pushing her glasses up her nose and thrusting her chin at the mayor who, although not overly tall, still towered over her petite frame. 'I put them up as soon as I got them. Like I *always* do.'

'For goodness' sake, woman! I'm telling you, they aren't there.'

'What's the matter?' The raised voices had brought Fabian through from the shop and he was met by the sight of Tante Josette and Serge Papon scowling at each other.

'Serge seems to think I haven't put the minutes up from the last meeting.'

'I saw you do it,' said her nephew and Josette folded her arms with an air of triumph.

116

'Well,' said Serge between clenched teeth. 'They. Aren't. There. Now.'

'Why don't you check, Fabian?' suggested Christian, concerned to see two friends arguing. It was this blasted hot weather, of that he was sure. It was making everyone tetchy. Agitated. Paranoid.

'Come on, Tante Josette. Let's go have a look.'

And like a patient father with a fractious child, Fabian led his aunt out of the bar to the communal noticeboard. Which was a rather grand name for the faded wooden cabinet with glass doors that Oncle Jacques had made a long time ago. Serving as a communication point, it displayed posters for events in the area and, of course, housed the minutes of every meeting of the Conseil Municipal, as was required by law. It was tucked in the narrow alley that ran alongside the épicerie and as Josette and Fabian approached, there, before the noticeboard, was a man who made the reedy Parisian seem fat. Long nose pressed against the glass, he was peering at the contents and scribbling on a small pad. With their arrival, he nodded briskly, wheeled round on his heel and strode off, his shadow more substantial than himself.

Paying him little heed, Josette moved over to the cabinet and promptly gasped, her surprised face looking back at her from its polished front. 'What on earth — ?'

Stuck to the board inside and stained with greasy Blu-tack marks, Fabian could see a flyer for a *vide-grenier* that had taken place last month, a small card advertising Le Jardin de

Chloé, Stephanie's garden centre, and a 'Wanted' poster offering a reward for the capture of the butcher burglar. Between them was a blank space of faded plywood where only the other morning the minutes had been displayed.

'How bizarre,' murmured her nephew.

'You saw me — '

'Yes.'

'Yet now . . . ' Josette slid the doors open, as though the minutes might be concealed behind their transparency, but revealed only a dazed honeybee staggering gratefully out of its imprisonment.

Fabian watched its drunken flight as it dipped and swayed across the road to the glorious display of flowers and plants at the garden centre. And then he thought about the man. His long nose. And that he had been taking notes. By the time he got back to the bar, he was no longer concerned about the missing minutes.

★ ★ ★

'You think this is the same man?'

Fabian nodded. 'I'm sure of it. That's exactly how Stephanie described him. The nose, in particular.'

The farmer grimaced. 'Lorna mentioned that too.'

'Lorrrna?' Annie Estaque's voice was sharp with too.

'She rang me on Saturday. Said a man had been in the Auberge and seemed to be taking notes. While Stephanie was there.' Christian ran a hand through his curls and let out a long breath between his teeth. Idiot. He'd dismissed the English woman's disquiet as summer fever. Or hormones. 'She also mentioned that Stephanie thought he was spying on her.'

'I reckon Stephanie could be right.' The assembled group looked at Fabian. 'She thinks her estranged husband might be trying to seek custody of Chloé.'

Josette gasped and Annie went pale, Serge Papon immediately covering her hand with his.

'But that's ridiculous,' he said. 'How can he possibly get custody when he's in prison for attempted murder?'

'She thinks he might have persuaded his parents to apply for it in his place. I've tried telling her that even if that's the case, they're unlikely to succeed. But she won't listen. And now . . . ' Fabian trailed off and gestured to the window where he'd seen the man walking away. 'This bloke. He was quizzing her in the garden centre. He was snooping around at the Auberge. And he was making notes at the noticeboard where her business card is on display.'

'He's been taking photographs of her too!' The five of them turned at the new voice and saw Véronique in the doorway, face flushed from the sun, hands covered in soil. 'Stephanie gave me some geraniums to brighten up the grotto outside the church. We were over there just now, bedding them in, and I saw the man you're talking about. Tall? Thin? A nose that would make De Gaulle feel inadequate?'

'That's him all right,' confirmed Fabian.

119

'Well, he took a photo of us. Stephanie didn't notice him but I did. He was loitering at the end of the alley and then next thing he got out his phone, took a picture and then slunk off.'

'How can you be sure the photo was of you two?' asked Serge.

Véronique gave her father a piercing glance that was pure Papon. 'He was at the wrong angle to get the church and I hardly think the grotto with two weeping Marys and a missing Jesus would attract attention, do you? No matter how lovely the geraniums are.'

Christian, who'd forced his gaze away from the sight of a dishevelled Véronique, her tousled hair and snug T-shirt making him feel even hotter than the infernal heatwave, saw Serge's lips twitch as though fighting a smile.

'So what do we do?' asked Fabian. 'Because we *have* to do something.'

Serge drummed his fingers on the edge of the table. 'While we can't be sure about any of this, I think Fabian's right. We need to do something.'

'Like what?' asked Josette.

'Catch him. Then ask him a few questions. In a mannerrr he can't rrrefuse to answerrr.'

This time Serge let his smile ripen, nodding at Annie. 'Exactly. We'll keep our eyes open and whoever spots him next, call me and I'll gather the troops. We'll show him that Fogas takes care of its own.'

And with that, the group got up to go.

'You won't forget to put up another copy of those minutes, will you, Josette?' Serge asked with a sly grin as he headed to the door.

120

'Talking of forgetting,' said Christian, 'I haven't had a letter about the next council meeting yet and it's on Thursday. You're cutting it a bit fine.'

'Neither have I,' added Josette, clearly gloating. 'And you do know a meeting is invalid without three days' prior notification?'

Victory short lived, Serge glowered at the pair of them. 'Céline was supposed to have sent those letters out last week. You haven't had them?'

They both shook their heads and he stomped off, muttering.

'I wouldn't want to be Céline,' said Josette, pitying the secretary at the town hall.

Christian smiled. 'I think she can handle him.'

'It takes exceptional talent to handle a Papon!' came the reply.

And as Christian stepped out into the furnace beyond the épicerie, he couldn't agree more. He watched Véronique make her way back to her apartment, shorts revealing long brown legs, her backside moving tantalisingly as she walked, and he wasn't sure whether he would ever be able to handle that particular Papon.

8

By Saturday, the weather had yet to break. Black clouds simmered on the horizon behind the distinctive flat peak of Mont Valier, and although the sun had lost some of its ferocity as evening approached, an oppressive heat had settled on the region, stifling the mountain breezes that normally brought respite to the village of Fogas. Despite the conditions, the car park at the town hall was busy, four marquees punctuating the corners, three of them hosting trestle tables covered in cheery oilcloths and flanked by rustic benches. The fourth contained an improvised bar, cans of soft drink and bottles of beer stacked inside an old chest freezer with a cable snaking round the back. At the opposite end of the car park, a rickety wooden stage drew a line between two of the tents and a string of coloured lights zigzagged from tree to tree over it all. As the clock that adorned the municipal building struck six, every space on the benches was already filled and the festivities were well and truly under way. Fogas was *en fête*.

'I don't know how they dance in those things,' said Véronique, as with a whirl and a stomp the folk dancers on the stage pirouetted to the music of an accordion, their heavy sabots thumping the boards beneath their feet.

'It's hardly dancing,' remarked Josette. 'Just a turn here and there and a stamp every now and then.'

'Hmph! Just as well! They'rrre not exactly cut out forrr anything morrre strrrenuous.'

Véronique and Josette laughed and Christian Dupuy, who was leaning against the wall of the ugly prefab *salle des fêtes* abutting the town hall, had to concede that Annie had a point. The traditional dance troupe gracing the stage had an average age of sixty-eight, a figure generously skewed by the presence of Monique Sentenac's nephew, who was only in his mid-thirties and had been press-ganged into performing by his aunt. From a distance, the colourful dresses and the old-fashioned attire were enough to fool spectators; close up it was all too clear that the performers weren't as agile as they had been when they'd set up the group several decades before. One or two of them were now shuffling with an arthritic gait and Christian suspected the music had been slowed down over the years to accommodate them.

'They don't get any better, do they?' muttered René, who was standing next to him, beer in hand, finger and thumb twitching nervously in a manner Christian had noticed of late.

'So why do you book them every year?'

René shot him a glance. 'Who the hell else is there?'

'Other valleys have better dance troupes. Why not invite one of them?'

'Because we can't afford them.' René thrust a thumb in the direction of the tall dancer at the back with the head of silver hair who at least looked dignified as he coaxed the elderly lady in his arms through a series of turns. 'Thanks to

Alain Rougé being on the Conseil Municipal, we get them for nothing.'

'They'rrre prrrobably grrrateful to be asked,' scoffed Annie.

'Well, if you're such an expert, perhaps you'd like to take over organising this lot next year,' huffed René and stalked off in the direction of the beer tent, hand still agitating and a slight stagger to his steps.

It was the same every summer. Had been for as long as Christian could remember. People grumbled and mocked, yet they returned the following August, never missing a single fête. And as he surveyed the crowds sheltering from the heat under the marquees, it was easy to see why. The residents of Picarets, having made the long trek down to La Rivière and up the mountain to Fogas, were clustered in one corner, their number bolstered by the return of one of the Rogalles from Toulouse and Christian's sister from Perpignan, both with their families in tow. Across the concrete, the second-home owners, who typically migrated back to their ancestral villages for the holidays, were grouped around Pascal Souquet and his wife, who, before bankruptcy had forced them to make Fogas their permanent home, had once been among their circle. Next to them were the old brigade of Widow Aubert and the Lavoir Gang. And under the third tent were the rest of the commune and other returnees, including the Estaque women, Josette, Fabian, Stephanie and even the British couple from the Auberge, Lorna looking hot and uncomfortable and very pregnant. They'd taken the unusual step of closing the restaurant for the night and many of their guests had accompanied them up the hill for the party.

Circulating among them all and uniting the different factions like the father of the bride, was Serge Papon. With a handshake here, a hearty welcome there, he pulled the prodigal sons and daughters back into the fold and made those who had remained, either through choice or necessity, proud to call Fogas home. A political maestro, he worked the crowd, his bonhomie never wavering, even when he had to endure several kisses from a tipsy Widow Aubert or a whispered conversation with Gaston the ancient shepherd, who was known to make a bar of soap last a decade. The only time his good humour slipped was when he greeted Henri Dedieu and the small group of men, all members of the hunting lodge, who'd accompanied him. Then, a certain wariness came over Serge, and Christian couldn't blame him.

Good-looking and with the rugged physique of an outdoors-man, the mayor of Sarrat's appearance was marred by only one feature: his eyes. Their icy gaze gave credence to his reputation as a ruthless hunter and a merciless competitor. Along with a couple of the men sitting next to him, he'd been involved in the incident that had led to the death of a bear within the borders of Fogas a couple of months earlier. And while no one really believed that the beast had been accidentally caught in the fire set to burn off undergrowth, nothing could be proven. Hence it was hardly surprising that Serge Papon treated

125

his opposite number with caution.

A boisterous shout came from the road and a gaggle of kids ran screeching up the hill towards the end of the village, a larger lad at the back chasing them in his capacity as 'the wolf'. Christian remembered playing the very same game with the lad's father, a man who now lived in Quebec and only returned home on holiday every other year. Today, with the population swollen to twice its normal size by his presence and that of others like him, the commune felt vibrant once more, just as it had when Christian was a child.

It was why he loved the fête, and had fought passionately as a member of the council to retain it when the economy turned sour and cutbacks were called for. In an effort to keep ticket prices low enough for all to afford, he'd persuaded his fellow councillors to reduce the festivities to one day instead of two and to forgo the usual banquet. In its place, he had suggested a picnic, revellers bringing their own food to the party. It had been a huge success the year before, ticket sales up and René's stress levels significantly lowered by not having to deal with outside caterers. This year was proving no different, women moving between tents, swapping dishes and sharing food across tables already laden with savoury tarts, platters of cheese, home-made terrines, jars of cornichons, cuts of *saucisson* and *jambon-sec* and baguettes aplenty. Someone had even brought pizzas from the pizza van in Seix.

But, as Christian knew too well, come next week most of the familiar faces that he'd shared

126

his childhood with, and their miniature replicas who ran screaming and shouting through the village, would be gone. Fogas would return to the stagnant commune that it had become in the last twenty years.

'The problem is,' mused Josette, as she watched the dancers come to the end of their routine, 'there is a distinct lack of young people. The group will die out without them.'

Christian, still contemplating his beloved birthplace, saw the pertinence of her words, not just to the aged troupe now departing the stage to enthusiastic applause, but to the community as a whole. When the fête was over, only a handful of the children present tonight would remain. Just like the dancers, Fogas was getting older by the day, with no means to slow down the tempo. And there seemed to be nothing the big farmer could do about it.

His gaze came to rest on the back of Véronique's neck. She was leaning to one side, talking to Lorna, her auburn hair pulled up into a clasp, revealing the smooth skin under the red straps of her dress. Of course, there *was* a way to help rectify the problems Fogas faced. Something he wanted to do more than anything. But would the woman before him be party to it?

He felt a flush of desire, his eyes still fixed on her, his fingers itching to trace the line that ran from her firm jaw, that stubborn jaw, down to the slope of her shoulders. And beyond. To feel that beautiful skin, to revel in the texture of it.

A burst of laughter at the table. No one was paying him any heed. He could reach out and touch her. Claim he was brushing off an insect.

Another gust of merriment and Véronique sat back, laughing, mere centimetres from him. He stretched out a finger, the warmth of her tangible. And then Fabian asked a question.

'Have you heard from Arnaud Petit, Véronique?'

Luck would have it that Fabian was to the right of the post-mistress. As was Christian's outstretched hand. So when she whipped around at the mention of the tracker's name, the farmer's thick finger jabbed her in the neck.

'Ow!' She twisted to see Christian standing behind her, face burning, hand frozen. 'What was that for?'

'Mosquito,' he muttered, mortified, his hands dropping to his sides.

'Oh, right.' She rubbed the skin where a red blotch had spread to mark the imprint of Christian's clumsy touch, and turned to Fabian. There was a bite to her tone as she responded to his question.

'No, I haven't. Should I have?'

He spluttered. 'I just thought . . . you know . . . you were dancing that night at the Auberge . . . '

Even from behind, Christian could tell she was blushing, a trace of pink stealing up the nape of her neck and the tips of her ears tinting red.

'It was one bloody dance. That was all! And yes, for the record,' she glowered at the entire table, 'he asked me to leave with him. But I turned him down. Which apparently makes me an idiot.' She threw a glare over her shoulder to

128

encompass the farmer, who was wishing the arthritic folk group was still on the stage simply to act as a diversion. 'So, I have no more of an idea where Arnaud Petit is than anyone else here. Okay?'

'Was therrre a specific rrreason forrr yourrr question?' asked Annie, taking pity on the floundering Parisian who had wilted under Véronique's wrath.

'Chloé asked, that was all. It was in the *Gazette* that the prosecution against the men involved in the death of that bear had been dropped. She wanted to know if Arnaud had heard the news.'

'I wouldn't put it past him to have his finger on that particular pulse,' said Serge Papon as he joined the group and took a seat beside Annie. He stared across to the opposite tent where the small delegation from Sarrat was getting ready for the next event, Henri Dedieu laughing loudly and slapping someone on the back. Pascal Souquet happened to be passing and one of the hunters barged into him, causing another outburst of rough laughter, a couple of jibes at the effect first deputy's expense and a caustic comment from the mayor of Sarrat as Pascal scuttled past. 'And I wouldn't mind betting that our Arnaud Petit is planning a fitting retribution for those involved!'

'God help them if you'rrre rrright,' murmured Annie. 'But it'd be grrreat to have him back herrre.'

Christian couldn't disagree. He missed the huge tracker and would be happy to see his familiar figure walking up the road, movements as graceful as a wildcat, dark features quick to lighten with a smile. Instead, he got to watch tubby Bernard Mirouze, the *cantonnier* for Fogas, whose odd-job duties included hosting the fête, waddle out onto the stage to call up the first four teams for the pétanque tournament. The farmer switched his attention to Véronique, her head bent, eyes steadfastly glued to the table as she ran a finger idly through the beads of moisture left by her bottle of beer, the blush yet to fade from her skin. Clearly Christian wasn't the only one wishing Arnaud Petit was still in town.

With a twist of his guts that gave full meaning to the expression 'sick to the stomach', he wandered over to where René was standing, a set of silver pétanque boules in his hands.

Battle was about to commence. And as far as Christian Dupuy was concerned, he would far rather wage war than love. Even though he was uniquely suited to neither.

★   ★   ★

'Merde alors!'

René's strangled cry cut through the humidity, followed by the clink of boules, muted in the heavy air, and a collective gasp from the spectators.

'He's miscalculated again.'

'What's he playing at?'

'He's not bloody playing, that's the prrroblem!'

Out in the car park, where the shade had at last stretched lazy fingers across the dusty concrete, the general of the Fogas army surveyed his troops with fatigue. Next year, vowed Christian Dupuy, I'm not volunteering to captain the team. It was the same every time. The annual pétanque contest always started out with good humour but, by the final round, inevitably descended into a fraught competition, as René and his partner Bernard whittled down the field to leave Henri Dedieu and a fellow hunter as their opponents. Fogas versus Sarrat in a head-to-head. It could only lead to trouble.

Officially, the two teams were battling for a prize, which this year, again owing to the recession, had been reduced from one hundred euros to fifty euros and a free meal at the Auberge. But no one believed that was what motivated the four men standing in the middle of the pétanque *terrain*. They were playing for honour, using every ounce of skill they could muster to coax their boules next to the jack or to slam the opposition boules out of contention. At stake were the bragging rights for the next twelve months. And, as the inhabitants of the mountain commune had become accustomed to over the last decade — with René Piquemal in the team — that honour rightfully rested with Fogas.

Taking over from Jacques Servat and Serge Papon, who'd ruled the pétanque tournaments of the seventies and eighties, René and Bernard were a formidable pairing. But everyone knew that whilst the chubby *cantonnier* had talent — his ability to scatter his opponents' boules was

131

unparalleled — René was the one with the gift. He understood the game. Took his chances. And with an exquisite twist of his wrist, he could place the team right next to the jack, nuzzling his boule into seemingly impossible situations.

But for the last twenty minutes René had been playing like a man who'd never thrown a boule in his life, conceding an eight-nil lead in a succession of horrific ends to be eight all with three points remaining. And it had his team captain tearing out his curly blond hair.

'What's the matter with you?' demanded Christian as he joined the two players in a huddle between ends, the Sarrat team looking confident across the car park. 'You had them on the run and now you've gone and let them right back in!'

'I don't know,' muttered the scowling plumber. 'I jusssh can't consssshentrate.' He reached to take the beer that Bernard was holding out to him and stumbled slightly.

'Are you drunk?' hissed Christian.

'No! Asssh if.'

'Well, what then?'

The plumber shrugged, fingers rubbing together.

'And what's with the twitchy fingers? That can't be helping any.'

'On the contrary,' said René, chest puffing out. 'That'sssh how I ssshtopped ssshmoking.'

Christian and Bernard shared a disbelieving glance.

'How?' asked the farmer.

'Hypnossshish.'

'You've been *hypnotised?*' Christian's voice rose on the last word.

'Ssshh!'

'When?'

'Over a month ago. I bought a CD — '

'Wait a moment. You hypnotised *yourself?*'

René nodded.

'And the fidgeting fingers?'

'When I crave nicotine, I have to rub them together and think of a ssshpecial ssshmell. Ssshomething to take my mind off ssshmoking.'

For a heartbeat Christian could think of nothing to say, the plumber's answer so unexpected. Then Alain Rougé, umpire for the day, was calling the players back to the *terrain* for the final time, the Sarrat team swaggering forward with newfound confidence.

'Well,' said the Fogas captain to his star player, 'in the minutes we have remaining, do you think you could hypnotise yourself back into being a pétanque player? Because as it stands, that smug bastard Henri Dedieu is about to win *our* tournament.'

René and Bernard strode out to where the mayor of Sarrat was already preparing to throw the jack, and Christian made his way back to the marquee by the stage.

'What's going on?' asked Josette as Christian stooped under the cover of the tent and took his place leaning against the wall of the *salle des fêtes*.

'Damned if I know,' he muttered as the first Sarrat boule landed centimetres from the white jack. 'He sounds drunk but swears he isn't.

133

Although he did reveal he hypnotised himself to stop smoking.'

All eyes turned to the farmer and a succession of jaws dropped.

'René *hypnotised* himself?' asked Véronique.

'Apparently. He bought a CD and now all he has to do is rub his fingers together, bring to mind a chosen smell, and his need for a cigarette disappears.'

René was standing in the circle looking steady, arm raised, and with perfect balance he lobbed his boule into the air and let out a satisfied grunt as it fell to the far side of the silver ball already there and closer to the target. His skill was met with a cheer. One point in the bag and Sarrat up next.

'At least he seems to be playing better. But do you think it was the hypnosis that was affecting his game?' Véronique's question was aimed at Stephanie, the only one of the group likely to know anything about the subject.

'It could be. There have been cases where people have used self-hypnosis and suffered side effects. It's a powerful tool and shouldn't be treated lightly. Especially by the uninitiated. And I wouldn't imagine,' Stephanie added drily, 'that René is an expert.'

'Huh!' said Annie as a poor shot from the Sarrat team ensured they had to play again, Henri Dedieu at the circle. 'Knowing Rrrené he's prrrobably chosen the wrrrong smell orrr something.'

The laughter from the tent was short lived as Alain Rougé bent down where the mayor of

134

Sarrat's boule had just landed. He reached into his pocket and pulled out his callipers, spread them between boule and jack and, with a grave face, gave the bad news. Henri Dedieu had taken the lead. Fogas would have to bowl next.

Bernard Mirouze gave his beagle, Serge, a pat for luck and waddled over to the rough arc drawn on the concrete, sweat dripping down his moonlike face. He was grimacing before the boule had even made contact with the ground and had turned away before it rolled harmlessly past the two Sarrat balls.

'Come on, Bernard!' called a voice from the back. 'Do it for Serge!'

A ripple of laughter at the deliberate ambiguity of the appeal fell quiet as the *cantonnier* took his place again. This time you could tell the minute he drew back his arm. A flash of silver, an almighty crack and both Sarrat balls were removed from play to leave René's first one still in the lead. But with three boules per team remaining, the game was far from over.

A whispered conference between the Sarrat duo, and the hunter stepped forward, Henri Dedieu moving behind him to watch his partner throw, a cigarette in the mayor's hand. Taking a long inhalation, he let the smoke curl out from his lips and Christian couldn't help but notice that the white cloud was drifting on the slight breeze that had picked up over the past hour. Drifting across the car park and into the face of Fogas's star player, whose right hand immediately started twitching.

A groan rumbled through the tents and

135

Christian pulled his attention back to the *terrain* where the hunter had placed a boule in a winning position on the right-hand side of the jack. Sarrat had wrestled the lead back once more.

Wasting no time, Bernard approached the circle, took a deep breath, and then bowled. The smack of metal on metal resonated off the town hall and a raucous shout hit the air as the *cantonnier* sent the hunter's boule spinning off the car park, leaving his own in its place.

'*Carreau!*' called the crowd in recognition of his achievement. Bernard grinned and René slapped him on the back, Serge the beagle barking in excitement. Two points on the board for Fogas with only four shots left.

Again Henri Dedieu accompanied his partner to the circle, whispering to him as the man prepared to throw. Then the mayor of Sarrat stepped back, leaving the hunter to play, and once more he drew heavily on his cigarette, René and Bernard right behind him, the smoke floating past both of their faces. They were so caught up in the game they didn't notice. But Christian did. Because René's hand was in overdrive. And as the plumber leaned forward to see where the hunter's boule landed, he stumbled slightly.

'No,' muttered Christian. 'Not now! Just hold on for a couple of minutes.'

While Fogas was still leading, the hunter had cleared Bernard's boule so they were back to one point and were going to need René at his best to win. Three shots left. Fogas closest to the jack.

136

Sarrat with two a bit further back. And the two best players still had boules in their hands.

With the order of play dictated by the distance from the jack, Sarrat had to play next. Henri Dedieu walked out into complete silence. Eyes narrowed, knees slightly bent, with perfect motion he threw. The crowd sucked in its breath. And then exhaled. The shot had been brilliant. But not brilliant enough. Even with three boules forming a half circle around the target, Sarrat still couldn't win, thanks to René's first effort. Bernard was already grinning. René had two shots left. And there was a narrow avenue between the opposition boules where the jack was visible. It would take skill. But René had it. Already a point up in this end, with his remaining two throws René could secure the three points needed to win the tournament for Fogas.

The crowd was shouting encouragement as the plumber walked forward. A route that took him past Henri Dedieu. Who leaned over and muttered something. Christian couldn't catch what was said but he saw René glower. Then he saw Henri Dedieu exhale, a cloud of cigarette smoke engulfing the pair of them, and the plumber's face seemed to dissolve.

René turned to the terrain and tried to compose himself, but his shot, while on target, had too much speed and rolled through the back. One point lost. Still one on the board. He shook his head as though in a trance. And then he rubbed his finger and thumb together.

Last one. With a deep breath he pulled back

his arm and the audience went quiet. But just as he released the boule, René staggered, like a drunk at a wedding party. Twisted by his sideways lurch, the ball arced upwards, flashing brilliantly in the setting sun. Too high. Too strong.

There was an outbreak of noise as the spectators surged to their feet and then a cry of anguish from the plumber as with a thud, his last boule smacked into his first and took both of them out of the game. Left behind in the dust of the car park was the jack and three silver balls, all engraved with the head of a boar.

9

'How the hell was I supposed to know?'

René took another long drag on the Gauloise gripped between his now steady fingers and exhaled in anger. On the stage, a smug Henri Dedieu was accepting the Fogas pétanque trophy, a trophy that had resided in René's house for the last ten years but, thanks to the plumber's catastrophic last throw, would now be crossing the river. As the mayor of Sarrat brandished it aloft, a cheer hailed from his supporters, which was quickly drowned out by hisses and catcalls and a distant rumble of thunder from the darkening sky. Sensing a volatile audience, Serge Papon hustled his gloating counterpart off the stage and a dejected Bernard Mirouze announced a short break while the band set up.

'It's not like there was any small print to warn me,' continued René, heedless of the smothered laughter at the table behind him, which Christian was trying to quell with the odd glare. 'I mean, it just said to choose a smell. Something that makes you happy and would take your mind off smoking.'

Even Christian's lips were twitching now. 'And you chose — '

'Pastis!'

A snort and a hiccup and then the barrier broke and a wave of hilarity washed over the plumber.

'It's not a laughing matter!' he stormed, short arms on ample hips. 'That bloody hypnosis CD cost me the tournament.'

Christian had been the one to figure it out. The fidgeting fingers. The drunken demeanour. Every time René longed for a cigarette and so invoked the 'cure', which, thanks to Henri Dedieu's underhand tactics, was often during the game, he thought of only one thing: the liquorice rich odour of pastis. And he promptly became inebriated.

According to Stephanie, the problem was that René was *too* susceptible; he was a hypnotist's dream. By listening to the CD, he had not only managed to suppress his cravings with the powerful smell of his favourite drink, but had also taken on the side effects of the alcohol. Without a drop touching his lips.

When Christian had pointed out what was happening, the plumber had been distraught. That emotion had quickly turned to rage. Then he'd marched over to Gaston the shepherd and taken a Gauloise from him. Now, sober and disconsolate and back on the cigarettes, he looked a sorry sight. Even the sudden brilliance as the fairy lights strung between the trees came on and received appreciative applause from the revellers, couldn't shake his mood.

'Don't worry about it.' Christian put a consoling arm around his friend's shoulder. 'There's always next year.'

But René shrugged off the farmer, face as sullen as the clouds that had closed in, bringing down the temperatures and causing the wind to tug and tear at the sides of the tents.

'Therrre's a storrrm coming,' Annie announced, eyeing the mass on the horizon that was turning the evening into night.

Christian only had to take one look at the plumber's fierce countenance, his unwavering focus on the celebrating group from Sarrat, to know that she was right. In more ways than one.

★   ★   ★

Just as Bernard Mirouze wasn't cut out to be a ninja, so Pascal Souquet wasn't suited to sabotage. Although he was becoming better acquainted with it.

From the other side of the building that rose behind him in the dark, the first deputy mayor could hear the strains of music and the animated sounds of the crowd as they danced and sang along to the decrepit band that René had seen fit to book for the evening. The same band of four ageing rockers that he booked every year. And they were playing the same songs. Pascal had left the jollity of the gathering of second-home owners, a group of people he genuinely couldn't abide with their prattle of new kitchens and renovations, and was currently at the back door of the town hall, staring out into the inky depths of a moonless night. His heart was already thumping and his hands were clammy. He'd thought he was done with all this. And with some success too.

The impromptu inspection of the Auberge, which had taken only a discreet phone call to set

141

up, had yielded the irregularities he'd known it would, and while the owners' lack of proper documentation might not make the official police report, it had been noted. Likewise, the disappearance of the two sides of A4 — typed up by council secretary Monique Sentenac and pinned up on the noticeboard in La Rivière by Josette — had caused problems. And it had been overheard that none of the councillors had received due notification of the council meeting that had been held on Thursday. Not that they needed a letter to tell them, bush telegraph still having a wider network than mobile phones in this part of the world. But it was the principle of the thing. And the legality. Plus it made Céline Laffont, secretary at the town hall and a woman Pascal Souquet couldn't tolerate, appear negligent. How was she to know, as she was being berated by Serge Papon, that the letters she had faithfully put in the postbag had ended up on a bonfire in the back garden of the first deputy mayor? Along with the missing minutes that had so perplexed Josette.

Having carried out his orders with such positive results, Pascal had thought he could sit back and enjoy the entertainment. Although the Fogas fête, with its endless pétanque and God-awful folk dancing, didn't hold much to captivate a man used to nights at the Opéra Bastille. Or anyone with any semblance of a palate, his own repulsed by the rough fare that was being passed around the tables. But either way, he'd expected to spend the evening in peace. To do his duty and smile and endure the occasion because, as his wife pointed out, it was the second-home owners who held him in power. Then, at an appropriate time, he would sneak home unnoticed.

But earlier in the evening as Pascal had excused himself to go to the bathroom, one of the burly hunters from Sarrat had deliberately knocked into him and, while the rest of the Sarrat group was roundly abusing the shaking deputy, he'd slipped him a piece of paper. Pascal waited until he was in the solitude of a toilet cubicle before unfolding the note. Instructions. From Henri Dedieu. Precise ones at that. Now, using the light from the hallway behind him, he stared at the crudely drawn diagram in his hand and looked again at the jumble of cables leading out of the back door, which he could tell with one glance was the handiwork of the *cantonnier*, Bernard Mirouze.

There were three extension cords. Two modern ones — still carrying the sale tags from Mr Bricolage down in St Girons — offered four plug outlets on a drum that wound out the extra cable. A third was of a more traditional type, with a flat rectangle housing six plug sockets and a flex threading back from it. A flex that obviously hadn't been long enough as it had been spliced to another cord, a bulky section of black tape revealing the join. While its newer counterparts were completely full, the older one held only a solitary plug. That, on Henri Dedieu's command, was about to change.

Electricity. Messing with that was a step up from removing documents and stealing letters.

143

Neither of which could kill anyone.

Pascal felt a prickle of sweat on his scalp, his throat dry. On the other side of the building he heard the last chords of 'Ne Me Quitte Pas' fade into silence and, over the applause that followed, the lead singer announced a short break.

That was his cue.

With a last check to make sure he was alone, he bent down and quickly rearranged the plugs as the diagram instructed. Then he hastened back to his seat. When his wife, Fatima, registered his lengthy absence with a sharp look, Pascal Souquet did his best to assume the pained expression of boredom that he wore at all such functions and hoped that it would mask the apprehension that was gripping him.

★   ★   ★

The members of the band were picking up their instruments again after the interval when Christian, with two beers inside him and the romantic fairy lights twinkling overhead, decided he was going to make his move. He would ask Véronique to dance.

He'd stood at the edge of the dancing all evening, watching his neighbours and friends moving with varying levels of skill across what had earlier been the pétanque *terrain*. And all the time he'd been aware of her. She'd jived with Alain Rougé, the older man one of the best dancers in Fogas, and had allowed Bernard Mirouze to lead her out for a more modern number. But when the slow strains of the last

144

song had started, she'd been approached by one of the Sarrat hunters. And to the man's chagrin, she had turned him down. With a smile. But firmly.

Then she had come to stand next to Christian, who'd cracked some joke about her not trusting the man to stay clear of her toes. She'd laughed and they'd stood in an easy silence while the Ariège's answer to Jacques Brel crooned out 'Ne Me Quitte Pas'. But the lyrics had eaten into the farmer. There she was. The woman he loved. Right next to him. Only, he was too spineless to do anything about it.

He'd started practising in his head. 'Would you like to . . . Care to . . . Shall we . . . ?' But not one word had made it past his frozen throat and before he knew it, the song was over and the band had announced an intermission, the lead singer looking like he needed a lie-down.

So Christian had gone over to the bar, thrown his money in the honesty box and fished a beer out of the freezer, which had promptly juddered to a halt. He'd given it a thump, his universal remedy for temperamental appliances, and seconds later it started up again as a flash of lightning lit the distant skyline. Knowing the vagaries of the electrical supply during a storm, he'd thought nothing more of it. Instead, intent on bolstering his courage, he'd popped open the beer and drank it in one terrified gulp. Another had quickly followed and now, with the music about to recommence, he was depending on the fortifying effects of alcohol.

Véronique was talking to Annie and Serge, her

back to him as he approached. The three of them were laughing at something. And then, as though sensing his presence, she turned. She was beautiful. Her hair was shimmering under the coloured lights; her skin was glowing. And that dress! It fitted tightly over her bust and then skimmed over her hips into a flare of red. He just wanted to twirl her round and round and into his arms.

'Véronique,' he managed, mouth of sawdust, 'I wondered — '

A shrill whistle from the microphone cut through his words.

'Are you ready, Fogas?' called the lead singer, and the crowd cheered.

'Sorry?' Véronique was leaning in towards him, the soft scent of roses on her hair nearly intoxicating him. 'What did you say?'

'I was wondering — '

'Well, get your dancing shoes on, because we're about to rock the place down!' roared the singer, and the audience roared back.

'I can't hear you,' she said, lips brushing his ear and sending a shock through his body.

'How does a bit of Johnny Hallyday sound?' shouted the singer, and the cheers got louder.

Merde! A rock number. Christian hadn't counted on that. But Véronique was there, hand on his arm, an eyebrow raised as she waited for him to finish what he'd been about to say. He'd be a fool to back out.

'I was wondering — '

'That's him!' Her grip tightened on his forearm, her focus shifting to over his right

146

shoulder. 'Look! The man who's after Stephanie.'

He wheeled round and saw the long nose, the thin figure; a shirt flapping over a scarecrow's body down near the beer tent. 'Are you sure?'

'Certain!'

On the opposite side of the car park, Fabian had also spotted the man. The Parisian caught Christian's eye and on a nod from the farmer, they both began to thread their way through the crowds making for the dance floor. René was brooding over by the tent that housed the Sarrat group, his face dark as he suffered their celebrations. At a shrill whistle from Christian he looked to where the farmer was pointing and his expression grew even fiercer. He too began to move, gathering up Bernard Mirouze and his dog as he went. With Véronique and Stephanie falling in behind, the Fogas posse converged on the target in a pincer movement. There was no way the corpselike man could escape.

'So, Johnny Hallyday it is!' yelled the singer and a lone chord wailed from an electric guitar. It was promptly followed by a shriek from the elderly guitarist, an explosion on the stage, a flash of yellow and the stench of smoke. Then the world was plunged into complete darkness.

'Get him!' roared Christian into the blackness of night, lunging forward for the thin figure he'd been so close to. His meaty hands closed around a frail wrist and he hung on, buffeted and swayed by the panicking crowds. God it was dark. No moon. Clouds overhead. He felt the man wriggling, trying to free himself, no more than bone in the farmer's grasp, his cries drowned in the melee. But Christian wasn't letting go. They'd all been culpable last time Stephanie was in trouble. He wasn't about to allow that to happen again.

It seemed like an eternity before a blaze of lights split the chaos, Serge calling for calm from the front steps of the town hall. Then he shouted over to Christian.

'Did you get him?'

'No he bloody didn't!' shouted back an enraged Fabian, who was being held down by both the farmer and Bernard Mirouze while Serge the beagle licked his face.

'Christ!' Christian released the skinny Parisian and turned to see if René had fared any better. But he'd obviously seized the blackout as an opportunity to avenge his wounded pétanque pride as he was being pulled off the hunter from Sarrat by Alain Rougé and Henri Dedieu, the man on the ground looking stunned at having been felled by the much smaller plumber.

'Bloody hell!' muttered Christian. 'We're useless.'

'You lot might be,' came a smug voice from the other side of him. 'We, however, know what we're doing.'

A triumphant Véronique was sitting astride the thin outsider, his arm wrenched up behind his back while Stephanie had an evil-looking lock on his left leg. The man was begging for mercy and howling in pain.

'Okay, let's have some answers,' said Serge, taking charge to a backdrop of thunder. He leaned over the man, the crowd having formed a

148

circle around him, menace filling the sulphur-tinged air. 'Let's hear why you've been following Stephanie around.'

The man managed to lift a puzzled face up from the ground. 'Who?'

'Me!' hissed Stephanie, giving his leg a tweak and making him yelp.

He twisted around to see her and then faced Serge. 'I . . . I . . . I haven't!' he stuttered.

A yank on his arm this time and the man whimpered.

'Perhaps you might want to think before you answer this one,' growled Serge. 'Who are you working for?'

The man gulped, his Adam's apple sharp against his skin. Then he spoke into the silence.

'The sous-préfet. I work for the sous-préfet.'

Véronique was so shocked she let go of his arm and Stephanie dropped his leg. The man crawled out from underneath them and slowly got to his feet, bony hands brushing down his clothes.

'You're a *fonctionnaire*?' Serge asked.

The man nodded, his title draping his angular frame with some of the dignity he'd lost at the hands of the Fogas women.

'So what are you doing creeping around my commune?'

Thin lips pursed together. 'I'm afraid you'll have to ask the sous-préfet that. Now, if you don't mind, I think I would like to leave.'

On a sharp nod from their mayor, the bemused crowd parted and the thin figure walked away into the night, limping slightly.

'I don't understand,' said Christian. 'Why

would a man who works for the sous-préfet be skulking around the place taking notes?'

'I don't know,' muttered Serge as thunder cracked above them and the first fat raindrops began to fall, bouncing on the concrete and sending people running for cover. 'But on Monday morning I will bloody well be finding out!'

10

It wasn't Monday when Serge Papon was granted an audience with the sous-préfet in St Girons. Nor was it Tuesday. In fact, thanks to the hectic nature of *la rentrée*, the period from late August to the beginning of September when the French abandon the beaches and their second homes in ancestral villages to embark once more on the treadmill of work in the metropolis, the disgruntled leader of Fogas had to wait four days before he could begin to understand what was going on in his commune. Hence, as a man entirely unsuited to patience, he was in a sour mood as he drove down from his mountain home and through La Rivière.

The heavy rains that had passed over the region at the weekend had taken with them the sultry temperatures and the humidity, leaving a clarity to the air that made the mountains sharp against the cloudless skies. But the beauty of that Wednesday morning was wasted on the irate mayor. His temperament wasn't helped by the melancholia he always succumbed to at this time of year either. While his neighbours and friends rejoiced in the departure of the seasonal crowds, he found it depressing; he missed the children underfoot, the gaiety that infected the commune. And he hated that the year was sliding towards its demise. His wife, Thérèse, had always managed to cajole him out of his autumnal depression but, eighteen months since she had passed away, he no longer had the benefit of her cheerfulness.

With the calendar announcing that summer in France had officially come to an end, all around were signs that the long, carefree *vacances* were over. The roads, for a start. The mayor had negotiated the twists and turns of the meandering route down to the Romanesque church at the back of the village without encountering a single car. No lost motorhomes struggling up the mountain, fear-stricken tourist behind the wheel forcing oncoming traffic to reverse into a passing place. No ostentatious 4×4s taking up more than their fair share of the tarmac either.

Here, in the valley, things were also noticeably quieter. The terrace outside the bar was deserted, fallen blossom spinning in the breeze between the empty chairs, and the shutters of several of the houses were closed tight despite the mild temperatures and the benign sunshine; they would remain that way until the next long stretch of holiday when their owners would visit again. At the Auberge, the impact of the exodus had given Lorna time to sit on the front steps, cup in hand, a profusion of montbretia in bloom next to her, the delicate orange flowers something Serge always associated with *la rentrée*.

He threw a wave at the British woman, getting a 'bonjour' in return, and then cast an eye over the lay-by opposite, expecting to see Chloé and the Rogalle twins waiting for the school bus. But it was empty. Silent. No children running around in a last game of chase before a day of confinement behind a desk. It took him a moment to work it out. And then he felt old. Chloé and the twins had started *collège* down in Seix today, and that meant an earlier departure. It also meant there were no children from Picarets at the primary school in Sarrat any more. Which made him inexplicably sad.

When he reached St Girons, there was the same sense of despondency. Streets that had vibrated with life only a week ago were now peopled by a solitary pensioner and his dog, as though the Pied Piper had swept through and lured the inhabitants after him. Shops that had flung open their doors to welcome the tourists were closed, handwritten signs taped to windows announcing that their proprietors had gone on holiday. Even the geraniums that graced window boxes across the town looked dejected, the red and pink flowers faded and tired at the end of a long season.

Serge cut around the edge of the town centre and the ease with which he found a parking space — in Place Jean Jaurès, right in front of the Salon de Thé — was yet another indication that the area had shrunk back to its normal population level. When he reached the austere offices of the Sous-Préfecture and pushed through the doors, however, he concluded that the flautist from Hamelin must be somewhere in the building. And he'd dragged the entire population of St Girons after him.

It was bedlam. Masses of people were gathered in the foyer, thick folders in hand, tempers frayed as two women worked hard behind the counter, trying to deal with a deluge of bureaucracy that had been neglected over the summer season and consequently was now urgent. Voices were raised in frustration, paperwork was being compared and a fierce discussion was taking place over the new queue management system, which had somehow got out of synch and was informing the waiting citizens via a flashing screen that number 500 was next to be served. Despite the fact that no one present was holding a ticket higher than 30.

Serge Papon made his way through the throng, stopping here and there for a quick 'bonjour' before turning into the quiet corridor at the back. At the third door along, he knocked authoritatively and entered.

'Serge! Come in,' said the sous-préfet, rising from behind his desk. 'What can I do for you?'

The mayor of Fogas closed the door and then fixed the *fonctionnaire* with a stare. 'You know damn well what you can do for me. Tell me why one of your lackeys has been snooping around my commune, for a start!'

The sous-préfet shook the proffered hand, the mayor's grip still vice-like despite his years and his arthritis, and gestured towards the empty chair.

'Take a seat,' he said as he placed a thick dossier on his desk. 'You're not going to like this.'

★   ★   ★

Up in La Rivière, Jacques Servat was trying to remember if the épicerie and bar had ever been so busy. It was as if word had gone round the commune telling everyone to descend on the place at mid-morning. Of course, they were all claiming they were there to celebrate the inauguration of the post office, Véronique finally installed back behind her counter almost two years since a fire had destroyed her old one. But Jacques didn't believe a word of it. None of them were buying stamps for a start.

No, it had to be Serge they were waiting for, anxious to discover exactly why the long-nosed man had been wandering around the community taking notes during the sweltering days of summer. Gathered in clusters, some on the terrace, others in the bar, with the number of people sitting around doing nothing it was difficult to believe that today was the first of September, a day which normally marked the return to work. Christian had abandoned the farm, Stephanie had closed the garden centre, posting a sign to say she was on her annual leave, Annie had walked down and Paul Webster had come up from the Auberge, despite the impending lunch hour. Even René had turned up, although judging by the repeated calls on his mobile, he'd probably left a customer stranded somewhere with a sink half-installed and no water on in the house. It wouldn't be the first time.

'How much longer can he be?' muttered the plumber as he stuffed his phone in his pocket, pulling out a packet of cigarettes in its place.

'He should have been back by now. I can't think what's holding him up.' Josette cast a concerned glance at the clock above the bar as she hurried past, a tray of drinks in her hands.

Véronique came through and started clearing tables, no pressing demand for philatelic items to keep her at the post office counter. Plus there was more going on in the bar.

'Well, whatever Serge finds out,' she said as she began to stack the dishwasher, 'at least it's a relief to know Stephanie wasn't being targeted.'

Stephanie pulled a face. 'Sorry about that. I don't know how I got it so wrong. That skinny *fonctionnaire* filled me with such an immense feeling of loss, it was as if I'd had something precious taken away from me.' She shrugged, unable to explain a phenomenon she couldn't understand herself. 'I jumped to conclusions.'

'Huh! You're not the only one.' Fabian rubbed his shoulder, which was still sore several days after his brief captivity at the fête. He glared at Christian, who merely held up his hands with a smile.

'You can hardly blame us for our mistake. One skinny person is the same as another in the dark.'

'Any news on the guitarist?' Véronique addressed her question to the plumber, who nodded.

'He's fine. A mild shock, the hospital said. Although I don't know how they can call it mild. What few hairs he has on his head are still standing upright!'

'He was lucky he wasn't killed,' said Josette as she came back in from the terrace and sat on the chair Véronique was holding out for her. 'Who would do something so reckless?'

Silence. No one had a clue. When the overloaded extension cord had been discovered as the cause of the commotion up at the town hall, blame had immediately fallen on Bernard Mirouze's chubby shoulders. But he had the perfect alibi: René had been with him when the electrics had been set up. And the plumber was adamant that the *cantonnier* had sensibly placed only the fairy lights on the extension held together by tape. The freezer and the cable for the band had been allocated their own sockets — the ones that Bernard had bought that morning in St Girons. But someone had changed that, placing all the demand on the fragile old extension cord. The minute the unsuspecting guitarist had hit the first chord of the Johnny Hallyday song, his guitar, the freezer, the sound system and the lights had all blown.

'But why would anyone do that?' Christian shook his head. 'It doesn't make sense. There was no reason to fiddle around with the plugs.'

'Unless it was deliberate.' Véronique's words hung in the air.

'Is the post office open?' Fatima Souquet stood in the doorway, indicating the abandoned counter at the back of the épicerie.

'It most certainly is,' said the postmistress and with a smile not normally reserved for the wife of the first deputy mayor, she willingly returned to her duties, still enthralled at having her job back.

Conversation moved on in the bar, Stephanie's impending trip to Toulouse for the meeting with her divorce lawyers and her estranged husband provoking discussion before speculation over the skinny man dominated once more. But in the inglenook, Jacques Servat was still mulling over the events at the fête, which he hadn't been fortunate enough to witness.

Deliberate? Could it have been? He'd seen a lot of things in his life. He'd lived through the occupation of the region as a young boy. Been unfortunate enough to spend his national service out in Algeria. And had lived and been dead long enough to know that people were unpredictable. So, despite Fogas being the sleepiest place on earth, a mere backwater in the mighty nation of France, it was entirely possible that the accident at the fête had been sabotage. The only question was, why? It wouldn't take long for the ghostly Jacques to work it out. Being able to tell people what he'd discovered — that was going to be trickier.

★ ★ ★

For many, early autumn in the Pyrenees is considered the best time of year. That particular autumn, the valleys south of St Girons were living up to such expectations. The trees were still in full leaf, some of them just starting to turn the shades that would set the hills on fire by the end of October. Birds were calling, the rivers were running fast after a burst of rain, and in a cerulean sky the sun was no longer the ferocious entity that it had been. The drive back to La Rivière along the winding road that followed the

Salat river should have inspired joy. But making that very journey, Mayor Serge Papon, his seasonal depression only exacerbated by his visit to the Sous-Préfecture, was consumed with sadness.

He'd been with the sous-préfet an hour and had emerged from the office stunned. He'd gone across to Café Kristal, ordered a pastis and had sat on a hard plastic chair outside thinking about everything he'd been told. Thinking about Fogas and the wonderful people who lived there. And wondering how he was going to explain it to them.

The drive home wasn't helping any. The blue flash of a kingfisher flickered along the riverbank to his left and he caught the ripple in the water where a trout surfaced briefly. From overhead came the coarse clacking of ducks flying past. Life. The valley was pulsating with it. Apart from his commune, which was slowly dying.

★ ★ ★

As with any small community, Fogas and its inhabitants thrived on conjecture. Never an event occurred that couldn't be explained — even if that explanation was pure hypothesis grounded in rumour. Over the years such mysteries as the sudden disappearance of the curé, the identity of Véronique's father, the provenance of Jacques Servat's *saucisson* and the inability of Madame Dupuy, Christian's mother, to cook a single meal without burning it, had all been resolved long before the facts emerged. That the solutions often veered widely from the truth never seemed to matter.

So, it was hardly surprising that, with a gathering of inquisitive minds and creative imaginations, by the time the mayor's car came round the corner down by the Auberge, the latest enigma had been unravelled. After all, it was obvious when you thought about it. Because, if you accepted the fact that the cadaverous *fonctionnaire* had been compiling a report and then added to it the knowledge that, as part of the recently established national park which had Fogas at its centre, a new round of government funding was about to be released by the préfet, there was only one conclusion: a windfall in grants for the mountain commune was imminent.

'We could renovate the church!' said Véronique.

'Buggerrr the churrrch! The *salle des fêtes* needs knocking down and rrrebuilding,' muttered Annie, condemning the prefab annexe on the town hall, which had seen better days.

'A children's play area would be good,' mused Stephanie. 'One with rope walks and treetop bridges.'

'Yes!' agreed Paul Webster, and with understandable bias, given his heavily pregnant wife, he added, 'I suppose a crèche is out of the question?'

Christian smiled. 'I'm not sure the money would stretch that far.'

'Well, if there's any left over, the folk dancers could do with some new sabots,' said Alain

Rougé, his suggestion earning him a burst of sharp laughter.

And it was into that laughter that Fabian's cry hailed from the shop.

'He's here!'

Sure enough, a silver Peugeot was pulling up outside and the solid figure of Serge Papon could be seen getting out of it, dossier under his arm, face serious. But it wasn't enough to quell the excitement and he was met with a babble of voices as he walked in the door.

'Pastis?' asked Josette, while he settled into a chair.

'Coffee. And strong.'

It was his voice that told them. Normally so robust, so resonant. Today it quavered, and as he reached to take the cup from Josette his hand was shaking. For the occupants of the bar, the optimism of moments before was quashed under a forbidding sense that something bad was about to befall their commune.

'There's no way to sweeten this,' said Serge, turning to encompass all of them in his gaze. 'Our esteemed préfet wants us to merge.'

'Merge?' René's interjection was a strangled yelp. 'You mean the commune?'

Serge nodded.

'Who with?' asked Annie.

Serge lowered his head. When he spoke it was barely a whisper. 'With those bastards across the river.'

His audience twisted to stare over the water at the fields on the opposite side, where Sarrat basked in the sun — and the castles they had been busy building in the Pyrenean air collapsed around them into dust and rubble. Then the noise began.

★ ★ ★

'One at a time, please!' shouted Christian above the din as the crowd in the bar all tried to claim the mayor's attention. 'Alain, you first.'

The retired policeman and current council member had no trouble making himself heard, the clamour abating as he began to speak. 'Surely it's too early to worry?' he suggested. 'I mean, the préfet can't force it on us, can he?'

'No,' admitted Serge. 'He can issue a decree but then it has to go to a local vote.'

'And presumably both our council and Sarrat's would have to approve it?'

Serge nodded.

'Well then, there's no problem. There's no way on earth that arrogant lot over there are going to accept this. They hate us as much as we hate them!'

'He's right . . . '

'It's true . . . '

Heads were nodding, a sense of relief filtering through the room at the wise words of the policeman. For everyone knew that the enmity towards the neighbouring commune that was fostered in Fogas cradles and cherished until the grave was reciprocated, as strong on the pastureland on the other side of the river as it was here in the shadows of the mountains.

Serge sighed. 'Unfortunately, our neighbours

162

seem to have overcome their aversion to us. I'm afraid to say that Henri Dedieu is the person who proposed the union.'

This time there was complete silence as the enormity of what was happening sank in. Sarrat wanted to merge. If they were throwing their weight behind the préfet, Fogas didn't stand a chance.

'I don't understand. Why would Henri Dedieu sanction this?' Christian voiced the question most of them were trying to answer.

'I have no idea. But it would have been polite if he had thought to consult us before he ran to the Préfecture. As it is, we have a fight on our hands.'

'So it's not definite yet?'

'No. Not quite.' The mayor tapped the thick folder on the table. 'Before he makes any formal representation, the préfet is having a report drawn up to see whether Fogas is *viable* as a commune.'

'And?'

Serge selected a page from his file and started to read. ' "In conclusion, it is no longer expedient to maintain Fogas as an independent commune; both economic and social concerns support this view. Overall, the inhabitants would be better served by an amalgamation with a neighbouring commune. Geographical and economic factors suggest that Sarrat would be the ideal partner." '

'*Expedient?*' Véronique shot up out of her chair. 'It makes us sound like diseased cattle in need of putting down!'

René was nodding furiously in agreement and

163

a rumble of discontent ran through the onlookers, Annie's voice rising from it.

'I'm prrresuming it was the snooping *fonctionnairrre* who compiled this. What evidence does he give forrr his damning verrrdict?'

Serge pulled another couple of pages from the dossier. 'Let's see. Firstly, there's the matter of employment. Apparently there is a lack of both meaningful opportunities and workforce, which results in prolonged hours for small business owners and an aged population having to work beyond retirement.' He looked at Stephanie and Josette who were leaning against the counter.

'I choose to work — '

'Is he saying I'm too old — ?'

The mayor cut short their indignation with a raised hand. 'Then there are the facilities. Poorly maintained and inadequate are the words used. The *salle des fêtes* up at the town hall is described as shoddy and not fit for purpose, the grotto with its missing Jesus comes in for criticism — '

Véronique gasped. 'So *that's* what he was taking a photo of!'

' — and seemingly we are in dire need of a tennis court and a children's playground.'

'And is the préfet offering to pay for all this?' demanded René.

'Lastly, we come to the small matter of an inefficient and unlawful Conseil Municipal,' continued Serge, and heads snapped up around the room. 'According to this, the Auberge, with the full sanction of the mayor, is operating without proper alcohol licences in place.'

Paul Webster paled and started spluttering, Stephanie laying a sympathetic hand on his arm.

'Furthermore, there was a failure to display the minutes of council meetings in accordance with the Code Général, Article L2121-25.'

René groaned at the reference to the dreaded Code, the national rule book that governed how the commune was run. Josette, however, was fuming, hands on hips.

'Someone took those minutes!' she spat. 'And look what trouble they've caused.'

'But that's not all,' Serge said, his voice now weary. 'We've also been cited for not sending out sufficient notification to council members of forthcoming meetings.'

'You mean the letters I mentioned last week? The ones Céline said she'd sent but we never received?' asked Christian. 'How did that make it into this report?'

Serge raised both hands and shrugged.

'Seems like that bloody *fonctionnaire* had a bit of help with his information gathering,' muttered René, and several others mumbled support.

'However, that's not the worst of it.' The mayor's words silenced the growing discontent and he pulled a set of graphs out of the folder and placed them on the table so everyone could see. 'These are from INSEE, the national office for statistics,' he added for Paul's benefit. He pointed a thick finger at a line that fell rapidly and then disappeared. 'And *that* is the real reason why we are being targeted for a merger.'

'The birth rate?' Christian glanced at the mayor, whose face looked grey and pained.

'No new babies.' Serge Papon stared at the assembled inhabitants of the commune, his tone accusatory. 'Not one in five years! Our young people are leaving. And Fogas is dying.'

The mayor was right. When was the last time a baby's cry had been heard in the valley? Josette, who had never been able to have a child, felt tears prick her eyes and was glad of the strong arm Christian placed around her shoulders. The farmer meanwhile was assailed with a sense of guilt he couldn't explain. He was one of the younger generation. He should have had a family by now. Should have given Picarets the joyful sound of children laughing and playing. Instead, the only people providing continuity were the incomers like Stephanie, who had brought Chloé to the commune, and the British couple, who were expecting a baby in the winter.

Across the room Véronique was also looking abashed, taking her father's rebuke personally. Although it was hardly fair. She wanted children. A whole tribe of them. All with curly blond hair and a beautiful smile. But time was running out. She was already thirty-six. She felt her mother's hand slide into hers and had the strange sensation of wanting to cry. Next to her, Fabian was equally frustrated. He too was happy to repopulate Fogas. If only he could find the courage to ask the woman he wanted to be his wife.

'Finally,' said Serge, 'we are in danger of losing two members of the Conseil Municipal, which, given our precarious position, we cannot afford to happen.'

'But we have over a hundred people in the commune. How can they take two councillors off us?' asked René.

'That's the point. We don't. Our population stands at ninety-nine permanent residents.'

Gasps of surprise echoed around the bar.

'How — ?'

'When did — ?'

'I thought — '

'Who died — ?'

'Ninety-nine? Are you sure?' Christian asked. Serge indicated a second chart, one with yet another line nose-diving off the page.

Christian scratched his head. If this was true — and he wasn't about to start questioning the verity of INSEE's statistics — then they were in a perilous state indeed. Because the size of the council was dictated by the size of the commune. At present, adjudged to be in the second lowest population band, which started at one hundred people, Fogas was permitted eleven councillors. If the inhabitants did indeed number only ninety-nine, however, then by rights Fogas should drop into the band below, where the maximum number of councillors was only nine. Which meant they would lose Alain Rougé and Monique Sentenac, the two who had garnered the lowest votes in the last election. As staunch supporters of Serge Papon, this would mean a shift in the power base. And Pascal Souquet, surrounded by his clique of second-home owners, would benefit.

As would Sarrat across the river. Luxuriating in a Conseil Municipal that carried fifteen councillors, thanks to a vibrant population, any debate over a merger would be balanced in their favour. And any potential union would to all effects be a takeover, Fogas submerged beneath its bigger counterpart.

'We do, however, have a lifeline,' Serge divulged to the now worried crowd. 'The sous-préfet has guaranteed that he will not raise the issue of the population, given that we are expecting a baby in Fogas within the next few months.'

A ragged cheer went up and René raised Paul's arm into the air like a prize-winning boxer, making the hotelier blush.

'So, if our numbers stay as they are, we will lose no councillors. For now. Which should give us a better chance of dealing with this potential merger. Even if it looks like a done deal.'

'But can't we just vote the proposal out?' asked Alain Rougé.

Serge shook his head. 'It's not that simple. Not if the préfet decides to issue a decree. Of course, it will have to be put to the Conseil Municipal, and if we reject it by a majority — '

'Which isn't certain, given there are some on the council who would vote for it if they thought it would bring political gain!' René said and shot a dark look at Fatima Souquet, who was hovering at the edge of the gathering, shopping basket in hand. But she didn't rise to his bait about her husband, forehead creased with a frown as she took in the news.

'If we did reject it,' continued Serge, 'it would then go to a referendum, which means everyone will have a say. Including the second-home owners.'

Mutterings started up again at the thought that the future of the commune could be in the hands of the people who came and went with the summer sun and yet held an equal say. They were, on the whole, more concerned about fêtes and festivities than the mundane aspects of running a commune, such as budgeting and road maintenance, not understanding the worth of having a functioning snowplough come the winter or a town hall roof that didn't leak. But they made up a significant enough body to have a powerful voice.

'It's risky,' admitted Christian. 'We could end up with our future being decided by the people who don't live here all year round.'

'But what are our options? We can't just roll over and give up!' Véronique was pacing up and down what small section of floor was unoccupied.

'You know me, Véronique.' Serge smiled for the first time that morning. 'I'm not one for giving up.'

'So what then?' She jutted out her chin and the amassed people of Fogas were reminded yet again of how like her father she was.

'We don't let the préfet get as far as issuing a decree.'

'We could blackmail him,' suggested René, totally serious.

And with equal solemnity, Serge replied. 'Not a chance. I've done a bit of investigating and young Jérôme Ulrich is squeaky clean. No skeletons in his cupboard. Not a hint of scandal. Nothing.'

'Which leaves us with what?' asked Christian.

'We nip it in the bud now. The sous-préfet has agreed to delay submitting his report, and as long as our population remains stable and we show signs of improvement in the areas I outlined, he's willing to put our case forward and suggest that the merger is not a good idea. So we have until *Toussaint*.' Serge took a breath and gazed around the room at the concerned expressions of his friends and neighbours. 'Which means we only have eight weeks to show those bastards over in Foix that we have a thriving community and we are self-sufficient. Who thinks we can do that?'

A flurry of hands shot into the air and Véronique produced pen and paper. The campaign to save Fogas was launched as the church bells rang out the midday hour.

11

After precisely four and a half hours Chloé knew that she was going to hate *collège*. Which was a shame, given that she was such a short way into her sentence at the place. With neither of the Rogalle twins for company, she was the only child in her class from the small school in Sarrat — a school that was roundly looked down upon by the other pupils, who mostly hailed from the bigger communities of Oust, Seix and Massat. Consequently, she was already the butt of jokes about hicks and mountains. And goats. Only half a day into her life as a student at the big school and she was having trouble keeping a rein on her temper.

Temporarily released by the lunchtime bell, she scuffed at the stones that pitted the car park as she slouched towards the village centre, her annoyance made worse by the fact that she wasn't allowed home for lunch any more. Instead, she had to suffer the canteen. The noise, the meal and the surroundings were a far cry from the simple fare at the wooden table in the garden with Fabian and Maman that she was accustomed to, the mountains spread out before them.

Although, with the way Maman was treating her lately, perhaps the canteen was preferable. She'd said this morning that she was going to Toulouse the following day. On business, had been her reply to Chloé's obvious response. She wouldn't say any more.

But Fabian was incapable of subterfuge, and when questioned by an intense eleven-year-old he'd stammered and stuttered and had eventually walked off. It was clear right then that this was no business trip. Maman was going to meet the madman who had tried to kill them. The man who might be trying to get custody of Chloé.

She stood on the bridge that spanned the Salat river, watching fat, lazy trout float effortlessly in the deep water of the mill run-off. But even the sight of their speckled bodies in the warm sunshine couldn't lift her mood. She hated that Maman and Fabian didn't trust her. She was old enough to be told the truth, especially as this involved her too. Which it did, given her birth certificate.

After overhearing Maman's conversation with Fabian that evening in July, Chloé had crept downstairs the next night and rifled through the drawers in the dresser until she found the flimsy record of her birth, a letter tucked beside it. With both papers in her hand, she'd been overcome with a sense of guilt in a house where mutual respect made locks redundant. But she'd told herself that Maman's mantra of openness and trust, instilled in Chloé from birth, no longer applied. Not now Maman had secrets of her own.

And so, in the beam of the bike light Fabian had bought her for Christmas, Chloé had read the letter from the lawyers instructing Maman to attend something called a conciliation session. She'd not totally understood the meaning but knew it involved meeting Bruno Madec, and she'd felt sick at the thought of it. Maman in a room with him. After what happened last time.

Shaking, she'd unfolded the second piece of paper. Her birth certificate. Hoping she'd misheard Maman, she ran her finger down the page to the box that should contain the name of her father. But it was empty. No signature. No printed name. So it was true; she was unclaimed. Unless Bruno Madec and his family got their way. Was it possible that, without the identity of her real father to protect her, she could be packed off to Brittany to live with grandparents she couldn't remember, a long way from the people she loved and her precious mountains? Fearful of what her future might hold, she'd shoved the papers back in the drawer and returned to bed.

The next morning she'd told Maman she wanted a bolt on her bedroom door, and they'd had their first row. Fabian had looked stunned and Maman disappointed. But Chloé insisted and got her way. By the following weekend she was able to lock herself in her room, and by the end of the summer holidays she had perfected the behaviour of the average teenager, showing dissension and throwing tantrums until she barely recognised herself. And behind it all was that piece of paper with its nameless box and the vulnerability it engendered.

Believing the world was set against her, she turned from the river and had started back towards the school when her reluctant progress was halted by a poster in the window of the tourist office. Mesmerised, she stepped off the kerb into the path of an oncoming cyclist, who shouted at her as he braked, swerved and narrowly avoided a collision with the bridge. Throwing an apology over her shoulder, she ran the remaining distance to the small, wooden building in the centre of the car park, her breath catching in her throat.

An acrobat. Muscles stretched as he balanced nonchalantly on a high wire, a broad smile on his face. Below him, way below, were the pale spheres of faces in the crowd. He was so high up. And there was no safety net.

Chloé's heart was beating fast, her face flushed as she stared at the poster, imagining how it would feel to be him. It was what she wanted. All she'd wanted for as long as she could remember. To be an acrobat. But Maman wasn't keen. When she'd first found Chloé, at the tender age of five, entertaining the Rogalle twins by hanging out of a tree and declaring she was a trapeze artist, Maman had told her off. She'd made her child promise she would never play at being in a circus again. For a while Chloé had obeyed. However when it proved too difficult to ignore this strange obsession she'd been born with, she had simply kept her performances out of sight. Perfecting cartwheels and tumbles and handsprings in the fields around the village using an old manual she'd found in a second-hand bookshop in St Girons, Chloé had taught herself well. And when her exceptional skills had come to light over a year ago, Maman had relented and allowed her daughter to practise at home. But still, she wouldn't entertain the notion of Chloé joining a circus. Nor would she ever take her to one.

Chloé ran a hand over the glass, hearing the roar of the crowd, the sudden hush as the acrobat began to walk along the wire. The spotlight. The gasps. And then she glanced again at the man's face. He was looking straight at her. Laughing. Enticing her to come along and watch a performance.

'If you stare at it any longer, you'll miss the start of the afternoon classes,' came a dry voice, and Chloé turned to see a woman standing in the doorway, tapping her watch in emphasis.

'I don't care,' muttered Chloé, gaze swinging back to the big top. 'I want to quit.'

'Quit? It's your first day at *collège*, isn't it?'

Chloé nodded dejectedly, eyes still on the acrobat. The woman folded her arms and Chloé could feel the weight of her regard.

'Would you like a copy?' the lady finally asked, tipping her head towards the poster.

A smile lit up Chloé's troubled face. 'Yes!' she breathed.

'Well, get to school. And give it a chance. It might not be as bad as you think. Then come and see me next Friday and I'll have a poster for you.'

Chloé grinned and was gone, legs propelling her across the car park towards her class. She was hurtling through the door to take her seat when she realised she hadn't made a note of the performance dates. She'd get them tomorrow. There was a circus coming to town and she was going to go and see it. No matter what Maman said.

★ ★ ★

'That went well.' The energetic meeting over, Christian stood up from the table and stretched, his T-shirt riding up from his jeans and exposing a strip of brown stomach. 'Don't you think?'

Véronique nodded, eyes dropping quickly to the notepad in her hand and a flush of pink covering her cheeks as he turned to her.

'Very well,' agreed Serge Papon. 'So good in fact, that I'll have that pastis now, Josette.'

The bar owner laughed and headed for the counter.

'It's great to have new names stepping forward to get involved,' said Christian, leaning over Véronique to read her notes, his large frame dwarfing her. 'Who'd have thought newcomers like Paul and Stephanie would be so passionate about saving our commune?'

'Often it takes an outside perspective to appreciate what you have,' murmured Serge.

With lunchtime still not over, a lot had been achieved. Deciding that the best way to tackle the problem was to finally form a *comité des fêtes* — something that Fogas had never had before and which poor René, in charge of all the festivities for the last decade, had been demanding for a while — a group of five people had been elected onto it: Christian and René representing the Conseil Municipal, and Paul, Stephanie and Véronique chosen unanimously by a show of assembled hands. Fatima Souquet, despite being put forward by none other than Serge himself, had declined to take a post. Having agreed they would meet formally that evening in the Auberge, the new committee had solicited ideas from the people gathered in the bar. They had been besieged.

The first suggestion had been to imitate the more dynamic villages in the area by developing a website for the commune. Much to the relief of the technically less able committee members, Fabian and Paul had volunteered to set it up. Then Alain Rougé had proposed another fête. Something that would showcase the abilities of Fogas. Still unsure as to the theme, they'd all agreed that late October would be ideal, at which point, in a Newton-esque moment, Josette had said apples. A fête tied in with the apple harvest. It was perfect. With her brainwave acting as inspiration the ideas rained down.

Stephanie and Alain were going to organise entrance into the regional Villages in Bloom competition and give the abandoned orchard next to the épicerie a makeover, while Paul had offered to host a monthly cinema club. This had led to Josette, Serge and Annie reminiscing about the nights they'd spent at the Auberge in their youth, the entire commune packed onto benches watching the likes of Clark Gable and John Wayne parade across a sheet hung on a wall while a projector whirred away in the background.

With the news that footage from the webcam on Sarko the bull had gone viral — a phrase that had to be explained to Gaston, the old shepherd, who thought the Limousin beast was dying — Véronique had suggested this could be exploited to grow the commune's image. She was confident she could source a toymaker to produce mini-Sarkos for sale in the shop, and Fabian was willing to set up a second website just for the cantankerous bovine. Christian had merely shaken his head in bemusement, unable to accept that his old nemesis was becoming such a star.

Serge meanwhile had taken on the mantle of making sure that the municipal buildings were given an overhaul, in so far as they had the budget to do so, and had delegated to Véronique the task of finding a replacement Jesus for the grotto. He'd ignored suggestions from the crowd that Bernard Mirouze could always be hung up there in a loincloth for the duration until something suitable was found.

When laughter and rumbling stomachs began to outweigh practical suggestions, Serge had called the meeting to a close and the bar had emptied, many of those present heading down to the Auberge for lunch, a panicked Paul racing ahead of them to warn his wife that numbers might be higher than expected. Serge, Véronique and Christian were the only ones to remain.

'Is that why you asked Fatima to join the committee?' asked Véronique, shifting slightly so Christian could have a better view of the notepad he was still reading over her shoulder.

178

'For an outside perspective?'

Serge laughed and took a sip of his pastis. 'No. I did that to keep our enemies closer! Shame she turned us down.'

'What did you expect? Pascal's power rests on the shoulders of the second-home owners. He's not going to make a move until he has sounded them out about the merger. Fatima neither.'

'Don't be so sure.' Serge leaned forward and placed his hand over Véronique's. 'There is more to that woman than you know.'

Véronique snorted. 'I'll take your word for it.'

'Don't you agree, Christian?'

'Hmm?' Christian straightened up with a jolt. He'd been lost. Staring at the page of Véronique's handwriting, which he was unable to read at that distance, he'd become caught up in the smell of her hair, the slope of her shoulder, the faint line of white skin where her bikini straps had held back the sun. He'd entered a trance. One filled with her laughter, her warmth. Her love.

He ran a hand over his face, brushing away the last cobwebs of daydream. 'Sorry?'

'Fatima. I said we shouldn't underestimate her.'

'I agree. I've always thought she should be the one on the council, not Pascal. She's definitely the brains behind that operation.' He stepped away from the table, surprised to find the withdrawal from Véronique's proximity causing a sharp pain in his ribs like a stitch. 'Right. Don't know about you two but I need my lunch. I'd best get home and see what Maman has

179

managed to incinerate today.'

'You're not coming to the Auberge? Serge . . . I mean . . . *Papa* and I are heading down there and you're welcome to join us.'

Christian's reply rose unbidden to his lips, overjoyed at the thought of spending more time with her. Then he caught sight of the mayor's face. Having thrown an arm of delight around his daughter's shoulders at her first public acknowledgement of his paternity, Serge now looked crestfallen.

'Yes . . . no . . . sorry. I'd love to. But . . . ' The farmer stalled, not the best at improvising. 'Er . . . I'm expecting the vet. For a cow. Not for me.' He spluttered his apologies and left, no more able to withstand Véronique's disappointment than he had her father's.

Exasperated at being the kind of man who put a father's desire for time alone with his daughter ahead of his own concerns of the heart, he drove all the way home making resolutions to be more selfish. To be more ruthless. This resolve was immediately tested when he arrived at the farm to be greeted by his mother's latest cremated meal. Of course, he sat down and made the best of it without complaining. Because, no more than Sarko the bull could curb his everlasting desire to escape confinement, could Christian Dupuy change the type of person he was.

★ ★ ★

Many hours later, with a waning moon hanging drunkenly in the ebony sky, Jacques Servat was wide awake. One of the curious aspects of this afterlife he'd been granted was the sleep. Or the lack of it. If he'd spared the matter a passing thought when alive, he would have said that ghosts probably didn't need to rest. That the exertions of daily life, which rendered a night-time slumber so essential to the living, simply didn't apply to those who had passed over. But it wasn't true. He felt as tired at the end of a day in this strange existence as he had when he was alive. And just as the later years of his time in the mortal world had seen his sleeping habits become fitful — the solid eight hours' repose that he'd known as a younger man denied him as a pensioner — so too he now found himself waking at odd hours, shuffling through the empty bar and épicerie and occupying himself by watching the deserted road.

Not that there was much by way of entertainment. He'd seen deer of course, the odd boar. Once he'd even seen a bear lumbering down to the lay-by, its bulky shape caught under one of the few street lights as it headed for the communal bins. Sometimes he was lucky and his boredom was relieved by the company of Josette, she too unable to sleep as soundly as she once had. She would make a hot chocolate and sit and chat to him until one or the other of them began to feel drowsy. He liked those nights best of all.

But tonight she hadn't appeared. Nor was she likely to, as he could hear gentle snores coming from the room they'd once shared. Plus they'd had an argument before she went to bed. An argument without words. On his part, anyway. She'd known he was unhappy though. She'd known she'd hurt him.

He sighed. If he was able to he'd head up the stairs and wake her up. Talk through what they'd bickered about, as they used to. They'd had some amazing rows over the years. And had amazing fun making up, too! He grinned at the thought, remembering the time when he'd ended a disagreement by closing the épicerie and carrying her upstairs to bed. In the middle of the day. They'd taken a bit of ribbing for that from locals calling in to collect their baguettes only to find a *Fermé* sign on the front door.

That was beyond him now, his present existence confining him to the épicerie and bar. If he tried to go any further he fainted. And then found himself back in the inglenook, which was very disconcerting. So he had no choice but to reflect on the argument by himself.

The épicerie had been abuzz after the mayor's return from St Girons, people popping in to discuss the shocking news of the merger, and Josette, even with Véronique's help, was shattered by closing time. With Véronique heading down to the Auberge for the first formal meeting of the *comité des fêtes*, Josette had managed the last few hours on her own until the sky darkened and the sliver of moon could be seen above Cap de Bouirex. At nine on the dot, she'd latched the windows and bolted the door and had stood for a moment, looking across the now indiscernible river to the scattering of lights that represented Sarrat at night. She must have forgotten Jacques was there. Or thought he was asleep. Because what she said next, she couldn't have meant him to be party to.

'Would it really be such a bad thing?' she'd murmured. 'Merging with Sarrat?'

He'd been up out of his seat like a shot, head striking the mantelpiece with a clatter only he could hear and a pain he'd thought impossible considering he was dead.

'What the hell do you mean?' he'd roared silently to her back.

She'd seen his reflection in the window, jumping up and down on the spot, arms flailing, he was so incensed. And he'd seen her shoulders slump as though she didn't have the energy for any more battles.

'Sorry, Jacques, I know what Fogas means to you. It means the same to me,' she'd said as she turned to face his angry features. 'But perhaps we should be thinking about the future.'

'Future? What kind of a future will we have with Sarrat ruling us?' He slapped his forehead, merely making it throb all the more, and began to pace the floor. 'I can't believe you would say that. You, who've lived here all your — '

'The figures don't lie, love. This place is dying. At this rate it won't be long before we don't have the right to self-government. Surely it's better for us to join forces with Sarrat now when we have a say, than to have it imposed on us when we no longer have a Conseil Municipal?'

' — life. How can you think that things would be better with that bigoted Dedieu in charge? Because no matter what they promise, that's how it would be. And how many councillors do you think we'll get on the council? No more than two if we're lucky. One of them being that dandy, Pascal Souquet. Is that who you want — '

'I can't hear you, Jacques. Not a word. So there's no point working yourself up any further.'

' — governing you? Of all the people who live here? Him and his ambitious wife and neither of them with a sense of this community? How can that — '

'Jacques, love. I'm off to bed. I can't bear it when you get upset. I'll see you in the morning.'

' — be good for the future? There'll be no future for Fogas if this goes . . . Josette? Josette?'

He'd called out to her but of course she hadn't heard, and she was already through the doorway behind the bar, the one he couldn't cross. He'd waved and shouted, pleaded with her to come back, but she hadn't turned around. The last sound had been her laboured tread on the stairs and a weary sigh as she reached the landing. Then nothing.

It had taken him ages to get to sleep, the inglenook proving uncomfortable, his mind churning with the heat of the row. Finally, he'd drifted off but had woken repeatedly from broken dreams of the pair of them arguing. Accepting the night was going to yield him no further rest, he'd got up and wandered through to the épicerie to stare out of the window. But as usual, there was nothing to see.

He slouched back into the bar, crossing to the square of dark glass, Josette no longer closing the shutters now that she was aware of his nocturnal prowling. Pressing his face against the cold surface, he breathed out, the exhalation leaving a circle of mist on the window. He breathed again and again, until he had formed a wavering shape in the middle of the glass. He'd just finished the excruciatingly slow process of adding writing to his artwork, all the inhaling and exhaling making him dizzy, when headlights dazzled him. A car was turning out of the Picarets road, opposite the Auberge.

Excitement! He concentrated on the lights, seeing nothing but the glare of them until the car slowed up before the épicerie. And indicated! Who bothered indicating at this time of night? Must be a woman, he thought with a chuckle. But it wasn't. Because as the car turned right, heading up the hill to Fogas, he saw the profile of the driver in the sulphurous yellow glow of the street lamp. It was Pascal Souquet.

Perhaps it was the argument with Josette. Or maybe the turbulent emotions of the day. It could even have been the bash to the head he'd taken earlier. But seeing the first deputy mayor like that jolted something in the recesses of Jacques' brain.

What was it René had said when Serge was reading out the contents of the damning dossier? That the long-nosed *fonctionnaire* had had help compiling his case.

In their eagerness to revitalise Fogas, those gathered at the bar today had overlooked the plumber's comment. But perhaps he had a point. All that malignant evidence that condemned the commune. The lost minutes. The letters that never arrived. The inspection at the Auberge. Even the electrical problems at the fête. Was it possible someone was behind it all in an attempt to make Fogas appear worse than it was? Who, though?

Removing the minutes was easy enough. The cabinet was never locked, so anyone could have had access to it. The same with the electrics. It wouldn't have taken much at the fête that night to nip around the back and rearrange Bernard's handiwork. But the letters that went missing after the town hall secretary had placed them in the outgoing postbag? And the inspection? That needed someone with insider knowledge. Someone with contacts. And quite possibly, someone who lived in Fogas.

Which meant they had a traitor in their midst.

The sound of the straining car engine faded into the distance as it continued the long climb up to the village. It was a strange time of night to be out. Though it wasn't the first time Jacques had seen Pascal Souquet at such an hour. Only last winter he'd witnessed the first deputy mayor returning from another late-night assignation, skulking down the road, hugging to the shadows. Given the effete manner of the man and the retribution his terrifying wife would be capable of wreaking, an affair seemed an unlikely explanation. But no other had come to mind.

Jacques paced over to the fireplace and back, letting his mind roam free. For he was sure there were other clues he was missing. Other things he'd noticed over the last twelve months or so that suggested all was not well at the heart of Fogas.

The incident with the bear, for one. That had never been resolved satisfactorily. But then no one else in the commune had seen what Jacques had seen: grainy footage from a camera up in the woods, which he'd watched over the shoulder of Arnaud Petit, the tracker. Clear as day, or night, because that was when it was taken, Jacques had seen Pascal's pale face on the video as he collected bear fur from one of Arnaud's surveillance points, unaware he was being filmed. The tracker had never raised this with the rest of Fogas. And Jacques had forgotten about it in the upheaval that followed the death of the bear.

But scraps of supposition weren't enough. Jacques was going to have to gather more evidence. And then he was going to have to find a way to transmit his findings across the gulf that existed between him and the mortal world. He was going to have to find a way to communicate.

'So you're up too?'

He spun round at her voice. Josette. Face sleepy, a dressing gown pulled tight around her small frame. He smiled.

'I'm sorry,' he said, arms open wide.

'I'm sorry,' she said, walking towards him.

Then she saw the window and she started to cry. For decorating the centre of the glass was a misty heart. And beneath it were the words '*Je t'aime*', breathed across the cold surface in shaking letters.

They sat in the inglenook holding hands, his touch no more than a sigh upon her skin. When dawn started to streak the sky with the promise

187

of another day, she was still there. Fast asleep, hand locked in his. And Jacques? He was wide awake, working out how he was going to catch the rat who was betraying Fogas.

★ ★ ★

By the break of day it was done. Fingers had flown across the keyboard, words pouring onto the blank screen. The passion was surprising. Once unleashed, it took over, stating the case with eloquence. With vigour. With a voice that was going to be heard. A resolute click of the mouse and the text was out in the ether for everyone to read. There was no turning back now.

12

'Do you know who's behind it?'

'No. But it is someone who knows Fogas very well. 'Ow else could zey write zis?'

Bracelets clattered as Stephanie gestured at the laptop in front of Lorna, the screen covered in text beneath a heading that screamed *SOS FOGAS*.

'What does this bit mean?' The Englishwoman began to read. "*Il ne faut pas vendre la peau de l'ours avant de l'avoir tué.*"

'It says you must not to sell ze skin before you 'ave killed ze bear. Like you English and counting chickens, *n'est-ce pas?*' Stephanie smiled. 'Whoever wrote zis, zey are very clever. Zey say ze merger is not definite and at ze same time — '

'They link Sarrat and Henri Dedieu to the death of the bear! Which isn't good for his image.'

Stephanie clapped her hands and grinned. '*Fantastique*! You are becoming a true local, Lorna. I 'ave taught you well.'

Lorna laughed, her baby tumbling inside her in response as though her mirth had woken him from a slumber. 'And still I have so much to learn. So has everyone seen this?'

'By now? I think so. Fabian discovered it yesterday when 'e was making ze website for ze commune. 'E sent it to Christian and to

Véronique, and from zere . . . '

'Everyone who used the post office today or even set foot in the shop will know about it by now.'

'Exactly.' A long finger pointed at the hit counter in the corner of the screen, which, despite Fogas having a mere ninety-nine inhabitants according to INSEE, showed that over two thousand people had already visited the anonymous blog. 'Sarko ze bull is not ze only one going viral.'

Lorna closed the laptop, shaking her head as she got slowly to her swollen feet. 'I can't believe Fogas might have to merge.'

'Pah!' The sound was filled with derision. 'Zose imbeciles in Foix, zey 'ave underestimated us. We will fight zis all ze way.'

Not sure where she was going to find the energy to fight, pregnancy and a summer season running the Auberge having already sapped her of every reserve she had, Lorna changed the subject. 'I've not had a chance to hear how you got on in Toulouse. Did everything go okay?'

A cloud passed over her friend's face at the reference to her overnight visit to the big city the week before and Lorna regretted asking.

'It was 'orrible. Zat man . . . ' Stephanie shuddered, the malevolent presence of her estranged husband still clinging to her like a slick of oil marring a pristine lake. 'But it is finished. Now I simply wait for ze paperwork.'

'He didn't try to get custody?'

'No. 'E never mentioned it at all.' Her furrowed brow was at variance with her news.

But Stephanie was baffled by how she'd managed to get her wires so crossed. Despite her fears, there had been no attempt by Bruno Madec, or his parents, to take Chloé into their care. In fact, Bruno hadn't said one word about her. Although he'd said plenty about his wife. None of it repeatable. Exhausted by the encounter, Stephanie had returned to Fogas, grateful that she'd had the sense not to share her unfounded suspicions with her daughter. At least Chloé had been spared any unnecessary turmoil.

'But that's good, isn't it? Your divorce should be straight-forward now,' said Lorna.

'Oh yes, it is excellent. Still, I don't understand . . . ze feeling I 'ad of losing Chloé. It was so strong. And connected to zat *fonction-naire*.' The frown on Stephanie's forehead deepened.

'Perhaps you picked up that he was a threat to the community? Maybe that was the feeling of loss you had?'

'Per'aps.'

'*Merde!* The tart! It's still in the oven.'

Lorna rushed through to the kitchen to rescue dessert, the mouth-watering smell of *tarte au citron* wafting into the restaurant. It wasn't enough to distract the young Frenchwoman. Because while her reaction to the long-nosed civil servant could be explained by the dreadful news that Fogas — the place that had given Stephanie and her daughter sanctuary — was under threat, the sensation she'd had of losing Chloé couldn't. She'd felt that long before she'd even met him.

Perhaps, she wondered wryly, that particular intuition referred more to the change that had come over her daughter since the summer, leaving behind a young person that Stephanie sometimes didn't even recognise and whose sole ambition seemed to be to provoke her mother at all turns. But even this couldn't allay Stephanie's fears, and it was with a troubled sixth sense that she began setting the tables for the lunchtime service.

★ ★ ★

'Does anyone know who's behind it?'

'Not a clue.'

'But they're on our side?'

'Most definitely. Unless describing Sarrat as a nest of duplicitous vipers could be construed as supportive of the merger.'

Serge Papon chuckled. 'And how many people have seen it?'

'By now? Considering that Véronique emailed me last night and since then has had a morning behind the counter of the post office to broadcast the news, pretty much the entire commune. And most of Sarrat.'

It was only as Céline Laffont, secretary at the town hall, looked up from the computer screen and saw the grin on the mayor's face that she remembered the recently uncovered family connection. But Serge was far from offended at her portrayal of his daughter as a gossip.

'That's my girl!' he murmured. He took one more look at the *SOS Fogas* blog and with a satisfied grunt, headed for his office.

It had been a long ten days since the news had broken. Many of them he'd spent in this very room, behind the large desk that occupied a fraction of the grand space allocated to the first mayor of Fogas just after the Revolution. What would that man have made of this development, wondered the latest incumbent as he sat in the familiar chair that had worn to his contours over the twenty-six years he'd been in power. Without question, that august leader would have been horrified. To learn that the commune he had helped found — a collection of mountain villages wrestled after a vicious and prolonged bureaucratic battle from the grasp of the people who ran Sarrat — was about to be reunited with his ancient foe would have been enough to kill him.

It was also quite likely that it would kill the man trying to do his job over two hundred years later.

Serge had met with no success in trying to turn back the ticking clock. Using his network of alliances, which had tentacles reaching into the darkest corners of Ariège officialdom, he had achieved nothing more than confirmation that Préfet Jérôme Ulrich fully intended to unify the two communes of Sarrat and Fogas. Not one of Serge's informants implied it was vindictive. No one suggested there was an ulterior motive. In fact, there hadn't been a bad word uttered against the man, and Serge had come away with a growing respect for the miner's son who had risen so rapidly through the ranks of the French civil service. To all appearances, in proposing the merger the young préfet was simply doing exactly what he had been asked to do by the President of the Republic: he was making cutbacks.

This was a conclusion that Serge Papon too had reached, in his call to the man who had placed the future of Fogas in the balance. Monsieur Ulrich had been polite, respectful and had put forward a persuasive argument; persuasive as long as you weren't one of the people on the wrong side of the river that formed the communal boundary. He had also, unfortunately for those very people, been steadfast in the face of Serge's attempts to change his mind. The préfet was determined to see this plan through. And the mayor of Fogas sensed that the report being compiled by the sous-préfet in St Girons, the document that Serge had persuaded his electorate to pin their hopes to, was no more than a formality.

But what had also emerged from the feedback submitted by Serge's moles was that Jérôme Ulrich, who hailed from Lorraine and knew nothing of the politics of the Ariège, had been offered a helping hand. Serge had heard all about the letter that had instigated the proposed merger. He had been told how accommodating his opposite number in Sarrat was being. And he had seen for himself the documents Henri Dedieu had willingly passed on to the powers in Foix, outlining the efficacy of his proposal; the cost-effectiveness of a single commune.

It shouldn't have surprised him, after all his years in local politics. But even so, Serge had been disappointed — and perturbed — to discover that his counterpart across the river had been instrumental in precipitating the crisis that Fogas now faced. From a long dynasty of councillors, Henri Dedieu had followed in the footsteps of his father and his grandfather by becoming mayor. In fact, he was a direct descendant of Louis Dedieu, the leader of the much larger, pre-Revolutionary commune of Sarrat that had stretched beyond the watery border and enfolded the two modern-day districts into one; the very man who'd suffered the ignominy of having his neighbours elect to withdraw from his domain in favour of setting up their own. Thus, the present-day Dedieu was steeped in centuries of political cunning and was a formidable opponent whom Serge had thankfully never had cause to confront.

Now, however, they would finally be crossing swords and already Serge had had to revise his opinion of the Machiavelli across the water. For when he'd called Henri Dedieu about the merger, the man had been unexpectedly charming, brushing aside accusations of unprincipled behaviour with a rhetoric far removed from the coarse hunter that Serge knew him to be. And while Serge didn't trust Dedieu an inch and was furious at his underhand tactics, he could understand how the préfet could be swayed by such an urbane show of support for a plan that met with approval at the highest levels.

Hence, after more than a week of relentless digging, Serge had reached the unavoidable conclusion that Fogas would soon be no more. It

195

was inevitable. The préfet wanted the merger. Henri Dedieu and the people of Sarrat wanted the merger. Given the size of the only objector, a puny commune of less than a hundred inhabitants, Serge wasn't willing to wager on the outcome being in his favour.

He wouldn't share his speculation with his electorate, of course. Instead, he would encourage them in every way to fight the well-oiled machine of French bureaucracy, no matter how futile it seemed. To demonstrate. To agitate. To spread the word of the anonymous blogger who was championing their cause. Because that was how they were bred. And that was what would keep them going. But in the back of his mind he was already planning the future. He would retire. Propose Christian for the new council. And Josette. The others? What chance did they have? A combined Conseil Municipal of fifteen people, with Sarrat making up the biggest voting share. Fogas would be lucky to get two representatives on it. The voices of the mountain villagers would be lost in the cacophony of those who lived on the pastureland across the river.

Serge Papon sighed and reached for a pen. He had letters to write, petitions to influential citizens who were indebted to him for ancient favours the mayor never forgot. He would keep trying. Go through the motions. But inside his heart was ripped apart. To think that the commune he had presided over for more than a quarter of a century was to be dissolved while under his stewardship. It was more than he could stand.

There was, however, one bright star on the

dismal horizon. Serge paused and allowed a smile to pass fleetingly across his lips at the thought.

The merger with Sarrat would put an end to Pascal Souquet's career. The ineffective first deputy, who had always seen his position as a way to further his political ambitions — one eye on the Conseil Général, the elected body that governed the Ariège, and the other on the Conseil Régional up in Toulouse — would find his way blocked by the shifts in power. Because if there was one thing Serge Papon was sure of, Henri Dedieu, Mayor of Sarrat and the future leader of the combined commune, couldn't stand the man. And once the union was made official, Henri Dedieu would wield his substantial clout and Pascal would be cast out into the political wilderness.

Unaware of how wrong he could be, Serge got back to work. He had yet to break the bad news to the populace that the route up to Fogas would soon be out of action, the electricity board having just informed him that they were upgrading the line to the hilltop village. Which meant closing the road for the duration of the work and providing shuttle buses to ferry people up and down. Two weeks of upheaval and no doubt lots of complaints. Shaking his head at the prospect, for Serge the political wilderness suddenly didn't seem so bad.

* * *

'Do you know who's behind it?'

Pascal Souquet had been enjoying a rare thing:

a decent espresso at the bar in La Rivière. Ever since Fabian had arrived with that amazing machine and educated the ignorant locals in the fine art of coffee making, the standard of refreshments on offer had improved dramatically. The ambience, it had to be said, still left a lot to be desired.

Sitting at a table on the terrace, the chill wind on his neck at odds with the mild temperature, the first deputy mayor was assailed by the boisterous laughter carrying through the open window and the odorous presence of the old shepherd and his dog in the far corner. Fatima, however, had insisted that he sit and have a drink while she did the shopping. Thus he'd been mulling over his future, revelling in the upheaval that the news of the merger was causing, when his phone rang. It was Henri Dedieu. And as always, he dispensed with the niceties of introductions and got straight to the brutal point.

'I said, do you know who's behind it?' growled the mayor of Sarrat.

'Behind what?' asked a flustered Pascal, voice low.

'The bloody blog, moron! *SOS Fogas*.'

Pascal didn't have a clue what he was talking about.

'Don't tell me you haven't seen it?'

'I, er . . . I mean . . . '

'Find out who's responsible. And sort it. By whatever means necessary.' Menace oozed through the receiver.

'Yes. Of course. I'll — '

But the line was already dead.

With a trembling hand, Pascal reached out to drain the last of his coffee, not entirely sure how he could solve a problem he knew nothing about. The man was insufferable. A bully. Worse than that. A demon. And he had the first deputy mayor dangling over the abyss of hell with threats of exposure. Threats that would confine Pascal to prison if carried out.

Another burst of laughter from the bar drew his wrath and he turned to glare through the open window at the bunch of locals gathered around a laptop on the counter.

'Imbeciles,' he muttered.

And then it clicked. A laptop. He could see a lurid title emblazoned across the screen: *SOS FOGAS*.

He stood and for the first time in Fogas history, Pascal Souquet did what most locals did to save Josette's legs. He picked up his empty cup and returned it to the bar.

★   ★   ★

'Do we know who's behind it?' demanded René, wiping tears of mirth from his eyes.

'No idea. But they have a wicked sense of humour.' Christian turned the screen so the plumber could see the cartoon that portrayed Serge as a hunter in full camouflage aiming a rifle at the préfet's target-embossed backside, and another wave of laughter washed over the room.

'It's ingenious,' declared Véronique, who had

been doing her utmost all morning to spread word of the radical new blog. 'But I'm still racking my brains as to the author. The posts started the day the merger was announced, so it's got to be someone in the know.'

'It's not Fabian?' asked René.

'No! For the hundredth time, it isn't me,' came a disgruntled voice from the épicerie.

'Everyone keeps asking him,' whispered Véronique. 'What with his IT expertise, he seems the obvious candidate, but he's getting rattled about it now.'

'What about Paul? He designs websites in his spare time. Surely he must be a contender?' Christian gestured towards the Auberge in the distance but the postmistress was already shaking her head.

'He might have the technical know-how but his French isn't this good. And I doubt he'd have the insider knowledge this person does.'

'Well, who does that leave?'

They looked around at each other, suspicions flourishing.

'It could be any one of us, couldn't it? I mean, that's what makes it so interesting,' said Véronique.

Alain Rougé disagreed. 'You're forgetting that most of us don't know how to set up a blog. Surely that's important?'

She shrugged. 'If you can use the internet, how hard can it be?'

'So I guess that counts out Gaston, then?' René cast a roguish glance at the snoozing shepherd.

'But everyone else is suspect,' concluded Christian. 'Even you, Pascal!'

The first deputy, who had joined the back of the throng and was leaning in to get a better view of the screen, jumped.

'Me? Set up *SOS Fogas?* You're joking.' Coloured by his feelings for the yokel-filled commune, the words came out with rather more vehemence than he'd intended and he was left backtracking. 'I mean . . . why would I . . . how — ?'

'Pascal, we're late.' The command came from the épicerie where Fatima stood, basket in hand, an impatient finger tapping her watch. Glad to be rescued, the first deputy scurried after her, leaving a burst of fresh laughter in his wake.

'SOS Fogas? SOS Pascal, more like! Merde, but that's some woman he's married to.' René finished his pastis and wiped his moustache, preparing to go. 'A man should get an instant papal annulment if he ends up with someone like that.'

'But how do you know beforehand?' asked Christian. 'That you're compatible?'

'You just do.' Fabian had wandered in, his face sombre as he approached the group. 'Take it from me.'

'Huh! Hark at him dishing out advice, and he's so in love he can't even manage to propose!' René winked at the Parisian, who looked sheepish.

'It's true,' he moaned. 'I'm petrified Stephanie will say no.'

'How will you ever find out if you don't pluck

up the courage to ask?' Véronique's voice was incredulous. 'It can't be that hard to tell a woman you love her?'

Christian grunted and eased up off the bar. 'You should try being in our shoes for once,' he muttered. 'You women have it easy. You cast your nets and ensnare some poor sod and then give no indication as to how you really feel, making us blokes do all the running.' He shook his head, glowering beneath the curls. 'And my parents wonder why I'm still single.'

And with that, he stormed out, a stunned silence settling behind him.

'If I didn't know better . . . ' mused René, watching the farmer squeeze himself into his Panda 4×4 in the distance. 'Nah! There's no way. Christian Dupuy? In love? That'll be the day.'

With the love-struck Parisian still bemoaning his lot to his aunt, René left the bar. He wasn't to know that his random speculations would cause such torment. That the postmistress, over a particularly idle afternoon when the shop was quiet and the post office closed, would while away the hours trying to work out if what the plumber had said could be true.

Was Christian in love? It would explain his moods of late. But if so, who was the lucky woman? Because, thought Véronique Estaque as she stared down the road at the hills in the distance, judging by his recent behaviour, it certainly wasn't her. And that was enough to make her thoroughly miserable.

★ ★ ★

202

'Do they know who's behind it?'

There were two people in the tourist office in Seix when Chloé pushed open the door. The woman she'd spoken to the week before was behind the desk and a man was leaning over it, looking at her computer.

'Not as far as I know.' The woman glanced up and smiled when she saw Chloé standing there. 'Have you come for the poster, love?'

Chloé nodded, heart beating rapidly.

'Here you are. And how was school? Better now that you've done a full week?'

The fat roll of paper in her hand, Chloé contemplated lying to make the lady feel better. But lying wasn't something she did.

'Not really.' She shrugged. 'I suppose I just have to get through it.'

The lady laughed and ruffled Chloé's hair. 'You sound so old!'

'I am. I'm eleven.'

'What's your name?'

'Chloé.'

'Well, Chloé, I'm Angélique. And I'm supposed to tell you that your school days are the best days of your life. But they're not.'

Chloé's eyebrows shot up at this honesty from an adult.

'What comes afterwards is so much better.'

'So why do I have to go, then?'

'Because what you get out of school is what makes your adult life great.'

Chloé wrinkled her nose, debating whether that could actually be possible; that school could yield anything of merit. After the introduction to *collège* this week, she sincerely doubted it.

Angélique smiled. 'You're going to have to trust me on this. And if you want to book tickets for the circus, come and see me. I might be able to get you a discount.' With a final pat of Chloé's head, she turned back to the man.

'So someone in Fogas is putting up a fight at least,' she said.

'Lot of good it will do them . . . ' The man's voice faded as Chloé let the door close behind her.

It was Friday. No school for two days, the weekend stretching ahead of her promising unforeseen pleasures. Maman was due to pick her up anytime soon and had promised pizza, which was always a great start. And in her hands Chloé was holding the poster. The poster that had determined her future. About that bit she knew Angélique was right — the best days of her life lay ahead of her. Under the canvas of a big top.

★ ★ ★

'So who's behind it?' asked Chloé as Stephanie took a chair next to her by the pizza van in the centre of Seix.

'No one seems to know. Although Fabian's worried he's the number one suspect.'

Chloé laughed at the idea of the lanky Parisian being capable of such deceit. 'No way. He'd have told you.'

'You think so? I can just imagine him creeping downstairs at night and tapping away at the computer until dawn.'

Chloé laughed again and Stephanie revelled in the sound. Her child, precocious from birth, which was hardly surprising given the circumstances she had been born into, had hit her teens two years early. Over the summer she had transformed from a carefree youngster into a sullen young woman who seemed to carry the world on her thin shoulders.

'Do you think he has a cape?' Chloé asked.

'Who? Fabian?'

'No, the person who created *SOS Fogas*.'

'Like a superhero, you mean?'

Chloé nodded, eyes twinkling. 'And his underpants outside his tights!'

'Ugh!' Stephanie groaned. 'If that's the case, let's hope it's not Bernard Mirouze or we'll all be sick!'

A snort escaped her daughter and she collapsed in giggles.

'Have you had a good day at school then?' Stephanie couldn't help herself. And instantly regretted it as the laughter dried up and the dark face returned.

'It was okay.'

She reached over to tuck an errant curl behind her daughter's ear and tried not to notice that Chloé pulled away.

'Are you going up to Toulouse again? On business?'

There it was. That tone. Stephanie didn't know how to deal with it. She hadn't told Chloé the real reason for her visit to Toulouse. She had no intention of upsetting her daughter by raking up the past when there was no need. But Chloé kept pushing her.

'Why? Did you miss my cooking?'

It was a common joke between them, that Fabian was a better cook than Stephanie. But Chloé didn't laugh. She just stared at her mother with hard eyes, as though there had been a test there somewhere and Stephanie had unwittingly failed.

Keeping her voice light, Stephanie tried to change the subject. 'So, what's the poster?'

'Nothing.' Chloé kicked her school bag, roll of paper sticking out of the top, further under the table.

'How can it be nothing? You're bringing it home, so it must be something.'

'It's just a stupid art project, okay? Come on, our pizzas are ready.'

Stephanie watched her daughter grab her things and walk over to the counter where the pizza woman passed her two boxes. The faint trace of pink around Chloé's cheeks and the heavy lids that had come down over her honest eyes told Stephanie she wasn't the only one with secrets. The long, sullen drive back to Picarets was spent racking her brains as to how she could re-establish something resembling a relationship with this stranger who, until recently, had been her daughter.

* * *

No one had a clue who was behind it. By nightfall, despite fervid speculation dominating every chance encounter, even though the topic had been dissected at every dinner table that evening, not a soul had guessed the true identity of the anonymous blogger. Even Jacques, who'd had the luxury of an entire day and had been privy to many huddled conversations, couldn't decide on a likely culprit. Or hero. Because that's what they were, the person who had set up *SOS Fogas*.

It was impossible not to see the effect the blog was already having. People who had been left like rabbits in the headlights of an oncoming juggernaut by news of the merger had woken up. They'd been kicked into action. And that's what this place needed. A bit of action.

There'd been another meeting of the *comité des fêtes* that evening in the bar, the quorum of members supplemented by enthusiastic locals, and there'd been talk of protests, posters, media interviews. For Jacques Servat, invisible and impotent, it had been like the latter days of the war, when the Resistance had taken hold down here in the south and ten-year-old Jacques and his best friend Serge had lain in a bedroom upstairs, watching the clandestine meetings through a crack in the floorboards. He'd felt the same level of frustration then as he did now at his enforced exclusion.

Yet his undetectable presence did yield some advantages. Like today when Pascal Souquet had graced the bar with a rare visit. Jacques had been sitting up on the windowsill right behind him, taking childish pleasure in blowing cold air on the first deputy's arrogant neck, when his mobile rang. It had startled Jacques. Damn near tipped him off his perch. But he'd got a look at the screen as Pascal picked up the phone. And he'd heard the voice at the other end, berating the first deputy, ordering him to investigate *SOS Fogas*.

Jacques had felt his skin prickle, a tingle of excitement racing along his nerves as he realised the significance of what he'd witnessed. Then Pascal had stood up and taken his empty cup to the bar. It was a dead giveaway from a man who never lifted a finger to help others. He'd slipped around the back of the group gathered around the laptop and had paid rapt attention as the locals discussed the possible identity of the person behind the website.

It wasn't much to go on. But it added to Jacques' growing suspicion. Pascal Souquet was the man selling Fogas down the river. And now, thanks to that call, Jacques knew the initials of the person he was collaborating with.

MS. That's what had been on the mobile as Pascal reached to answer it. All Jacques had to do now was find out who they were. Which was why he was stooped over behind the bar, blowing frantically, the pages of the phone book shifting slowly on the breeze he was creating. He straightened up for a moment, his back creaking in protest, and took a rest. He'd had to get through twenty-five pages of useless information about the Ariège before he even got to the first residential listings. And as the phone book was organised by commune, in alphabetical order, it was going to be a long night before he got to

Sarrat. Which was where he was sure he would find the name he was looking for.

He bent back to the thin pages illuminated by the security light above the door, placed his pursed lips close to the corner of the book and began blowing once more. He'd just reached La Bastide-de-Sérou when a weak beam of light became visible out on the road.

A torch? No, it was moving too fast. A bicycle? Jacques crossed to the window and saw the unmistakable rangy figure of Fabian pass under the street lamp. The Parisian's normally svelte shape was somewhat distorted, and it was only as he dismounted opposite the bar that Jacques noticed the shovel. Leaning his bike against the gates to the garden centre, Fabian sloped across the road and into the abandoned orchard.

What now? Jacques waited a few moments but there was no sign of his nephew. With a despairing shake of his head, he returned to his tiresome labours. He had got as far as Ercé when he heard the clatter of metal and looked up to see Fabian clambering back on his bike. No wiser as to what the Parisian had been doing, Jacques focused back on the phone book. With spots before his eyes, he continued, puffing and panting until the pages turned, bringing his quarry ever closer.

13

By mid-September, streaks of red flashed among the trees lining the steep slopes of the mountains and the long spell of fine weather, which typified autumn in this part of the Pyrenees, continued unabated. It was perfect for a stroll in the hills. Unless it was a Sunday and the opening day of the hunting season.

'Neanderthals! That's what they are!' Stephanie glowered at the camouflage-clad men gathered by the side of the road, rifles slung over their shoulders, as she drove the van down towards La Rivière. 'What pleasure can you get out of shooting a defenceless animal? An endangered one even? I mean, how can you get a thrill out of killing a beautiful capercaillie or an izard?'

Fabian was too busy gripping the dashboard to reply, the combination of speed, hairpin bends and a decrepit vehicle driven by a mad woman conspiring to rob him of the power of speech.

'You'd think they'd have lost their appetite for such barbarity, after that poor bear. But no. There they go with their guns and their hip flasks, making the forests no-go zones for our kids every weekend. Pah! It's ridiculous.'

'Slow down,' muttered Fabian as the Estaque farm whizzed past in a blur and the tight corner beyond it approached rather fast.

It was precisely the wrong thing to have said because Stephanie now turned her fierce gaze on him and took her attention from the road. Luckily they were on the inside of the bend, far away from the gorge that dropped down to the river. And luckily it didn't matter that the battered ex-police van gathered another scar as it grazed the mountainside.

'See what you made me do!' declared Stephanie as she wrenched the vehicle back onto the tarmac. She flung her red curls over her shoulder and frowned through the windscreen at the passing trees.

Perhaps this wasn't a good idea? Fabian had been planning it for a while. He'd even ridden down to La Rivière in the middle of the night the week before to set everything in motion and had passed numerous sleepless nights since in the fear that a wandering boar might unearth his preparations. But now that he'd finally found the courage to proceed, he seemed to have picked the precise moment that Stephanie was in a foul mood.

'We don't have to do this,' he suggested as the Auberge finally came into view.

Stephanie stamped on the brakes as they arrived at the T-junction and cast a dark look at the thin man next to her who had been jerked back in his seat by the fully functioning seat belt as the van came to a sudden stop.

'You brought me all this way and now say you don't want to do this?'

Fabian quailed. 'I just . . . if you like . . . we could . . .'

Stephanie shoved the van into gear and pulled out onto the main road with a squeal of tyres, throwing Fabian against the side window. The crack of his skull against the glass was sharp but the Parisian didn't say a word. He did notice, however, that Stephanie eased up on the accelerator, and when they parked at the garden centre she was looking slightly calmer.

'It'll be fine,' he told himself as he jumped out of the van, heart racing at the enormity of what he was about to do. 'Nothing is going to stop me this time.'

★ ★ ★

Stephanie felt like a cow. She'd been behaving like one all morning. It was the argument with her daughter that had started it. Chloé had wanted to go for a walk with the Rogalle twins in the forests behind the cottage up in Picarets. A perfectly reasonable request on a Sunday morning. But Stephanie had refused. It was the opening day of the hunting season and everyone knew that it was the worst day of the year to be out in the hills, even if you were dressed in bright orange. The hunters would be more testosterone fuelled than normal after a summer of inactivity and the chance of accidents was high. The last thing she wanted was a phone call telling her that Chloé had been shot. Her firm stance, however, had led to a row.

With neither mother nor daughter in the best of humour, the debate over a woodland walk had escalated into a tirade of condemnation, Chloé accusing Stephanie of treating her like a child and Stephanie accusing her of acting like one. Fabian had hopped around trying to calm them both down, not knowing how to deal with two enraged females who shared the same temper. Finally, Chloé had stormed out of the house, shouting something about secrets being kept from her. She'd gone straight to Annie Estaque, who'd been good enough to call Stephanie and let her know that Chloé was there. She'd also talked Stephanie out of driving straight round to pick her daughter up.

'Perrrhaps you'd both benefit frrrom some distance,' she'd suggested in her usual pragmatic way. 'And besides, Chrrristian is down herrre finishing off the worrrk on the solarrr panels, and we need all the sparrre hands we can get.'

So, against her better judgement, Stephanie had acquiesced and allowed Chloé to remain at Annie's farm. Which was when Fabian had suggested they take a trip down to La Rivière. He wouldn't say any more than that. But he had put a spade in the back of the van.

She'd been in too dark a mood to be intrigued. And then she'd seen the hunters in their orange berets lining the road in Picarets, getting ready for their day in the woods. It was the final straw. Already upset and puzzled as to her daughter's behaviour, she'd vented her growing spleen on Fabian. Which was beyond unfair. The man was a saint. Always cheerful. Always there for her. Even now he was willing to abandon whatever plan he'd concocted just because she was in a bad temper. She didn't deserve him.

She got out of the van and crossed over to where he was standing with his spade, a wary look on his face as though he didn't know if she

213

was going to berate him or embrace him.

'I'm sorry,' she said, looking up into his face, where her words instantly chased away his frown. She put her arms around his neck and pulled him down into a kiss, his own arms reaching around her and the spade falling to the ground with a clatter as his lips met hers.

'Bonjour, you two!' came a cheeky shout from the terrace, René raising an early pastis to them, cigarette in hand. 'Nice morning for it!'

Fabian lifted his head and grinned. It was indeed. A perfect morning for it. Feeling more confident than ever, he reached into his back pocket and pulled out an envelope.

'Here,' he said, offering it to Stephanie.

'What's this?'

'Open it and see.'

She lifted the flap and took out a piece of paper, covered in what looked like a map.

'Is that the orchard?' She glanced from the drawing to the rectangle of aged trees next to the épicerie, grass grown long between them, fruit struggling on the withered branches. Then she looked back at the instructions below the map. 'It's a treasure hunt?'

The pleasure in her voice made him both ecstatic and anxious. What if she didn't like the particular treasure he had in mind? He handed her the spade and she crossed the road, a bemused René watching from the terrace.

''Enter the orchard and stand next to the tree that is no more.'' Stephanie read the first line and then pointed at a stump just inside the wall. 'There! That must be it.'

214

'What's going on?' Josette had joined René on the terrace, apron on, an empty tray in her hands.

'No idea,' replied the plumber, transfixed all the same.

'"Take three long strides to the tree due east." East . . . ?' Red curls tipped back, Stephanie looked into the sky at the sun and got her bearings, pointing towards Véronique's apartment in the old school. 'That way.'

'No,' called René. 'East is that way.' Rather than the building itself, he was indicating its back garden.

'Don't listen to him,' countered Serge Papon, who'd arrived for his morning croissants. 'You were almost right the first time, Stephanie.'

'Does she not know which way east is?' Bernard Mirouze asked, baguette in hand, Serge the beagle at his feet.

Véronique, on her way back from church, couldn't help butting in. 'East? It's that way.' Her pointed finger gave yet another orientation. 'What do you need to know for? And what's Stephanie doing in the orchard?'

Fabian was trying his best to ignore the backseat drivers now absorbed in Stephanie's ordeal. He had more things to worry about. Especially as none of them was guiding her in the direction she was meant to be going in. So it was left to Josette to explain.

'It's a treasure hunt,' she said, before leaning over to whisper. 'I think Fabian's going to propose!'

While her news was met with hushed excitement from the majority, René simply scowled.

'Not any time soon with the rate that map's

215

being turned,' he muttered. He called across to the Parisian, who was still by the entrance. 'You should have known better, Fabian! Never give a map to a woman.'

As if spurred on by the plumber's scorn, Stephanie decided to trust her instincts and took three steps forward towards the old school. She threw a cheeky grin at a dissenting René and read out the next line.

''Turn ninety degrees and take ten long paces to the tree marked with an 'X'.''

'She'll not know what ninety degrees are,' called out René. 'Not when she doesn't know which way east is.'

'Honestly. You are incorrigible!' Josette whipped his legs with a tea towel.

Serge chuckled. 'Knowing what they are is one thing. Knowing which way to turn them is another.'

And he was right. Stephanie didn't know if it was clockwise so she would face the hill behind the épicerie or anticlockwise so she would face the road.

'Which way?' She raised her hands in appeal, and that was all it took.

Within minutes the group gathered on the terrace as spectators had become uninvited participants, René holding the map and directing Bernard around the orchard while Serge and Véronique deplored the poor quality of the instructions and Serge the beagle snuffled his way around every tree on the abandoned land. Fabian, meanwhile, had taken a seat on the edge of the terrace, chin on his hand as he watched the community take over his plan. He didn't mind. In fact, it was what had drawn him to Fogas in the first place. But he wasn't sure he wanted a running commentary from the likes of René and Bernard when the big moment came.

If it ever came. At present the group of treasure seekers was so far off the mark it was untrue. Luckily Fabian had thought to designate the tree or they could be here forever.

'Do you want me to get rid of them?' Josette had sat next to him and put her arm through his, a knowing smile on her face. 'You might want some privacy?'

'Privacy?' He laughed nervously. 'I don't think Fogas does privacy.'

She nodded, eyes twinkling. 'I'm so excited. I can't wait to see her face.'

'Neither can I. If we ever get that far.'

'Here! It's here!' Stephanie cried from the far end of the orchard, where René and Bernard had also arrived with the map. 'This is the tree.'

Puzzled, Fabian shot to his feet. Surely she was in the wrong area?

'Spade? Who's got the spade — ?'

'Start digging — '

'Get that blasted dog out of the way — '

Josette squeezed Fabian's arm and kissed his cheek. 'You'd best get over there,' she said, gesturing towards the buzz of voices. 'You don't want Bernard Mirouze to be the first person she sees when she finds it!'

Heart thundering, he started towards the group. He couldn't see Stephanie. She was stooped over, wielding the spade, a crowd of curiosity around her. But he could see the tree. The one she was digging under. It was old, wizened apples hanging from gnarled branches, leaves already wilting. Apples. He didn't remember apples. But then it had been dark and his torch not too powerful.

Another couple of steps and through the bodies he glimpsed the 'X', a small mark low down on the bark. Strange — he'd carved it at waist height. Which for him was quite a way off the ground. And surely he'd made it bigger? Was it possible . . . ?

'I've found something!' Stephanie cried as the spade hit metal.

'Get the soil off it — '

'Do you want me to have a go — ?'

But Stephanie was more than capable. Fabian heard the thud of the spade a couple more times and then an intake of breath from the onlookers. Knowing he must be insane to think of carrying out such a personal act in front of the entire community, he pushed his way through, cleared his throat and, as he prepared to get down on one knee, she pulled the treasure out of its hiding place.

'It's heavier than it looks!' she exclaimed, holding up a dirt-covered tin that Fabian had never set eyes on before. 'Should we take it to the bar to open it?' She was looking at him as if he knew what was going on. Which he was supposed to. But he didn't.

'Erm. Yes. Why not?' he mumbled and she led the way across the orchard, her helpers following. Only Fabian stayed behind, confused and deflated.

He picked up the discarded map and, starting from the stump, took a true bearing of east — which actually lay more towards the road than any of the locals realised — before turning ninety degrees anticlockwise and pacing his way towards a completely different tree. One that was marked with an 'X' a metre from the ground. Making sure no one was watching, he used the spade to uncover a small jewellery box inside a plastic zip-lock bag. He filled the earth back in the hole, stuffed the box in his pocket and, feeling like the world owed him a favour, made his way towards the excited voices coming from the bar.

★ ★ ★

'What is it?'

'She hasn't opened it yet.'

'It looks antique.'

'Pastis, Josette. Digging is thirsty work.'

'You didn't even touch the spade!'

'No, but he watched a woman wield one and that's even more tiring.'

The voices roused Jacques Servat from his mid-morning slumber and he wasn't best pleased to see an excited pack of locals troop into the bar behind Stephanie. Already in a sour mood thanks to several laborious nights of blowing pages in the phone directory — all of which had yielded nothing, no name in the Sarrat listings matching the initials MS which he'd seen on Pascal Souquet's mobile — he wasn't happy when they made their way to the table in front of the inglenook, crowding out his resting place until he was obliged to move. It was either that or have fat Bernard Mirouze's backside in his face, which wasn't the pleasantest of ways to wake up.

With an invisible glower cast at the entire entourage, Jacques shuffled to one side, where he had an excellent view of the box, a discarded copy of the *Gazette Ariègeoise* protecting the table beneath it. Metal and about twenty centimetres long by ten wide, even through the layer of dirt the tin was clearly old. As Stephanie carefully brushed off the earth still clinging to its edges, an intricate pattern of Celtic knots was revealed and then the words 'Biscuits Olibet'.

'Oh, Grand-mère had a tin just like that!' said Véronique. 'I think Maman still has it somewhere.'

'It's beautiful,' sighed Stephanie, tracing the twisting lines that took her straight back to her Celtic homeland of Finistère. 'So thoughtful, Fabian. Where did you find it?'

'I . . . er . . . '

'For goodness' sake, open it!' demanded René, face puce with ill-contained excitement.

'Okay, okay!' Stephanie laughed and with long fingers laced over the top, she began to lift. At first it didn't move. But then, with the squeak of rusting metal, the lid came slowly away and everyone leaned forward to see inside.

'It's a bunch of old rags — '

'Why would he have given her a bunch of old rags — ?'

'That's just the wrapping — '

'So what's inside it — ?'

They jostled and strained, Josette using her elbows to get to the front and René standing on a chair so he could see over their heads as Stephanie lifted the cloth-covered object out of the box. She was careful but even so, a piece of the material snagged on the rough metal corner of the tin. It caught fast and jerked the bundle out of her hands, and like a baby rudely pulled from its swaddling, something was ripped from the cloth and fell to the table with a thud.

'GUN!' screeched Bernard Mirouze, jumping back and clattering into René on his chair. Losing his balance, the plumber stumbled and fell into a heap as others leaped away from the stubby object that now lay pointing at them. Only Jacques and Serge didn't move, both staring at the pistol, both pale as ghosts.

'Why on earth have you given me a gun?' Stephanie asked into the silence, eyes on Fabian.

'And an old one at that,' said René, back on his feet and peering at the lump of metal on the table. 'That's a bloody strange way to prop — ' A sharp elbow from Josette knocked the breath out of the plumber and ensured his silence.

'I didn't . . . ' Fabian stuttered. 'It's not — '

The Parisian's protestations were cut short by Serge Papon who leaned in and picked up the weapon, making everyone duck for cover.

'Careful, Papa! It could go off,' warned Véronique.

'I know what I'm doing,' he muttered, face still wan as he handled the pistol.

And Jacques knew that to be true. He watched

221

as his old friend checked the gun thoroughly, fingers covering every inch of it before he placed it back on the newspaper.

'It's not loaded,' the mayor said. 'But what I want to know is where you found it?' His piercing gaze rested on Fabian as the others crowded the table to get a closer look at what Stephanie had dug up.

'I didn't. There's been a mistake. That's what I was trying to tell you.' Fabian threw a beseeching glance at Tante Josette, who came to his rescue.

'I don't think this was what Stephanie was supposed to find,' she said. 'Although how she came upon this is a miracle. It must have been there for years.'

'Possibly since the war,' said René, turning the gun over in his hands. 'It's a Unique, manufactured over in Hendaye until ten years ago. They mass-produced this particular model in the run-up to 1940. Then the Germans took over the factory and changed the design. See this?' He twisted the gun so they could all see the small circle containing a lion on the grip. 'This shows it was made before the occupation. Which means it's at least seventy years old.'

'And what's that?' Véronique was pointing at a small engraving on the other side. 'Is it a boar's head?'

The plumber peered closer at the weapon and nodded. 'I'd say so. But it's not a manufacturer's mark. It must have been added by the owner.'

'Whoever he was. And why was it hidden under a tree in the orchard?'

'Perhaps it was Monsieur Garcia's gun?'

suggested Josette, referring to the Spanish exile who had owned the plot next door and was long dead. He'd fled his native Catalonia during the civil war and had settled in Fogas, planting fruit trees to soothe his frustration at his inability to grow oranges in his adopted land. 'But goodness knows why he would have buried it.'

'A boar's head?' Bernard Mirouze looked at René. 'We both know someone who likes to mark things with a boar's head.'

René whistled and stared at the gun. 'It could be his father's.'

'Who?' asked Véronique.

'Henri Dedieu,' said Bernard Mirouze. 'Whenever we go hunting he always wears a ring with a boar's head on it. Says it's his family emblem.'

'Well, it can't be his father's,' said Josette. 'Not if it's as old as you think it is. He was only a young child in the war, like me. Isn't that right, Serge?'

The oldest member of the group merely nodded.

'So if there is a connection, it's more likely to be Grand-père Dedieu's. Which could be possible because, as far as I can remember, he was in the Resistance. Wasn't he killed just before liberation?' Josette looked at the mayor as though expecting him to elaborate, but he didn't. He was staring at the pistol, a frown creasing his prominent forehead.

'It still doesn't explain why his gun would be hidden under a tree.' Stephanie reached forward to take the weapon from René, but as her fingers met the metal she recoiled with a gasp.

223

'You all right?' Fabian was by her side in an instant.

She nodded but made no move to touch her unintended prize again.

'What do we do now, then?' asked René.

'Shouldn't we at least call the gendarmes in Massat and tell them what we've found? Although that will mean you won't get to keep it, Stephanie.' Véronique turned to the other woman in apology.

'I don't want it,' she replied. 'There's something evil about that thing. In fact, I think we should bury it again.'

René, ever respectful of Stephanie's gypsy background, shuddered and dropped the pistol on the table. 'Maybe she's right. If it's connected to the war, no good will come of finding it. You know what people are like around here. They're reluctant to talk about things that happened in those days and we've just unearthed someone's secret. So perhaps we should just shove it back in the tin and throw it in the ground?'

'We can't do that. It's too dangerous. What if some child found it?' Josette shook her head. 'Best we contact the authorities and let them deal with it.'

Stephanie shrugged. 'If you say so. But I'm warning you, that gun will bring trouble.' She moved through the crowd of onlookers and headed out into the sunshine, wanting nothing more to do with her macabre treasure. Fabian, chastising himself for having had such a stupid idea in the first place, raced after her, leaving an eerie silence to descend on those still in the bar.

224

Serge Papon finally spoke. 'I'll give Dedieu a call. See if he knows anything about it. Until then, if you could keep it behind the bar, Josette . . . ?'

He picked up the pistol, bundled it back into the rags it had been wrapped in and placed it in the biscuit tin, closing the lid firmly. As he passed it to Josette, she was aware of his intense regard, as though he suspected she knew more than she was saying.

'What is it?' she asked as she took possession of the box.

'Nothing,' he mumbled, letting his gaze drop to the tin. 'Just old memories. You know . . . '

But she didn't know. Thanks to being eight years younger than Serge and Jacques, Josette had been a toddler when the south of France was finally occupied during the war. And thanks to Jacques, she was as innocent as they came with regard to the item found that morning. In a long and happy marriage, it was the only thing he had never told her.

Like René before him, Jacques shuddered as his wife slipped the biscuit tin on a shelf behind the counter. Stephanie, he feared, was right. That gun would bring nothing but trouble to a commune already beset with problems.

As the crowd dispersed, the original intention of the treasure hunt forgotten in the excitement of the morning, Jacques Servat settled back in the inglenook, hoping to catch up on the nap that had been so rudely interrupted. But it took him a while to doze off and when he did, his dreams were punctuated with images of the past.

225

It was enough to make his wife comment to
herself, as she watched him jerking and
muttering in his sleep, that he was behaving like
a man who had rather a lot on his mind. And
none of it good.

14

'A gun? In Monsieur Garcia's orchard?'

René nodded, cigarette in hand as he inspected the new solar panels on Annie's barn. He'd arrived in perfect time, just as Christian was packing away his tools after a long day. It had taken a week for the panels to be installed, the company from Foix agreeing to a reduced price in return for Christian's labour. With all of the technical work completed by Friday, the farmer had been left to dismantle the scaffolding. Alone. As he stretched out the kinks in his back from a weekend of lifting the long poles, he wondered if the savings had been worth it. Especially as his fear of heights had made the work slow going.

'Fabian had Stephanie on a treasure hunt this morning, apparently leading up to a proposal.' The plumber was heedless of the farmer's fatigue. Or the head of dark curls that had been dangling over one of Annie's dogs but sprang up at his news to reveal a surprised young face. 'Only, she didn't find a ring. She found something else entirely.'

Christian grinned despite his tiredness. 'A gun? That's novel.'

'A second world war antique.'

'Can I tempt anyone with a cold drink?' asked a voice from the doorway.

Hot and weary, Christian wiped his hands on

a rag and reached for a beer. 'Thanks, Véronique. You know the way to a man's heart.'

She smiled and turned her head to look at the brilliance of the barn roof, the sunlight dancing off the panels and dazzling her eyes. It wasn't enough to banish the image of the large farmer from her mind, his shirt off, tanned chest broad and muscular. She gripped her beer and forced herself to admire her mother's latest investment for a little longer. At least until her face had stopped burning.

Unaware of the effect he was having, Christian took a seat next to Annie on the bench by the back door and pulled his T-shirt back on.

'Stephanie freaked out when she saw it. She wanted us to throw it back in the ground,' the plumber continued.

'Huh. She might have been rrright. Therrre arrre lots of people rrround herrre who won't want the past drrragging up. Especially if it involves a gun.'

'Did it work?' asked Chloé from her seat on the grass, where she was dwarfed by the two Pyrenean mountain dogs lying next to her in the shade of an oak tree.

'What do you mean?'

'Did you fire it?'

René raised an eyebrow. 'Of course not. Why?'

Chloé shrugged. 'Just thought it might make an interesting focus for my history project. I could take it into school and show them.'

Annie laughed at the thought of a pistol-wielding Chloé strolling up to *collège*. 'That would liven up lessons, forrr surrre!'

228

'So whose gun is it?' asked Christian, happily gazing at his handiwork, the vista interrupted by the contours of Véronique and none the worse for it.

The plumber shook his head. 'We're not sure. But there's a boar's head etched into the grip. We think it might belong to the Dedieu family.'

'Henri Dedieu?' Christian cast a glance at the plumber. 'He does have a thing about boars.'

'Only dead ones,' muttered Chloé, who had inherited her mother's disdain for hunting.

'Serge is going to contact him. But it's no use until the hunt is over for the day. He doesn't like interruptions when he's up there.' René cast a hand at the forests that raked up the mountainsides around them.

'How come you're not with them?' Véronique finally turned around, relieved and yet disappointed to see that the farmer was now wearing a T-shirt. 'You always go hunting on the first day of the season.'

René became fascinated by the label on his beer bottle. 'I didn't fancy it. Neither did Bernard. After all that happened over that bear . . . and now with talk of a merger . . . ' He pulled a face. 'It's difficult to hold my tongue when I'm out with them, and as there are more from Sarrat in the hunting lodge than from Fogas, it's an argument I'm never going to win. Not without resorting to violence.'

'Damn merger! It's all anyone talks about in the post office.'

'And what's the general consensus?' Christian asked.

Véronique pouted. 'Depends where they come from. Everyone across the river seems to think it's a done deal and are in favour. Whereas those from Fogas tend to be against it.'

'*Tend* to? So not everyone here believes it's a bad idea?'

'No. But they're fools. I mean, Monique Sentenac was in the other day and said she thought it could be good for the commune. Pah! I don't know how she's come to that idea. And if Henri Dedieu presumes he can soft-soap us with this open forum he's arranged . . . '

She tailed off, a look of disgust on her face at the thought of the meeting that had been widely advertised over the last few days, posters appearing on communal noticeboards and flyers pushed through postboxes. It was to take place in the not-so-neutral Sarrat town hall in ten days' time.

'I take it you're not going, then?'

'No way! Why, are you?'

'I have to really. As deputy mayor. But I thought it might be good to hear the other side too.' Christian looked at Annie for support and she nodded.

'It's not as black and white as some would make out,' she said. 'We should considerrr it at the verrry least.'

'*Consider* it?' Véronique's hands had moved to her hips in a stance Christian knew well. As he anticipated, next thing her chin lifted and she stared at them both. 'What is there to consider? There is nothing Henri Dedieu can say that would make me change my mind. And if there was, I wouldn't believe a word of it. The man is a snake.'

'She's right,' stated René. 'The only thing we should be doing is concentrating on how to fight our way out of this mess, like the person who set up *SOS Fogas*. And you, Christian, as deputy mayor, should be leading us. Not contemplating jumping into bed with the enemy.'

'I'm not saying it's right,' said Christian, hands up in surrender. 'I'm just saying we need to give both options equal thought. After all, it's the future of kids like Chloé that we're deciding here.'

'I'm not a kid,' said Chloé, jumping up to stand next to Véronique with a look that would have stopped Sarko the bull in his tracks. 'And for the record, I've already conducted a poll and us *kids* don't want to join Sarrat. But when was the last time any of you asked what we wanted?'

Faced by the three of them, all set against him, Christian sighed and hauled himself off the bench. 'Thanks for the beer, Annie. Don't spend all evening watching that electricity meter spin round.'

Annie cackled, her fascination with the fact that her barn roof was now providing an income being something that wasn't going to wane anytime soon.

'Are you going home? You won't stay for dinner?' Véronique's indignation had gone, replaced by something else, which Christian couldn't put his finger on. But he was too tired for any more arguments and too lovestruck to trust himself in this state. He was quite capable of grabbing the irate postmistress by those lovely shoulders and kissing her until the laughter returned to her eyes. Which would be a disaster and would probably get him slapped. So he shook his head and started for the car.

'I'll come with you,' said Chloé. 'If you don't mind dropping a *kid* home, that is.'

Christian held back another sigh and opened the passenger door for her. Not for the first time, he felt that a comprehensive understanding of the female mind was way beyond him. He stood more chance of fathoming the erratic behaviour of Sarko, whose foul moods were at least predictable.

★   ★   ★

'What did you do that forrr?'

'What?' snapped Véronique, slamming plates down on the table outside that looked over the pasture.

'Scarrre him off. We could have had a lovely meal togetherrr, which is the least I owe him afterrr his help this week. But no, you had to go and rrraise politics and send him home to his motherrr's bad cooking. You arrre morrre like yourrr Papa than I everrr thought.'

Véronique threw the cutlery beside the plates and thrust a bowl of salad in the centre, her temper not assuaged by this accurate assessment.

'Politics are important,' she muttered, more to convince herself than Maman. 'I can't believe he is considering the merger.'

'He didn't say that. He said he was willing to

see both sides. Which I think is perrrfectly rrrational. Morrre than I can say forrr you.'

The cry of a kite overhead made them both look up, and when it had wheeled out of sight over the mountains, Véronique let out a long sigh. 'I'm an idiot.'

Annie nodded and poured two glasses of rosé as they took their seats.

'It was this morning. Fabian and Stephanie. It's so difficult seeing them together and so happy, especially when he was clearly planning on proposing.'

'Look how that turrrned out! You'rrre not the only one stumbling arrround in love. And won't be the last eitherrr. It's made a fool out of most of us at one time orrr anotherrr.'

'Even you?'

'Hmph.' Annie concentrated on getting the salad onto her plate while Véronique spread paté on her slice of baguette, one eye on her mother. 'Let's just say I've had my moments. Yourrr conception being one of them.'

'That was love? I thought you said — '

'Corrrnichons, please.'

Véronique passed the jar of pickles, knowing from her mother's tone that this conversation was going no further. They ate in silence for a few moments, the air ruffled by the lightest of breezes, the sky unmarred by a single cloud, and the barn roof a gleaming mirror of the evening sun. But the serenity was squandered on the pensive postmistress.

'So what should I do?' she asked.

'Give him time. The man's lived the life of a

233

monk since he took overrr that farrrm. Worrrking all hourrrs. Helping to rrrun the commune. He's not had the chance to learrrn anything about women. Let alone one as complicated as you.'

'I'm not complicated!'

Annie gave a wry smile. 'You'rrre half Papon, half Estaque. It doesn't get morrre complicated than that.'

'You think that's what he needs, then? A bit of time?'

'I'm surrre of it.'

Véronique looked out across the field, the mountains the same as when she was a child, the forest unchanged in those thirty-odd years and the oak tree in the garden looking no older. The same couldn't be said for her though. For her, time was marching on and, if she wanted those curly-headed children in her life, fast running out. She pushed her plate away, appetite gone, and turned to face her mother.

'Only thing is, Maman, I can't wait forever.'

And Annie, knowing exactly what she meant, covered her hand with her own.

★ ★ ★

The ring in Fabian's pocket might as well have been a burning lump of coal, so conscious was he of it all the way home. Stephanie, her mood not much improved from the journey down, had driven just as manically back to the cottage at the far end of Picarets, and Fabian knew from experience that it was no time for talking. Consequently, he'd had time to dwell on his stupidity. To kick himself metaphorically up the backside. And to regret ever having listened to Josette's romantic anecdotes.

What had he been thinking? Burying something so special and expecting Stephanie to find it in front of a crowd of interfering Fogas onlookers. It was bound to go wrong. He should have predicted that not one of the locals would have a clue as to the bearing of east, which Fabian, true to his nature, had calculated exactly. As for the ninety-degree turn that had so confused them, the Parisian hadn't appreciated that others might not automatically take anticlockwise as the default direction. To go the other way would, in the strictest of mathematical senses, yield a negative angle of ninety degrees. And Fabian always observed the rules of maths.

But the tree. That was the killer. Who could have guessed that there would be another 'X' carved into a trunk just metres away from the intended target? *He* could have. Should have, given his meticulous nature. But he hadn't.

Annoyed at his uncharacteristic lack of precision, he'd had to surmise that his emotions had led him astray, causing him to err from his usual exactitude. And the results had been catastrophic. Stephanie had discovered a gun with a possibly nefarious history and had sensed such horror when she touched it that she hadn't spoken properly since. She'd retired to the bedroom with a migraine the second they'd got in, eschewing lunch, and now as evening approached, the shutters remained closed. Thus, instead of celebrating a future of wedded bliss with the woman he loved, Fabian was kneeling in the back garden, working on his bicycle.

So much for romance.

He contemplated the bike, aware that his tinkering with the gears was a displacement activity. It helped calm him. Soothed his nerves, which were still on edge. Because he was sure that when Stephanie surfaced, she would want to know what the real objective of the treasure hunt was. Which meant he had to make a decision. Did he tell her the truth and propose? Or did he brush it off as a meaningless diversion intended to raise her spirits?

'Bonsoir.' Chloé slouched into the garden, face no more animated than it had been when she'd stormed out that morning.

'Did you have a good day?' he asked, nevertheless.

She shrugged. 'S'pose so.'

'How did Christian's work go? Solar panels all up and working?'

She nodded and dropped onto the bench. 'I hear Maman found a gun.'

Fabian stifled a sigh. That was the trouble with this place — the news usually made it home before you did. There weren't many times he missed the anonymity of Paris but this was one of them.

'Yes, she did. In the orchard.'

For the first time, Chloé's features lit up. 'Will she get to keep it?'

'I doubt it. René thinks it belongs to Henri Dedieu.'

'What was she supposed to find?'

Fabian froze. He hadn't thought of that. 'Er . . . just something to cheer her up.'

'Like what?'

There was an intensity to the young girl's questions and Fabian had the distinct impression that she was testing him. Although what she could possibly be testing him about he had no idea.

'Look, I can't tell you. It's a secret.'

The shutters closed down over Chloé's face, but before he could ask her what was wrong, Stephanie's voice came from the doorway.

'I think we've had enough secrets for one day, Fabian. So tell me, what was my real treasure?'

Wan, red hair framing a tired face, she still managed a smile, and he heard the thudding of his heart in response. Surely they could hear it too as it hammered at his ribcage? Now was his chance. Here in the garden she loved, in front of Chloé, the most precious person in her world. But the ring . . . it was in the shed, hidden in a box of old inner tubes.

Spontaneity. It wasn't something he'd been blessed with. In fact, it was probably the aspect of Stephanie's character that had drawn him to her, like a moth pulled irresistibly to the fire. But just because he loved her volatility, her ability to react on emotion, it didn't mean he could reciprocate.

'It was . . . '

'Well?' She stood over him and ran her fingers through his hair, letting them graze down his cheek, and he leaned into her touch like a cat. When he opened his eyes, he was staring at an advertisement in the old newspaper he had placed under the bike to catch the oil.

'It was tickets for the circus.' He looked up with a grin, pleased with his ingenuity, and was rewarded with the first proper smile he'd seen from Chloé in days. But while she was ecstatic at the idea, Stephanie snapped her hand away, arms folding across her chest.

'Seriously?' she asked, voice sharp, eyes flashing.

'Is there a problem?'

Stephanie's lips were a thin line of disapproval. 'Sorry, Fabian. I should have explained. While I allow Chloé to practise her acrobatics, I won't allow her to go to the circus. You'll just have to take them back.'

'But Maman — !' Chloé's entreaty was cut short by a glance.

'No. We are not going to the circus. You know better than to ask.'

'You're not being fair!' Chloé jumped to her feet and they heard her pounding up the stairs and then the slamming of her bedroom door.

'That's all I need,' muttered Stephanie, a hand going to her forehead. She turned back into the house and Fabian was left alone in the garden.

How had it all gone so spectacularly wrong? A simple proposal. That was all that was required. And instead, he had somehow turned it into a family dispute. He stared at the offending page of the paper, a handsome man on a high wire smiling out at him and beckoning him towards the big top in the background. With a deliberate hand, Fabian squirted oil over the man's face until he could no longer be seen.

At least, he thought, trying to see the bright side as he packed his bike away, he didn't have to rush out and buy tickets for the circus.

★   ★   ★

Chloé was fuming. She flung the door shut, bolted it and threw herself onto the bed, anger sparking inside her like lit fireworks in a sealed tin. Feeling her eyes stinging with tears, she brushed an impatient hand across them. Crying was for babies and she was no longer a child. Which was what she was trying to tell everyone but no one was listening. Not even Fabian.

From the moment she'd met him he'd treated her differently. He always spoke to her like an adult, asked her opinion on things as if it really mattered. In fact, sometimes she felt older than him. And she was a lot less clumsy than him. Only yesterday he'd dropped two plates while doing the washing-up, his arms so long that his brain had difficulty getting messages to his hands. He'd been so upset, as though it was fine china instead of stuff Maman had bought at a flea market. Chloé had taken over, sitting him down out of harm's way while she finished the dishes. When Maman had arrived home from work, she'd laughed as they related the tale, and then Fabian had started kissing Maman, Chloé making a quick exit before she was sick.

But today, Fabian, the man she'd had on a pedestal for the last eighteen months, had proved he was no different from the rest of them. An adult, and therefore not to be trusted. They lied and made up rules which they later broke. And they were mean.

A *secret*. That's what he'd said when she'd given him the chance to tell her that he was going to ask Maman to marry him. Something he'd decided he couldn't tell Chloé because she was a little kid.

She thumped the mattress in frustration. How could it be a secret when all of Fogas knew about it? And why would he have told the likes of René Piquemal before he told her? She knew Maman better than anyone. Definitely better than Fabian did. Like just now when he'd bungled into that mess instead of telling the truth. How could he not know about Maman's stupid dislike of the circus?

Maman was no better. She still hadn't admitted the real reason for her trip to Toulouse. And her daughter hadn't found the courage to ask whether it was all resolved or whether Bruno Madec and his family were going ahead with their custody claim. It was as though by remaining uninformed, Chloé was able to keep at bay the horrible prospect of having to move to Brittany. Then, of course, there was the question of that blank box on the birth certificate. But Chloé didn't think she'd ever be able to ask about that.

Why couldn't they trust her?

Leaping off the bed in one lithe movement, she crossed to the poster of the trapeze artist Jules Léotard that dominated the wall. Pulling out the drawing pin in the bottom left-hand corner, she allowed the paper to curl up and reveal the much smaller poster she'd been given by Angélique down in Seix.

He would understand. This acrobat with the cavalier smile and the twinkle in his eyes who disdained the safety of a net. He knew all about trust. And no matter what Maman said, Chloé was going to see him in action.

She folded up the twenty euros that Christian had given her for helping at Annie's, tucked it behind the poster, kissed the acrobat, and covered him back up with Jules Léotard. With the scent of lasagne stealing past the locks on her door, she wondered whether she could maintain her sulk and do without dinner. A gurgle from her empty stomach told her otherwise, and so, affecting the martyred face of the misunderstood, she slid back the bolt and headed downstairs.

★ ★ ★

By early evening up in Fogas, the weather was just as beautiful as it was over in Picarets. It had been the kind of day where a soft seat in the garden and the latest copy of *Le Point* or *La Revue du Vin* was all that was required to while away the hours. But instead, Pascal Souquet was stuck indoors, hunched over the computer in the spare room that served as his office. He'd spent his entire Sunday in the same position and was probably going to be here until nightfall. All because of that damned *SOS Fogas*.

He clicked another link on the website in front

241

of him, but it told him nothing. Or perhaps it would have if he knew how to go about uncovering the identity of the person behind it. Henri Dedieu had been insistent. He'd rung several times demanding to know who was writing the blog's posts, which had been delivered with startling frequency and biting satire. The latest had the mayor of Sarrat's head superimposed on a boar running amok in a garden that symbolised Fogas. Needless to say, the man in question had been enraged, given that he'd tabled a preliminary meeting to discuss the merger and this wasn't the image he wanted to portray. Therefore, Pascal was receiving even more abuse than usual.

The first deputy had tried to explain that he wasn't the man for the job. He didn't know enough about computers and the internet to trace the origin of the posts. Henri Dedieu, however, wouldn't listen. As far as he was concerned, Pascal Souquet, with his limited experience of modern technology from his previous life in Paris, was the Ariège equivalent of Bill Gates. The mayor was demanding results.

'It's *apéro* time.' Fatima was at the door, a plate of canapés in one hand and a glass of muscat in the other. He tried to shield the computer screen from her but it was too late. She was already smirking. '*SOS Fogas?* Wouldn't have thought *he* would approve of your taste in reading. Or has he got you doing the dirty work again, trying to figure out who's behind it?'

'Do you know?'

'No. But I have my suspicions. Come outside

242

and we can talk about it.'

Grateful for a reprieve, Pascal closed down the computer and followed his wife. She might not approve of Dedieu's methods, but she understood that the means justified the end and Pascal was grateful that she had come round to his way of thinking.

'So,' he said as they clinked glasses on the terrace. 'Who's the strongest suspect?'

She leaned forward conspiratorially. 'You're not going to believe this, but rumour has it . . .'

A chainsaw in the nearby forest drowned out her words for all but her husband who listened intently, a half-smile settling on his face as Fatima relayed all she had picked up in numerous visits to the épicerie. When she'd finished, they toasted his future, and Pascal sat back and relaxed, content that with his wife fighting by his side everything would turn out exactly as it was meant to.

15

As September drew to a close, the transformation that was slowly taking place in the mountain commune of Fogas became manifest. The town hall looked resplendent with newly painted shutters, the old men at the *lavoir* had worked diligently to remove decades of graffiti from the back wall of their gathering place and replace broken and missing slates on the roof, and the graveyard down in La Rivière had been tidied up, lopsided gravestones made straight and paths and neglected graves weeded. Stephanie had been busy, working with Alain Rougé in the disused orchard, pruning trees and clearing out dead growth until the derelict patch of land began to resemble the garden that Monsieur Garcia had planted long ago. She'd also made up hanging baskets for all municipal buildings, colouring the three villages in splashes of red and orange and yellow and scenting the air with the fragrance of late summer.

Turning right towards the épicerie, Christian couldn't help but marvel at the changes. Even the railings in front of the old school, which had remained twisted and buckled since the bad winter two years ago when Bernard Mirouze had careened into them with the snow plough, had finally been repaired and were decorated with geraniums. The place was positively gleaming.

Which was more than could be said for

Christian. He'd spent the best part of the morning running around the hillsides with his mobile, trying to find his bull. Alerted to Sarko's absence by a text from Chloé — who'd been getting a surreptitious mountain fix during class by monitoring the webcam and had noticed that there were more trees on screen than there should be — Christian had raced to the field where the bull had been enclosed since he'd been brought down from the summer pasture. As Chloé had feared, it was empty, the length of electric fencing that served as a gate left trailing on the ground. Someone, probably a tourist, had taken a shortcut through the field, met the bull and raced out again, leaving the fence open behind them. Sarko, true to his nature, had made the most of it.

But thanks to the Ariège tourist board, Christian now had help finding his truculent bovine. Using his smartphone, he'd logged on to the webcam and quickly deduced where the bull was. That is to say, he'd narrowed it down to an area of forest not more than four square kilometres. Thrashing through undergrowth and battling through brambles, he'd mourned the absence of Arnaud Petit. The tracker would have found his quarry in a matter of minutes, alert to the slightest disturbance of the natural habitat. Lacking such prowess, Christian had to rely on technology and his knowledge of the area. Thankfully, despite intermittent images on his phone as the signal came and went, both had proved up to the task. An hour into his search the view from Sarko's camera had yielded a clue.

A jumble of ivy-covered stones that had once formed a wall and a small stream burbling past them.

The old mill that lay high in the valley between Fogas and Picarets. Praying that the grass would be sweet enough to keep Sarko occupied for another thirty minutes, Christian had started climbing. When he'd arrived at the derelict mill, not only had the bull been sated with the lush vegetation, he was also worn out from his efforts and it was a slow walk back to his official pasture.

With no time for a shower, the farmer had jumped into his car and raced down to La Rivière for a lunchtime gathering of the *comité des fêtes* which had been rescheduled to accommodate the evening meeting about the merger over in Sarrat. Aware, as he parked in front of the épicerie, that he probably smelled as bad as a cowshed in high summer, he ran a hand through his curls to remove any souvenirs of the woods and, in the absence of deodorant, grabbed the cardboard pine tree off the rear-view mirror and dabbed it liberally on his shirt. Nostrils stinging with the sharp scent of a Nordic forest, he headed into the bar.

'Bonjour!' he called out as he crossed to the group gathered around the big table by the fire-place.

'Bonjour, Christian.' René stretched out a hand to greet him and promptly pulled it back, slapping it over his nose instead. 'Mon dieu! What's that stench?'

'Merde!' said Paul, eyes wide as he stepped

away from the farmer. 'You smell like — '

'A mixture of hospital floors and cow shit,' finished Stephanie with a grin, pulling back from the kisses Christian was offering.

'Sorry,' he mumbled. 'Sarko escaped and I didn't have time to clean up.'

'Well, I'm not sitting next to you,' remarked René as he took a place at the opposite end of the table, leaving the seat nearest the bar — and Gaston the smelly shepherd — for the deputy mayor.

'Me neither!' Paul laughed.

'Why, what's the matter with him?' Véronique had wandered through from the épicerie, her morning duties behind the counter in the post office over, and Christian wished the ground would open up and swallow his malodorous body. Or provide him with a shower.

'He stinks!' said René. 'Enough to put a man off his beer.'

Véronique turned to look at the blushing farmer, who had a shimmer of golden stubble on a jaw smudged with dirt, a scarlet complexion and a smear of something that could be oil on his forehead. Or possibly not, given the smell. Sensing his discomfort, she crossed the floor in quick strides and stood on tiptoe to brush her lips across both cheeks. She stepped back with a smile. 'It's a good country fragrance. No harm in it.'

And at that moment, Christian knew she would be the only woman he ever loved.

Jacques Servat, whose olfactory senses had remained intact after death, thus requiring him to clamp a hand over his nose as Christian approached the inglenook, came to a different conclusion as the postmistress took a seat next to the farmer. As he suspected, Véronique Estaque was in love with Christian Dupuy. Because only an infatuated woman could kiss a man who smelled that badly.

★   ★   ★

The meeting didn't last long. A quick report from René showed that everything was going according to plan. The three villages were looking rejuvenated, the orchard was nearly finished and volunteers had been organised to help put up bunting over the coming weekend. Véronique gave an update on the progress with the church, confident that the statue of Our Lord she had ordered online should be with them in a matter of days and the grotto restored to its original glory — once she found someone willing to go up the ladder and place him on the cross. Christian, spurred on by the recklessness of the besotted and with cheeks still tingling from Véronique's kisses, offered to assist, momentarily forgetting his aversion to heights. René, who had no desire to climb a ladder for Christ or anyone, declined to remind his friend of his oversight. But made a note to himself to be a witness when the time came to install the new Jesus.

Meanwhile, plans for the fête were well under way. René had booked a band for the evening — one proposed by Stephanie rather than the aged group that had played at the last one, the guitarist having retired following his shocking performance — and was confident they would set the right tone. He'd also lined up a traditional dance troupe from a nearby valley who were younger and more able than the group that normally graced Fogas festivities. And Christian had got hold of an apple press and various other equipment that they needed for the big day.

Stephanie and Paul had been busy too and unveiled the posters that would soon be displayed all over the region announcing a *croustade* competition to be overseen by the British couple. This prompted René to reiterate his warnings about the dangers of such a contest, the local women fiercely proud when it came to their traditional apple pies and unlikely to take kindly to being judged by outsiders. At the last such event in a nearby village, the adjudicator had been verbally abused by the runner-up, who'd bridled at his criticism of her flaky pastry and then attacked him with her second-place prize — a rolling pin. Assuring the nervous plumber that Lorna would be delicate in her assessment and that the prizes could not be turned into weapons, Paul got the go-ahead to distribute the posters.

With everything going smoothly, they wrapped up with a quick discussion of the website Fabian had created for the commune, which was attracting a healthy number of visitors.

'I think the link to *SOS Fogas* is helping,' explained the Parisian, joining them to reel off statistics that mostly went over the heads of the others listening. 'It's definitely gaining us a lot of attention.'

'Hopefully all of it beneficial,' said Christian.

'Don't forget Sarko is pulling in the crowds too,' added Véronique. She grabbed a plastic bag off the bar and passed it to the farmer. 'Here. Perhaps this one won't give you the runaround!'

Paul and René laughed as Christian opened the bag and pulled out an exact replica of the beast he had spent the morning chasing. Only this one was soft and cuddly. He looked up in amazement.

'We got them in on Monday,' continued the postmistress, 'and thirty have gone already. I've put in another order and Fabian's going to start selling them online. All proceeds to the *comité des fêtes*.'

'And when people see the footage from today, with Christian arriving all hot and sweaty on the mountaintop, we'll sell even more!' said René.

Christian slapped a hand to his forehead and groaned. 'I forgot all about the camera once I found him. Merde! I'll be a laughing stock at the next Farmers' Union meeting.'

'Why? What's wrong with you finding a lost bull?' asked Stephanie.

A blush stole across the farmer's grubby cheeks. 'Nothing. Just I . . . might have . . . been singing.'

'So?'

'To Sarko,' mumbled Christian, looking miserable as the laughter began, the noise attracting Josette and several customers in from the shop.

René was the first to manage speech. 'Was it a duet?'

Christian scowled. 'Don't mock. I discovered at the post office protest in July that Sarko goes as sweet as a lamb when you croon to him. Since then . . . '

'So you're saying we have footage of you serenading Sarko?' asked Fabian, reaching for his laptop with a grin.

'Can you delete it?' asked the farmer hopefully.

But Fabian had no intention of deleting it. He found the relevant section and hit play and they all gathered around the screen, leaving the farmer to squirm as the first strains of an off-key warbling came from the computer.

'You sang 'Ne Me Quitte Pas'?' roared René with hilarity. 'To a *bull*?'

'It was the only song I could think of,' muttered Christian, not willing to confess that he hadn't been able to get it out of his mind since the night of the fête. Nor the image of Véronique in that red dress.

'And you didn't say you had your shirt off! *That's* definitely going to attract the women.' Stephanie threw him a wink and the farmer wanted to die.

'So, can you delete it? Please, Fabian?'

'Delete it?' René shook his head, pointing at the screen. 'Have you seen how many people have watched this already? Sorry, Christian, but this is exactly what the commune needs, something quirky to pull people in. At this rate, we're going to have to order even more Sarko toys. And perhaps a topless farmer to go with it, eh Véronique?'

'Um?' The postmistress lifted her gaze from the computer, eyes dazed, face crimson. 'Sorry, what did you say?'

'Perhaps we could get one that sings!' added Fabian and the laughter started again.

'I've had enough of this! If we're finished, I'm off.' Christian stood to go, mood soured by the merciless teasing and by his need for a shower. As he passed Véronique, he paused. 'Have you changed your mind about attending the meeting tonight?'

He caught her off-guard, visions of the man in front of her striding across a sunlit glade with his chest bare still dominating her thoughts. 'Tonight?'

'Up in Sarrat. The meeting about the merger.' He lowered his voice. 'Please come. I don't think I can face it on my own after this.' The note of desperation, a result of the persecution he had just suffered and was about to endure even more of once wind of the video got out, was enough to sway her.

'As long as you don't mind me disagreeing with it all.'

'I'll pick you up at seven, okay?'

'Fine.' She smiled up at him and he had to restrain himself from bending down to meet her lips with his.

As he walked across the road to his car, he forgot all about his internet fame. He was oblivious to the rustic odour emanating from his tired body. All he was conscious of was that in a few hours' time he would be with Véronique. Alone in his car. And that was enough to brighten up what had otherwise been an exceptionally lousy day.

★ ★ ★

Across the hills in Foix, Jérôme Ulrich was also having a bad day. It had started over breakfast, when his wife had announced that she wished to have a baby. He'd frozen, an already-dunked pain au chocolat hovering over his coffee, and before he could come to his senses, the sodden pastry collapsed into the bowl, necessitating a change of his shirt and tie.

A baby. He thought they'd discussed this a year ago when they'd first arrived in the Ariège. It wasn't the right time. It would hold him, and therefore them, back. Already one of the youngest préfets in the country, his future looked assured when you considered that the average age of his peers was fifty-seven. In the next five years, more than half the current crop of préfets would be retiring, leaving the route open for an ambitious young man who was willing and able to move around the country. So, as long as he didn't make a mess of his first posting — in which case he would be on a fast track to a dead end appointment in somewhere like Creuse — his career prospects were very rosy indeed. But this morning, when he'd reiterated these logical arguments, his wife had countered by claiming that if it was left to him, there would never be a right time.

She had a point. Starting a family was the last thing on his mind. He had a desk covered in dossiers that needed his attention. He had meetings every day for the next six months. And he had the business with Fogas and Sarrat to conclude, which, if recent events were anything to go by, would not be as smooth as he would wish it to be.

He glanced down at the copy of *La Dépêche* that was spread across his desk, yielding a perfect example of the trouble he was facing. On one page there was a photograph of Henri Dedieu dressed in hunting gear and holding a pistol. A close-up of his left hand showed a boar's head signet ring, the design an exact copy of the engraving on the grip of the gun. According to the newspaper, the weapon, which had been uncovered in the orchard in La Rivière, had belonged to the mayor of Sarrat's grand-père, a member of *La Résistance* who'd been shot by an unknown assailant towards the end of the war. The current mayor expressed his joy at being reunited with the family heirloom and, in citing the discovery of the pistol as an example of the mutual co-operation and respect that existed across the two communes of Fogas and Sarrat, lost no opportunity to exploit it in support of amalgamation.

But whatever good his propaganda did, it was nullified by the article next to it. A full page devoted to the mysterious *SOS Fogas*, which, the write-up claimed, was already generating national attention, several left-wing blogs championing the anti-merger troublemaker who had struck again and again with a barbed pen at the leaders of Sarrat and even the préfet himself.

Closer to home, Mayor Papon was quoted as saying that, while he would prefer the instigator of the popular site to come out from behind the cloak of anonymity, he supported the gist of its message. And René Piquemal, the drunkard Jérôme had bumped into at the Sous-Préfecture, was pictured at the bar in La Rivière, two beers before him, saying he would be the first to buy the author a drink when their identity became known.

If that wasn't bad enough, the paper had seen fit to give details of the blog's latest instalment — a tirade against the forthcoming meeting, which was dismissed as an attempt by Henri Dedieu to woo his neighbours. Four paragraphs of biting satire were underlined by a picture of the eleven members of the Fogas Conseil Municipal sitting around a table in the town hall. Entitled 'The Last Supper', it cast Serge Papon as Jesus, the halo out of keeping atop his roguish face, while the rest of the council were draped in robes as his apostles. It was inspired. And if the person behind it wasn't curbed, this unknown entity could undermine the entire unification proposal. Which wouldn't look good for Jérôme as préfet and architect of the process.

He paced his office floor to the window, weighing up his options. Clearly, he needed to know more about this mystery blogger. But how?

From below, the gleeful shrieks of a toddler distracted him as a young father held his child on the bridge to watch the water tumbling beneath them. The boy's delight was infectious and for a moment, less than a second perhaps, the préfet felt what could only be described as envy. Then he turned back to his overladen desk and came to a decision.

Tonight. He would attend the meeting in Sarrat tonight and spread the word that he wished to meet the author of *SOS Fogas*. See if he couldn't flush them out. And then see if he couldn't talk them round.

Just as he would talk round his wife. Because having a baby was the last thing he wanted right now.

★　★　★

'Rest assured we want to make this process as painless as possible for all concerned. Then, together, we can move towards a brighter future with a new and invigorated commune, large enough to provide inhabitants with a better standard of living and small enough that we will still know our neighbours and be there to offer a helping hand when required.'

'And to sing to them,' called out a voice from the back of the hall. Laughter ensued, the muted strains of '*Ne Me Quitte Pas*' audible.

Christian Dupuy, who was sitting at the top table with the leaders of the two communes and the préfet, met the jibe with a forlorn face, making even the inhabitants of Fogas laugh, something Véronique had never expected at such a potentially volatile meeting. But then, it had been in process for just over thirty minutes and far from being the riot she had anticipated, the audience had been putty in the mayor of Sarrat's hands.

Henri Dedieu smiled from his position behind the microphone, allowing the teasing at Christian's expense to ease any remaining tension from the room. Then he called the large gathering to order with a raised hand.

'Perhaps this would be an opportune time to call for questions,' he said. 'Although any queries about bull management I will of course refer to the second deputy mayor of Fogas.'

'He's as smooth as a politician,' muttered René, a surly eye on the striking figure up on the platform.

'Bet his promises are just as valid,' murmured Véronique.

René's mobile pinged, earning him a reproving glance from Josette. The plumber apologised, glanced at the screen, and cursed softly. 'Mon dieu!'

Véronique raised an eyebrow in response but René was too busy reading. Then his stocky arm rose in the air.

'René? Would you like the honour of the first question?'

'What about the name of the new commune. How will that be decided?'

'It's simple. There will be an open debate. As with every decision, it will be a process of negotiation between Fogas and Sarrat.'

Before René could respond, the mayor called on another person, who asked whether property taxes would be affected. René's hand was in the air throughout the long-winded answer and started waggling the minute the mayor finished speaking.

'And again, to my friend the plumber. Yes, René?' This time Véronique thought she detected a note of irritation in the hitherto polished performance.

'Could you explain what's going to happen with the town hall? Are we, those of us in Fogas I mean, going to have to trek all the way down to La Rivière and up to Sarrat to access the administration? A journey our ancestors deemed inconvenient enough to instigate separation in the first place, I hasten to add.'

'That's a point . . . '

'Hadn't thought of that . . . '

Muttering traversed through the Fogas contingent, who were mostly clustered towards the back of the large room.

'That won't be the case,' answered Henri Dedieu, forestalling the grumbles. 'We will keep a satellite office in Fogas in the current town hall, thus maintaining the present service.'

'But won't that make the merger redundant?' Véronique asked. 'Surely the point is to save running costs, and running the town hall has to be one of the biggest outlays for any commune. There's the secretary's salary for a start.'

The mayor of Sarrat narrowed his eyes, his smile strained for the first time. 'Don't you worry about the accounts, my dear,' he said. 'We've got experts to take care of that.'

'Perhaps you've got someone to pat me on the head too, while you're at it?' bit back the postmistress, and a bark of laughter came from Serge Papon at the table across the front of the hall.

'It's a valid question,' agreed Christian, getting to his feet. 'Could you make the accounts public so we can all see your prospective running costs?'

'I'm afraid the report isn't complete as yet. But as soon as it is, we will most certainly be publishing it. Next?'

René's hand shot into the air once more, but Henri Dedieu ignored him and pointed instead to one of the hunters who had an inane question about refuse collections. The reply took up the next few minutes and by the time it had been dealt with, René was bouncing in his seat.

'Yes!' barked the mayor of Sarrat, glaring at the plumber.

'Can you verify how many councillors from Fogas will be on the first Conseil Municipal?'

Heads lifted around the room because this would be the real test of the merger. Realistically, being smaller by a wide margin, Fogas couldn't expect to be granted many of the fifteen places. But rumours had been circulating that it could be as few as two.

'In the initial administration, there will be five seats allocated to Fogas, with ten held over for Sarrat. These will be determined by votes gained at the last elections. This will provide the new administration with a two-year honeymoon period before the next municipal elections. At that point, voting will take place as normal and the Conseil Municipal will be decided in the usual way. On votes cast.'

Surprise rippled through the audience, the suggestion more generous than the mountain residents had hoped for, many villagers nodding in approval at the plans outlined.

'So, if that's it — ?'

'One last thing.' René hopped to his feet and the sigh from the man at the front was audible. 'How much is this going to cost?'

It was such a simple question but, marvelled Véronique, one that none of them had thought to ask. And for the first time that evening, Henri Dedieu had the air of someone caught off-guard.

'Can you clarify your point?'

René shrugged, eyebrows raised. 'What is there to clarify? You must have done a cost analysis of the expenses such a merger would incur. What are they?'

'I'm afraid I don't have that information to hand.'

'Can you give us an estimate?'

'I'm unwilling to do that. But I assure each and every one of you, this will be made clear when the report is published. Now, I think we've talked enough. There's wine next door — '

'How will the costs be shared?'

The mayor of Sarrat paused, half turned from his audience, but still Véronique could see the cloud of thunder that passed across his face and then vanished like a storm behind Mont Valier on a summer's day. When he faced the people again, he was smiling.

'It will be done equitably, according to population size. Therefore, Sarrat will incur the majority of the costs. But as I said, this will be further outlined in the official report. So let's take the rest of this evening to celebrate the amazing opportunity we've been presented with.'

Without waiting to see if René was satisfied, Henri Dedieu turned to the préfet and with a guiding hand, ushered him through the double doors at the back of the hall and into the reception room beyond it.

'Well, that was a lot better than I expected!' announced Josette as she gathered her handbag and coat and stood to join the mass exodus heading for the refreshments. 'I must say, I'm quite impressed.'

As they made their way out of the hall, Véronique couldn't disagree. It had been a skilled performance from a man who had left little room for dissent. All around she could hear her neighbours praising the grandeur of Sarrat's town hall, commenting on the quality of the furniture and the flooring, and comparing it to the dowdy building on the mountain ridge that was badly in need of repair.

They had been shown a glimpse of what a merger could bring them. And it seemed as though many were tempted.

16

'I had help.'

'Who from?'

'You wouldn't believe me if I told you.'

'So tell me, then!'

René grinned and stroked his moustache, enjoying the attention, unaware of Véronique's left foot impatiently tapping, a warning sign Christian knew well. She'd been trying to find out how the plumber had come up with his questions, all of which had been pertinent and probing and had provided the only opposition to what had been a seamless sales pitch from the mayor of Sarrat.

'I'd tell her if I were you,' said Josette, sipping a glass of red wine. 'Remember what she did up at the fête!'

A look of concern creased the plumber's face and he transferred his plate full of food to his left hand and reached into his pocket.

'Here. These were sent to me.' He held out his mobile and the group crowded round to peer at the screen, four emails displayed in the inbox. When Christian saw the account name they had come from, he whistled.

'*SOS Fogas?* They emailed you the questions?'

René nodded. 'Funny thing is, they sent them one by one. With perfect timing. Whenever Dedieu completed an answer, another query arrived. Which suggests — '

'Our anonymous supporter was in the meeting! And is probably here now.' Véronique swung her gaze across the huddles of people standing chatting, glasses and plates in hand, making the most of the generous hospitality that the town hall of Sarrat had laid on. 'Did you notice anyone using their phone a lot while Dedieu was speaking?'

'No. But then once these started arriving I didn't have time to think about who could be behind them.'

'Well, all this technology rrrules out ourrr generrration, eh, Josette!' declared Annie.

'Huh! Speak for yourself.' An indignant Josette produced her mobile with a flourish. 'Fabian talked me into getting it. Apparently it does everything.'

Annie cackled. 'When it can milk cows, I'll be interrrested.'

'Mon dieu! Another one,' said René, eyes on the screen of his mobile which had just lit up.

'From *SOS Fogas?*' Christian was already leaning in over Véronique to get a better view.

'What does it say?' asked Josette. René handed her the phone and she peered at the text, Annie reading over her shoulder. Then she looked up at the others, who were all staring at the handsome young man engaged in a conversation with Widow Aubert.

'What a brilliant idea,' murmured Véronique. 'Why didn't I think of that?'

★ ★ ★

'Find out who fed him those questions. The man is too thick to have thought all that through by himself.'

In the corner of the room where the wine was being served, Henri Dedieu was standing next to Pascal Souquet, looking for all the world like one councillor chatting innocently to another. But while a bright smile was fixed on the mayor of Sarrat's face, his icy stare was pinpointing René Piquemal, who was balancing a plate piled high with vol-au-vents and crudités, eating his fill while having an animated discussion with a crowd of his neighbours.

'Someone's been passing him information and I want to know who, before he discovers more than he needs to know,' continued the irate mayor. 'Because that wouldn't be healthy. For René or his informant.'

Pascal nodded, palms sweating. Privy to Henri Dedieu's plans, it wouldn't take much for the finger of suspicion to be pointed at him, and despite the fact that he hadn't spoken to a soul about them, the first deputy still felt nervous under the malicious gaze of the mayor of Sarrat.

'Merde!' The mayor's focus shifted to Jérôme Ulrich, who was heading across the floor towards Christian Dupuy, one of the group gathered around the plumber. 'We have to keep that rabble away from the préfet. Last thing I need is them trying to sway him. I'll distract him. You start making enquires. And be discreet!'

With quick strides, Henri Dedieu reached the préfet and steered him towards a group of Sarrat locals, which included the curé, the mayor's good-humoured tone a rapid change from the voice that had been dripping venom moments ago.

Hastening to carry out his orders, Pascal drank the last of his wine with a grimace, dismayed to learn that the people of Sarrat had no more appreciation for the finer things in life than their bucolic neighbours. Still, if the wine was bitter, the evening was providing unexpected sweetness in other ways. He'd already derived a warped pleasure from watching people like Josette Servat being beguiled by the promises held out before her. She wouldn't be so approving when she realised that the post office was going to be relocated. Over the river. Likewise, the old boys from Fogas wouldn't be so content when they found out their town hall was going to be sold off as flats. As for René and his questions . . .

With a self-satisfied smirk he couldn't conceal, Pascal approached the group clustered around the plumber, his natural condescension towards them magnified by the future he knew they were blindly facing.

★   ★   ★

Jérôme Ulrich was feeling coerced. Twice now he'd attempted to approach the blond farmer to get a better measure of the man than first impressions yielded, and both times he'd been scuppered.

In the two and a half months since they'd crossed paths and Deputy Dupuy had sent him

265

home via a torturous route, Jérôme had heard only good things about the big man. He was highly respected in the Farmers' Union, the Ariège tourist board thought both him and his bull were wonderful, and he was considered to be a dynamic and inspirational leader among his community. Perhaps the greatest testimony had just come from Madame Aubert, an old widow who had known Christian Dupuy all his life.

When the préfet had found himself standing next to her at the reception, following what had been an uneventful meeting, he'd made an innocent remark about the deputy mayor of Fogas and she had been quick to sing his praises. Seemingly the man, who had come across as a curmudgeon that day back in July, had brought Madame Aubert a stray kitten after her husband died, and this thoughtful gesture had sealed Christian Dupuy's place in her heart. Several years later this treasured feline, Réglisse, had got stuck in an ash tree at a great height. When the fire brigade refused to come all the way up to Fogas on a rescue mission, the big farmer climbed the tree and carried the terrified cat down, despite suffering from vertigo.

Sensing that the widow could keep him all night eulogising the deputy mayor, Jérôme had made his escape, intending to talk to the subject of her rhapsodic tales. But he'd been intercepted. Henri Dedieu had come striding up to him and wheeled him away to discuss the new church roof with the curé. Using skills honed from years in diplomatic circles, the préfet had managed to extract himself after ten minutes of anodyne conversation and had been within touching distance of the big farmer when the mayor of Sarrat had swooped again. This time, the préfet had been ushered towards the members of the hunting association. Not sharing their thrill of the chase, he'd struggled to engage with the monosyllabic men, one or two asking hostile questions about the government's policy of reintroducing bears to the region. He'd been as tactful as possible in his replies but knew he wasn't making any friends, when he heard the gruff tones of mayor Serge Papon.

'Hope you don't mind if I steal this young man,' he said to the hunters, an avuncular arm wrapped around the préfet. 'I know some people who wish to meet him.'

They had barely taken a step when Henri Dedieu appeared before them, a wide smile on his face.

'Good of you to look after our VIP, Serge. Perhaps you would introduce him to Louis Claustre over there. He wants to know how the proposed merger would affect planning permission.'

'Later, Henri. Right now I'm taking Monsieur Ulrich to talk to some of my electorate.' Serge glanced at the préfet. 'If you don't mind?'

'Not at all. It would be lovely to meet them. Again!'

Serge laughed and slapped the younger man on the back. 'They won't recognise you without your PSG cap.'

They moved on, the icy chill of Henri Dedieu's stare following them. 'I get the feeling he's not happy,' Jérôme murmured and Serge shrugged.

'He doesn't want you talking to my lot. He knows they're against the merger on the whole. They can be passionate. And very persuasive.'

'I think I can safely say I've already seen evidence of that in my short time in the Ariège.' The préfet's dry tone made Serge laugh again.

* * *

Pascal recognised the booming laughter and glanced up from his huddled conversation with his wife to see Serge Papon guiding the préfet towards Christian Dupuy and his entourage. The first deputy mayor had been trying without much success to ascertain the origin of René Piquemal's shrewd questions, hanging around the edge of the group the plumber had attracted and listening for all he was worth. But he'd heard nothing of substance, a heated discussion about the merits of smartphones finally driving him to try other avenues. Spotting Fatima at the edge of the Fogas delegation, he'd drawn her aside and was rewarded with information.

'René was contacted by *SOS Fogas*,' she'd whispered and he felt an overwhelming sense of gratitude at her loyalty. 'They sent him the questions.'

'How?'

'By email. They came through to his phone.'

'Did you get the email address?'

She shook her head. 'He showed it to Monique while I was in the ladies. Sorry.'

Which was when the mayor's laughter caught Pascal's attention. With no time to revel in solving the mystery behind René's sudden eloquence, he scuttled back to the Fogas group. If he couldn't prevent Jérôme Ulrich from talking to them, at least he could monitor the conversation. And perhaps sneak a look at René's phone while he was there. He had a feeling that the identity of *SOS Fogas* might be within his grasp.

★ ★ ★

'Delighted to see you again,' said Christian, red-faced as the préfet shook his hand.

Jérôme Ulrich smiled. 'Likewise. Only this time I won't be asking you for directions home!'

'Humph! If we'd known what you were planning that day, we'd have sent you back over the Col de Péguère,' Véronique retorted, referring to an even trickier climb out of the valley that wasn't for the faint-hearted.

'I take it you're not in favour of my plan, then?'

Véronique threw back her head and glared at the préfet. 'Not many in Fogas are. Your proposals will destroy our community.'

'I'm afraid I have to disagree. The merger is an ideal opportunity for Fogas to grow. Instead of struggling to provide amenities all on your own, you will be able to share resources like this superb town hall, and use the savings you make to develop other facilities. Which in turn will attract more people to the area. This union is exactly what Fogas needs.'

'You seem to be very knowledgeable, based on

269

one visit,' muttered René as the préfet's dark gaze switched to him.

'Ah, the man with the astute questions. I was very impressed with your rigorous examination of the facts.'

René fidgeted at the undue praise and Josette couldn't help setting the record straight. 'All thanks to *SOS Fogas*!' she stated.

'The blog? What did that have to do with it?'

Ignoring the sharp Estaque elbow in her ribs, Josette continued. 'They emailed him the questions during the meeting.'

'You've got an email address for the author?' The eager note of interest from the préfet was unmistakable.

'Yes, René's — ' This time the nudge from Véronique was enough to make Josette pause.

'Perhaps we could do a trade?' said the postmistress. 'We give you the details for *SOS Fogas*. And in return . . . '

She smiled, head tipped to one side, and with a look in her eyes that Fogas residents knew was inherited from her father, leaned in to whisper her demands.

★ ★ ★

Pascal was just in time to see Véronique Estaque lean in to the préfet and whisper in his ear.

'What's she asking him?' Knowing the post-mistress, a quaver of concern tainted the first deputy's voice, but Alain Rougé didn't seem to notice.

'Something about the merger, I suppose. Have

270

you seen this?' The councillor held out a mobile and Pascal could hardly believe his luck. On the screen before him were five emails, all from *SOS Fogas*.

'It's René's phone,' explained Alain. 'He was emailed by the author of that blog. Seems like he was at this meeting. For all we know, he's probably still here.'

But Pascal wasn't listening. He was scrolling through the emails, reading the questions that had been sent to the plumber and making a note of the address they had originated from. He had reached the fifth email when he heard more laughter and looked up to see Véronique and the préfet shaking hands.

'It's not very orthodox and I won't be in uniform,' the government's representative in the Ariège was saying, 'but you have a deal.'

A frisson of excitement passed through the group as though everyone present knew what was happening. Pascal Souquet didn't. But he was about to. He opened the last email from *SOS Fogas* and a dreadful comprehension dawned.

INVITE THE PRÉFET AND HIS WIFE
TO THE FÊTE.

A look of horror crossed the first deputy's face. Thanks to *SOS Fogas*, far from being kept a healthy distance from Fogas and its rabble-rousers, Jérôme Ulrich had just accepted an invitation to the commune's forthcoming celebrations. How was Pascal going to explain this to Henri Dedieu?

'Such a beautiful night,' sighed Véronique, gazing out at the stars festooning the sky.

Christian kept his focus on the road, the twin beams of light not really sufficient to combat the depths of darkness they were driving through. He'd already made the mistake of glancing at her on the twisting journey down from Sarrat town hall and his attention had immediately wandered, with the Panda 4×4 following it, right-hand wheels bumping off the road momentarily. He'd passed off his erratic driving as exhaustion, which, given his day, was feasible. But the truth was, with Véronique sitting next to him, he found it hard to think about anything else but her.

She'd been amazing as always. Passionate about her community. Willing to step up and say something when she felt there was injustice. And able to twist the préfet, a debonair man of the world, around her little finger.

Christian had seen the overt admiration in Jérôme Ulrich's eyes, the way his hand had lingered on hers as he'd said his farewells. Not knowing the family connection, the préfet had still been extolling the virtues of the postmistress of Fogas to Serge Papon as they walked to their cars, Serge putting him none the wiser but clearly proud of the impression his daughter had made.

But the farmer was willing to forgive the younger man's appreciation. Especially when he had unwittingly given Christian Dupuy the first flicker of hope when it came to Véronique Estaque. It happened just before the end of the evening, when the préfet made reference to Christian's newfound fame as a singer. He'd turned to Véronique and jokingly asked if the farmer had ever serenaded her in the same way.

The mistake was easy to make. After all, the man had first seen the pair of them emerging from the woods fresh from a swimming session. He'd obviously assumed they were an item. But it was Véronique's reaction to the préfet's misinterpretation that had set Christian aquiver.

'No, no!' she'd said, face aflame as René rocked with laughter at the idea. 'We're not a couple.' But while her words refuted the notion, she'd smiled shyly at the farmer from beneath lowered eyelashes and his throat had constricted, his heart racing so fast he thought it might burst out of his chest at any moment.

So he'd decided there and then. When they reached the communal recycling bins at the end of the Sarrat road, he would pull over into the lay-by and ask her out.

They were only minutes away from his designated spot. His hands were already starting to become clammy and he was filled with anxiety. He was really going to do this. He was going to reveal his feelings to the woman he revered and risk her trampling all over them.

The thought made him feel sick.

'I could drive like this forever,' murmured Véronique, still gazing out of the window, and the car lurched forward as though the driver's foot had jerked on the accelerator. Which it had.

'Sorry. Need to get the car serviced,' muttered Christian.

'It's stunning, isn't it? I mean, even when it's dark. The different shades of black give a sense of the mountains. It's comforting. Romantic.' She gave a small laugh and glanced at him, her features nothing more than a pale blur. Enough, though, to make him want to pull the car over and take her in his arms.

He said nothing, forcing himself to concentrate. Three more bends and they would be there. And in his silence, he opened up the route for his own destruction.

'The préfet is charming, don't you think?' she said quickly, as though to erase her idle notions which had failed to elicit a response.

He shrugged, the thorns of jealousy quick to prickle. 'It's his job. To be charming.'

'What do you mean?'

The answer came without thought. Because all thought was on the last bend ahead and the lay-by that was beyond it. 'Well, he didn't meet much resistance, did he?'

'I'm sorry, I don't understand what you're saying.'

He should have sensed the plummeting temperature, the ice forming on her words. But he was on autopilot. 'No one really challenged him. Or the idea of the merger. But then again, after tonight, maybe we'll all see it differently,' he mused.

'Differently? You mean support it?'

He nodded.

'You're joking.'

He was indicating, pulling into the small parking area next to a lone street light, the rush of the river audible beyond the window. 'No, I'm serious. I think a lot of people might begin to reconsider the union now they've heard Dedieu's proposals and seen for themselves how much better off Sarrat is than us.'

He stopped the car and turned to face her, taking a deep breath. 'Véronique, there's something — '

'I can't believe you just said that!' A deep line was etched between her eyes, brow pulled together in annoyance. 'Are you genuinely suggesting that tonight's sham by Henri Dedieu was enough to fool the people of Fogas?'

'No, but — '

'Then what are you saying? Because that's what it sounds like. A cop-out, Christian Dupuy. And something you should be ashamed of.'

'It's not like that. But can we put this to one side for a moment? There's something — '

'It's exactly what it is. Complete capitulation. I never for one moment — '

'Capitulation? All I'm suggesting is that we listen to what Sarrat has to offer. It's a novel concept for you Estaque women, I know, but listening can be a good thing.'

'Oh, I listened all right. I'm just not naive enough to believe everything that comes out of Mayor Dedieu's mouth,' she snapped. 'Unlike some around here, I'm not that gullible.'

'Well, I'd rather be gullible than insufferable!'

'And I'd rather be at home alone, which would be better company than I have right now! So why on earth have we stopped?'

There was a brief hiatus, a slight moment when the tension crackling through the Panda could have swung either way. All it would have taken was a gesture from one of them. A reaching out. A casual connection that would have tipped the balance in the favour of love. But the farmer was caught on a wave of desire-fuelled frustration and the postmistress was restrained by a fear of getting hurt. And so they stared at each other, two terrified lovers, the lamplight not enough to reveal the passion behind the fury.

Then Christian crunched the car into gear, and they drove over the bridge and up towards La Rivière, engulfed by silence and unspoken regret.

★ ★ ★

'Promise you won't tell?' Chloé gave Jacques her sternest look and the ghost crossed the area generally believed to have held his heart and nodded his agreement.

She reached into her satchel and pulled out a tattered cutting from the local newspaper. Checking that Fabian was busy in the épicerie, she unfolded it and laid it out on the table, smoothing it down with affection.

'There's a circus coming to town,' she whispered needlessly, the acrobat astride the high wire and the big top in the background enough of an explanation. 'I've looked them up on the internet and they're famous for their trapeze acts. And they're going to be here, in St Girons!'

Jacques smiled at the enthusiasm, leaning over to ruffle her curls, which yielded nothing more than a sense of warmth. He'd had a lovely evening with young Chloé, her mother dropping her and Fabian off when she called in to take Josette up to the meeting. The girl was a joy to be with and although she hadn't seemed her usual chirpy self at first, a hot chocolate from Fabian and a long conversation with Jacques while she was doing her homework had raised her spirits. A couple of hours on and she was back to the Chloé he knew well.

Of course, conversation was a bit of an exaggeration. It was more like a monologue given Jacques' inability to talk, but over the two years of his spectral existence they had developed a basic means of communication that consisted of mime, dramatics and a lot of laughter.

'I'm giving Maman one more chance,' Chloé muttered as she stowed the paper back in her bag. 'But if she says no, I'm going anyway!'

With her chin tilted up, eyes flashing defiance, Jacques could see the formidable woman that Chloé would become. He wagged a finger at her, making sure she understood that he couldn't condone deceit of any kind, but she just grinned.

Headlights blazed across the wall above them and they both jumped up, eager to have news of events in Sarrat. Crossing to the window, they were in time to witness a small blue car pulling up, Véronique and Christian visible in the

277

interior. The postmistress turned and said something to the farmer and his lips moved in response. Then she tossed her head and thrust open the door, got out and slammed it behind her, the noise bouncing off the épicerie walls. Without turning to wave goodbye, she walked down the road to her flat, her hand wiping her eyes as she went.

Back in the car, the large shape of the farmer was slumped over the steering wheel, head resting on the back of his hands. With what seemed an enormous effort, he sat up and stared across the road at the old school, as though debating following Véronique. But then, with a shake of his blond curls, he thumped the dashboard a couple of times before turning the car around and heading off towards Picarets, leaving Jacques wishing he could knock sense into the pair of them.

'What's wrong with Véronique and Christian?' asked Chloé. 'Why was she crying?'

Jacques pulled a face like a swooning lover, clasped his hands to his chest and puckered his lips.

'She's in *love*? With *Christian*?'

The ghost nodded.

'Does he love her?'

Wearily Jacques nodded again.

'Then why is she crying?'

A gesture to his heart and a zip across his lips was all it took.

'They haven't told each other?'

Another affirmative.

'Why not?'

A shrug of the shoulders was all he could do in response to such wisdom. Why indeed? The pair of them were idiots. Causing each other misery when they had it in their power to give such joy.

'Wow,' breathed Chloé, watching the lights of the Panda fade up the hill. 'Christian and Véronique love each other and they don't know it!'

Jacques smiled and then put a finger to his lips and pointed at her with a wink.

'It's a secret? That's okay. I'm good at keeping secrets.'

'Is that your maman, Chloé?' Fabian was at the bar, watching the young girl with a slightly concerned look.

He'd entered the room just in time to hear her declaration about being a good secret keeper, and although he knew he shouldn't worry about her, it was difficult not to. After all, how many eleven-year-olds stood in an empty room holding conversations with thin air? Stephanie had told him it was normal. That Chloé probably had an imaginary friend. When he'd tried to suggest it was unusual that she only ever conjured this friend up when she was in the bar, Stephanie had given an enigmatic smile and said there was more to the bar than he would ever know.

He'd left it at that, aware that Chloé's behaviour was probably some manifestation of the preternatural powers she had inherited from Stephanie's maternal line. But even so, it was still somewhat disturbing when witnessed first hand.

'No, it was Christian dropping Véronique off.

279

But this might be them now.' She pointed to another set of headlights approaching up the road and sure enough, a minute or so later Stephanie and Josette were coming through the door.

'Thanks for minding the shop,' Josette was saying before she even had her coat off. 'Have you got time for a coffee, Stephanie?'

'Best not. It's time we got this young lady to bed.' She bent down and kissed her daughter, running a hand through the riot of curls and overjoyed to get a beaming smile in response. As always, Chloé was in a good mood after time in the bar.

'Come on then. Let's get home.' Fabian reached for his jacket and Josette put a hand on his arm.

'Are you sure you won't stay for a drink?'

'Sorry Tante Josette, but Stephanie's right. Chloé needs to be in bed. It's a school day tomorrow.'

Reluctantly Josette conceded and walked to the door with them, staying in the doorway until the car had been swallowed by the winding road.

'Right. Best head to bed myself,' she said, bolting the door and turning off the lights in the épicerie. But when she walked into the bar, Jacques was before her, blocking her way, a questioning look on his pale face.

'What?' she asked, attempting innocence. He frowned, pointing at the table with intent.

'Oh, all right!' she sighed, knowing she wasn't going to get away with slipping up to bed without giving him a breakdown of the night.

'But I warn you, Jacques, you are not going to like this. The evening wasn't at all what we expected.'

And Jacques took a seat, dread stealing into his heart, because it sounded like the fight had gone out of Fogas.

17

'Chloé Morvan!'

The voice came from far away, muffled through the fog of sleep, but the prod in her ribs was fierce enough to jerk the young girl out of her dreams.

'Um? Pardon?'

'Is this an example of a pictogram or a hieroglyphic?' The teacher stood at the front, patiently holding up a picture of a lump of rock covered in squiggles.

'A hieroglyphic,' muttered Chloé, ignoring the giggles of her classmates.

'Good. Now perhaps you could do us all the favour of staying awake for the rest of the class?'

Chloé cast her eyes onto her desk, face scarlet. She waited for the lesson to recommence before whispering 'merci' to Thomas, whose timely intervention had saved her from further embarrassment. He grinned and did a quick impression of her, eyelids drooping, head lolling. She kicked him under the table and he pretended to be mortally hurt, making her smile.

It was the first time she'd smiled all day. Up before either Fabian or Maman, she'd crept downstairs and into the garden to practise her acrobatics, as she had been doing every day for a month. Tumbles, handstands, aerial cartwheels, backflips and even some basic trapeze work using the lower branches of the oak tree. Over an hour of secret exercise, necessary if she was to be ready for next week, and then back inside before either of the adults suspected a thing.

By the time she'd reached the school in Seix, she'd already been exhausted. Thus, at the end of a long morning in a closed-up classroom looking out onto a car park, it was difficult to concentrate. Even more so when the subject in question was ancient writing systems. Never a fan of history, Chloé had discovered that there were periods requiring study which were even more tedious than the Napoleonic era. The Egyptians were but one of them.

'And what does this style of writing tell us about the civilisation behind it?'

The teacher's voice droned on and Chloé tried to focus. But her mind kept slipping. In seven days — none of them spent at school as the half-term holidays started at the end of the afternoon — she would be at the circus. It barely seemed possible. To go from such monotony to such excitement.

'Thomas?' The teacher was looking at Chloé's rescuer, who was squirming under the attention. 'Shall I repeat the question?'

He nodded.

'Where did cuneiform script originate?'

Chloé heard him swallow, spade-like hands gripping the edge of his chair. He was large for his age, a farmer's son from Ercé whose chores at home bookended school, leaving him tired and with as much appetite for the ancient world as Chloé had.

'Mesopotamia,' she whispered.

'Meso ... potato ... mania,' he struggled, sending the class into hysterics and making even the teacher smile.

'Good try, Thomas. In Mesopotamia. And approximately when was that? Amélie?'

The danger passed and the cobwebs began to form again, draping Chloé's consciousness in layers of voile, the sounds of the class receding as the shadows claimed her. She tried to fight it, to claw her mind back to the civilisation on the banks of the Tigris. But it was no good. Soon she was slouched in her chair sound asleep, cheek propped on her hand, black curls covering her face. And the smitten Thomas, who far preferred staring at Chloé than paying attention to the teacher, could do nothing to help when her head slipped off her hand and fell onto the desk with a loud smack. It was the end to what had been an awful morning. Things weren't about to get any better.

★　★　★

Christian was having a rotten day. Three weeks on from the meeting in Sarrat, the question of unification was far from resolved. While some in Fogas had been swayed by the smooth presentation from Henri Dedieu and others won over by the display of relative opulence at the neighbouring town hall, there was still a diehard core of dissent focused on the préfet's plans. Predictably, the tension between the factions was causing problems in the commune, with neighbours and friends falling out over the future of their community.

Josette and Fabian were two that had wavered from their original commitment to tradition. With a business to run, they could see the potential that a bigger, more vibrant population could bring, and while they were both still enthusiastic about the forthcoming fête as a chance to showcase Fogas, they were also putting forward the positives for a possible merger.

Of course, this was like a red rag to the bull-headed René, who would brook no discussion about the benefits of an amalgamation. To him there was nothing to be gained from joining forces with Sarrat. And he broadcast his opinion at every opportunity. He'd found support in Véronique, her adherence to the past surprising Christian, who'd expected the younger Estaque woman to be less conservative in her views. Her mother, Annie, having witnessed first hand the dangers of convention and the narrow-mindedness that can spring from it, was much more open-minded. A stance that infuriated her daughter.

Like Véronique, Stephanie Morvan was vehemently against the proposal but, predictably, with reasons which were unique. Having been granted shelter by the commune and its inhabitants at a time when she had nowhere to turn, she was indebted to them and so refused to countenance anything that would threaten the wonderful place that had given her and her young child asylum. Meanwhile, down at the Auberge, the Websters had heard nothing at the meeting which could convince them to alter their opinion and they wanted little to do with the changes that were coming.

Because, as far as Christian could see, changes were coming. There was no way to stop them. Having met the préfet under more formal circumstances, he now had a better measure of the man, who was nothing if not determined. And ambitious. Beneath that handsome exterior and the personable style, there was a centre as hard as the seams of coal that typified the landscape he'd been raised in. There was no way Jérôme Ulrich would be coerced by the sentimental arguments of a small group of villagers when he had plans for his own future to consider. That, the farmer was sure of.

He was pretty sure Serge Papon must be aware of it too. Since the meeting, the mayor had continued with his rhetoric, sending letters to anyone he could think of who might be in a position to help the endangered commune, and rallying the locals to support the fête, but underneath it all Christian sensed a formality, as though even the power that was Serge Papon had accepted what fate held in store for his fiefdom.

Which left Christian himself. He was torn. Split down the middle like the pine tree that had been struck by lightning only last week, leaving neither half viable. On the one hand, he had always fought for a better future for the children of the community, and perhaps a merger with Sarrat would offer that. With a more sustainable population, the likes of Chloé might not be driven from their birthplace in search of work as the majority of Christian's generation had been. But this pragmatic approach was at odds with his passion for Fogas, his pride at belonging to that mishmash of villages that clung to the mountainsides in the same way their inhabitants clung to their heritage.

So, in a replica of the commune, Christian was at war with himself. And with victory impossible, it was making him thoroughly miserable. It didn't help matters that his spat with Véronique on the night of the meeting had yet to be resolved. Neither had made any overtures of peace, the postmistress treating him with an icy formality when they met and Christian too tormented by feelings of love and pride to broach the topic of their argument without causing another one. Add to that the farmer's sudden-found fame as an internet sensation, and life was just not fun at present.

'So how many emails have you had this week?' asked Josette, as Christian shouldered the ladder he'd taken out of her shed.

'Two hundred. And it's only Friday.' He shook his head, despairing at the thought that a video captured on a camera around his bull's neck could have brought him such notoriety.

'How many from women?' demanded René with a lascivious grin.

'All of them. I've had twenty marriage proposals and countless offers for dates in the month since that video went live.' The farmer shrugged, perplexed. 'If I'd known this was how to win women over I'd have done it years ago!'

'Pah!' Véronique came out of the épicerie carrying a box under her arm. 'Don't let it go to your head. There's a reason why they're chasing a man over the internet.'

Christian heard the sourness in her voice and

couldn't help responding. 'Actually, some of the photos would suggest these women wouldn't have a problem dating in the real world. Stunning, most of them.'

'Feel free to share!' said René.

'Don't be fooled by photos,' retorted Véronique. 'Anyone can paste a picture of a pretty young thing on their profile. But it's probably some old crone on the other end of the keyboard.'

Christian tried not to shudder at the thought.

'And I hearrr you've had one orrr two visits,' commented Annie as the group walked up the alleyway to the church. 'Tourrrists looking forrr the Singing Shepherrrd?'

The nickname triggered laughter. But not from the farmer. He had no idea who'd coined it but suddenly it was all anyone was calling him. Even though he couldn't sing. And he wasn't a shepherd. But it had caught the public's imagination and in the last four weeks the épicerie had been besieged with people asking for Sarko dolls and visitors demanding to know where they could catch a glimpse of the famous crooning *berger*. Only that morning, he'd been accosted in a field above the farm by two elderly women from Belgium. They'd been on holiday in the region and had trekked up to Picarets in the hope of meeting him. Of course they'd asked him to sing. And asked to see his Limousin bull. Both requests had been brusquely turned down. Although he remembered to tell them to buy their souvenirs down in the shop in La Rivière.

'It could be the answer to your problems,' said René.

Christian propped the ladder in place against the empty cross that dominated the grotto, careful not to knock either of the weeping Marys, who had waited a long time for this day. Then he turned to the plumber. 'I don't have any problems.'

'Could have fooled me. When was the last time you were on a date?'

The farmer's skin darkened.

'In March. With that estate agent from St Girons.' Véronique's reply was barbed and Christian rued yet again the drive down from Sarrat. If only he had pulled up earlier and shown her how he felt, perhaps things would have been fine. Instead a tension had developed between them that night, which had been further fuelled by the friction souring the commune. She was baiting him, but he wasn't about to rise.

'Jesus Christ,' said the farmer, hand held out as he placed one foot on the ladder.

Véronique set the box on the ground and carefully lifted out the figurine that was to finally restore glory to the neglected Romanesque church, which had been without its Messiah for over two decades following the accident with an errant football.

'Don't drop him,' she said, and he replied with a stare, tucking the statue under his arm without so much as glancing at it. Carefully, he started climbing, reminded as each step saw the ground beneath the rungs recede, that he wasn't the best at this. He was halfway up when he began to feel light-headed.

Focus on the cross. Eyes on the wood. As long

as he didn't look down, he should be able to cope.

'Are you all right?' called Josette, seeing the big man pause.

'Course he isn't. He suffers from vertigo. And he's a communist. Can't understand for the life of me why he volunteered to do this.' René's accurate assessment of the situation did nothing to help the atheist who was climbing a cross with a deity under his arm.

'He has vertigo?' Paul had joined the group at the grotto. 'Why is he up there?'

'Because he's a good man!' replied Annie, staring meaningfully at her daughter. 'He'd do anything forrr anyone.'

'Not anyone,' corrected René. 'I don't think he'd have done this if Bernard had asked, for instance. Or even me. In fact, without Véronique's fluttering eyelashes — '

'René!' The shout from above halted the plumber. 'Hold the ladder still and shut up.'

The farmer glanced down to see if his words had been heard and felt the vile sensation of the ground rushing up to meet him. A tide of nausea swelled in his chest and he snapped his focus back onto the cross. Don't look down. Not even to ascertain whether it was possible from this angle to hit René on the head with a falling Jesus.

Breathing deeply, he steadied himself and climbed the final few rungs to the bracket from which Jesus would hang. He hooked the statue over it and reached for the screwdriver in his pocket, tightening the screws that would hope-fully keep Our Lord in place when the wind came. Concentrating only on getting the job done, he was back on the ground and taking deep breaths when he looked up at the cross to admire his handiwork.

'It's a bit . . . ' Josette faltered.

'Ridiculous?' offered René, finishing her sentence with brutality as the others stared up in silence. 'Like he's been put through a hot wash?'

Christian had to concede that the plumber had a point. Jesus was looking a bit on the short side, his arms barely reaching the vertical bar and his figure a fraction of the size of the two women kneeling below him.

'Where did you get it?' the farmer asked a frowning Véronique.

'Online from America. It was much cheaper than buying it here.'

'And did you check the measurements?'

She glared at him. 'Of course I did. It's supposed to be just over a metre and a half.' She pointed at the dimensions on the side of the box where 1'6" was clearly marked and René let out a snort of laughter.

'What?' she snapped.

'That's feet and inches,' explained Christian gently. 'An easy mistake to make.'

'You mean . . . ?'

'He means we'rrre stuck with a shrrrunken Jesus,' said Annie and the group started laughing. Apart from the postmistress, who was mortified by her mistake.

'I'll have to send it back,' she said. 'Do you think you could . . . ?' She turned distraught eyes on Christian.

'Yes,' he heard himself say. 'I'll get it down.' He had a nauseous hold of the ladder when Annie spoke up and granted him a reprieve.

'If you orrrderrred it frrrom the USA, therrre won't be time to get a new one beforrre the fête. And this was one of the things mentioned in the rrreport. So we'd best leave Jesus up therrre forrr now.'

'Oh, you're right,' conceded Véronique. 'But it looks so silly.'

'We'll get used to it,' said Josette, picking up the empty box while Paul and René took hold of the ladder and the three of them walked off towards the épicerie.

'I can't believe I was so stupid!' muttered Véronique, still standing at the bottom of the cross, her face troubled as she glanced up at the offending statue.

'Josette's right. Soon we won't even notice the size difference,' said Christian, wishing he had the courage to put his arm around her shoulders as he would have done before their argument. 'And look at it this way. It'll take exceptional skill to decapitate this one with a football!'

She laughed despite herself and he had to fight the urge to pull her to him and bury his face in her auburn hair. Chest tightening under the scrutiny of her dark gaze, he was debating whether he should apologise when René's whingeing voice saved him from having to make the decision.

'Christian, you going to help carry this ladder or what?'

'Coming,' said the farmer and turned to the

plumber, who was leaning against a wall and breathing heavily.

Annie, who was exasperated by the cold war that had developed between Christian and her daughter over the merger but had wisely kept her counsel on the subject, wasn't surprised that Véronique was unusually quiet on the walk back. It was the first time the young couple had exchanged more than a few words with each other in a long while. And Annie couldn't remember when her daughter had last laughed. Now though, Véronique's silence suited Annie fine. Because she was busy mulling over something René had said.

What would drive a man with vertigo up a ladder?

After Christian's display this morning, Annie was beginning to suspect it might be love. Although he had a bloody strange way of showing it!

★　★　★

Stephanie's day had been going fine until she decided to tidy Chloé's room. Normally it wasn't something she did, Chloé having been allocated the task of keeping her own space in order from an early age. But her daughter had looked so tired this morning heading off to school that Stephanie took pity on her, and in the two hours she had for lunch, she decided she would do something to cheer her up. A quick dust and vacuum, a change of bedlinen, so that when Chloé came home from school, she wouldn't have to think about it. She'd have the entire half-term ahead of her and no one nagging her about her room.

Chloé not being an unruly child, it didn't take long. There were a few items of clothing to hang up, a gym kit that needed to go in the laundry, and a couple of books on the floor. The rest was immaculate, Jules Léotard, the haughty trapeze artist, looking down in approval from the poster that Fabian had bought to replace the one destroyed when terror had entered their lives in the form of Stephanie's estranged husband.

Stephanie sank onto the bed at the memory. There hadn't been much left in this room after that awful day. But they'd rebuilt it piece by piece, just as they were rebuilding their lives. And when the papers finally came through for the divorce, it would at last feel like that episode was over.

The divorce. She ought to tell Chloé but superstition held her back. Until those documents were in her hands, she didn't want to tempt fate. Or raise the subject with her child who had been through so much at the hands of that mad man. It wouldn't be long now. And then they'd make a celebration of it. This little family they had created.

She stood up and ran a hand across the poster in affection, knowing that Jules Léotard had helped save her daughter's life. Which was when she felt it. Ridges under the bottom left-hand side, as though there was something under it.

With no thought for privacy in a house that was unused to secrets, she pulled out the drawing pin, the poster curled up and Stephanie gasped.

It couldn't be.

She stared at what was taped to the wall and her knees collapsed, tumbling her back onto the bed.

★　★　★

Across the mountains from the small cottage in Picarets, Pascal Souquet was staring at a computer, his features jaundiced by the glowing screen. He'd spent most of what had been a frustrating day sitting in front of the damn machine trying to complete an impossible task. But, try as he might, discovering the identity of the person behind *SOS Fogas* was beyond him.

He'd found out bits and pieces all right. He knew when the blog was created. He knew the company hosting it — a global organisation, which led him nowhere. He could even tell the time the posts were uploaded. But, despite Hollywood making it seem so easy to track the exact location of people through their internet trail, there was little more he could glean about the author. Not without a court order. And as for the email account used to send the messages to René, it was an off-the-shelf address with one of the main providers. Which yielded nothing.

He dropped his head into his hands and stared at the list on the desk. Fatima had helped him compile it, going through the electoral register for the commune, patiently discussing each and every person and the possibility of them being

295

the brains behind what was becoming a serious problem, until they had narrowed down the potential culprits to just seven names: Alain Rougé, René Piquemal, Fabian Servat, Véronique Estaque, Stephanie Morvan, Paul Webster and Philippe Galy.

While Pascal wasn't confident about the inclusion of Philippe Galy, the beekeeper having proved a firm ally in recent months during the debacle over the bears, and doubted that Monsieur Webster, as a foreigner, was capable of hitting local nerves so accurately, Fatima had insisted no one was above suspicion. So one of these seven, Pascal was sure, was responsible for the sarcasm and scorn that poured out of the ether onto the heads of those leading the march towards unification with Sarrat. Today's blog post had been typical, a video of Henri Dedieu taken surreptitiously at the meeting three weeks ago. Only, instead of the speech he'd given proposing the benefits of the merger, the audio had been cunningly changed so that now he was uttering statements like 'I love Fogas as much as I love bears.'

It was hilarious. Unless you were Henri Dedieu. Or Pascal Souquet, who had endured a long tirade from the man under attack that had been even more venomous than usual. With the sporadic postings on *SOS Fogas* having escalated into a daily ritual of abuse, each more elaborate and acerbic than the last, the mayor of Sarrat wanted results quickly. Pascal, aware that his future was in the hands of this man, was afraid not to give them to him.

But how to determine which of these people was the guilty party?

The first deputy mayor sat back in his chair and stared bleakly at the blog once more. It was put together simply. A list of previous posts by title on the right-hand side. A brief background of the author, which was totally tongue-in-cheek. And a counter showing the number of visitors to the site, which had been steadily rising since the blog started and had already hit an alarmingly high tally. There was nothing to yield any indication as to identity. Although . . .

Pascal jerked forward, reaching for the mouse to scroll down through the most recent articles. There, as he'd noticed before, at the bottom of each one was the time it was uploaded. Only he hadn't really *noticed* it. He clicked through to the older entries, getting excited as he went. Every post was published at around the same time, which of itself wasn't of any use. Except, in this case, the time was two o'clock in the morning.

He reached for a pad and started making notes. He was looking for someone who had to do their furtive work at night. Why? Perhaps they were too busy during the day? Or could only get privacy in the small hours? Which could mean his target worked. Or was a family man, having to wait until nighttime to access the family computer.

He looked at his list again. All seven possibilities fitted this new information apart from Alain Rougé, who was retired and whose children had long since left home. With great delight, Pascal picked up a red pen and put a firm line through the name of the ex-policeman.

One down, six to go. And now he knew how to catch his prey. Surveillance. He would stake out their houses in the hours before dawn and in doing so, he would ferret out *SOS Fogas*. What ruthless Henri Dedieu would do with the information once he had it, Pascal preferred not to dwell on. For now, he was content to end his afternoon on a high.

★ ★ ★

Home. No more school for two weeks. And the circus just around the corner. Chloé crashed through the front door, shouted a quick hello to her mother in the kitchen, flung her bag to the floor and then raced up the stairs to her room. She hadn't even got over the threshold when she saw it. Jules Léotard. The left-hand corner of the poster was curled up, revealing nothing but the bare wall beneath.

'Chloé. Come down here now.'

She'd found it. Maman had been snooping around in here and had discovered Chloé's secret.

'Chloé? I won't ask you again.'

Heavy steps down the stairs gave evidence of the temper that was building behind the sullen young face.

'Can you explain this?' Maman was holding out the circus poster, her features pale and drawn, and Chloé felt a flicker of guilt. She quickly replaced it with self-righteous indignation.

'You've been sneaking around my room?'

'No. I was cleaning it for you. As a treat.'

'So how did you find that then?'

'It doesn't matter how I — '

'So you *were* snooping. So much for respecting others — '

'*Chloé!*' It wasn't the tone that stopped Chloé. It was Maman's expression. She looked like she was about to faint, the veins in her temples blue under taut grey skin. 'Just tell me why you have it.'

Chloé looked down at the floor, toes prodding at the edge of the rug. 'The woman at the tourist office in Seix gave it to me.'

'Why?'

She shrugged.

'I found this behind it.' Maman pulled twenty euros out of her pocket. 'Were you planning on going behind my back? And don't even think of lying to me.'

Chloé blinked. Hot tears forming behind her eyelids. She didn't look up. Couldn't. Because Maman would know the truth.

A long sigh and then the sound of the poster being ripped up and thrown in the recycling basket.

'I want you to promise me, Chloé.' A finger gently tipped her chin and Chloé was facing her mother's tired gaze. 'Promise me you won't go to see this circus.'

'But I don't underst — '

'*Promise* me.'

A tear trickled down Chloé's face and she swallowed. 'I promise.'

Maman reached out to pull her into her arms

but Chloé spun in a pirouette of black curls and ran for the door. Outside, she tore up the hillside, hiccupping and struggling for breath as she fought her way through the undergrowth, tears of frustration marring her vision. It was so unfair. She hated school. She hated Maman and her secrets. She hated the blank space on her birth certificate. In fact, the only light in her life was the circus, and even that had been taken away from her.

When she could no longer maintain her furious pace, she slowed to a walk, wiping her face on her sleeves. Beneath the simmering anger, guilt flared momentarily because she knew that for the first time in her eleven years, she had just made a promise to her mother that she had no intention of keeping. But Maman had put her in an impossible position. Because one way or another, Chloé had to find her way to that circus. It was something she couldn't explain, a pull akin to a magnetic force drawing her in. And once she got there, she decided as she looked out over the valley where life had become so miserable, she was going to join them.

★ ★ ★

Serge Papon just wanted this day over and done with. It had started in his office at the town hall with a shrill call from Agnés Rogalle in the butcher's van. She'd lost another rabbit and was threatening legal action if he, as mayor of Fogas, didn't apprehend the thief. Then he'd spent

300

most of the morning liaising with the electricity company over the imminent closure of the road into Fogas. They were quibbling over the provision of transport, trying to suggest that shuttle buses would only be needed during working hours, and he'd had to patiently explain that, with the road closed, there was no other way of accessing the mountaintop village, nor the hamlets beyond it. The buses would have to run around the clock or the essential repairs to the electricity lines would not be going ahead. They'd finally reached a compromise, the electricity company agreeing to leave a lane passable through the work zone overnight.

Satisfied, Serge turned his attention to the mountain of paperwork that always accompanied such endeavours. The church bells were sounding lunchtime as he finished. But his peaceful interlude in the back garden of his house, enjoying the autumnal warmth with a glass of red and a hunk of bread to accompany the excellent saucisson from the épicerie, was interrupted by an unexpected visit from Fabian Servat. A month on from his disastrous attempt to propose to Stephanie in the old orchard, he was anxious to give it another go. So he'd come to Serge for advice.

The mayor wasn't surprised. He'd had a reputation in his prime as a man capable of wooing the ladies, more than one at a time in his heyday. And he still felt the appreciation of a red-blooded male when he saw shapely calves kissed by the hem of a skirt or the soft curve of bosom under a blouse. He'd poured the young man a drink and given him the only wisdom he had on the matter: make her feel special. Put on a big display. Flowers, champagne, the works. And a ring. You had to have the right ring.

Fabian typed notes onto his phone as he listened and Serge had to bite back a laugh at the earnest expression on the man's face. He was doomed. Entering the battle with no knowledge of how to fight and no shield for his heart. Still, you had to admire his pluck. And envy him the extremes of emotion that love brought with it.

When the Parisian cycled back down to La Rivière, head full of plans for the perfect proposal, Serge was left behind in his garden, looking at the empty chair opposite him, the single plate on the wooden table and the bottle of wine he would drink on his own. It had plunged him into a dark mood that he hadn't encountered in a long while. Not since Annie Estaque had walked all the way over here and broadsided him with the news that Véronique was his daughter, banishing all his doleful thoughts with that amazing revelation.

Back at the office, he'd thrown himself into his work, trying to brush the cobwebs of depression aside. He'd signed off on the deeds for a house sale in Picarets, some fool having bought old Widow Loubet's derelict property, and had answered three calls from irate residents who were only just hearing about the road closure that would come into effect in ten days' time, Philippe Galy particularly incensed as it would impact on his ability to get to the local markets which were essential for selling his honey.

Then he'd sat and read the report into the bear attacks last spring, which had arrived that morning. It didn't make for comfortable reading, stating that two of the incidents — the one in Sarrat and the one at Philippe Galy's beehives — had been faked and were the subject of an ongoing police investigation. There was no suggestion that the beekeeper or the Sarrat farmer had been complicit. But nevertheless, some troublemaker had staged the attacks and provoked the backlash that brought Fogas to its knees and proved fatal for one of the bears.

Perplexed by such reckless behaviour, Serge decided the best thing to do with the report was to bury it until the police had completed their inquiries. The last thing he wanted was for the commune to get all stirred up again in the knowledge that someone had deliberately targeted the bears. So he'd photocopied it, knowing that Arnaud Petit would want to see it if he ever got back in touch, and then he'd placed the original at the bottom of his desk drawer, where he hid anything he didn't want his meddlesome first deputy to find.

Twenty minutes later, thinking that the day, which was thankfully almost over, had reached its nadir with the incendiary report, the mayor of Fogas answered the telephone. And the floodgates on his despair were opened.

'Serge?'

He recognised the whispered voice, an old friend from across the river, whose loyalty to Sarrat had waned when he'd lost the mayoral election to Henri Dedieu.

'I've got some interesting news,' the man continued.

'How interesting?'

'They're having a vote on the merger on this side of the water.'

Serge stiffened. 'A referendum?'

'Just the council.'

'When?'

'This is the cunning bit. Next Friday.'

'Bastards!' muttered Serge, not needing to look at his calendar to know the significance of the date. 'Thanks for letting me know, Jean-Claude. I owe you one.'

He replaced the receiver with great care, trying to breathe through the fog of frustration building in his chest. Bloody Henri Dedieu. Not content with having caused mayhem in Fogas by putting the idea of a merger in the préfet's head, the mayor of Sarrat had twisted the knife even further. He'd called a vote on the proposal to coincide with the fête in Fogas. It was a stunning manoeuvre. Timed to divert attention from the mountain commune as it battled for its existence, it could be the final blow. Because if the Conseil Municipal in Sarrat threw their weight behind the amalgamation, the préfet would have the green light he needed to go ahead, regardless of any opposition. And the feeble attempts to save the mountain commune would amount to nothing.

Serge forced himself to focus on the last pieces of paperwork that needed signing, and then he placed the lid on his fountain pen and leaned back in his chair.

He couldn't take any more. The weight of office, which he used to shoulder with such nonchalance, had suddenly become insupportable. Already tired from the turmoil over the post office and the bears, not to mention the shock he'd got from Stephanie unearthing that revolver after all these years, which had plunged him into an unwelcome past, he'd been further dragged down by the animosity that had poisoned the three villages ever since the meeting in Sarrat. Aghast, he'd watched as friends turned on each other, the thorny issue of the merger tearing them apart. Only yesterday he'd walked into the épicerie to hear René and Josette arguing, Josette close to tears as the plumber harangued her over her views. And from what he could gather, Alain Rougé and Philippe Galy had come to blows over the topic in the market in St Girons the Saturday before. Two of his councillors brawling in public. It was making Fogas a laughing stock.

But what was hurting him the most was the impact the proposal was having on two of his favourite people: Christian and Véronique. Where they had been firm friends, now a veneer of frost coated their interactions and the pair of them were almost unbearable to be around. Christian was morose, walking about with a face like a whipped puppy, and Véronique was on the shortest of fuses, many an unwitting customer triggering her caustic tongue.

Serge rolled his shoulders back as though he could physically dispense of the burden he was carrying. But it was useless. It sat there, heavy and oppressive, too much for him to endure on his own and he could feel his chest tighten with stress.

Time to go home. He'd done enough for the day. Done enough, full stop. When this was over, which wouldn't take long given today's news, he would resign as mayor. Not that he'd have a choice, he thought wryly, as there would only be one mayor in the new commune and it wouldn't be this side of the river.

He left his office, bid *au revoir* to his secretary, Céline, and wandered down the street to the empty house that was awaiting him, weighed down by the concerns he had for the future — both that of the commune and his own. He got as far as reaching out for the wine to put on the half-set table when he decided he couldn't face being alone any longer. He rushed out of the house, still clutching the bottle, got in the car, and was down in La Rivière before he could change his mind. He'd been intent on going to the Auberge, but as he slowed to pull into the car park he suddenly veered left instead, up the road to Picarets. When he turned the last bend before the plateau and the Estaque farmhouse came into sight, he knew that this was where he'd been heading all along.

Greeted by two bounding dogs, he stood on the path, bottle clutched to his chest, wondering if he'd made a mistake. But the door to the farmhouse was already open and there she was, a knowing smile on her face.

'I had no one to share this with,' was all he said as he held out the wine.

'Took yourrr bloody time!' She held her face

306

up to greet him and he felt the load fall from his shoulders.

⋆   ⋆   ⋆

From the Estaque farm to the border with Spain is a mere matter of twenty kilometres but a tough walk for a man in his prime, over mountain passes and rough terrain. Once across the high peaks that separate the two countries, the soft green of the Ariège gives way to a harsher landscape where, even by late October, there is still a sting to the heat of the day.

On this particular day, in a village tucked high into the Spanish Pyrenees, that heat was abating as the evening lengthened and the shadows fell across the tiny square. There, at a table outside the bar, a man was sitting working on a laptop. Strong hands, broad shoulders straining at his shirt, he had a physique more suited to an outdoorsman than a computer expert. The bar owner's wife watched him with interest. He'd been living among them for the best part of three months, this giant Adonis of a man who'd wandered in off the high hills one day looking for work. He'd found it and a place to stay. And still they knew nothing about him. Except that he had an amazing appetite and could work the stock like no other farmhand had before him.

'There you are,' she said as she placed a simple stew on the table, a basket of bread next to it. 'Don't be afraid to ask for more.'

'If it's as good as always, I will!' He smiled,

white teeth stark against the brown skin of his face, his pronunciation burred by his native French. 'Thanks.'

He moved his laptop to one side, the same website on the screen as always when he visited the bar on a Friday night — some local French newspaper from the place where he used to live. She knew no more than that and had been unable to winkle any further details out of him despite her persistence. But tonight, as he went to close the computer, something must have caught his eye because he froze, his entire body tensed like a hunter getting scent of a trail.

'*Merde!*' she heard him mutter.

Moving so she could see what held him so entranced, she didn't waste any time on the page of text, which made no sense to her, French being nothing more than a series of sighs and lip pursing that had passed her by at school. Instead, she focused on a photo of a middle-aged man holding a revolver, good-looking but with a sadistic twist to his gaze. And in a small inset there was a close-up of the man's hand showing a tacky ring with a boar's head on it.

So ostentatious. So French!

She was about to turn back into the bar where her three regular customers were waiting for refills when, with the fluid movement which defined him, the Frenchman reached back and gathered his long black mane of hair into a sleek ponytail.

'Is that to keep it out of your dinner?' she quipped as she started towards the bar.

He didn't reply. He was still staring at the computer screen. When she came to collect his plate some time later, she noticed with despair that he hadn't eaten a thing.

18

The last Friday of October dawned with ribbons of mist threading between the hills, plunging the valleys into obscurity while the higher peaks remained impervious above them. At this hour, a good while before the sun would haul itself over the mountains, the sky was dusted with fading stars as the night began to lose its hold on the heavens. It was a time for sleeping. That last snatch of dreams before the waking hours chased away the delights of the slumbering mind. But in one of the houses in Picarets, someone was already astir.

With careful feet, the stairs were negotiated and the tiles crossed, then shoes were put on before small hands unlocked the front door and eased back the shutters, wary of creaking wood. Once outside, the figure swung a rucksack onto its back and scampered down the road, keeping close to the verge until it reached a path that led into the forest above. With quick steps, the steep incline was climbed and only when the trees had closed around her, did the young girl stop to look back at the shuttered cottage disappearing behind the leaves.

Propelled by a force she didn't understand, Chloé Morvan was doing the only thing she could. She was running away. Although it actually felt like she was going home.

Christian Dupuy was torn from the tender caresses of the postmistress by the shrill call of the rooster. He peeled open his eyes, threw back the bed-clothes and stumbled across to the window. With a clatter he thrust open the shutters and cast a malevolent glare down at the arrogant bird that was astride the fence, sounding the break of day. Then he stared at the empty bed, imagined kisses lingering on his lips.

How much more of this could he take? The woman who barely spoke to him in waking hours invaded his dreams every night in a world where mergers didn't exist and Christian was the light of her life. Which meant it was with great reluctance that the farmer awoke each morning, dragging his body from her warm arms to embrace reality in a cold shower.

Enough, he decided as the water cascaded over his massive frame. This confounded passion for Véronique was making him thoroughly miserable. And as there was little chance of his wild imaginings turning into anything substantial, given the state of things between them, it was time to let it go. He considered the practicalities of this as he dressed. He would see the fête through and then he would resign from the *comité des fêtes* and take a step back from commune life, giving up his seat on the council. If he threw himself into work on the farm and reduced the chances of seeing her, perhaps his heart might yet recover. Because he didn't think it could stand many more nights like the last one.

He was dressed and down the stairs, heading out to his car before the sun had fully lifted over the hills behind the farm. As he drove down the valley road, past Stephanie's house and on through Picarets, the mist closed around him, as close as the arms that had held him so tightly in his dreams. It was no wonder that he missed the flash of red that dived into the bushes just above the lay-by opposite the Auberge. He had other things on his mind.

★　★　★

'Christian!' Chloé breathed the words into the ground as the blue Panda rumbled past.

She'd heard the car at the last minute, the engine muffled by the white clouds that had settled in the valley, and with a desperate leap, she'd thrown herself down the embankment at the side of the road. It was her second lunge into the undergrowth that morning, the other one coming when she'd heard the soft hiss of tyres on tarmac on a bend behind her. She'd just made cover in time to see Fabian go whizzing past on his bike.

She waited a heartbeat or two before lifting her head, and only when she was sure she was safe did she scramble back up. This was the tricky bit. To get past the Auberge and onto the main road. But with the meteorological conditions playing into her hands, she stood a good chance of remaining undiscovered. Taking cautious steps, she covered the remaining distance to the T-junction, staying close to the trees, and then crossed the road in a burst of speed to take refuge in a clump of bushes. She would wait here for the right car. Hopefully it wouldn't take long.

*   *   *

Paul Webster was taking a cup of tea upstairs to his wife when he saw the cat, Tomate, stalking across the expanse of lawn that ran parallel to the road. A flash of black and white, she was low to the wet grass, belly almost rubbing on the ground. A mouse, no doubt. Yet another present to be left at the back door for them by a feline who didn't comprehend that they had no need for her generosity.

He turned from the window with a rueful smile, knowing he would be cleaning up the remains, Lorna no longer able to bend down now that her pregnancy was nearing the end. It was her final scan this afternoon and then, in another six weeks, they would have a baby, *their* baby, living with them. It was a thought that both thrilled and terrified him with equal measure.

Six weeks. It was nowhere near long enough to get everything sorted. After an extended tourist season, Paul had taken on several commissions for websites, trying to make as much money as he could so Lorna could take it easier in the first half of the following year. Which meant he still hadn't redecorated their bedroom, the one room they hadn't touched since they'd moved in. It was going to be a push to get it done in time.

He eased open the bedroom door and crossed

to the bed where his wife was sleeping, the covers arched across her swollen stomach. So much for fretting about the room being ready. What about them? Were they ready to be parents?

Bit late to be wondering that now, he thought, as he placed the cup down. Lorna's eyes flickered open in response and she smiled.

'It's scan day!' she said, excitement already replacing the traces of sleep on her face. 'And then the fête. So much to look forward to.'

Paul did his best to smile back, although he wasn't sure which alarmed him more — the prospect of being a father or of being one of the judges for the *croustade* competition later that day. As he headed downstairs, he was contemplating the feasibility of declaring all the entrants winners. Which was why he didn't notice the cat's tail sticking out of the undergrowth at the end of the garden. Or the flash of red as a hand reached out to tuck it away.

* * *

'You're going to give me away, Tomate!' Chloé did her best to scold the manically purring cat that was sitting next to her, barely concealed by the bushes. 'At least pull your tail in.'

The cat ignored the suggestion, so Chloé quickly curled the offending length of black fur up against the warm body that was pressing into her. Despite reprimanding her unexpected companion, she was glad of the company. It felt like she'd been crouched here forever, waiting

314

for the right car to come along, one driven by people who didn't know her. She was beginning to think she might have to resort to walking. Sixteen kilometres — how long would that take? A couple of hours? A day? She had no idea.

She heard the sound of an engine in the distance and peered out to see a Range Rover approaching through the mist. No good. That was Pascal Souquet's car. She watched it speed past, Fatima hunched over the wheel, sharp face close to the windscreen, and she tried not to panic. But if she didn't get to St Girons by one o'clock she would miss the last performance and the circus would be leaving town without her.

In the shade of the bushes she twisted her wrist to peer at her watch. It was coming up to eight-thirty. If she started walking, she should be able to make it. But she was also more likely to be seen because the road offered no protection down to the Sarrat bridge as it twisted between the two boundaries of mountainside and river, and once the sun cleared the hills, the cluster of cloud that was lingering along the valley would be burned off, leaving her exposed.

She stroked the cat and concentrated on the stretch of tarmac that led to the épicerie, willing someone to come along. She was still young enough to believe that if she willed it with all her might it would happen.

* * *

'Have you got the ring?'
Fabian nodded, already nervous some twelve

315

hours before the event. Wanting to put the finishing touches to his plan, he'd cycled down ahead of Stephanie and before Chloé had even emerged from her room.

'Flowers?'

'Yes, Tante Josette. And there's a bottle of champagne in the fridge.'

She heard the thread of impatience in his reply. 'Sorry. It's just so nice to have something lovely to look forward to after all this nonsense with the merger. I'm excited, that's all.'

He grimaced. 'Glad someone is. I just feel sick.'

'You're not the only one,' muttered a grumpy Christian, who was slouched over a coffee at the bar.

'Ignore him,' said Josette, shooting the farmer a furious look. 'You have nothing to worry about. What on earth could go wrong?'

A raised eyebrow met her words. 'Well, let's see. She could get a letter from her solicitors telling her she has to meet her psycho husband, which is always a passion killer. Or she could find a gun in the orchard that is so evil it brings on a migraine. Or . . . I don't know. Something even worse than that?'

'Have you never heard of third time lucky?' quipped Josette.

Her nephew laughed and leaned down to kiss her cheek before heading for the door. 'Let's hope you're right. I'm just going over to the garden centre to make sure everything is in place. I'll be back before the meeting starts.'

'Fabian?' The farmer's voice stopped the

Parisian and he turned to see a broad hand held out towards him.

'Take no notice of me,' said Christian, shaking hands. 'And the best of luck for tonight.'

'I thought you didn't approve of romance?' said Fabian, touched by the gesture.

Christian shrugged, a rueful smile chasing away the shadows on his face. 'It's not that I don't approve. I'm just not very good at it. So here's hoping you fare better than I have.'

He drank the last of his coffee and followed the Parisian out of the door to meet René who had just arrived, leaving Josette to ponder the portent of his words. Jacques Servat, resident in his habitual spot in the inglenook, had no reason to ponder. He knew exactly what the farmer was talking about. He also knew what he sounded like: a man who had given up all hope.

★ ★ ★

Down at the Auberge, from behind a clump of leaves, Chloé could just make out the tall figures of Fabian and Christian in front of the bar. The mist was dispersing. If she didn't catch a lift soon it would be too late to walk. She was debating making a dash for it when she saw a car approach from the far side of the bridge, a bright yellow number plate affixed to the front. Dutch! Perfect. She reached for her rucksack, getting ready to step out and hitch, and then watched in agony as they pulled up at the épicerie and went inside.

She let the bag fall to the floor and slumped back beside it. She was never going to get away.

'I can't believe they've cancelled at such short notice!'

René was pacing up and down the terrace outside the bar, cigarette jerking between lips and hand, his fierce visage enough to make the couple of Dutch tourists who'd popped into the épicerie pick up their pace as they headed back to their car.

'Merde! There's no way I can find a replacement at this hour.'

'Perhaps we could fall back on the dancers we normally use? They'd be better than nothing. Try calling Alain Rougé,' said Christian from the safety of the doorway, the plumber being too enraged to be approached.

'No good. He's done his back in gardening and two of his troupe are in hospital. I'll just have to improvise.'

'What, get up on the stage and dance yourself?' Véronique said as she approached, notebook in hand, ready for the final meeting of the *comité des fêtes*. 'I'd pay to see that!'

'It's not funny! With less than seven hours to the start of the fête, we don't have any entertainment to open it.'

'Stephanie might know someone who could fill in,' suggested Christian, gesturing at the blue van nearing the T-junction down at the Auberge. 'Failing that . . . ' He scratched his head, blond curls all over the place thanks to his disturbed night and head empty thanks to the presence of the woman of his dreams.

'Failing that, we'll improvise like René said. Now let's get this meeting started or the préfet and his wife will be here before we've got anywhere.' Véronique brushed past the farmer to enter the bar, leaving his left thigh on fire and a tortured look on his face.

Soon this torment will end, Christian promised himself as he took a deep breath before following her. It had to or he wouldn't be responsible for his actions.

★   ★   ★

'Yes!' hissed Chloé, as she saw the Dutch couple get back into their car. Deciding to wait for the vehicle to reach the bridge before she stepped out of her cover, she brushed off her clothes, picked up the rucksack and eased into a crouch. But a squeal of brakes opposite, announcing the arrival of a battered blue police van, spoiled her plans.

Maman!

Chloé froze, frustrated. Her best chance in over an hour and she couldn't move. She watched her mother turn her head to the left to check for traffic and then to the right where the Dutch car was just pulling away from the épicerie.

'Go. Now!' muttered the girl, willing the blue van to make the turn.

Maman's head flicked left one more time and then her green gaze swung to the undergrowth where Chloé was hiding and a frown formed on her forehead. Chloé didn't breathe, hunched over, staring back at her mother from behind the foliage, knowing the mystical abilities Maman possessed. It was Madame Rogalle and the twins who saved her. Pulling up behind the blue van, a sharp pip on the horn from Madame Rogalle and Maman shook her head, raised her hand in apology and turned right towards the épicerie, Madame Rogalle following.

But it was too late. The Dutch car was already abreast of Chloé's hiding place. She had no time to step out, not without being hit. She lowered the rucksack back to the floor and was preparing to sit back down when a last-minute blink of an indicator gave her hope. They were pulling into the lay-by and she could see the woman looking at a map.

Checking the route was clear, Chloé dashed out of the bushes and ran across the road through the last wisps of mist. Now all she had to do was persuade the foreign tourists to take her.

★ ★ ★

In St Girons the sun had already dispersed the haze and was shining down on an expanse of red and white canvas that covered a patch of ground on the edge of town. Alexei Bénac surveyed his mobile fiefdom and couldn't help but smile.

One more show, the matinée performance, and they would be back on the road, heading east to Font Romeu, where his father came from, the place where Alexei had spent many a summer and learned everything he knew about acrobatics. He couldn't wait. While he loved performing — balancing on a trapeze far above the crowd an exhilaration that never waned — he adored being on the move, winding along the tree-lined roads of France, each destination offering the possibility of adventure.

He checked his watch. Ten o'clock. If all went well and they managed to dismantle everything with no problems, the entire troupe should be on the road by five. Plenty of time for them to make Font Romeu before dinner. And time enough now for a last tranquil practice before the clowns arrived and anarchy descended.

He walked towards the big top past a large poster, his own image smiling back at him, a riot of black curls and a wide smile above a slender frame. Without so much as glancing at it, he pushed aside the canvas and disappeared inside.

* * *

She'd done it. Negotiated her way from Picarets to St Girons without bumping into anyone who knew her. Under the pretext of helping with directions, Chloé had approached the Dutch tourists in the lay-by, counting her blessings when they'd pointed at Foix on the map and asked, in halting French, which was the best way to get there. The man obviously wanted to take the scenic route over the mountains but Chloé's contrived expression of concern at such an undertaking had convinced his wife that going via St Girons was a better option. Chloé had then innocently hoisted her rucksack onto her back, making sure she staggered slightly under the negligible weight, and the man had asked where she was heading. Minutes later she was slouched on the back seat of the car as it sped down to Kerkabanac and out of the Fogas valley.

Not wanting the couple to have any idea of her real plans, Chloé had asked to be dropped off at the supermarket south of town. So she had a fair walk across the centre of St Girons and out the other side to reach her objective, keeping to back roads to avoid being spotted. With the time just coming up to ten-thirty, she saw it. A peak of red canvas that with every step grew more and more impressive. When she reached the bridge over the River Lez and the big top was fully revealed, tears filled her eyes.

It felt so right, being here, the edges of the tent fluttering in a slight breeze, posters announcing the circus decorating every lamp post and a fleet of brightly painted vans and caravans situated to one side. She watched for a few moments from afar. It was quiet. The occasional person coming out of a caravan and heading into another. Other than that, there was no one around.

Seizing her chance, she crossed the road and, with an air of authority she didn't feel, walked straight towards the canvas. Slipping through the opening unchallenged, she found herself inside the big top and there, swinging high from a single trapeze, was the man who'd brought her here. She crouched between the back two rows of seats, sliding down so she couldn't be seen, and watched as he rehearsed, effortlessly twisting and turning his lithe body in a series of stunts that held her breathless. More than anything, she wanted to be up there with him.

★ ★ ★

The pockets of depression that had been gathering in the corners of Serge Papon's mind were borne away like fallen leaves on an autumn breeze when he descended to La Rivière on the day of the fête. Admittedly, he'd already benefited from hearty doses of Estaque tonic dished out by Annie on what had become frequent evening visits to the farm on the plateau. But the sight that greeted him that afternoon was enough to dispel any lingering melancholy.

Stalls were being erected by willing helpers all the way along the road, Paul Webster and René were down at the lay-by wrestling with an enormous apple press, people carrying *croustades* of all flavours were already beginning to arrive and a stage had been set up in the grounds of the Auberge. As for the orchard . . .

Serge couldn't find words for it. Tiny lights were strung between the boughs, ribbons and garlands hung from the branches and wooden tables with vibrant covers were spaced between the old fruit trees displaying a variety of wares while Stephanie and Véronique were putting the finishing touches to a display of old photos that showed the changing face of Fogas over the years. They had transformed the derelict space into a fairyland.

'It's wonderful!' he announced to Christian, who was sitting at a table on the terrace, which had become the impromptu headquarters of the *comité des fêtes*. 'I take it we're almost ready?'

'As ready as we'll ever be,' said the farmer, looking up from the clipboard in front of him. 'We're still missing an entertainment for the aperitifs. Don't suppose you know anyone willing to step in?'

Serge waved a dismissive hand. 'If that's the only hitch, then we're fine. But you could ask Philippe Galy to play the accordion.'

'Excellent idea!' The farmer replied and Serge wandered off to inspect the orchard.

★ ★ ★

The drumbeat throbbed around the arena, the lights caught the sequins and scattered a thousand sparks into the darkness behind him, and the atmosphere grew taut with anticipation. In her brief eleven years on the planet, Chloé Morvan had never experienced anything like it.

Hunkered down in the back row, she'd remained undetected throughout rehearsals and even managed a nap before the paying public began to arrive. Then, as the big top started to fill, she'd simply chosen an empty seat between two families, both sets of parents believing she was with the other. When the lights dimmed and the ringmaster entered in his top hat and red coat, she'd been transported to another world.

Along with the children around her, she'd laughed until her sides ached at the clumsy clowns, had been amazed by the skills of the knife-throwing cowboy and had watched with envy and awe as a beautiful woman dangled from a rope by only her toes. But when the drums rolled and the spotlight swung onto a lone figure on the scaffold high above the crowd, her heart began to thunder.

It was him. The Great Alexei. A slight man, his sinewy frame sheathed in a leotard trailing a flame of sequins across his chest, he waved to his cheering audience and smiled. That smile. The one from the poster that had bewitched Chloé and brought her all the way here from her mountain home. Then he gave a bow of acknowledgement and took hold of the trapeze as the drums began to roll once more. On a burst of cymbals, he let go of the scaffolding and swung out over the arena.

The crowd gasped as he arced over them, forwards and back, forwards and back, building up momentum before flinging himself free, his body knifing through the air, turning over and over. Once. Twice. Somersaults perfectly executed until, just as it seemed he must fall, out of the dark came the arc of another trapeze and he was grasped by the firm hands of his fellow acrobat.

The crowd swooned. Chloé didn't. She was clapping and cheering. Such skill. Such technique. All made to look so easy. And without a net beneath him.

The Great Alexei, back on the scaffolding, took a bow and accepted the applause with a huge smile and a nod of his black curls. The drums rolled again and the beautiful woman from the rope act passed the trapeze to him. This time he was standing even higher up. He raised his arm and silence descended. Concentration. His focus on the man on the other trapeze who was already swinging, body hanging down ready for the catch.

Alexei rose onto his toes, placed both hands on the thin bar and thrust himself out into space. The rush of air. The silence. Chloé was with him, her muscles tensing for the flick of energy needed to propel himself off the bar and into thin air. Once. Twice. Three times! She twisted and turned and felt the jerk on her body as he was caught on the clash of cymbals.

The crowd went mad. Chloé couldn't breathe.

'And now, mesdames et messieurs, the most daring act of all.' The ringmaster's deep tones cut through the applause. 'Complete silence please, while the Great Alexei performs a feat no other act dares imitate.'

A murmur of expectation swelled and then faded as the lights went out, leaving a single beam on the acrobat at the top of the scaffold. He took a deep breath, shook his curls back off his face and then hands reached out from the darkness to place a mask over his head.

The crowd inhaled, a sound of trepidation. Chloé's nails were digging into her palms.

Guided to the trapeze by his assistant, Alexei groped for the bar, hands doing duty for his sightless eyes. This time, no drums. No cymbals. Just silence.

'Ready,' Alexei shouted and a pendulum of light split the dark, highlighting the trapeze of the catcher who had begun his swing. To and fro he swayed, upside down, focused on the masked figure still standing on the scaffolding. Then Alexei stretched upwards and swung himself off the platform. He arced forwards, backwards, and as he came forwards once more he released the bar. Blind. Trusting his ability and his sense of timing. The small figure turned effortlessly in the air and was caught.

The crowd began to clap and then realised the act wasn't over. The beautiful assistant had swung the empty trapeze back over the two men who were still swaying above the arena.

He couldn't . . . no way . . . oh my God . . .

The applause trickled to stunned silence and on a backwards arc, the catcher released the masked Alexei, who turned twice in the air before grasping his original trapeze. All without being able to see a thing.

The crowd let out their held breath in a roar. Chloé jumped to her feet and started cheering and pretty soon the entire place was doing the same, a storm of noise greeting the acrobat as he whipped off his mask and bowed down to them.

For Chloé Morvan, self-taught acrobat of many years, it was like coming home. Which was why she had no intention of leaving.

★ ★ ★

All day, Stephanie had been plagued by a nagging worry. It wasn't something she could put her finger on but it lingered in the background like the dark clouds that gathered on the horizon on a humid afternoon: you might have sunshine on your face but you knew something bad was coming. She was taking a breather, standing back with Véronique to admire the transformation of Monsieur Garcia's orchard, when Serge approached.

'You've made the place look amazing,' he said to the two women.

'It was all Stephanie's idea,' said Véronique. 'I just followed orders!'

'Actually, some of the ideas were Chloé's,' admitted Stephanie.

Serge laughed. 'It takes a young mind to create something like this. Where is she, by the way?'

'She spent the morning at the swimming pool in Foix with the Rogalles. She should be down here any minute.'

And that was it. Bang. Stephanie was back at the T-junction earlier that morning, engine idling, a sensation that something was wrong stealing over her. Her gaze had been drawn to the clump of bushes that marked the grounds of the Auberge but before she could pinpoint the feeling of unease, Madame Rogalle had been there, tooting her horn.

Stephanie could remember looking in the rear-view mirror. Could see the reflection now before her in the orchard. Three faces in the car behind. Not four.

'Is everything all right?' Véronique was looking at her with concern.

'Chloé,' said Stephanie, hands shaking as she pulled her mobile out of her pocket. 'I just need to check on Chloé.'

★   ★   ★

'Have they called Madame Rogalle?' Josette asked as she placed a cup of coffee in front of a very pale Annie Estaque.

'Fabian just got thrrrough to herrr. Chloé's not with them. She was neverrr meant to be.'

'She lied to Stephanie?'

Annie nodded. 'That's what worrrries me. That child neverrr lies. And she's not answer-rring herrr phone.'

'So you think she's been planning this for a while?'

'It's looking that way,' said Christian as he entered the bar with Véronique. 'We've just heard from Fabian, who's up at the cottage with Stephanie. They found Chloé's phone on her bed and some of her clothing has gone, along with a rucksack and her acrobatics book.'

'She's taken herrr *book?*' Annie drew air between pursed lips, knowing how important the gymnastics manual was to the young girl. 'That's not a good sign.'

'But where would she go?' asked Josette.

They all looked at each other, none of them having a clue. Apart from Jacques, who had listened to the conversation with growing horror. He knew where young Chloé might be. She'd told him the last time she was in here and sworn him to secrecy. While he had no intention of keeping that promise given the circumstances, he realised that the constraints on his existence could mean that he had no option but to observe it. Particularly as his attempts to communicate didn't seem to be having any impact on Josette at all.

The big top was empty. Filled to the brim only half an hour before, now the tent was silent, the sides billowing slightly as the wind filtered through. This was her chance. She could test herself before she approached him. Because he was bound to want to see what she could do before taking her on.

With one last glance to make sure she was alone, Chloé crept out of her hiding place in the back row and hurried down to the arena. The ladder was there, stretching up above, the top of the scaffolding almost out of sight. It looked a lot higher from here. Before her courage could fail her, she started climbing.

* * *

Josette was on edge. She'd been on edge since the meeting in Sarrat when Henri Dedieu had made his case for the merger and she'd found herself impressed by the man and his promises. Foolish enough to voice her change of heart in public, she'd been caught up in a maelstrom. Véronique and René, among others, had taken exception to her betrayal, as they termed it, refusing to accept that Henri Dedieu could bring prosperity to Fogas. So Josette had spent the last four weeks biting her tongue and trying not to get drawn into the arguments that seemed to spring up out of nowhere like a summer storm. Tension pervaded every conversation and with Véronique working in the épicerie, it had made for an uncomfortable time. The situation wasn't helped by having the ghost of her dead husband in high dudgeon at her stance, accusatory looks and a turned back replacing the smiles that used to greet her.

Therefore, it was with some surprise — as everyone began to congregate in the bar at the news of Chloé's suspected disappearance — that Josette noticed Jacques trying to catch her eye. Waving one arm around in front of his nose and then flapping both hands by his ears, he was clearly trying to tell her something but she had no idea what it was. He was insistent though. Because every time she shifted so he was out of her sight, he moved back into her line of vision. When he jumped onto the table and threw himself off in what looked like an attempt at a somersault, he finally got her attention.

★ ★ ★

The Great Alexei was feeling great indeed. Another fine performance from all involved and a crowd of happy people sent on their way. Circus life didn't get better than that. He'd signed autographs, posed for photos, and had gently disentangled himself from a couple of young women who were willing to offer him more than just a smile, all because he dangled from a few bits of rope way above the ground.

It never failed to amaze him how women reacted to the dangers of his world. But it was something he'd never taken advantage of. Except once. That time up in Brittany, a warm October

331

night when he'd been overcome by passion. To be fair, he'd had a sense that the ravishing woman in his arms was the one taking advantage. He just hadn't known how. Or sought to find out.

He grinned at the memory and pushed back the canvas of the big top. He had time to warm down before they began dismantling. With his mind still in Finistère all those years ago, he didn't notice her at first. But when he did, his heart leaped to his throat.

A young girl was standing on top of the platform, holding onto a trapeze. And it looked like she was about to step off.

19

'Any word?' Serge entered the bar, apprehension emanating from him.

Christian shook his head. 'René has called everyone we know in case Chloé is off practising her acrobatics, but so far, no one's seen her. And we've organised search parties to go door to door across the commune.'

'But where could she be?' asked Véronique. 'I mean, even if she got as far as here, she wouldn't get much further without someone seeing her. There's nowhere to hide on this road.'

'Perrrhaps she thumbed a lift?' offered Annie.

'Even then, she'd have to stand at the lay-by and Josette would have seen her from here. Wouldn't you, Josette?'

'Sorry?' Josette's attention was elsewhere, a furious look of concentration on her face as she stared at the fireplace.

'I said, you'd have seen anyone down at the lay-by trying to hitch.'

'Not this morning,' came the distracted reply. 'It was too misty. I could hardly see the garden centre.'

The rest of the villagers shared a concerned look. It suddenly seemed possible that young Chloé had got further than they thought.

'Perhaps it's time I called the police,' said Serge.

'The police?' enquired a jovial voice. 'Don't

tell me your fête has got out of hand before it's even started?'

As one, the people of Fogas turned to see the Préfet of Ariège in the doorway.

'Christ!' muttered Serge. 'That's all we need.'

* * *

'It's no different to jumping out of the window onto the oak tree,' Chloé muttered.

With one hand already clasped on the bar of the trapeze, all she had to do was lift the other hand off the scaffolding and with a small push, she would be away, doing exactly what she'd always dreamed of doing.

But her right hand was cemented to the metal railing that was keeping her tethered to the ground. And her eyes were fixed on the empty space where the safety net should be, the circus ring tiny beneath her. To her deep disgust, she was paralysed by a fear which had mushroomed out of nowhere.

* * *

He could see her lips moving as though she was talking herself into this, a fierce look of determination on her face, which made him smile despite his concern. Small, with dark curls cascading over tense shoulders, there was something about her . . .

Quietly, moving like a cat across an open field, he made his way to the bottom of the ladder and began to climb.

It meant nothing. Her years of practice in the back garden and the fields around Fogas. The long hours. The twisted ankles. The bruises. All worthless because she couldn't tear her gaze away from the fearsome drop beyond the platform.

She simply wasn't cut out to be an acrobat. She was way too scared.

And at that realisation, Chloé's temper surfaced, a scorch of anger at herself that fired along her veins and cut through her fear. Her cheeks flushed, she gave a toss of her head and her eyes snapped onto the offending fingers that were tightly curled around the scaffolding.

'Just let go, you wimp,' she hissed. 'You might never get another chance.'

With a deep breath, she stretched up onto her toes, and in one unflinching movement, grabbed the trapeze with both hands and pushed off. She was airborne. She was flying!

But she wasn't alone.

A strong arm was locked around her waist, a hand grasped the bar alongside hers, and a voice was whispering in her ear.

'It's not as easy as it looks, is it?'

The Great Alexei. He was sharing the trapeze, swinging them both out above the empty arena, the ground beneath a long way down. Chloé felt the thrill of the air rushing past and the intense joy at being with the man whose smile had pulled her to this circus with a force she hadn't been able to deny.

Fabian stole a glance at Stephanie as he drove the van back down to La Rivière. She was understandably quiet. There was no sign of Chloé up in Picarets. Or rather, there were plenty of signs, all of them pointing to the conclusion that the young girl had run away. What they had to work out now was where she'd gone. Then they had to find her. And quickly, before any harm befell her.

But, unbeknown to Fabian, Stephanie was pretty sure she knew where her daughter was. The fates had been screaming this would happen for eleven years and while Stephanie had done all she could to protect Chloé, it hadn't been enough. In fact, that overprotection had driven her child to the very thing Stephanie had been trying to keep her from.

'Head back to the épicerie,' she said as they reached the T-junction. 'I think I know where Chloé might be.'

★　★　★

It was bedlam. Jérôme Ulrich and his wife, Karine, had walked into the bar in La Rivière expecting to find a warm welcome to the fête. Instead, the place was upside down with worry over a missing child.

Serge Papon was calling the police, three search parties had been organised and dispatched to scour what they could of the villages that made up the commune, and everyone else seemed to be on the phone, putting out the word. Apart from the woman who ran the bar, who was sitting in a corner watching the empty fireplace, a frown on her face.

'There must be something we can do,' Karine Ulrich said to Véronique Estaque, who'd explained the situation to them.

Véronique gestured at the heavily pregnant lady standing next to her. 'Lorna and I are going out on the road to stop cars as they pass. We're hoping to find the person who gave Chloé a lift coming back the other way. Let me text you a photo of her and you can help us.'

'What about me?' asked Jérôme, as his wife followed the two women out of the bar.

Christian Dupuy pointed to a man with a mobile to his ear. 'That's Paul Webster, who runs the Auberge. We figure Chloé will have tried to hitch a lift with someone who doesn't know her. Chances are, it might be a tourist. So Paul is calling all the hoteliers and tourist offices nearby. He could do with a hand.'

'Consider it done.'

Without even thinking, Christian slapped him on the back in thanks.

'The gendarmes are on their way,' said Serge, approaching with a grin as he saw his second deputy putting the préfet to work. 'Any news from Stephanie and Fabian?'

'They should be herrre any minute,' said Annie from behind the bar, where she was helping Monique Sentenac keep everyone supplied with coffee. Normally Josette's domain, her old friend seemed to have been knocked sideways by the news of Chloé's disappearance and was sitting by the fire, muttering to herself. Annie was just thinking that she had never seen her so withdrawn when Josette leaped to her feet with a shout, knocking over her chair in the process. It was enough to silence the room.

'I think I've got it!' Josette exclaimed, gaze fixed on her ghostly husband who was lying on the floor panting after his latest mime, which had involved tripping himself up and walking into a wall.

'Got what?' asked René, back from a fruitless search of Fogas.

Josette closed her eyes and concentrated. An elephant. Acrobatics. A clown. It had taken her a while but she was sure it was what he meant. She turned to the room, face alight.

'I think Chloé has gone to the circus.'

'How can you be so sure?' asked Christian.

It was only then that Josette realised she couldn't explain how she knew this. Couldn't tell them about the madcap antics of her husband as he attempted to communicate with her. 'I just . . . I don't know — '

'This would seem to confirm it.' The commanding tones of the préfet cut across the buzz of excitement generated by Josette's revelation. 'The woman at the tourist office in Seix says a young girl answering Chloé's description was interested in buying tickets for the circus. She seemed quite obsessed with it in fact.'

A squeal of brakes outside heralded the arrival of the battered blue van, Fabian racing into the bar in a flurry of long limbs, Stephanie close behind him.

'The circus!' he shouted. 'We think Chloé has run away to join the circus.'

Still on the floor, Jacques Servat smiled at his wife and nodded his weary head. At last they stood some chance of finding the child before it was too late.

★ ★ ★

'You've really thought this through, haven't you?'

The admiration in the Great Alexei's voice warmed Chloé to the core. He was taking her seriously. He hadn't told her off for being on the trapeze, and once they were back on the ground he'd watched in quiet contemplation as she demonstrated somersaults, handsprings, backflips and aerial cartwheels. Now that she had laid her master plan before him, he studied her intently.

'But you do realise it would mean being on the road for most of the year?'

She nodded.

'No nipping back home to see Maman or Papa.'

'I don't have a Papa.'

'Right. Well, friends then.'

Chloé shrugged indifferently.

'There's no one you'd miss?'

'No.' The word rang hollow even to her ears.

Fabian. She'd miss him. And Annie. Who'd walk the dogs with her? The Rogalle twins too, even if they got on her nerves sometimes. There was Josette as well. And, of course, Maman.

Then Chloé thought about Jacques, her silent companion, the only one who'd trusted her with a secret, and she felt her throat constrict. Who'd talk to Jacques while she was away? Only Josette, because no one else could see him.

The Great Alexei saw the tears but pretended not to as a fierce hand slapped them away.

'Come on,' he said, reaching out to ruffle those curls which had caught his heart. 'Let's take you home.'

'I still want to run away with the circus,' said Chloé defiantly as she got into his van. 'Just maybe not yet.'

'Well, when you do,' said the Great Alexei with sincerity, impressed beyond measure by this young acrobat who had found her way to his side, 'there'll be a place for you here. Just remember that.'

★ ★ ★

'They had their last show this afternoon and have started packing up to leave,' announced Christian as he put the phone down.

'No one has seen her?' asked Fabian.

Christian shook his head. 'But that doesn't mean she's not there. She could be hiding somewhere.'

'Oh God, Chloé . . . ' With the sense of loss she'd anticipated back in July now bitterly real, Stephanie put a shaking hand to her mouth, only Fabian's strong grip keeping her from slumping to the ground.

'So what are we waiting for?' demanded Véronique, turning to the gathered crowd. 'Let's get down there and start looking. The more hands the merrier.'

340

'But what about the fête?' Fabian asked as his neighbours began to head for the door en masse. 'It's due to start in half an hour.'

Serge Papon put an arm around the lanky Parisian. 'Some things, Fabian, are more important than a stupid fête.'

'Even when the survival of the commune depends on it?'

Christian smiled. 'This is the commune, Fabian. All of this.' He waved a hand at the large group of friends and neighbours who had come together at the news of Chloé's disappearance, Monique Sentenac and René standing side-by-side despite recent differences of opinion over the merger, Véronique and Josette united through concern. Even Fatima Souquet was there, jangling her car keys impatiently. 'A simple change of name won't affect that.'

'Come on,' said René, voice gruff with emotion. 'At this rate the circus will be gone by the time we get there.'

'Actually,' said Véronique looking down the road at a gaily coloured van bedecked with clowns that was approaching, 'I think the circus has just arrived!'

★   ★   ★

'Maman!' Chloé was out of the van and running before the handbrake was even on. She'd forgotten about their arguments. Forgotten about the secrets. She'd forgotten why she'd run away in the first place.

'Oh my love!' Stephanie fell to her knees, arms

341

clasped around her daughter, fingers entwined in soft curls. 'You had us so worried.'

'Sorry,' came a voice from beyond the throng that had gathered around the reunited family. 'I should have called the minute I found her. I didn't think.'

The people of Fogas parted to get a look at this newcomer, the slight man with the muscular frame, jet-black curls around a dark face.

'I'm Alexei Bénac,' he said.

'The Great Alexei!' proclaimed Chloé, stretching out a hand to hold his. 'He's the best acrobat in the world, Maman, and he said I can join his circus when I'm older.'

Heads swivelled to Stephanie, knowing her opinion of that particular profession. But she didn't say a word. She was still on her knees, staring at the man who had walked through the crowd to stand next to Chloé, two dark heads together as the girl chatted away.

It was him. She'd known when she saw the poster in Chloé's room. Now he was here in the flesh. Despite her state, she was aware of people doing double takes, then one or two gasps of surprise, and she knew they too must be making the connection. Because it was so clear when you saw the pair of them together.

★　★　★

Alexei hadn't noticed her. He'd seen the bowed head, the red curls. But it hadn't rung any bells. His attention had been claimed by Chloé. It was only when she stood up that he realised. That

342

slim figure, the way she had of holding herself which conveyed an air of mystery. And then he heard the helter-skelter of bracelets chiming on her arm.

He looked at her and he was back in Finistère all those years ago. 'Stephanie?'

'You know each other?' An incredulous Chloé was staring at both of them.

'Perrrhaps I should take Chloé into the barrr and make herrr a hot chocolate?' said Annie, wise eyes watching Stephanie dealing with the shock.

'No!' Stephanie reached out and put an arm around her daughter. 'No more secrets. That's what caused this mess in the first place. She deserves the truth.'

Puzzled, Chloé's gaze swung round the ring of adults, the Great Alexei staring at Maman, Maman staring back at him, everyone else staring at Chloé. They all seemed to know what was going on, apart from Fabian who wasn't the quickest person in the world. He was standing to one side, eyes on the ground, looking sad.

'What truth, Maman?'

'Chloé, love, I'd like you to meet your father.'

★ ★ ★

Fabian knew exactly what was going on. He'd seen the resemblance the minute the two of them had stood side by side. Then it had all clicked into place. Chloé's innate acrobatic skills. Stephanie's weird dislike of the circus. Had she somehow known, this amazing woman who

343

could see the future? Had she worried that she might lose her child, the genetic pull of ancestry calling Chloé from birth?

He edged to the outside of the gathering, able to see over the heads to witness Chloé's mouth drop open as she heard the momentous news.

'So, if he's my real father, then that Bruno man and his family can't claim me?' she asked her mother, who looked as though she'd been slapped.

'No, love . . . he can't . . . you're safe,' Stephanie stuttered and there was a blur of red and black as Chloé hurled herself at the Great Alexei who, despite his evident shock, managed to catch her.

'She's my daughter?' the acrobat murmured in wonderment, his strong arms closing around the sobbing child.

Then Stephanie was crying too, a rare sight in Fogas, and Fabian watched Annie, good old Annie, gather her into an embrace while those around them found their voices, an excited hubbub filling the air.

'Are you okay?' A small hand clasped his arm and he looked down to see the worried face of Tante Josette.

'Fine. Why wouldn't I be?' He knew his smile was pained.

'Right!' Serge Papon stepped forward to control the growing excitement. 'I think we need to give these people a bit of space. Which is just as well, as according to my watch, we are supposed to be opening the fête!'

'Merde!' Christian slapped a hand to his

forehead. 'I forgot to ask Philippe to bring his accordion. We don't have any entertainment for the aperitifs.'

'I think we do,' said René, never one to overlook an opportunity. He turned to the Great Alexei. 'Seeing as you're part of the Fogas family now, perhaps . . . ?'

Laughter. People dispersing to their stalls, shaking their heads at the turn of events. And René's audacity. No one noticed the lanky figure slink into the garden centre. No one saw him dismantling the table he'd set up, candles, cloth, champagne glasses. He silently packed all of it away before throwing the red roses into the river. For while he wasn't the best at figuring out human relationships, Fabian Servat knew for certain that there wasn't a chance in hell he would be proposing to Stephanie tonight.

★ ★ ★

Bedlam? Jérôme Ulrich laughed to himself. If that had been the situation before, what followed on from the search for young Chloé Morvan was even more chaotic. Asked by Serge to officially open proceedings, the préfet had obliged and then found himself roped into judging the *croustade* competition by the Englishman who ran the Auberge. Suspecting the honour was a double-edged sword and wary of the tension simmering around the women standing behind their exhibits, he'd announced it was an impossible task. Declaring all the pies winners, he'd left a hapless Paul Webster to sort out the allocation of prizes.

Meanwhile, Karine had been persuaded to help out on the stall run by the *comité des fêtes*. Issued with an apron, she'd stood and made *beignets aux pommes* with Véronique Estaque and René Piquemal, the queue devouring the doughnuts as fast as they emerged from the hot oil.

With the arrival of the sous-préfet from St Girons, Jérôme and Karine had been released from their duties and Serge Papon and Pascal Souquet had escorted the three dignitaries down the road to the apple press, which was being operated by Bernard Mirouze. Daft beagle at his feet, the *cantonnier* was bright red in the face as he wound a handle on the contraption while fruit gathered from orchards and fields — and surreptitiously from the gardens of absent second-home owners — was tipped into a vat above him. At the far end of the complicated piece of machinery, Christian Dupuy was filling bottles full of golden apple juice and distributing them to the locals.

After the delicious juice had been sampled and praised, Serge Papon then took the sous-préfet on a guided tour of the village, leaving Jérôme and his wife to enjoy the fête.

'It's amazing, isn't it?' said Karine as she slipped her arm through her husband's and they wandered back over the bridge towards the orchard. 'What an atmosphere.'

She was right. As well as the stall selling *beignets aux pommes*, there were others laden with honey, local cheese, jam, a brazier of hot chestnuts, a table covered in handmade knives, damask blades aswirl in the dimming light, leather goods, herbs and spices and even one selling toy bulls, which was besieged with customers. Then in the orchard, underneath the strings of fairy lights, there was a *marché aux puces*, wares ranging from knick-knacks to old records to vintage clothing. And all around, milling from stall to stall, were hordes of people, the road almost overtaken with the crowds that had turned out for this last fête of the season, which, Jérôme suspected, was only just getting started.

★ ★ ★

'Have you brought a tiger?'
  'No.'
  'An elephant then?'
  'No. We don't have animals.'
  'What kind of bloody circus are you, man?'
  Backstage, the exasperated sigh and the inhalation on a Gauloise were met with a burst of laughter and a shake of dark curls.
  'We'll show you.'

★ ★ ★

René stepped out onto the stage, not entirely sure about the quality of the act he was about to introduce, but confident, despite the absence of animals, that it had to be a better opening than moody Philippe Galy squeezing the life out of his grandfather's music box.

'Mesdames et messieurs,' he said into the microphone. 'Welcome to the Fogas Fête des Pommes!'

A hearty cheer greeted him, made even louder when Christian and Paul Webster began circulating with trays of aperitifs.

'And to kick off tonight in style, I give you — ' He glanced over at Bernard Mirouze beating a wooden spoon on a metal beer keg in imitation of a drum roll ' — the Great Alexei and Sons.'

'And daughter!' came a disgruntled female voice from backstage.

'And daughter too, of course!'

★ ★ ★

'I can't believe we missed the scan!' said Lorna with a laugh as she sat down to relieve her swollen ankles. 'It's all I've been thinking about for weeks and then, poof! It just went clear out of my head.'

'Same here.' Paul gave a wry smile. 'It's hardly surprising, given all that was going on. Did you get through to the hospital and explain?'

She nodded. 'They were great. But they can't fit me in next week thanks to the bank holiday. So we'll have to wait until the week after to see this little one on the screen.'

Stroking a hand over her stomach, she felt two solid kicks as though her baby was mimicking the youngsters performing acrobatics on the stage. What a place this was, she mused. They had settled here partly by chance and now their child would be joining this community. Becoming part of Fogas.

She realised, with a shock, how passionately she wanted to keep it that way.

★ ★ ★

'She's amazing!' said Annie as the four tumbling figures came to rest to rapturous applause.

Stephanie smiled. She could hardly believe it. All those years she'd tried to deflect Chloé from her heritage, worried that she would lose her to the lure of the circus, and here she was, this child of hers, giving her first public performance. With her father and her two half-brothers.

A flash of sequins and a blur of movement, more somersaults and aerial cartwheels and other things that Stephanie could barely watch, hands over her eyes until they had all landed safely.

More applause and then, at Alexei's urging, Chloé and the two boys, who were a couple of years younger than her, stepped forward to take a bow and the place erupted.

That was Chloé up there. Her Chloé. The one who had gone missing over the summer. She was back with a broad smile on her face.

It was only at the word missing that Stephanie realised — she hadn't seen Fabian in ages.

★ ★ ★

'What a night!' said Christian, trying to shout over the music, the group Stephanie had organised younger and livelier than their predecessors.

'What a day too,' said Véronique with a laugh.

'Life doesn't get any quieter around here, does it?'

Christian smiled, as happy with the success of the fête as with the fact that whatever tension had been between himself and the postmistress, it seemed to have been submerged under the pandemonium of the afternoon. 'Did our VIP guests have a good time?'

'They seemed to,' said Véronique, who had just escorted Jérôme Ulrich and his wife to their car. 'Despite how it all started. The préfet spent most of the evening listening to Papa reminisce about his time down the mines. His wife had to prise him away.'

'Two glasses of René's home-made hooch and anyone would find Serge's stories fascinating,' remarked the farmer with a grin.

'And now, it's Johnny Hallyday time!'

The lead singer's announcement triggered a wave of movement as, caught up in fête fever, a surge of people made for the dance floor. Alain Rougé and René led the charge, a protesting Annie being dragged along by Chloé and her half-brothers while Stephanie was trying to persuade Alexei to join them. Even Gaston the shepherd was strutting away. As it seemed there was no escaping France's favourite rock star, Christian abandoned all the resolutions he'd made that morning and decided to seize this second chance with the postmistress.

'Véronique, would you care to — '

'Christian!' Serge Papon was striding towards them, his face a worrying shade of purple.

'Papa!' Véronique stretched out a hand to her

350

father, not at all happy with how he looked. 'Whatever is the matter?'

'The results are in,' he said.

It took a moment for Christian to catch on. Sarrat council. The meeting to vote on the merger had been tonight. 'And?'

Serge shook his head, looking out over the jiving bodies, laughter and singing carrying into the star-strewn sky. 'It's all been a waste of time. The bastards voted unanimously in favour.'

Véronique sank onto a chair and Christian's hands balled into fists at his sides. Then he noticed the commotion down on the dance floor.

'Call an ambulance!' shouted René, bent over a prostrate form. 'Quickly. I think it's a heart attack.'

★ ★ ★

Pascal Souquet stood on the sidelines as the stretcher was rushed in. The crowd parted to let the medics through. But it was too late — the first deputy knew from the way everyone was looking at each other, a sombre air replacing the jollity of only minutes before.

He assembled his face to match their sorrow. Hid the sense of relief. Because he knew what this meant. First the vote in Sarrat and now Fogas had lost another vital member of the population. The sous-préfet wouldn't be able to support them anymore. No one would.

Fogas was as dead as the blanket-covered form being wheeled out of the gardens.

20

'I can't help you, Serge. You know that.'

The mayor of Fogas gave a grunt of acknowledgement. He knew all right.

'My report will go in as planned and it will be favourable, thanks to the efforts you've made,' continued the sous-préfet. 'But following the tragic end to the fête, I can no longer conceal the fact that your population has dropped below the required margin for the number of councillors you have. That's going to weigh heavily against you when it comes to the question of whether or not you are viable as a community.'

'So what do you suggest?'

Splaying his fingers across the surface of his desk, the *fonctionnaire* contemplated them before replying. 'Spike the préfet's guns.'

'A vote?'

'Yes. And soon. Put the matter before your council now while you still have people on it that support you. Come the next local elections, with a reduced Conseil Municipal you might find you no longer hold the balance of power.'

'But a vote is risky.'

'Riskier than having the préfet issue a decree and take the decision away from you? Because once he puts pen to paper on this, you are committed to a merger, like it or not. At least if you call the council together to vote on it, you might still change his mind.'

'Not if we vote for it.'

'There's a chance of that?'

Serge shrugged. 'Possibly. People have been swayed by the promises being made across the river.'

A look of distaste crossed the sous-préfet's face. 'By Henri Dedieu?'

'Who else? The man is masterful. Makes me feel I'm past my prime.'

'That'll be the day!'

Serge mustered a smile and got to his feet. 'A vote it is then. But it's likely to tear the rest of what's left of my commune apart.'

* * *

Jérôme Ulrich stood at the window of his office, watching the river below and feeling the burden of his position. He had a decision to make. One which wasn't going to be easy after the unexpected pleasure he and his wife had derived from the Fogas fête.

Having anticipated the usual sterile fulfilment of duty that such occasions necessitated, they'd been unprepared for the gusto with which the locals had celebrated. Or for the way they'd welcomed Jérôme and Karine and treated them as neighbours, no fuss made of rank or status. The hospitality had even extended to a liberal pouring of René Piquemal's *eau de vie*, although given that the clear liquor lay somewhere between vodka and paint-stripper in potency, the honour was a dubious one.

For the young couple, the *joie de vivre* had

carried over into the weekend. They'd stayed in the area, booking into a small auberge up in Salau in the valley above Seix to make the most of the *Toussaint* bank holiday, and had enjoyed two days of hiking and good food. It had been like a second honeymoon, the mountain air rekindling the passion between them that had lain dormant under the pressures of his office. It had been enough to leave Jérôme grinning all the way to work.

His smile had quickly faded when he'd reached his desk and realised that things had developed in his absence. With the commune of Sarrat having decisively come down in favour of unification, the sad news out of Fogas meant the road was open for him to complete the process; the merger would be going ahead.

With this in mind, the préfet was contemplating the next step. Should he issue a decree to speed things along and quell any lingering resistance in the mountain villages? Although, it was a resistance that was dwindling, if this morning's audacious email from Pascal Souquet could be trusted. The first deputy had made it clear that he would support the préfet's anticipated motion and suggested that a fair chunk of the council could be persuaded to join him. He had therefore urged that the official wheels be set in motion.

The obsequious tone had irked Jérôme. As had the notion of a deputy undermining his mayor in this manner, even more so when that mayor was Serge Papon. An unlikely affinity between the leader of Fogas and the préfet, possibly born of their shared mining backgrounds, had developed into mutual respect over the last six weeks, making this deception distasteful. But Jérôme Ulrich wasn't one to let sentimentality get in the way of duty. And so the email had further strengthened his resolve.

A light knock at the door prefaced the entrance of his secretary.

'Your ten o'clock appointment is here, Monsieur Préfet.'

'Thanks. Show them in, please.'

He resumed his seat with a sense of anti-climax. He'd been looking forward to meeting the person who'd dared to clash swords so openly with him, the force behind the blog that had created such a furore. The events of the past four days, however, had rendered this conversation redundant. But at least he would be able to put a face to the anonymous postings of *SOS Fogas*.

The door opened and when he realised who was standing there, it took all his years of diplomatic training not to blurt out, 'You?'

* * *

'Who'd have thought it? And on the dance floor of all places.' Josette shook her head mournfully and cleared away the empty coffee cups cluttering the bar.

'With a Gauloise in his mouth and a drink to hand. Can't think of a better way to go myself,' said René in all seriousness.

'It could be arranged!' said Christian.

'You've got to admit, though,' said Annie with

355

a wicked grin. 'It smells a lot betterrr in herrre now.'

'Maman! You can't say things like that.' Véronique's protest was tempered with a laugh.

'She's right, though. Gaston's aroma was definitely an acquired taste.' Christian's face turned serious. 'And his death might have more of an impact on us than we think.'

'How?' asked René.

'Serge is meeting the sous-préfet today to discuss the report following the fête.'

'Huh! I don't see how it can be anything less than favourable thanks to the magnificent show we put on. Fogas has never looked so good.'

Christian shrugged. 'That's not enough now. Not after the vote over in Sarrat. Add to that the fact that our population is dwindling and we've dipped below the quota for the number of councillors we have, I'd say we're in more trouble than before.'

'Merde!' René struck the bar with his fist, clearly not having thought through the implications wrought by the sudden demise of Gaston the shepherd on a commune that was already dying. 'It's going to go ahead, isn't it?'

'Not until we've voted on it,' said Serge Papon, entering the room with a thunderous demeanour.

'We're having a vote? When?' asked Christian.

'Next Wednesday. So those of us on the council have a week to make up our minds. I'm heading up to the town hall now to tell Céline to prepare the notification letters. And this time I'll bloody deliver them by hand.'

356

'Probably just as well you do,' said Véronique. 'The electricity company is about to start ripping up the road and it's really going to have repercussions on the post. Seeing as the van won't be able to get through, we've had to arrange for a motorbike to be left in Fogas for the postman to pick up once he's off the shuttle bus. It's bound to delay things terribly.'

Serge cursed. He'd completely forgotten. Work was due to commence that morning, meaning that the only way to reach the mountain village during working hours would be to wait for the shuttle bus to take you from La Rivière to where the road was dug up, cross the work zone on foot and then catch the shuttle bus on the other side to the *lavoir* in Fogas. He could do without his car being stuck down in La Rivière for the day.

'Are the buses in place already?' he asked.

'Not yet. Philippe Galy was in a moment ago, moaning about the disruption,' said Josette. 'But he managed to drive down. So if you're quick you might get through before they close it.'

'Come on. I'll give you a hand with the letters,' said Véronique and she slipped her arm through his and accompanied him out to his car.

In the tense silence left behind, Josette started filling the dishwasher, keeping her head well below the bar and out of sight. After a fantastic fête, she'd hoped that the tension over the merger would evaporate into the autumn air. Now it seemed as though it would be back with a vengeance and, with no clue as to which way she was going to vote, she was going to be caught up in the middle of it.

'So, I'm from a long line of acrobats,' Chloé said, concluding her account of Alexei's amazing pedigree as a performer, his grandparents on both sides with the circus in their blood and his mother and father having starred in *La Piste aux Étoiles*, the famous TV programme dedicated to the arts of the big top. 'No wonder I'm a natural!'

Her grin tempered the arrogance as she helped her mother lift the unsold pots of chrysanthemums off the display racks. They'd spent a hectic weekend at the garden centre, Chloé manning the till while Stephanie and Fabian tried to keep up with demand for the traditional *Toussaint* flowers, the solemn grave-yard around the corner now alight with their colours the day after All Saints' Day. But mother and daughter had still found time to talk and unravel all the tangled threads that had led to Chloé running away.

'No wonder indeed,' said Stephanie, hugging her child, something she hadn't been able to stop doing over the last few days, partly because she was so relieved to have her home unscathed, but also because Chloé no longer pulled away from her embrace.

It had been a shock to find out that the poor girl had been living in fear of being claimed by Bruno Madec's family, thanks to an overheard conversation and a birth certificate with no name on it. What hurt more was that Chloé hadn't felt she could talk about it, aware that the adults in her life weren't being honest with her. In trying to protect her child, Stephanie had turned their home into a labyrinth of secrets. It was only natural, then, that Chloé had joined the ranks of those with something to hide.

The other great shock of the weekend had been Alexei Bénac. Seeing him on the poster in Chloé's room hadn't prepared Stephanie for meeting him again, eleven years on from that fateful encounter in Finistère. Her husband, Bruno, had been away at a funeral in St Malo, the evidence of his temper too vivid on her pale skin for him to want her by his side. She hadn't baulked at his suggestion that she stay behind, not wishing to be seen or for questions to be asked. Because she hadn't been in a state to answer them.

She'd spent the day indoors, trying to come to terms with a relationship she was beginning to suspect was beyond redemption. But as dusk fell, she'd been overwhelmed by a need to be near the sea, to let the wind sweep across her and wash her clean, the way the waves washed the beach. Pulling up the hood of her sweatshirt to shield her bruised face, she'd headed down to the shore.

The lights had been visible from a long way off. A circus. Bright red canvas flapping against the backdrop of a darkening sea. She'd been drawn despite herself, pulled towards the gaiety that had become so alien to her. The performance was already under way, sharp bursts of applause carrying over the wind as she approached. Not feeling up to entering, she'd walked around to the back of the tent to sit on the ground facing the beach, the lights dancing across the white crests of the waves, visible despite the approaching dark.

He'd tripped over her. Fresh from a performance, he'd left the big top to catch his breath and smell the sea. With that stealthy gait of his, she hadn't heard him coming over the cries of delight from the audience as the clowns entertained. And in her dark clothes, tucked up against the tent, he hadn't seen her. He'd stumbled, cursed and then realised she was there. He'd held out a hand to help her up and her hood had fallen away from her face.

A hand on her cheek. That was how he'd reacted. No questions. No condemnation. He'd simply put his hand on her cheek, fingers brushing lightly over the discoloured skin as though trying to heal it. She'd closed her eyes at his touch. It was all it took.

They'd spent the night together. The next morning she'd snuck out of his caravan and made her way home, not asking for contact details and leaving none behind. Bruno had returned from the funeral vowing to change, and Stephanie, racked with guilt at her treachery, had made every effort to meet him halfway. Three weeks later, she'd known she was pregnant. She'd also known that her baby had been conceived in the shadow of the big top. When Bruno resorted to his old ways, this stranger's child had made Stephanie strong. Strong enough to escape a brutality she wasn't sure she would have been able to on her own.

Now Bruno was in prison, serving a long sentence for attempted murder. Her divorce papers had come through that morning. And Chloé had somehow found her father and brought him, a widower with two young boys, back into their lives.

It had been fantastic to see Alexei again. Having sent the circus on ahead to their next stop, he'd booked into the Auberge in La Rivière with his boys, choosing to spend the two days between performances in the company of Chloé and Stephanie. Not that they'd had much free time, *Toussaint* meaning long hours working for the Morvan ladies. But on Sunday afternoon they'd all managed to get together and had enjoyed a riverside picnic down at the 'beach', the kids splashing and squealing in the cold waters on a bright sunny day. Watching from the rocks, the two adults had swapped histories, her violent marriage and the tragic loss of his wife in a car accident proving sombre tales against the backdrop of children's laughter. When Alexei and the boys had left for Font-Romeu yesterday morning, they'd promised to be back soon.

But as always, life was never completely smooth. Just as one corner of her world acquired some sense of order, so another was thrown into chaos. Normally Stephanie was willing to accept such capricious behaviour on the part of the Fates. This time, however, the chaos was in the corner of her world that concerned Fabian, and it was making her uneasy.

Apart from helping out at work, he'd hardly been around since the fête. He'd moved out of the cottage and back into the old Papon house at the other end of Picarets, saying that she needed time with her daughter. But she knew that he was really giving her space to resolve her relationship with Alexei. It was typical of him. So considerate. Despite living on a different planet, he was the most sensitive man she had ever met. She didn't want to lose him.

Brooding over the Parisian, she almost missed it. A smudge of scarlet on the ground where she had just placed the last unwanted chrysanthemum. It was a trampled rose. She didn't sell roses at this time of year. Curious, she bent down to pick it up and noticed four evenly spaced indentations in the grass as though a table had stood there recently.

She twirled the rose between long fingers, puzzled. Fabian had the only other key to the front gates. What could he have been doing that required a table and red roses? And why hadn't he mentioned it? She needed to talk to him. Soon. Or this gulf that was growing between them would only widen.

'What's up, Maman?' Chloé was regarding her with concern.

'Nothing, love . . . ' Stephanie paused, about to deflect the question, but her daughter's open face forestalled her. What had they said about no more secrets?

'It's Fabian,' she confessed. 'I'm worried about him.'

Chloé tipped her head to one side, suddenly wise beyond her years. 'So am I. Why don't I go and get us both a hot chocolate and we can talk about it.'

Stephanie watched her run across the road to

the bar and wondered when her daughter had become so grown up.

* * *

The Great Alexei. It was so typical of his luck that his rival in love would have the prefix 'Great'. Fabian wiped down the coffee machine, hands moving on autopilot as he stared across at the garden centre where Chloé and Stephanie were sitting on a bench, his hot chocolate warming them against the chill wind that had arrived with November.

'You're a good man, Fabian.' Josette was by his side, a hand on his arm. 'You're doing the right thing, giving her time to think.'

Fabian snorted. A good man. That was nothing when he was up against someone great. If he'd taken his chances and managed to complete one of his three proposal attempts, she would be his now. But instead . . .

He let his eyes rest on the flash of red hair, the beautiful face that was so earnest, bent towards Chloé, confiding in her daughter everything she couldn't tell him. Would she leave with this man who had appeared out of nowhere? Given he was the father of her child, it seemed probable. In fact, statistician to the bone, Fabian knew that the odds were definitely stacked against him.

* * *

Lorna Webster felt fat. And tired. And grumpy. Another five weeks of this. That was all she could think as she lowered her immense body onto a chair outside a restaurant and tried not to cry out loud at the relief. The trauma of Chloé's disappearance, followed by the festivities of the fête and then the drama surrounding the death of Gaston the shepherd in the grounds of the Auberge had sapped her of her last vestiges of energy. Yet foolishly, she'd agreed to accompany Paul to Foix to go shopping while he attended the alcohol awareness course to obtain the vital certificate the gendarmes were so keen he have.

She'd lasted an hour. Long enough to buy a pack of three adorable sleepsuits and a soft cot blanket covered in cheeky little birds. Then she'd had to nip to the toilet in a café, so she'd stayed and had a herbal tea. Then she'd been hungry so she'd had a millefeuille from the bakery.

Walking back through the market, she'd spotted a stall selling handmade wooden toys and had been taken by the mobiles of farmyard animals, flowers, cars, all in primary colours, twisting in the breeze that danced down the Cours Gabriel Fauré. Unable to choose between trains or tractors, she'd bought one of each, a rash decision that she would keep from Paul's ridicule until after the baby was born. Finally, she'd collapsed on a chair in the November sunshine and decided to have an early lunch.

She pulled one of the mobiles out of its bag, the reds and blues and yellows like a burst of spring, and her grumpiness subsided. She imagined the toy hanging in the open bedroom window, the green fields and the peak of Cap de Bouirex beyond. It would be the perfect distraction from the state of the room. She smiled. If only she could convince Paul of that. Make him see that there was no point in panicking because they hadn't got round to redecorating. With the love of both parents, their baby wouldn't notice the sagging ceiling, the garish floral wallpaper or the frayed carpet.

At least, that's what Lorna hoped. Because in a chain reaction of setbacks, the conversion of the Auberge's huge attic into a living space for their growing family, which Paul had scheduled for this autumn, had been delayed until the New Year. It made no sense to start on it until the leaking roof had been replaced and the grant they'd been awarded by the Chambre de Commerce for that very purpose was taking a long time to process. In the meantime, they would make do with their ramshackle bedroom and would spend another winter emptying buckets that were strategically placed beneath the worst of the slipped slates.

But none of it would matter. Because their son would be here.

'Mind if I join you?'

She looked up from the mobile in her hands to see Véronique Estaque leaning in to greet her with a big smile.

'It would be a pleasure,' said Lorna, her spirits lifting even higher at the sight of the postmistress.

'Are you shopped out?' Véronique gestured towards the bags with a laugh and got a groan in return.

'Yes. I'm ready for home but I'm not meeting

Paul until after one. What about you?'

'I'm on an errand for Papa. He had some letters that he wanted delivered by hand, so I offered to pop over with them.'

'About the merger?'

The postmistress nodded, the sunny disposition of moments before disappearing to leave a cloud of apprehension.

'Is it going to go ahead?' asked Lorna.

'It all depends on Wednesday next week. Serge has called a meeting of the Conseil Municipal and they'll vote on it.' Véronique shrugged. 'It's too close to say. And even if we do reject the proposal, there's nothing to stop the préfet from issuing a decree anyway, and then that would be that.'

'So you're here on a mercy mission?'

The postmistress laughed. 'Yes. I suppose I am. Although going on one knee and begging isn't usually my style.'

'Merde!' A face of sharp bones and pinched skin had caught Lorna's attention. She flicked open her menu and ducked behind it, gesturing for Véronique to do the same. 'Don't look. It's Fatima Souquet heading this way.'

But Véronique Estaque hadn't got to be the news gatherer she was by hiding behind menus. Intrigued, she watched Fatima, brow creased in concentration, cross the road and pass right by the two Fogas women without even seeing them. Then she walked through the Halle aux Grains to a café where a tired-looking Pascal Souquet was waiting for her, hailing her with a raised arm.

'Damn him,' muttered Véronique with the conviction of a believer. 'Looks like I'm not the only one over here making a last-minute case. And I doubt he's trying to save Fogas.'

Filled with despair, she ordered a *salade au jambon* knowing she wouldn't be able to eat a thing. She was relieved to discover that the Englishwoman had an appetite big enough for both of them.

*   *   *

By late afternoon, eleven letters of notification about the forthcoming council meeting had been distributed to the members of the Conseil Municipal for the commune of Fogas. Serge had personally delivered three of them, Pascal Souquet and Bernard Mirouze within walking distance of the town hall and Philippe Galy a ten-minute drive to a small hamlet further up the mountain. Serge had also taken the precaution of instructing the secretary, Céline, to include his own name in the list of addressees, determined that there would be nothing about the procedure that could come back to bite them should they be so lucky as to win the vote.

With the Fogas end of the delivery taken care of, Bernard Mirouze had been dispatched to endure the shuttle bus down to La Rivière to hand over five more. One went to Monique Sentenac in the first house on the way down, another to Alain Rougé beyond the old school and, since Bernard was on foot thanks to the roadworks, he left the letters for Christian and

367

René in the bar, along with Josette's.

The final two envelopes, destined for Toulouse and the second-home owners Lucien Biros and Pascal's cousin, Geneviève Souquet, had been entrusted to Véronique. Knowing the allegiances of these particular councillors lay with the faction that might support the merger, Serge was taking no chances. As she was already going to Foix at his behest, his daughter would go to the main post office in the town and have the council letters sent registered delivery. That way there could be no claims that due notification hadn't been received, and whatever the outcome, the vote could not be nullified by an administrative glitch.

Satisfied that all procedures had been followed correctly, Serge pulled a piece of paper towards him and drew two columns down the page. Labelling one 'For' and the other 'Against', he pondered the forthcoming meeting.

Pascal and his cohorts from Toulouse, they were an easy call. In favour. Serge wrote the names down in the appropriate column. And on the opposite side he included himself, René and Bernard, who would do anything Serge asked him to. Philippe Galy was a difficult guess, the beekeeper having joined forces with the first deputy mayor in recent months. Erring on the side of pessimism, Serge added another to Pascal's side. Which meant, given the growing hostility between beekeeper and ex-policeman, Alain Rougé would probably vote with Serge.

Four each. That left Christian, Monique Sentenac and Josette. Serge had a gut feeling about the first two, but Josette? She was the one unknown.

Her husband, Jacques, would be rotating in his grave if he knew that his wife was considering condoning a merger with Sarrat. And while Serge understood some of her concerns as a business-woman and respected her opinions as a friend, he was the mayor of Fogas and all his years of politicking were telling him that the future of his commune quite possibly lay in her hands. Which meant he had to deter her. Pull her off balance somehow and back into his fold.

It came to him in a flash of Papon brilliance. Using the disruption caused by the road being out of action as a legitimate excuse, he could dictate that the town hall wasn't a suitable venue for the meeting. And accordingly invoke his power to name another setting. Having already announced that it would be a closed session with the public barred from attending, size wasn't a problem. So he could hold the election down in the bar, a place where the lingering presence of Jacques might be enough to stay Josette's hand and make her vote the way her husband would have, out of loyalty to his memory if nothing else.

The bar it was. He would get Céline to write memos informing the councillors of his decision and he would deliver them himself this evening when the road reopened. It would give him an excuse to go past the Estaque farm, after all.

*   *   *

Once October passes in the high Pyrenees, the warm summer evenings rapidly become a distant memory and the nights turn cold and frosty. On the second evening in November, as soon as the sun disappeared behind the mountains above La Rivière, the temperature fell sharply and the wind picked up. For those like Annie Estaque who could interpret the vagaries of the weather in this region, there was even the threat of an early snowfall in the air.

It was hardly the night to be on a stake-out. But Pascal Souquet had no choice. He yawned widely, slapped a hand against his cheek and tried to will himself awake. Two o'clock in the morning. He'd been parked up for over an hour, watching the home of the last name on his list, waiting for a sign that he had finally identified the culprit who was causing him such trouble. So far, there had been nothing but the dark space of window up above him and the creak of an unlatched shutter flapping gently in the wind.

Ten nights in a row. All of them spent cooped up in the Range Rover, a flask of coffee by his side, Fauré's *Requiem* featuring the sublime baritone of Michel Piquemal — how the Ariège had produced two musicians of such quality astounded him — floating softly from the stereo while he fixed his eyes on his neighbours' homes and hoped for a break. He hadn't been lucky to date. Four times in the last week *SOS Fogas* had posted blogs, all four uploaded between one-thirty and two o'clock, the time period Pascal was targeting. During all of these postings he had been sitting outside one of the houses on his list. And not once had it been the right one.

It meant of course, that he'd ruled out all but

one name. Which also meant, if he had been correct with his instincts in the first place, he was finally going to succeed. Only thing was, he needed it to be soon. Like tonight. With the vote on the merger having been announced, Henri Dedieu had been on the phone threatening him in no uncertain terms. He wanted *SOS Fogas* out of the way so that the mischievous blogger could cast no more influence on proceedings. Already this week there had been posts raising concerns about the cost of the merger, echoing René's questions from the meeting back in September and encouraging the inhabitants of Fogas to demand the answers that had been promised. With the vote hanging in the balance, the mayor of Sarrat wanted no more revelations.

Especially as there was plenty to be revealed.

Pascal smirked in the darkness, his confidence in the future he'd marked out for himself growing by the day. Once the vote was out of the way next Wednesday, he would be safe, his treachery to Fogas no longer an issue as the mountain commune got swept aside and into history and he stepped up to become first deputy mayor of the new community, earmarked to become mayor by Henri Dedieu himself on his retirement five years hence.

A burst of light spilling out of an unshuttered window pulled him to attention and a shadow crossed the room above. The timing was right. But that wasn't enough. How long would it take to write a post? Ten minutes? Twenty if there was video to upload, which seemed to have become a feature of the blog of late.

He waited, eyes fixed on the backlit half-arch of glass, the wayward shutter cutting back and forth across his view in the breeze. Not that he could see much. An occasional shift of light on the ceiling as the person moved. He was just beginning to think it was another false alarm when his phone beeped and he snatched it up.

An alert from the blog *SOS Fogas* telling him there was a new post online.

He threw his head back against the headrest and laughed. He had her. *SOS Fogas* had been caught. He would call Henri Dedieu first thing in the morning and let him take care of it. Pascal didn't want to know the details. Elated by his achievement, he clicked through to the blog to double-check there had indeed been a post, and as his eyes skimmed the text, the brief taste of victory soured in his throat.

It was impossible. How had she found out?

He read the post a second time to be sure. But it was clear enough. Somehow she'd got hold of information Pascal had only received in an email that afternoon.

Knowing his success in identifying *SOS Fogas* was unlikely to temper the wrath of Henri Dedieu at this latest untimely disclosure, a worried Pascal started the car and turned around to head for home.

★ ★ ★

The squeaking hinge on the shutter had woken her. She'd surfaced from a tortured dream where one moment she was running into the arms of

372

Christian Dupuy and the next, as his lips bent to hers, his features morphed into the suave face of Henri Dedieu, a sneer of condescension replacing the endearments she'd expected to hear.

Knowing the combined worries of the merger and her love life would be enough to keep her awake without the added interruption of the protesting hinge, Véronique had got up to latch the shutter. But once in the lounge, she'd decided to make herself a hot chocolate and had sat surfing the internet on her laptop while she drank it.

It was when she crossed the floor to the window that she saw him. Pascal Souquet in his Range Rover, face lit up like a ghoul by the mobile in his hand. An unhappy ghoul at that. Whatever he was reading, he didn't like it. She instinctively drew back out of sight as he started the car, turned it around and headed up the road to Fogas.

Puzzled, she opened the window and leaned out to trap the offending shutter, wondering what would cause the first deputy mayor to sit in a car looking so annoyed at two o'clock in the morning down in La Rivière. Taking one more look at her computer before going to bed, on the *SOS Fogas* blog she got part of her answer.

DEDIEU PUSHING FOR MERGER BEFORE CHRISTMAS!

Véronique knew then that she was never going to get back to sleep.

★ ★ ★

Jacques Servat had seen the Range Rover driving up and down the valley in the dead of night over the last week and a bit. Going past the bar at one o'clock and often not returning until gone three, Pascal Souquet was up to something, but Jacques couldn't make head nor tail of it.

Then, tonight, the first deputy had parked in front of the garden centre, car tucked out of sight by the fence and shielded from the street light. Jacques hadn't been able to see much. The occasional blur of movement behind the dark windscreen. But he got the sense that Pascal was watching something. Or someone. But who?

The way the car was facing it was focused on the old school. And with Arnaud Petit having vacated the flat at the front of the building when he left La Rivière in July, that meant it must be Véronique's place which was under the watchful gaze of Pascal.

But why?

Just after two o'clock, shafts of light stretched across the tarmac, suggesting that the post-mistress was up, the bar situated in such a way that Jacques had no direct sight of her windows. But the illumination was sufficient to let him see the shadowy shape in the driver's seat of the Range Rover, the first deputy watching Véronique's window with a smirk. He must have reached for his phone since the dim interior of the car suddenly lit up, Pascal's attention drawn to the screen. He'd laughed. Then he'd looked at the screen again and his eyes had widened, his hand had slipped to his head and he'd looked like a man about to be sick.

Not long after that, he'd turned the car around and gone home.

So, what, wondered Jacques Servat, was the Judas of Fogas up to now? And why was he so focused on Véronique Estaque?

Sensing that he had all the pieces to the jigsaw but not a clue as to the picture they should make, Jacques stared hopelessly into the distant dark. It was only when the first soft flakes of snow began to fall that he gave in and retired to his inglenook. He wasn't the only one to spend the night in restless dreams.

21

What started as a gentle dusting turned into an unseasonably heavy spell of snow. With trees still jealously guarding their leaves from winter's clutches, the woods surrounding the commune of Fogas resonated with the crack of timber and the crash of falling boughs, ashes, chestnuts and oaks succumbing to the unbearable weight loaded onto them by this early precipitation.

Three days after the first flakes and the ground was covered in a layer of white, the roads were treacherous without snow tyres or chains, and Bernard Mirouze had made the first of what would be many passes with the snowplough. He'd also had the first of many crashes, reversing into a street light opposite the old school and rendering it defunct.

Whether this had any impact on the fate that befell Véronique Estaque, no one could agree, but the following night, clouds smothering the stars, she returned from dinner with her mother to the unnaturally darkened surrounds of her flat. Still smiling at the unexpected pleasure of seeing her father seated at the farmhouse table, clearly at home, she turned the corner and realised she couldn't see a thing. Cursing the *cantonnier* for his clumsy driving, she carefully felt her way around the building to the outside staircase. She didn't notice the fresh prints in the snow. Nor did she see the flicker of light behind the closed shutters above her.

It happened in a flash. Or rather a thump, since she saw nothing. One moment she was part way up the stairs. The next, she was lifted off her feet by a solid force, her fingers left clawing at cold air as she fell to the ground. She heard the soft crunch of boots on snow as her attacker fled. She also heard the harsh crack of bone as her arm snapped beneath her.

Out walking his dog, Alain Rougé responded to her cries and came running. Christian, enjoying a solitary meal at the Auberge in his customary Saturday reprieve from his mother's cooking, saw the flashing lights go past and dashed to the scene. He accompanied a distraught Véronique to the hospital in St Girons, not having the heart to tell her in her current state that more bad news awaited. For it transpired that her flat had been burgled. Brutally so.

When she made it home the following day, she stood in the doorway and stared at the mess. Drawers tipped out on the floor, crockery broken, her laptop stolen. They'd left the TV but had put a boot through the screen. Thankfully, the statue of St Germaine that Christian had given her had survived. Little else had.

'Why me?' she'd muttered, hand on the doorjamb to support her trembling legs as for the second time in less than two years she surveyed the wreckage of what had been her home.

No one had an answer. The gendarmes said it was a simple matter of burglary. A single man, judging by the footprints, who, interrupted by Véronique's return, had knocked her down the stairs as he fled. Those discussing the incident over the days that followed had no reason to question this assessment. They blamed the missing street light. They blamed the decline in moral standards. And more than one voiced the wish that Arnaud Petit still lived amongst them. He'd have found the culprit in a matter of hours, the snow providing perfect conditions for tracking.

But Arnaud wasn't there and the thief wasn't caught. And Véronique couldn't rid herself of the feeling that the two hands planted firmly on her chest, which had precipitated her fall, had been deliberate. Jacques Servat, if he'd heard her views, would probably have agreed, convinced that the late-night vigil on her flat by the first deputy mayor had some connection to the despicable crime she'd fallen victim to. But neither of them was anywhere close to guessing the motivation for it.

Opinions on the attack were still keeping the merger from the headlines in the daily round-up of gossip when, on the Monday before the vote, calamity struck again. Already undermined by the work of the electricity company, the road up to Fogas had been further tested by the deluge of wet snow and a large section had collapsed, sliding into the gorge below and taking a telephone pole with it. As, for some reason best known only to France Telecom, the main exchange was up in Fogas, everyone below that point was left without a functioning telephone.

Which meant the entire village of La Rivière. Given that the landslip had happened right next to the roadworks, things were further complicated and Serge Papon couldn't guarantee that the phone line would be repaired before the week was up.

By the time a weakened sun began to struggle over the horizon on Wednesday 10 November, still a long way from cresting the mountains that surrounded the three villages, there was an air of fatigue about the beleaguered commune. Or even resignation. For that evening, in a closed council session at the bar, the eleven elected representatives of Fogas would decide its fate.

It was possible that Lorna Webster was the only one that morning who greeted the momentous day with a sense of relief. She'd woken early, the sky still dark, the silence peculiar to snow making it hard to judge the hour. She lay there for a few seconds, relishing the fact that she didn't have to get up and start breakfast for the guests, the Auberge closed for a week after a hectic *Toussaint*. Then her hand went to her stomach and she knew.

'Paul! Wake up.'

He groaned, worming further under the covers, so she switched on the light.

'Paul,' she hissed, pain beginning to pulse. '*Get up!*'

His eyes flashed open, squinting as the brightness hit them.

'Lorna?'

'Hurry!' She was already struggling for her clothes.

'Oh my God!' He shot out of bed, his foot caught in a trailing cover and he tripped over himself, catching the footboard to prevent his fall. 'Jesus. Lorna. Where are my keys?'

They made a huddle of shadow as they stumbled out into the dawn, Paul keeping a firm hold of his wife on the icy path. The car lights disappeared around the corner just as Josette threw open her bedroom shutters.

It had begun. The day that would decide Fogas was upon them.

★ ★ ★

Always bleary eyed at this early hour, Josette couldn't be sure across the distance and through the half-light, but she thought the car she'd seen haring round the corner down at the Auberge might be Paul's. What was he doing going to town at this hour? Nothing would be open.

It took her a moment, arm outstretched as she flicked the latch into place on the shutter, cold air spiralling into the bedroom behind her. Then she gasped.

The baby! Lorna was having the baby. Today of all days.

Shaking her head at the magnitude of it all, she descended to the bar and crossed straight to the fireplace to rake up the embers. Slivers of flame emerged from the ash, biting at the remnants of a log, snapping at the fresh wood she placed on top of it. Jacques was already awake, over by the window, gaze fixed on some point in the distance. Or the past. He'd been

380

preoccupied for days and as the council meeting approached, he'd taken to staring at her balefully as though he already knew what she was going to do.

How that was possible was beyond her, when she didn't even know herself. When Serge had announced the impending meeting she'd been thrown into a quandary. For months she'd been debating the pros and cons of the merger, trying to make sure that she understood the issue from both sides. But that had been easy when she didn't have to put pen to paper and take a stand. Her vote would be instrumental. Unchangeable. Its impact on the commune possibly catastrophic.

She hadn't signed up for this when she'd been cajoled into standing for the council, Jacques' sudden death creating a vacancy. Wiser now in the ways of local politics and the persuasive powers of Serge Papon, she could see that he had pressured her into it. For the mayor had gambled correctly that the affectionate regard and respect bestowed on Jacques Servat by all who knew him would be automatically transferred to his widow, thereby preventing Pascal from filling the position with yet another second-home owner.

A pawn. That's what she was. She unlocked the front door and twisted the sign to *Ouvert*. An ill-prepared pawn at that. She'd thought she'd have ten days to wrestle with the issue. To convince herself that what she was planning on doing was right. But the last week had been chaotic. First came the news that Henri Dedieu was trying to fast-track the merger, meaning that everything could be decided by Christmas, which had thrown her. Then there had been the attack on Véronique. The appalling weather and the lack of a telephone line didn't help either. Nor did the fact that the bar had become the natural focal point for all debate, more than one discussion over the last few days having degenerated into an argument. On a couple of occasions Christian had to intervene, the looming shape of the big farmer enough to extinguish the heated words.

None of this had brought Josette to a decision. So here she was, twelve hours away from the vote, and she was no clearer as to which way she would swing than she had been after the meeting in Sarrat.

Of course, if she let Jacques have her voice, she knew what the answer would be. His eyes had followed her around as she prepared for the day of business ahead and she sensed he was bursting with frustration at his inability to communicate verbally. She, on the other hand, was glad of his silence. She knew only too well the ear bashing she would be subject to if her ghostly spouse suddenly acquired the power of speech.

'I think Lorna's gone into labour,' she finally said when his beseeching look became unendurable.

A bushy white eyebrow shot up and delight suffused his face. Just as quickly it was gone, the sadness stealing back, his mouth curving downwards. She knew what he was thinking.

This baby was probably going to be the last one ever born in Fogas.

But was that really such a bad thing?

The bell sounded in the shop. Alain Rougé in for his morning baguette. She headed through the archway and prayed the day would be busy. Because that way she wouldn't have to spend it dreading the forthcoming meeting. Or being shadowed by a forlorn husband who, thanks to Serge Papon, would be present when she was required to cast her vote. It was something she wasn't looking forward to.

* * *

'You're up early.' Fabian Servat ran a hand over his face, hiding his yawn, and tried to focus on the small figure on his doorstep.

'You promised me a hot chocolate,' was all she said, pushing past him and throwing her school bag to the floor in the corner while she took a chair at the kitchen table, eyes fixed on him.

'Well, yes . . . but . . . ' He recognised her look and with a sigh began filling the small coffee machine with water.

'We haven't seen much of you lately.' Still that steady gaze, her focus unnerving him, making him wish he was dressed in something more suitable than the pyjamas he'd come down the stairs in. Armour, perhaps.

'I've been busy,' he muttered, not looking up. Quite possibly the worst liar ever, his only chance when choosing to deceive was to avoid direct eye contact. Which of course Chloé knew.

And parried brilliantly.

'Don't you love us anymore?'

His head snapped up, his eyes locked on to hers, and his heart lurched as though whatever was holding it in place between his ribs had disengaged. He was across the room in two long strides to gather her to his chest.

'What on earth makes you say that?'

She shrugged, bottom lip trembling. 'You moved out. And you took the coffee machine with you.'

He pushed a hand through his hair, not knowing how to proceed.

'It's complicated . . . ' he began. And it was. How to explain to an eleven-year-old that he was trying to be noble? That he was repressing every feeling he had to give the woman he loved the space she needed? 'You wouldn't understand.'

'Because I'm a child?' The defiant edge caught him off guard.

'No, Chloé. Never that.' He gave a small laugh. 'More like because I'm an idiot.'

'Perhaps I can help?' She was looking up at him now. Eyes big. Face earnest. And he realised just how much of an idiot he was.

Annie, Véronique, Christian, Josette, even Serge. He'd turned to all of them for help when it came to winning Stephanie's hand. Yet here was the person who knew Stephanie best of all and he'd not even told her of his plans.

'Perhaps you can,' he said, taking a seat opposite her while the coffee machine burped and burbled. 'Thing is, I've been trying to propose to your mother.'

'With a gun.' Chloé giggled.

'Ah, yes. You've heard.' Of course she had. This was Fogas. 'Well, the gun wasn't part of the plot. But anyway, I've not had much luck. Then on Friday, the day of the fête — '

'When I ran away.'

'Yes, exactly. Well, erm, I was planning on trying again.'

Chloé's lips formed a circle of surprise. 'Oh! Why didn't you?'

The wry smile was across his face before he could hide it. 'The Great Alexei turned up.'

'Papa? You didn't propose because of Papa? But what does he have to do with it?'

Fabian got up to make the hot chocolate, hoping she would be distracted. But this was Chloé. One of the most tenacious kids he'd ever encountered. Of course she wasn't distracted.

'Is that why you're staying away? Because of Papa?'

He could see her assessing everything, that mind of hers working away as she formed connections with an ease that left the socially inept Fabian envious.

'Ohhh.' Her hand went to her mouth. 'You think Maman might love him?'

'Don't you?' he countered, placing the drink in front of her.

She paused, took a slurp of the frothy chocolate, and then looked up. 'Maybe. I haven't really thought about it.'

'So there you go.'

She frowned. 'There you go, what?'

He kept the exasperation out of his voice.

'That's why I've stayed away. In case your mother still has feelings for him.'

The frown deepened. 'So you're not going to propose?'

'No. Not now.'

'Because you think Maman might say no?'

'I suppose that's it.'

'But did you know she'd say yes, before Papa turned up?'

Fabian froze. 'No . . . but . . . '

Chloé's arms folded across her chest and the light of victory was dancing in her eyes. 'So what's changed?'

He stared at the wooden table, a finger following the line of an ancient knife across the surface. He had no answer.

'Have you lost your nerve?'

'I don't think I ever had it,' he replied and she laughed.

She made it sound so easy. This situation that he found himself in, that he'd convinced himself was complicated. His eleven-year-old friend had worked out the knots in seconds and was watching him now, waiting for his response.

'If I was to try again . . . would you help me?'

She nodded, a bounce of black curls. 'It's quite simple really,' she said, her reply cutting through the romantic advice that the others had given him. 'If you want Maman to be your wife, you just need to be yourself.'

Then she gave him a wicked grin. 'And I know the perfect way to do that!'

★　★　★

386

The day was passing in a blur for Lorna Webster. Rushed into a maternity ward, she'd been examined by a midwife who'd fired rapid French at her, a combination of pain and panic leaving her understanding almost none of it. Paul hadn't coped much better. Grey with shock, he'd kept a tight hold of her hand and she was sure he needed the support more than she did.

'Will the baby be all right?' he asked repeatedly as the staff popped in and out of the small room over the hours that followed. A smile and 'don't worry' was the standard response.

But it was impossible for them not to worry. Their child was arriving a full four weeks before the due date. Perhaps, Lorna tried to reassure herself, a mistake had been made when it was first calculated? Which would explain why she was the size of a house.

She stared up at the ceiling, trying to do the maths between spasms, but it was hopeless. She could concentrate on nothing but the agonising cramps that made her feel as though her stomach was being rent in two by a vice. When the doctor arrived with an epidural, Lorna didn't even try to protest.

* * *

Stephanie was going through the motions down at the garden centre. She'd put the racks of plants out on the roadside, swept the snow off the path and checked that nothing was suffering in the inclement weather they were having. Now she was bent over a table, finishing off a couple of orders for Armistice Day wreaths, weaving blue cornflowers into garlands for tomorrow's ceremony up in Fogas. All the time she was conscious of only one thing. She was missing Fabian.

He'd become like a stranger to them since the day of the fête. He helped out when she needed him, and he chatted away to Chloé as before. But with her, he was . . . aloof. It was the only word for it. The Parisian had removed himself from her. Literally and metaphorically.

Space, he kept saying. He wanted her to have space. At first she'd understood this and been glad of it. But then she began to wonder. What if it was Fabian who needed the space? It wasn't hard to see that his ordered world must have been jolted when the truth about Chloé's father had been revealed. And by the manner in which it had happened. For a man who liked his life controlled, it was enough to send him spinning out of orbit.

Maybe that's what it was. It made sense. With Alexei appearing out of the blue, Stephanie's past had reared up out of nowhere and Fabian was having to re-evaluate the woman he'd fallen in love with.

She grimaced at the thought. What if it wasn't a positive appraisal?

Twisting the last flower into place, she wiped her hands on a rag and contemplated her work. They were good. A nice addition to a business that was steadily growing. If things kept going as they were, she'd be able to afford gymnastic classes over in Foix for Chloé and perhaps even get enough together to send her on an intensive course at a circus school Alexei had recommended. She'd ask him about it when he came back at the weekend, having rearranged the circus schedule to squeeze in another performance in St Girons for this coming Saturday before heading north for the winter. He'd claimed it was because of the amazing reception they'd had first time round. But Stephanie knew it was so he could see more of Chloé. And perhaps her too?

She wasn't sure how she felt about that. As the church bells began to sound the midday Angelus, she only knew one thing: that it was possible to feel lonely when there was too much space around you.

★　★　★

'Did you find out how Véronique Estaque knew about the merger being fast-tracked?'

Pascal shifted nervously, the blue stare piercing him. 'No . . . I . . . erm . . . not yet.'

The gaze flicked off him and out across the towering pillars of wrecked cars and spare parts that formed an avenue before them. It had been Henri Dedieu's idea to meet at the scrap yard in St Girons, the tangled heaps of metal providing a sinister backdrop in the growing dusk despite their pretty coating of white, and Pascal couldn't help but think that he was being sent a message.

The mayor of Sarrat raised his cigarette to his lips and narrowed his eyes against the smoke as he exhaled. 'I don't like leaks, Pascal. Or loose ends.'

'I understand.'

'Do you?' That look again, Pascal skewered on

the end of it. Then the smile, the one that swept across his mouth but never reached the rest of his face. 'Perhaps, after the unfortunate accident that befell your blog-loving postmistress, you do.'

Throat tightening, Pascal could make no response.

'What about tonight? Is it sorted?'

'Yes, I think — '

'*Think?* Tut tut, Pascal. You'll need to do better than that.'

'It's just . . . I can't guarantee — ' The first deputy broke off, his cheek smarting from the glancing burn of Henri Dedieu's discarded cigarette.

'Listen carefully, you idiot. You will make it happen.' With his head thrust close to Pascal, the mayor's voice was a sibilant hiss of menace. 'My ancestor might have been careless enough to let Fogas slip through his hands, but I won't make the same mistake. And you don't want to be the person who gets in my way.' He took a step back and rubbed a rough finger across the smudge of ash on the terrified deputy's face, as though marking him for penance. 'Secure the vote, Pascal, because this is your last chance. Next time, you won't get off so lightly.'

Boots crunching over oil-stained snow, Henri Dedieu walked away, leaving behind the scent of tobacco smoke in Pascal's nostrils and a sour coating of fear in his mouth.

He wiped his forehead with a shaking hand. The man was insane. The first deputy mayor of Fogas had always suspected it but now, after the events of last week, he had his proof. A simple burglary. He could have countenanced that. Véronique couldn't post on *SOS Fogas* without a laptop and would be hard pressed to get another in the intervening days before the vote. But the violence . . . he hadn't banked on the violence. Not even after the incident with the bear last year. And now Pascal was on the man's radar.

That bloody blog! If only he'd unmasked Véronique Estaque before she'd uploaded that final post. For as Henri Dedieu had pointed out, she could only have heard about his plans through a leak. But from where? Pascal had been notified of the mayor's intentions in an email sent to him mere hours before she wrote about it. And as the only other person to receive the email was a member of the hunting lodge — the man Pascal suspected had helped Véronique down the stairs the other night — then it stood to reason that the mayor was looking across the river for the source of the betrayal.

Still, it was over now. *SOS Fogas* was no more. There had been silence since the attack, the postmistress no doubt shaken considerably by her ordeal. So he had nothing to fear. In a couple of hours they would vote and afterwards he would be able to call Henri Dedieu and tell him that Fogas was finished. It was a call he was looking forward to making.

★ ★ ★

'You're doing really well.' Paul's face hovered above the bed, his hand clasped in hers.

It didn't feel like she was doing well. It didn't

feel like she was doing anything at all. Her entire lower half was numb, the contractions like ripples across a pond, leaving her awareness to scatter across a myriad of subjects.

Fogas. She kept thinking about Fogas. That wonderful place that had stolen her heart on a warm June day and had kept its grip despite the long winters and the impenetrable bureaucracy that would drive a saint to murder. By the time her baby arrived, the meeting would be over and if Stephanie was to be believed, the news wouldn't be good.

'Push, love, they're telling you to push.'

She complied, pushing with all her might, conscious all the time that she was about to give birth to the last child ever born in Fogas.

★ ★ ★

'Don't forget you're meeting in the bar!'

'I won't,' said Christian with a patient smile, knowing his mother's anxiety over the commune was manifesting itself in unnecessary solicitude.

'And don't let any of them deter you, Christian. You vote whichever way you think best,' said his father, leaning in to speak through the open window of the Panda.

'I will, Papa. Thanks.'

André Dupuy squeezed his son's arm and then stepped back to let the 4×4 go, its wheels slithering on the incline out of the farm.

'Rather him than me,' he said, reaching out to draw his wife to his side as they watched Christian depart.

'Do you think he'll vote for it?' asked Josephine.

'Hard to say. His head is telling him to, but his heart . . . '

Josephine nodded. She knew all about her son's heart. It was huge. Filled with generosity, kindness, honesty and a willingness to shoulder the burdens of everyone around him. She suspected it also harboured vast reservoirs of love, and that when Christian finally found an object for his affections, the dam would burst and it would be a marvel to behold.

'I hope to God his heart wins then,' was all she said as they turned from the cold landscape, snow beginning to drift down from the oncoming night sky, to the farmhouse and the fire that awaited them.

★　★　★

Christ, it was dark. Heavy clouds obscured the moon and the trees loomed over him as he drove past Stephanie's cottage and on into Picarets. Around the small square, all the houses were shuttered, lights visible through the cracks at only two of them: the Rogalles' and the old Papon house with its faded Dubonnet advert, where Fabian had taken up residence again in a move that had astounded everyone. Not wanting to dwell on the Parisian's love life in case it opened the box to his own, a distraction he had no need of this evening, Christian let his eye be caught by the flapping sign across the door of Widow Loubet's property.

Sold. The agent so surprised, he'd traipsed all the way up here to erect a sign announcing his achievements. Would it be a permanent resident that moved in? Or yet another second-home owner, the building left empty for the best part of the year and the community gaining little from its sale? Whoever it was, Christian wondered if they knew the commune was about to be merged. And if they did, were they bothered?

He turned his attention back to the road, wary of ice as the forest closed around him and the snow began to thicken. By the time he pulled up opposite the Auberge, he was no clearer as to how he was going to vote. On the one hand, the merger could offer new hope for people in the area. On the other, he could feel the tug of history and tradition, as strong for him as it was for his father and his ancestors.

He just wanted to do what was right. That was all. If only he could work out exactly what that was.

★ ★ ★

'Promise me you won't get upset, whatever the outcome?'

Serge Papon laughed, the sound echoing around the épicerie, and he kissed his daughter on the cheek. 'It's me who should be worrying over you,' he said, gesturing at the white sling that held her broken arm in place. 'I'll be fine.'

'Are you sure? This seems to have really taken a toll on you. You look pale.'

394

'Stop fussing! He's made of strrrong stuff. Now let's get back to yourrr flat and out of the cold.' Annie made to steer Véronique towards the door but the postmistress turned at the last minute and threw her good arm around the thick neck of the mayor.

'I love you, Papa. And I'm proud of you. Remember that.'

His hand went automatically to the back of her head, holding her in the embrace. When he finally released her, his eyes shone with tears. 'I'll call you,' he said, voice quavering. 'As soon as we have a result.'

Then, in a swirl of snow and cold, the Estaque women were gone, their hunched shapes making a careful path down to the old school.

'I think I might need a pastis, Josette,' said the mayor, passing through the archway into the bar, a dazed look about him. He surveyed the room, ten seats already occupied around the big table and a heavy silence prevailing. 'And then perhaps it's time to lock the door.'

Josette did as she was asked. Anything to get away from Jacques' steady gaze, which had followed her all day. How she could vote under these conditions, she didn't know. She flipped the sign on the épicerie door to *Fermé* and turned the key in the lock, returning to the bar as the mayor of Fogas began to speak.

'Let's make a start. But first of all, can you please turn off your mobiles? This is a serious business we are about tonight and we need no interruptions.'

Over in the inglenook, Jacques sat up straight.

395

He was about to be part of history. He only hoped it would be a version he approved of.

★ ★ ★

It was taking forever. But she sensed it would soon be over.

Outside the sky had gone dark, affording her a strange glimpse of herself in the snow-spattered window, knees raised, people huddled around, her own face staring back in puzzlement as though she didn't really belong here. Then a nurse had whipped curtains across the glass and she'd been left with a wall of blue to stare at.

'Lorna, it's almost here. Push, love.'

She pushed, watching Paul, trying to gauge from his face if she was doing this right. He was nodding, smiling, so she pushed some more.

'The head.' He grinned down at her. 'I can see the head!'

Other voices, telling her what to do. She tried to understand. Caught the odd word. But it was difficult. Then a strange sensation, as though her hips had clicked apart, and a rush of movement.

'He's here! Oh my God, Lorna.'

Paul was squeezing her hand, face turned away, transfixed by the bundle of skin and slime they were handing to her. Then it was on her chest. *He* was on her chest. For it was a boy, as she'd known all along. And like a light through fog, he cut through the haze of her senses, every nerve alive at his touch, every part of her awake at his cry.

Which was how she noticed it. The change in

atmosphere. The midwife and the obstetrician looking worried, a phrase passing between them that she couldn't catch.

'What did they say?' she asked.

Paul looked up from the baby, silly smile on his face. 'I missed it. Why?'

She didn't get a chance to reply as another contraction hit her and her baby was snatched away by the nurse. 'What's going — ?'

'They're saying you need to push, Lorna,' said Paul, face pale now, clearly worried.

'Push? Why do I need to . . . ooooooh!'

Another rush of pressure and then relieved laughter from the end of the bed. Paul reeling, having to put a hand out to steady himself, and outside, the Angelus starting its heavy toll. But for her, only one thought.

Fogas.

'Paul,' she said, tugging him down to her. 'The meeting. You have to tell them.'

And he understood. Leaving a room of surprised faces behind him, he rushed for the door.

22

The roads were getting difficult, fresh snow lying thick across the tracks of the snowplough. Paul was going as fast as he dared, propelled by adrenaline as the car slipped around another corner and he fought to keep it under control.

It was insane being out in these conditions. Especially for a new father. He gave a shocked laugh at the thought. But he'd tried calling and had been unable to get through to Christian or René on their mobiles. And the phone line was still down to La Rivière. So he was making a journey that only a fool would undertake.

Another slip and he tightened his grip on the steering wheel. He couldn't afford to make a mistake. On one side was the unforgiving shoulder of rock that led up to the hills above. On the other, a steep drop into the icy waters of the Salat river.

But still, he had to hurry. It was a quarter past seven. They would be voting by now. And he had to stop them.

★ ★ ★

'For most of us, the position we find ourselves in tonight is not one we would choose.'

The solemn words fell heavily into the silence in the bar.

'We have been handed a grave responsibility,'

Serge Papon continued. 'To decide the future of this commune. And while some of us might feel we are not up to that task, we must remember that when we stepped forward to join the Conseil Municipal, we were agreeing to be representatives for Fogas. By electing us, the people have given us their mandate. So all I will say is this . . . ' He paused, looking around the table at his councillors, their faces sombre in the flickering light of the fire, and his gaze lingered briefly on Josette before he spoke again.

'However you vote tonight,' he said, 'as long as you are voting with a clear conscience and for the benefit of all, no one can castigate you afterwards. With that in mind, I ask that we respect each other throughout, and to prevent intimidation, I have decided we will deviate from our normal procedure and have a secret ballot.'

A sigh of relief met his announcement. Apart from in the inglenook, where Jacques Servat was shaking his head in disapproval, knowing that an open show of hands would make it far more difficult for those wavering to have the courage to opt for the merger. But this change of plan wouldn't stop him finding out how people voted. Slipping to his feet, he started circling the table, Josette following his movements with a deprecatory look he chose to ignore.

'Bernard, if you could hand out the ballot papers, please,' said Serge, shivering as an unseen Jacques passed behind him. 'And René, throw another log on that fire. There's a draught in here from somewhere.'

While the *cantonnier* made slow work of

distributing the forms, Serge was left to wonder if the biggest gamble of his political career would pay off. Judging by the stoical expression on his face, Christian Dupuy looked a long way from allowing his emotions to overcome his sober practicality. And as for Josette, her eyes were shifting nervously around the table like someone carrying a guilty secret. She was showing no sign of being swayed by marital allegiances to a dead husband.

Bernard finally resumed his seat and Serge knew he was out of time. Pens clicked, papers rustled and when the mayor of Fogas spoke, it was with a sense of resignation.

'Let's vote.'

★   ★   ★

Kerkabanac. The roundabout appeared through the falling flakes, a flawless mound of white. Paul felt the tyres skidding as he took it too fast, the car flicking out at the rear and threatening to spin. He wrenched it back under control and negotiated the turn up to Fogas. Five minutes and he would be there.

He pressed carefully on the accelerator, feeling the snow crunching under the wheels, and peered into the swirling mass ahead. He had a horrible feeling he was going to be too late.

★   ★   ★

In a perverse way, Jacques was enjoying himself. He'd stood behind Pascal and had watched with

400

no surprise as the first deputy marked the box that would consign Fogas to history. Fists clenched in ghostly anger, he'd seen Geneviève Souquet and Lucien Biros, seated either side of Pascal, follow suit. No reflection. No indecision. A confident stroke of the pen and that was that.

He'd been swift of foot around the table, not lingering over René or Bernard, who were sitting back, decision made, the plumber shooting hostile glances at the first deputy despite Serge's fine speech. Likewise, Serge had made his mark and Jacques had been close enough to hear the quiet sigh that escaped his lips as he did the last thing he could to protect his commune.

Alain Rougé and Philippe Galy took longer. They were inconveniently seated directly opposite each other, which meant Jacques had to scamper from one to the other whenever it looked like they might commit their choice to paper.

Then he'd had a brainwave and had leapt onto the table, towering over them from the middle. In this manner he'd seen them vote, Alain against the merger, Philippe for it.

With a glare at the young beekeeper and a mutter about what his grandfather would have made of such treachery, Jacques spun round in time to see Monique Sentenac, with pursed lips and an air of defiance, tick the box that would bring Fogas to its knees.

A wail escaped his lips. Five in favour of the merger. Four against. Two left to vote. Pirouetting on the table, Jacques stared at Christian and Josette, sitting side by side, both heads down, concentrating on the paper in front of them. He willed his wife to look up. But she didn't. Then the farmer picked up his pen, and with a slow hand, placed his mark.

Jacques jerked back. Elated. Christian had voted against the merger.

But his joy was short lived for the result was now balanced. And Josette would have the final say.

★ ★ ★

'Sit down, you'rrre making me dizzy with all that prrrowling!'

Annie tapped the seat next to her on the sofa and Véronique reluctantly desisted from her restless patrol of her flat.

'Sorry. I'm not good at waiting.'

'Makes two of us.' Her mother smiled and ran a hand over the lingering colours of the fading bruise on Véronique's cheek. 'And we don't even have a TV to watch! Have the gendarrrmes got anywherrre with catching the buggerrr that did this?'

Véronique shook her head. 'No. Whoever it was came prepared. He wore gloves and the prints he left in the snow are standard issue hunting boots around here.'

The clock on the dresser, which had survived the burglary with only a broken glass face, sounded the half-hour.

'They must be finished by now,' muttered Véronique, getting to her feet once more to cross to the window where the lights from the bar turned the fallen snow yellow on the empty terrace. The ping of her phone had her back to the coffee table in a whirl.

'Is it Serrrge?' demanded Annie.

Véronique was staring at the mobile, reading intently.

'Well, is it the rrresult?'

'No.' Rushing to the hall, she slipped into shoes and awkwardly threw her coat on over her sling. 'It's more important. It's an email from *SOS Fogas*. I have to go down there. That vote needs to be stopped and now.'

The door slammed behind her and by the time Annie finally got her boots on, her daughter was already halfway to the épicerie.

★   ★   ★

She was refusing to look at him. He knew it was deliberate. The way she was holding her head, angled so he couldn't catch her eye. He'd even tried sliding across the table on his belly to get into her line of sight but she'd simply turned away.

So how could he tell her? How could he let Josette know that her vote was the final one? That she held the future of Fogas in her hands?

Jacques stared at the window, the glass giving out onto snow-punctured darkness, and he knew. He jumped off the table and was at work in seconds, cheeks puffed out as he blew on the cold surface in an attempt to save the commune.

★   ★   ★

The lights of the bar visible at last, Paul drove past the empty Auberge, across the bridge and slithered to a stop outside the épicerie. He was out of the car just as the unmistakable figure of Véronique, arm in a sling, came hurrying towards him, feet slipping on the snow.

'Stop the vote!' she shouted. 'We have to stop the vote.'

With the same purpose in mind they turned to the bar, where through the window they could see the councillors gathered around the table. Ten of them were sitting back in their chairs. Josette, however, was just picking up her pen.

'We're in time,' said Véronique, reaching for the door.

But it was locked.

'The épicerie. Try there,' urged Paul.

They raced across the terrace only to be met with the same resistance. When Véronique pulled out her mobile, Paul shook his head.

'No good. I tried calling Christian and René earlier but both of their phones are switched off. I reckon it will be the same for the rest.'

'Well, we'll have to catch their attention some other way,' muttered Véronique, hurrying back towards the bar to see her mother already banging on the window.

★ ★ ★

'It's not a school exam, Josette,' said Serge into the tense silence, smiling at the exaggerated way his friend was protecting her ballot, arm curved around it to shield it from view. 'No one's going

404

to copy your answer.'

'The walls have eyes,' she muttered enigmatically.

Refusing to look at her husband, who was doing everything he could to catch her attention, she clicked her pen and finally cast her vote, folding it quickly into a small square held in her clenched hand.

'Christian, could you gather the ballot papers, please?' requested Serge, holding out a small cardboard box with a slit in the top.

The farmer was sitting next to Josette. On the window side. When he stood, her paper already in the box, his large frame completely blocked her view. So it was only as he passed around the top end of the table, gathering votes as he went, that she turned her head and saw her husband standing next to the window. Her hand flew to her mouth.

A single line had been breathed down the glass, dividing the pane into two columns. On one side was the number five. And on the other, another five. She knew immediately what it meant. Hers had been the casting vote. And Jacques, with one look at her face, could tell that she had decided in favour of the merger.

'Are they all in, Christian?'

The farmer nodded but as he leaned across the table, about to pass the box to Serge, there was a terrible commotion outside. The councillors turned to the window, and there were the faces of Paul, Annie and Véronique pressed up against it, their fists pounding on the glass.

'Let them in!' barked Serge and René shot to

his feet, opening the door to a burst of noise.

'Stop the vote!' shouted Véronique. 'You have to stop the vote.'

'Véronique, whatever — ?'

'Read it!' She held out her mobile to Serge. 'It's from *SOS Fogas*. There's a leaked copy of the cost analysis for the merger up on the blog.'

A ripple of unease shot around the table.

'And?' asked Christian.

'Seems like Mayor Dedieu wasn't entirely truthful. A conservative estimate puts the bill for the merger at ten thousand euros.'

René whistled. 'Christ, that's a lot.'

'It gets worse,' continued the postmistress. 'According to the same document, Dedieu has proposed that the bill gets split fifty-fifty, breaking the promise he made at the meeting. Which means the residents of Fogas would be picking up half of the cost, despite the massive differences in population.' She turned to her father. 'But the thing is, if he's lied about this, what else has he lied about? Surely that's enough to cancel the vote?'

Voices erupted around the room, Pascal rising to his feet in indignation.

'Quiet!' Serge held up his hand and turned to the Englishman, who'd been hopping up and down behind Véronique, clearly bursting to speak. 'Paul, you have something to add to this?'

'She's right. You need to stop the vote. There's no need for it anymore.' Then, using a word he'd only just learnt that evening, he plunged the room into silence. 'Lorna's had twins!'

★ ★ ★

Cacophony. Pascal citing the regulations, saying it was too late to cancel the ballot and insisting they finalise it immediately. René and Véronique shouting back at him, saying that until the votes were counted, nothing was official and that the crucial change in population had to be mitigating circumstances. Alain Rougé and Philippe Galy having to be separated by Paul and Annie while Bernard, Monique and the two second-home owners added their opinions from the sidelines. Serge meanwhile was watching Christian, who was still standing to one side, the box of votes in his hand, his attention fixed on the window.

It puzzled the farmer for a few moments. Those numbers breathed onto the glass. Who'd put them there? That was his initial thought. Then he began to wonder what they meant. It took a minute for him to understand. The vote. Five for. Five against.

He swung his gaze to Josette, who had slumped onto her chair at the combined announcements from the latest arrivals, hand over her mouth, face grey. She'd voted last. The deciding factor. And suddenly the ballot box was heavier in his hand now that he knew the dreadful news it contained. If it was opened, Fogas was doomed. If it wasn't . . .

The noise. Christian couldn't think straight. Then he glanced across at Serge, who was staring back at him, a small smile on his lips as mayhem unfolded around them, and the farmer

407

felt something shift inside him, like the slip of soil down a wet embankment, leaving a part of him exposed that he had never encountered before. He knew what he had to do.

With a steady gait, Christian began to walk around the table towards the inglenook. Then slowly, deliberately, but in a way that no one could ever question, he tripped over a chair leg and threw himself to the ground.

The sound of the big farmer falling was enough to turn heads and everyone saw the cardboard ballot box fly out of his hands and into the fire. On a sudden draught, the flames flared up and in seconds the votes that had caused such acrimony were beyond reach, each councillor's decision cast into permanent secrecy as the papers were devoured.

'Sorry,' muttered Christian, face down on the floor to hide the massive smile on his face. It was the first time in his life that he'd done anything bad. And he decided he rather liked it.

★ ★ ★

From his position in the inglenook, Jacques saw the smile and matched it with one of his own. He'd seen the farmer making the connections. But he'd thought it was all too late. For Christian Dupuy was known to be a man of principle, someone beyond corruption.

Then, as though in slow motion, the second deputy mayor had made his lumbering fall and next thing Jacques knew, the ballot box was flying past his head and into the fire. Nimble

408

despite being dead, he'd quickly leaned down to blow on the flames, fanning them into a fierce inferno that no one would dare risk putting a hand into, not even Pascal.

'Are you okay, Christian?' Véronique was the first to react, rushing over to the farmer, concern on her face.

'You oaf!' cursed Pascal, rage boiling out of him. 'You did that deliberately.'

'He tripped!' declared René. 'Out of all of us here, Christian is the last man you can accuse of being dishonest.'

And it was true. Jacques could tell by the way they were reacting that no one suspected a thing. Not even Véronique, who was now helping the farmer to a chair, Christian resting heavily on her shoulder, an innocent look on his face as his hand draped cheekily over the front of her jumper. If she noticed, she never said a word, but simply took the seat next to him and dabbed her handkerchief at the cut on his cheek.

Jacques laughed out loud. It seemed like Christian Dupuy had gone bad indeed.

* * *

'So what do we do now?' asked Alain Rougé as Josette and Monique distributed drinks around the table.

'We have two choices,' said Serge. 'We hold a second vote — '

'No!' Josette's voice was firm. 'Let the préfet do what he will but I am not going through that again. I don't think my heart could take it.'

Voices joined in agreement, drowning out the protests of Pascal Souquet.

'In that case,' continued the mayor, 'let it be noted in the minutes that the vote was abandoned according to the wishes of the majority. And I'll go and see the sous-préfet tomorrow — '

'Tomorrow's a bank holiday, Papa.'

Serge grimaced at the enforced delay. 'Of course it is. So, the day after tomorrow, I'll go down and tell him to submit his report. Then we'll await the decision from Foix. We can do no more than that.'

'So we're as good as merged anyway,' muttered René, shoulders drooping.

'After tonight's charades, I for one think that's no bad thing.' Pascal Souquet stood and put on his coat. 'If the meeting is over, I'm going home. But I will be making an official complaint about this.'

'Complain away,' said Serge, dismissing the first deputy with a wave of his hand. 'If we're merged, most of us won't be in elected positions by the time the complaint gets dealt with.'

Pascal had no reply. Instead, accompanied by his cousin, Geneviève, Lucien Biros and Philippe Galy, he left the bar. As the door closed behind them, Paul spoke up.

'Is it okay if I leave too? Lorna — '

'Lorna!' Josette exclaimed, the significance of Paul's presence finally registering. 'Goodness, you've left her to cope with two newborn babies!'

'Trust a man to put politics before family,' said

410

Monique, equally outraged. 'You should have just called.'

'I tried!' said the Englishman, defending himself against a united front of indignant women. 'Your mobiles were all off and the phone line is still dead. So Lorna insisted I drive up here to stop the vote.' He shrugged, a true French hunch of the shoulders. 'She said she didn't want our children raised anywhere else.'

Serge reached over and slapped him on the back, moved by the loyalty from these outsiders who had made the commune home. 'A toast,' he said, raising his glass. 'To the first Fogas babies in a long, long time.'

It was only when Paul stood to go that he saw his car was parked in a snowdrift.

'Anyone got a shovel?'

'I've got better than that,' said Bernard, thrusting plump arms into his coat sleeves.

Minutes later, the snowplough rumbled past the bar, Paul sitting up high next to the *cantonnier*, waving as he went.

'Rrrather him than me,' said Annie as the vehicle headed over the bridge and down towards St Girons. 'Don't fancy theirrr chances of getting to town without at least one scrrrape.'

Serge groaned. 'With any luck the bill for the insurance will arrive after the merger.'

'Right, I'm off.' Alain Rougé said his farewells and left the bar, the others following, Monique getting a lift from Serge while René helped Annie across the snow to his 4×4.

'Are you sure you want to trust your heap of rust to start?' the plumber shouted back to

Christian, who was still standing in the doorway.

'Yes, I'm sure,' said the farmer. He waited for the cars to go before turning to Véronique.

'I'll walk you home,' he said. And taking her good arm through his, he guided them towards the old school.

'Well,' exclaimed Josette as she locked the doors and began to clear the table. 'That was too much excitement by half.'

Jacques didn't respond. Partly because he was watching the farmer and the postmistress head down the road, a sly grin on his face. But also because he couldn't face his wife right now. Not after what she'd done.

He didn't feel her hands reach around and encircle his chest. He saw them in the window. Then he heard her heart thumping away. And he felt the warmth that always accompanied her presence.

'I'm sorry,' she whispered. He knew she was crying. 'I've been a fool.'

He couldn't resist. He turned in her arms and they crossed to the inglenook, sitting side by side, her hand clasped in his while he stroked her hair.

It was still a long way from settled, this issue of the merger. But thanks to the duplicity of Christian Dupuy, there was a glimmer of hope to be had. Jacques was pinning his hopes on it.

★　★　★

Christian Dupuy was feeling reckless. He'd done something bad and it had felt right. Now, as he

412

walked along the road, Véronique tucked close to his side, he knew this was his moment. He'd walk her to her door and then he'd ask her on a date. If she rejected him, well at least he would have done something about it.

That was his plan. The plan of a virtuous man. But when they turned the corner at the old school gate and crossed the yard to the staircase, they were plunged into complete darkness.

'Damn,' muttered Véronique, pressing even closer to the reassuring solidity of Christian next to her. 'That blasted street light is still not fixed and I forgot my torch.'

The farmer, side afire to her touch and senses leaping in the dark, couldn't help himself.

'We don't need a torch,' he murmured and he bent down to the pale shadow of her face and kissed her, one hand buried in the silky locks of her hair, the other winding around her waist to hold her tenderly against him.

When she didn't slap him, but instead wrapped her good arm around his neck, returning his kisses with a passion he could never have guessed at, Christian Dupuy came to the conclusion that being bad was very good indeed.

23

By ten o'clock the following morning, the snow had stopped and a pale blue sky draped itself across the white-coated angles of the mountaintops. Down at the épicerie in La Rivière, people were gathering for a coffee — or something stronger in the case of René Piquemal — before making the journey up to Fogas for the Armistice Day ceremony. Dressed in their best clothes, neither the formality of their attire nor the sombre nature of the events they were marking could suppress the frisson of excitement that rippled through every conversation. For news had already got round about the dramatic happenings at the meeting of the Conseil Municipal the night before.

'He tripped?'

'And the ballot box went straight in the fire — '

'No! So does that mean — ?'

'I heard Pascal burned his fingers trying to — '

' — twins! The population is back up — '

'Surely Fogas must be safe — ?'

'But if the préfet issues a decree — '

For most people, there was only one topic of conversation. But for a small group clustered over by the window, the focus was on something else entirely.

'His car is still here. He must have walked home.'

'There are prints heading up the hill, so I think you're right. The Panda must have failed him again.'

'Well, I offered him a lift last night and he wouldn't take it. Insisted on walking Véronique home. Hey, Véronique!'

The postmistress looked over to where René was sitting, the plumber gesturing for her to join them.

'What's with Christian's car?'

'What about it?'

'Why is it still down here? Wouldn't it start?'

Aware that the flush burning across her cheeks would give her away, Véronique made the most of going over to the window to see the car for herself, a solid lump of metal encased in snow.

She shrugged. 'I don't know. Here he comes now, so you can ask him yourself.'

Excusing herself on the basis that Josette could do with a hand, she headed for the bar as Christian arrived, driving his father's car, his parents and Annie with him.

'Mind your step,' said the farmer as he opened the door for his mother. 'It's treacherous underfoot.'

'Let me take your arm, then.'

'And I'll take the otherrr one,' said Annie, placing a hand on the strong forearm offered to her.

'I reckon I'm the luckiest man in Fogas,' chirped Christian, beaming down at the ladies on either side of him. 'Escorting you two beauties on a morning like this.'

His mother laughed. Annie Estaque merely gave him a shrewd look, hoping that she had correctly guessed the cause of his high spirits.

415

She knew the moment she stepped into the bar that she had. For Véronique, tray of drinks in hand, jumped as they walked in, as though a dart of electricity had travelled up her spine. Then her eyes dropped to the floor and she smiled, at no one in particular, dimples forming on her glowing cheeks. For Annie, it was the most beautiful smile she had ever witnessed on her daughter's face.

Christian was smiling too. In fact, when the call of the cockerel had roused him from a deep sleep, he had found his lips curved in an upward position. Stumbling out of bed, leaving sheets he'd barely had time to warm, he'd luxuriated in a hot shower, all the while a grin slapped across his sleepy features. If his parents had noticed his exceptionally good mood over breakfast, they hadn't said, his mother more concerned about the fact he'd had to walk home. Now, with his eyes locking on to the tight curve of skirt bending over a table to deliver espressos, that smile had taken on a wolfish slant. It was all he could do not to walk over there, pick Véronique up, and carry her back to the old school to resume what he had been reluctant to leave in the early hours of the morning.

'Bonjour, Christian!' René's summons pulled the farmer's attention back to safer ground. 'Would the Panda not start?'

'Er, no. Heap of junk!' Mentally apologising to his maligned car, Christian shook hands with the group at the window and made to turn away.

'So you had to walk all the way home?' asked Alain Rougé.

The farmer nodded.

'What time was it?' Bernard Mirouze was looking at him, vaguely puzzled.

'I don't know. Not long after you all left. I saw Véronique back to her flat and when I returned to the car, it wouldn't start.'

'You should have knocked,' said Josette, coming over to clear cups. 'I was still up. You could have stopped the night here.'

'Er . . . I didn't want to bother you. So I started walking.'

'But it still doesn't make sense,' said Bernard.

'How do you mean?' René focused on the *cantonnier* while Christian could feel his smile slipping for the first time that morning.

'I had a look at his tracks. There's no snow on them.'

'It wasn't snowing,' said Christian, knowing as soon as he'd said it that he'd blundered.

'The snow didn't stop until five this morning,' said Bernard. 'I was already out on the snowplough when it finally eased off. So why are your footprints still visible?'

'Christ, who do you think you are? Arnaud bloody Petit?' Christian threw his arms up in despair and strode off towards the bar, where a coffee was waiting for him.

'What did I say?' asked Bernard, unsure as to why his nascent tracking skills had caused such a reaction.

'I'm not sure,' said René, staring out at the car and running the facts over in his head. It was only when he looked back and saw the post-mistress smile softly, her gaze lowered to the

417

floor as Christian bent down to greet her with two kisses, that he made the connection.

'Jesus!' he exclaimed, slapping a hand to his forehead, and then letting out a laugh. 'The sly fox!'

'What?' Alain and Bernard asked in unison.

'He walked home all right. Not because the Panda wouldn't start. But because it was snowed in after he'd spent most of the night sleeping somewhere else.'

They followed his gaze, both reacting as he had when they realised what he was suggesting.

'How can you tell?' asked Bernard, in awe of both the plumber's perception and the farmer's prowess.

'Because Véronique Estaque just looked demure. And there's only one thing on this planet that could make her look like that!'

Jacques Servat, listening in on the conversation from the inglenook, took a fit of laughing, tears still rolling down his cheeks as a bemused Josette closed up the bar twenty minutes later, leaving him alone with his merriment while she made her way to Fogas in a convoy of cars behind the snowplough.

★ ★ ★

Eleven o'clock. The bells sounded the hour and then silence fell, broken only by the fluttering of the blue, white and red ribbons that decorated the garlands tightly clutched in the hands of the children. Heads were bowed, thoughts resting on those who had gone from the three villages of

418

Fogas all those years ago and never returned.

For Serge Papon, standing in front of the war memorial next to the town hall, it was always a poignant moment. This year, as his eyes ranged out across the spectacular view, the crystal-coated mountains sparkling in the morning sunshine, it was even more significant for him. Because he knew, regardless of the fate of his commune, which still hung in the balance, this would be his last experience of presiding over the Armistice Day ceremony.

It was time for him to retire.

He'd been toying with the idea for a while, aware that his energy levels weren't what they used to be. But concerns over his successor had forestalled him. After last night, that had changed. When he'd seen Christian Dupuy throw the ballot box on the fire, his exaggerated fall not fooling the mayor, Serge had known that his second deputy was finally ready to wear the sash of office that was currently draped across his own robust chest.

He would do it in the new year, he decided. He would give the commune time to come to terms with whatever decision came out of the Préfecture over in Foix. And allow Christian time to settle down in his new relationship. For only an idiot could miss the attraction that had blossomed overnight between the farmer and the mayor's daughter. Even as they respectfully observed the ritual of the day, their arms were casually touching, Véronique leaning slightly in towards the larger frame next to her, her face alight despite her sombre expression. Serge knew, even if Annie hadn't whispered the news in his ear with a delighted laugh.

Christian and Véronique. He smiled to himself. As a father, he couldn't have been happier. As Mayor of Fogas, there was only one other thing that he could wish for. But with everything stacked against his commune, it would require a major miracle.

★ ★ ★

Over in Foix the sun was glinting off the brass buttons and the gold braid that decorated the uniform fitting the athletic figure of Jérôme Ulrich as he stood to attention at the war memorial, white glove touching the peak of his cap. It was a day that always brought home to him the privilege of his position, giving him the chance to talk to veterans and to serving soldiers, making him appreciate that his work could effect changes for normal people and wasn't always about the bickering and infighting that symbolised the political world.

Perhaps this was apt, given that Armistice Day had been established to celebrate peace as well as to commemorate the fallen of past wars. Not that there was going to be much peace around when the day was done. In his own life or in that of the people living up in the mountain commune of Fogas.

He would find a quiet moment between official duties to make the phone call. Then he would wash his hands of the whole affair.

The moment his official obligations had been dispensed with, Pascal Souquet made for home, spurning the traditional gathering in the *salle des fêtes*, where weak wine and some ghastly refreshments were being served to those who'd attended the Armistice Day ceremony. He had no time for it; he had no stomach for it either. In fact, he had no appetite at all.

Bloody Véronique Estaque. Still claiming to be innocent, insisting *SOS Fogas* had emailed her the leaked document last night, detailing Henri Dedieu's apportionment of costs for the merger. Pretending she knew nothing about the troublesome blog when it was her all along who'd been dropping poison into the ears of the commune and souring Pascal's ambitions. She must have used her mobile to upload the post. Why hadn't they thought of that when they'd ransacked her place?

Imbeciles!

They'd taken her laptop but forgotten to take her mobile as she lay prostrate on the ground. No doubt the man responsible was too thick to know about smartphones. If only he'd pushed the postmistress a bit harder. A lot harder. It would have made life easier for Pascal.

As the first deputy dropped into a seat in front of his computer and hung his head in his hands, he knew he was in trouble. He'd read last night's post on *SOS Fogas*. Three times. And there was no denying it. The information contained in the blog, which had been instrumental in derailing

421

the vote on the merger, had come from *his* computer. He'd recognised the pages. Pages he'd scanned in, thinking it was safer to have an electronic copy than a paper one. Pages that he'd numbered so he'd get them in the right order. And those scribbled numbers were now up on the internet for the entire world to see.

How the hell had Véronique Estaque, a mere postmistress, managed to hack into his PC?

His own image stared back from the blank screen, strained and grey. When Henri Dedieu got wind of what happened at the council meeting he would be furious. Dangerously so. And when he found out who'd been the cause of it . . .

It was the fear that this provoked which had robbed Pascal Souquet of his appetite.

A single trill from his mobile pierced his gloom. Afraid it might be the mayor of Sarrat, he was relieved to see it was an email from his internet provider, an advisory message to alert him that he was in danger of exceeding his monthly usage allowance. Friendly in tone, it stated that he had already used more than half of his 10GB allocation and advised him to restrict his activities if he wanted to avoid incurring charges.

What the — ?

His attention was momentarily diverted from his political problems. While Pascal's knowledge of computers was limited, as proved by his ineffectual attempts to trace *SOS Fogas* through digital means, he knew that 10GB was a generous amount. More than adequate for a household where neither occupant downloaded videos, played computer games or spent hours surfing the net. There must have been some mistake.

Clicking the PC into life, he accessed his provider's homepage and then his account, bringing November's usage record up on the screen. He stared at the columns for a few seconds, the numbers in front of him making no sense. When comprehension came, it brought with it a groan of abject despair.

He'd got it wrong. So wrong. All of it. And whatever he did now, he was damned.

★ ★ ★

The *salle des fêtes* was packed, a clamour of voices trapped under the corrugated roof. Christian had managed to make his way through the throng with a tray above his head, using his height to protect his cargo from the jostling and his bulk to forge a path. He'd never seen the place so busy.

'At last!' sighed René, helping himself to a glass of wine as soon as it was within reach. 'What took you so long?'

'Negotiating my way through that lot!'

'It is busy,' agreed Josette as the farmer passed the wine around the small group by the door. 'It must be the news of last night's meeting that's drawn the crowds.'

'They sense there's still hope.' Serge Papon had materialised next to Véronique and was reaching out for the last glass on the tray. 'Thanks, Christian.'

'That's not for . . . I mean . . . ' Christian was left with only the tray in his hands.

'You wouldn't deny me a drink?' asked Serge with a wicked smile as he raised the glass to his lips. 'Not when you're dating my daughter?'

Véronique spluttered, nearly choking on her wine, while Christian turned beetroot.

'We're not . . . it's not — '

'No need to deny it, Christian,' René joined in with delight. 'We all know.'

'How?' squeaked Véronique, her usual composure lost.

René grinned. 'Christian made a mistake about the snow.'

'And I guessed frrrom how he looked at you this morrrning,' said Annie.

'Then your mother told me,' said Josette, earning an elbow in the ribs from her old friend.

'And me,' added Serge, laughing as he moved out of Annie's range, mobile lifted to his ear to answer a call.

'And I guessed over a year ago.' The newly formed couple turned to their gypsy friend and Stephanie just shrugged in apology. 'I saw it in the tea leaves.'

'I knew too!' piped up Chloé, who had squirmed her way into the circle. 'But you wouldn't believe me if I told you how.'

'Is there anyone here who didn't know?' asked Christian in amazement.

Fabian Servat raised his hand, a bemused gaze fixed on the postmistress and the farmer and a delighted smile breaking out on his face.

'Bloody Fogas!' muttered Christian.

'Bloody Fogas, indeed!' said Serge, rejoining them. 'That was the préfet on the phone.'

René groaned. 'He didn't waste any time.'

'Has he issued the decree? Today of all days?' But Véronique's question received no reply. Serge Papon was elbowing his way through the crowd, making a beeline for the front of the hall.

'I don't think I can bear this,' she muttered as her father's stocky figure appeared on the stage. She turned her head into the broad chest of Christian Dupuy and covered her ears with her hands. She had no desire to hear the announcement that would signify the death of Fogas.

★ ★ ★

'If I could have your attention, please?' Serge's voice cut through the rumble of conversation and silence fell upon the room. 'I've just had a call from Jérôme Ulrich, Préfet of Ariège. And when a *fonctionnaire* calls you on a national holiday, you know it has to be important.'

Nervous laughter rippled through the crowd.

'The thing is . . . ' Serge faltered to a stop, visibly shaken by the news he was about to impart. 'For reasons best known to himself, the préfet has decided not to issue a decree on the merger of Fogas and Sarrat.' He paused, his audience speechless, unsure as to what they had just heard. 'Furthermore, he has declared a twelve-month moratorium on any such amalgamation.'

'You mean, those bastards across the river can't force our hand?' René shouted from the back.

Serge nodded. 'Not for a year, at least.' He shrugged, as nonplussed as his electorate. In all his years in politics he had never been so flummoxed by an opponent's move.

Then, like wind through the summer meadows, voices began to ripple across the room, excitement building as the inhabitants realised what this meant. It was the rumbling in Christian's chest that made Véronique raise her head.

'What is it?' she asked, uncovering her ears to discover he was laughing.

He grinned down at her. 'We're safe. The préfet isn't going ahead with the merger.'

'Honestly?'

Christian nodded.

She turned to see people talking, some celebrating, Bernard doing a dance with Serge the beagle in his arms and René calling for more wine. And then, as Widow Aubert would testify the next day to Agnès Rogalle at the butcher's van, the postmistress flung her arms, sling and all, around the farmer and kissed him in full view of everyone.

★   ★   ★

'I'll ruin you!' The voice hissed across the wires, slicing into the préfet's office and causing him to shudder despite himself. 'You will rue the day you crossed me, you jumped-up paper-pusher.'

The venom was unexpected. Jérôme had dealt with many a local official when he had disappointing news to impart, and never in his experience had he come across such antipathy,

426

most of them managing to hide their annoyance behind the necessary diplomacy. But not in this case. When he'd informed Henri Dedieu of his decision to suspend talks on the merger for at least twelve months, the suave veneer that coated the mayor of Sarrat had been stripped away to reveal the vindictive, dangerous man beneath.

'I'm sorry you feel — '

A bitter laugh cut through the préfet's attempt to pacify the mayor. 'It's you who'll be sorry. Remember that.'

The line went dead and Jérôme replaced the receiver with a slightly unsteady hand. He steepled his fingers and rested his forehead on them, staring at his desk.

Why? That's what Serge Papon had wanted to know when he'd heard that his commune had been given a temporary reprieve. The préfet hadn't provided a complete answer, just some waffle about official schedules and regional considerations. The real reason was a lot harder to articulate.

First of all, there was the letter on his desk. It had arrived two days ago, and when he'd seen the seal of the Council of Ministers on the envelope, he'd known what it was straight away. Pleased with his progress in Foix, the Council had decided he was to become the Préfet of Charante in January, a promotion far exceeding his expectations. It seemed unfair, therefore, to instigate the merger when he wouldn't be in the Ariège to oversee its implementation. Plus, given the identity of the new préfet, he rather thought his successor would have enough on their plate without the added friction of Fogas to deal with.

Then there was *SOS Fogas*. If the blog had been instrumental in swaying his opinion, his meeting with the author had been inspirational. He'd been impressed by her passion, her commitment to the commune and her determination to fight for what she thought was right. She was wasted in her present capacity, he mused, thinking how she would shake up local politics in the mountains if she ever stood for office.

But the biggest factor of all in his decision to shelve the proposed unification had been Fogas itself. Barring the unfortunate death of the shepherd, the fête had been splendid, an amazing achievement for such a small commune. However, it was the search for young Chloé Morvan that had the greatest impact on both the préfet and his wife. Those people, all gathered together despite their political differences, unifying to find a missing child. He'd felt privileged to have witnessed it, to have been able to take part. And when Chloé had returned, well . . . How could you describe that feeling?

His short sojourn in the mountain commune had changed his opinion. And his life. Because this morning, he'd awoken to see Karine standing in the doorway of the bedroom, a small white tube in her hand, a stunned look on her face.

'I'm pregnant,' she'd whispered. 'We're going to have a Fogas baby.'

And to his surprise, he'd been overjoyed.

He gathered up his papers and dropped them

in a drawer and then sent a quick email before turning off his computer. Picking up his official cap, he walked past the map of the department, pausing to let his eyes drift across the contour lines and the winding roads. He found it with ease. There. Tucked into the mountains, one of the smallest political districts in the whole of the Ariège. But the one with the most heart. It had overcome his Teutonic reticence and released the Mediterranean passion that his Italian grandmère had been famous for. And while he was moving on to pastures new, Fogas had left an indelible imprint on his soul.

Home time, he thought, with a smile as he closed his office door on the unchanged map. Time to head back and persuade Karine once and for all that they were not going to name their baby Serge.

★   ★   ★

When the wine in the *salle des fêtes* had run out, the celebrations had travelled down the hill to La Rivière, flooding into the bar and keeping Josette and Véronique busy. It hadn't taken long for Jacques Servat to ascertain the cause of the merriment, one look at René Piquemal's elated features sufficient. Although Chloé had been good enough to come up and whisper the news to him.

So, with Fogas safe and Christian and Véronique together, he was rather at a loose end. He still hadn't uncovered the identity of Pascal's co-conspirator, but given that talks of a merger had been dropped he wasn't unduly worried. Time was on his side. As was invisibility. Sooner or later the first deputy would slip up and Jacques would have him.

Which meant that Jacques was free to get back to his old tricks. Today, with his usual prey absent, he was making do with second best; he was standing behind Fatima Souquet and blowing cold air onto her neck. She didn't notice at first. Then she shivered. On the third exhalation, she whipped round, her ferret-like face inches from his. He yelped, jumping back in fear and only just caught his breath when her phone chirped.

He couldn't resist it. He leaned over her shoulder and saw her click on an email. It was from Jérôme Ulrich. Why would the préfet be emailing Fatima Souquet? Intrigued, he peered at the screen as she scrolled through, cursing his inability to wear glasses in his ghostly state. He'd tried but they simply fell through his ears. Therefore, it took him a while to piece it all together. In fact, it was only when he saw the words *SOS Fogas* that he began to understand.

Jacques tried to process it. Attempted to cast his mind back over the last two and a half months of acrimony, having to reassess everything he'd ever thought about the woman in front of him. It proved too much for him to cope with. And for the first time in life or death, Jacques Servat fell to the ground in a dead faint.

* * *

Chloé was over by the épicerie, handing out the last of the invitations to the circus performance in St Girons on Saturday. She'd tried to impress on everyone how important it was to attend, struggling not to blurt out the fantastic secret she was carrying. If only they knew the entertainment that lay in store for them.

She was about to go through to the shop and chat to Fabian when she sensed something and knew — thanks to the abilities handed down to her from her maternal ancestors — that she needed to turn around. She was in time to see him fall.

Rushing over to his side, she threw the rest of the invitations on the ground, giving her the pretext to bend down to what, for everyone else, was an empty patch of floor. For they couldn't see the body of her old friend sprawled across the floorboards.

'Jacques,' she murmured, as she picked up the pieces of paper. 'Are you okay?'

His head started to move and then his eyes opened and he saw her.

'Chloé.'

She could see the shape of her name on his lips, felt the draught of his words on her skin. He struggled to sit up, pulling a face at his proximity to Bernard Mirouze's backside, and Chloé giggled, knowing he was okay. Then he tapped her arm, a touch of cold, nothing more, and he pointed at Fatima Souquet.

'What about her?' muttered Chloé, standing with him, his hand still on her arm as they walked to the inglenook.

Jacques shook his head in amazement. Then he bent to the ashes of last night's fire and blew softly until the words were formed.

SOS Fogas.

He pointed at Fatima again.

'Nooooo,' breathed Chloé, head swivelling from Jacques to the first deputy's wife. 'No way!'

Jacques crossed his arms and nodded his head with resolution. Then he winked and put a finger to his lips. Chloé Morvan had garnered yet another secret. Which was just as well, she decided. Because if she unmasked Fatima Souquet as the person behind *SOS Fogas,* no one would believe her.

★ ★ ★

Up in Fogas, Pascal Souquet was having a hard time believing it himself. It didn't help that he'd consumed the better part of a bottle of whisky, his faculties not as clear as they should have been. But the evidence was there on the screen in front of him. A record of internet usage over the last three months. Nothing spectacular for the first couple of weeks, then a steady increase, until in the previous fortnight, 5GB of allowance had been used up.

On its own, he could dismiss it as his wife's sudden penchant for watching movies on her laptop. Or downloading music videos. He could explain it all away. Except for one thing. The time.

Each internet session was logged. And up until two months ago, the times were mostly mid-morning or mid-afternoon. Then, in September, his wife had turned into a night owl. One o'clock, two o'clock, the sessions short at first, until, around about the time that Pascal had started his nocturnal stakeouts, they ballooned in length, all coinciding with the timing of the posts on that blasted blog.

She'd had the house to herself, no doubt rising from the bed the minute he left to make the most of her seclusion, producing longer and longer posts with video clips and animations. No wonder she'd used up so much data.

And his computer. It wasn't the dimwit postmistress who'd hacked into it. It was his own wife, who'd simply had to switch it on. The woman he'd thought was supporting him throughout had been betraying him all along. Fortunately, most of his dealings with the mayor of Sarrat had been confined to clandestine meetings or phone calls, and the few emails Pascal had received he'd deleted. So there was a limit to how much Fatima could know. Nothing about the bears, for instance. But still, she knew enough to destroy him if she so chose.

His world already in tatters, he'd been dealt the final blow from *SOS Fogas* herself. A declaration of victory posted an hour ago, detailing the U-turn on the merger and thanking the préfet for his consideration. Seconds later, Pascal's phone had trilled into life, the initials MS flashing on the screen. With a shaking hand, the first deputy mayor had turned it off.

That was when he'd opened the drinks cabinet and pulled out the whisky, drinking straight from

433

the bottle as he assessed just how dead he was going to be if Henri Dedieu ever made the connection. *SOS Fogas* had successfully derailed the mayor of Sarrat's schemes. And he, Pascal Souquet, was married to the person who'd made that possible.

He felt sick. Not only at her deception. But at the position it placed him in.

Then, through the haze of alcohol, a sharpness of thought manifested itself. What if he did nothing? Buried this unpalatable truth he had uncovered? With the merger abandoned, *SOS Fogas* would disappear and it would become difficult for anyone to discover the truth. He could maintain the pretence that Véronique Estaque was the person behind the blog. Allow Henri to vent his wrath on her. And in the meantime, he would say nothing to his wife. Because, even when drunk, Pascal Souquet knew which way to fall. For if it transpired that Henri Dedieu wasn't able to deliver on the promises he'd made, Pascal was going to need his wife's political astuteness to get him to where he needed to be.

When he heard the key turn in the lock and her tut of disapproval as she surveyed his dishevelled drunken state, he kept his eyes closed and tried not to think of all she had cost him.

★ ★ ★

Drunk. What did she expect? Fatima stared at her husband for a few moments and then walked out of the room before her pity for him overcame her seething anger at his betrayal.

She'd warned him. When he'd first started messing with Henri Dedieu, she'd said the man was dangerous. And when Pascal had started toying with the idea of breaking Fogas apart, she'd told him it would be the death of their marriage. For Fogas was the birthplace of her maternal ancestors, a long line of women just like her, who had loved this mountain commune and finally bequeathed her a house here. The very house the Souquets had turned to when Pascal had plunged them into bankruptcy.

When she'd realised that Pascal was intent on following the path Dedieu was dictating, she'd contemplated divorce. But in the end, she'd done better than that. With help from online forums, she'd set up the means to disrupt the schemes coming out of Sarrat. And with a couple of false trails, she'd led Pascal off on the wrong scent. How many nights had he spent outside the homes of Fogas residents, convinced he was closing in on the secret? All the while allowing her free rein.

She laughed as she started to prepare the evening meal. He didn't have a clue. Even now, he was looking to the postmistress as the author of *SOS Fogas*. A fact that had led to Véronique's accident, Fatima had no doubt. While she regretted that unfortunate turn of events, she had no intention of declaring the truth. Because Fatima Souquet hadn't gone soft. She still had the driving ambition that had seen her husband propelled onto the Conseil Municipal. And she knew she still had enough energy to get him secured as mayor.

So for now, she would carry on as if nothing had happened. She would support Pascal through this, help him negotiate a way out of Henri Dedieu's clutches. Then she would start to steer him in the direction he needed to go. If he messed up again, however, she would get rid of him and do what the préfet, Jérôme Ulrich, had advised her to do in his email. To come out from behind the scenes and take her own place on the stage of local politics.

It was time that Christian Dupuy had some decent opposition to contend with.

* * *

With two babies and a steady succession of visitors, Lorna's day had been far from peaceful. But she didn't care. After a couple of hours in the neonatal unit, which the midwife had assured her was a mere precaution, the twins had been returned to her and from that moment on, nurses had made excuses to poke their heads around the door. As well as wanting to see the two Anglo-Saxon boys who had caused such a fuss on the maternity ward last night, they'd also gathered to stare at the errant husband who, rumour had it, had raced from his wife's side to attend a council meeting. Poor Paul had endured more than enough dark looks from the staff when the sound of a familiar cackle could be heard along the corridor and the weathered face of Annie Estaque appeared, accompanied by Serge, Josette, Stephanie, René, Christian and Véronique. And a bottle of champagne.

'To toast the new arrivals!' declared René. 'And to celebrate the news from Foix.'

Thanks to text messages flying between the hospital and the *salle des fêtes*, Paul and Lorna had been kept abreast of developments, including the news that Christian and Véronique were an item. As a new mother and therefore easily moved, Lorna had been reduced to tears by both announcements and thus was overjoyed to see the group gathering at the end of the bed.

'So these arrre the saviourrrs of Fogas!' said Annie, crossing the room to help herself to the baby Paul was holding.

Seeing the look of envy on Josette's face, Lorna offered up her own precious bundle and the two older women fell silent, cooing and sighing over the wrinkled faces poking out of the blankets.

'You really had no idea you were expecting twins?' asked Christian.

Lorna shook her head. 'Not a clue. It seems like the Fates didn't want me to know either. My second scan was messed up and I didn't get a photo, and my third scan was the day Chloé went missing. In all the commotion, I completely forgot. I've got an appointment for tomorrow if anyone wants it?' She shot a mischievous grin at Véronique, making the postmistress blush.

'Judging by the panic in here last night,' added Paul, 'I don't think we were the only ones in the dark. These devious little devils are going to be right at home in Fogas!'

'Have you thought of names?' asked Stephanie, handing over a bag of pains au chocolat and winning Lorna's undying affection in the process.

'We've got one.' Paul indicated the baby in Annie's arms. 'Sébastien. He arrived first so he gets the name we'd already thought of. As for him . . . ' Paul scratched his head, glancing fondly at the son that had surprised them all. 'The only other possibility we had ready was Mathilde!'

Everyone laughed but Josette fluffed up like a mother hen. 'You can't leave this darling without a name. We'll just have to put our thinking caps on and come up with something.'

'Bernard?' suggested René, earning himself a reproving look from the women.

'Or Jérôme, after our esteemed préfet?' said Serge.

'Very diplomatic, Papa!' Véronique took the baby from a reluctant Josette, marvelling at how light he was, nestled in the crook of her good arm. And how right it felt to be holding him. Perhaps . . . ? She let the thought drift. It was too soon. She didn't want to scare Christian away just as he'd plucked up the courage to approach her. She glanced up to see the farmer watching her with a smile.

'What time was he born?' she asked, to cover up the flush of emotion that simple smile had triggered.

'Seven on the dot. Just as the Angelus was sounding,' said Lorna.

'Well, that's sorted then,' said Josette. 'He entered this world on the bells of God's messenger. You should call him Gabriel.'

Lorna and Paul looked at each other and knew that their unexpected arrival had just been named.

'Gabriel it is,' said Lorna.

And Josette Servat, from that moment on, laid claim to the boy she had christened. Luckily Annie Estaque was just as smitten with young Sébastien, and as the babies were passed between the crowd of people in the room, fuss and cuddles being bestowed upon them, Lorna realised that this was what had come to her the previous evening, in the hours before her children were born: an awareness of how special Fogas was and how precious would be the childhood for any baby fortunate enough to be raised within its borders.

She lay back on the pillows and brushed away the tears that flooding the corners of her eyes, glad that in some small way she and Paul had been able to secure the future of the commune. And equally glad that they would never be short of babysitters.

24

Christian Dupuy woke up dead. He knew he was dead because there was an angel lying next to him, her hair falling across the pillow, her soft breath sweet on his cheek. And beneath the covers was a body that could only be heaven sent.

He grinned, looping a finger through an auburn lock, letting his touch slide gently down her face, down her neck, towards the swell —

'Oh no you don't!' She trapped his hand and was laughing at him. 'We don't have time. We've got a circus performance to catch.'

'It's a matinee,' he protested. 'We've got hours.'

'Yes, but I want to go to the market beforehand.'

'The market? Really?' He twisted free of her grasp and stroked the nape of her neck, his touch already making her arch backwards. 'What do you need that's so important?'

'Onions . . . ' she sighed, eyes closing. 'Some cheese . . . and . . . '

He pulled her towards him and kissed the hollow at the base of her throat, and she sighed again.

' . . . and . . . perhaps . . . I could miss it just this once . . . '

Then her eyes snapped open and she smiled a smile that made him melt.

'Christian Dupuy,' she said. 'When did you turn bad?'

★ ★ ★

The big top was back where it had been a fortnight ago, canvas sides bright against the patches of lingering snow on the ground. Inside, it was a full house, a large contingent having travelled down from Fogas. Chloé, in charge of seating, had arranged things to perfection. Serge and Annie were sitting together, next to Véronique and Christian. René and Bernard were on the row in front of them, with Josette sitting next to Chloé. Behind Chloé were Stephanie and Fabian and the rest of the invitees. The Websters had sent their apologies, Lorna and the twins due home from hospital that afternoon.

'Are you enjoying it?' Josette asked Chloé as the knife throwers jogged out of the arena, waving at the crowd.

Chloé nodded. But she was lying. She wasn't enjoying it at all. She was far too nervous. When the magician came through the curtain at the back, she knew it was time.

'I need to go to the toilet,' she whispered, turning to Maman.

'Now? The acrobats are going to be on after this.'

'I'll take her,' said Fabian, getting to his feet and holding out his hand.

'Well, be quick. It would be a shame for her to miss her father.'

Praying everything would go right, Chloé followed Fabian out of the tent.

'Good girl, Chloé,' said Alexei as she led the nervous Parisian into the caravan, the two men shaking hands. 'Now hurry back to your maman before she suspects. And remember, not a word!'

She grinned and then threw her arms around Fabian. 'Good luck,' she whispered.

His petrified face was the last thing she saw as she rushed out of the door.

★ ★ ★

'Where's Fabian?'

Chloé pulled a face, taking the seat next to her mother that the Parisian had vacated. 'He's outside talking to some cyclist from his club. Said he wasn't bothered about the acrobats.'

'Oh.' Stephanie tried to hide her disappointment. While Fabian wasn't being as distant as he had been, he still wasn't back to his usual self and she'd hoped a night out *en famille* might help him thaw a bit. Instead, he'd escaped at the first opportunity. But perhaps it was understandable given that the next act was none other than Chloé's father and Stephanie's former lover. Wondering if her complicated life would ever get any easier, she tucked Chloé's hand into hers. 'We'll just have to enjoy it without him, then.'

The lights dimmed and the spotlight focused on the back of the arena, where the Great Alexei had just emerged to thunderous applause. He bowed to the crowd and began to climb up to the platform. Chloé was about to whisper to her

442

mother that she'd been up there when she saw Maman cover her eyes with her hands.

Perhaps, considered the eleven-year-old as Alexei began his routine, the crowd gasping and Maman flinching, it was better if Maman didn't know.

★ ★ ★

Fabian was looking at himself in the mirror, unable to recognise the person staring back. What had he been thinking, taking advice from Chloé? He was insane. It was all going to go horribly wrong and he would make an idiot of himself.

The caravan door swung open and Alexei's eldest son was there, grinning, the resemblance to Chloé uncanny.

'It's time,' he said.

With a sense of dread, Fabian stood and followed him.

★ ★ ★

'Where has he got to?' murmured Stephanie, twisting in her seat to look around.

Fabian had missed all of Alexei's routine, which to be fair, she hadn't seen either, her hands clamped over her eyes for most of it. She hadn't allowed herself to think that in a few years Chloé would be up there, dangling from a rope by a big toe.

'You know what he's like when he starts talking bikes, Maman!' Chloé gave an exaggerated yawn and Stephanie laughed.

443

A drum roll silenced the crowd and then the back curtain lifted and into the spotlight came a clown riding a unicycle. Long legs in tartan trousers, enormous shoes, curly orange wig above a white painted face and a bright red nose, he teetered around the arena, gangly arms windmilling all the while, giving the impression that he wasn't quite in control. He managed a half-circuit before his flapping trouser leg caught in the wheel and he fell flat on his face. The crowd loved it, children shrieking with delight, adults laughing.

The clown pickled himself up, dusted himself off, and got back on the bike, this time cycling backwards. Reaching into his enormous coat pockets he pulled out three juggling clubs and with a dramatic flourish threw all three into the air. They spun in the bright lights, twisting and turning and then they began to fall, the clown underneath them, long arms thrashing as he tried to catch them. But he was useless. One after the other, with audible thuds, all three landed on his head.

The audience was in hysterics, Josette reaching for a tissue to wipe her eyes while René was holding his sides.

'He's funny, isn't he?' said Chloé to her mother.

Stephanie grinned. 'He's an idiot! Fabian would have loved this.'

Down below, the clown had resumed his cycling, the music slowing to a romantic number as the clown hung his head and tapped his heart.

'Ahhhhh,' sighed the crowd, sympathising with

444

his love-struck state.

Then he reached into his baggy coat and pulled out a bunch of fake flowers.

'Oooh!' said the audience.

He reached into another pocket and pulled out a giant-sized engagement ring, plastic diamond catching the lights.

'Awwwww,' was the response.

And when he jumped off the unicycle and went down on one knee, laughter rang around the big top. The clown was about to propose.

Like everyone else, Stephanie was transfixed by the thin figure looking so vulnerable down in the arena. She watched him reach into his coat a final time to pull out a banner, which, with a flick of a bony wrist, he unfurled.

It was upside down.

More laughter as the flustered clown realised his mistake and hastily turned it the right way, knocking his hat off in the process. Then a spotlight centred on the sign.

Stephanie, I'll always be your clown. Will you marry me?

The crowd caught on fast. This was real. Laughter turned to the buzz of anticipation, people twisting and turning to see who the recipient was. In the collection of seats allocated to Fogas residents, there was a dawning comprehension.

'Is that — ?' asked Véronique, trying to see beyond the painted face.

'It can't be!' exclaimed Josette.

'It is! I'd know that lanky frame anywhere,' said Serge.

And they all turned to see Stephanie, white

faced, hand to her mouth, staring at the clown.

How had she not known? That gait. The long limbs. The clumsiness! She felt her pulse racing, felt the weight of his gaze across the rows of seats.

She stood, a spotlight picking her out and sending the crowd into a frenzy, and even across the distance she could sense his anxiety, that sweet, defenceless nature the part of him that had stolen her heart.

'Yes!' she shouted, and squeezing past an ecstatic Chloé, she started running, taking the steps two at a time as she raced towards the arena.

★   ★   ★

Fabian couldn't believe it. She was hurtling towards him, red hair flying, bracelets jingling, and in one bound she was into the arena and in his arms, the audience all on their feet.

'Yes, yes, yes,' she whispered as he swung her around, his wig falling off and his feet tangling in the ridiculous shoes. He almost fell over, which had everyone laughing again.

Heart fit to burst, he looked out across the rows of faces to where the spotlight was still resting at the back, highlighting Chloé who was standing on her seat to see over the adults. She was crying, Josette next to her no better, tissue at her eyes.

She'd been right, that young girl who was wiser than he'd ever be. Be yourself, she'd said. And what was more natural for him than being a fool?

Scooping Stephanie up in his arms, he bowed to the crowd and made his exit, carrying his bride-to-be. He was the happiest clown alive.

★　★　★

She said yes!
Jacques had spent the entire afternoon staring at the mobile Chloé had left on the bar, willing it to tell him good news. Any news. Now, a couple of seconds after it vibrated loudly and scared the life out of him, the screen carried the words he'd been hoping to see.

She'd said yes. Fabian had finally asked her and she'd accepted.

He shook his head in amazement, his joy for his nephew equalled by his puzzled wonder that Fabian had managed to capture the exotic Stephanie Morvan. He stood there, eyes fixed on the phone well after the screen had dimmed and the text had disappeared, taking it all in.

Eager to know the details, when Josette returned much later he made her recount the story again and again, Josette happy to do so, crying each time she got to the end. She wasn't the only one. Jacques was surprised to note the sting of tears in his eyes and a familiar tightness in his throat whenever she reached the bit about Stephanie running down the stairs, hair flying as she leaped into Fabian's arms. Being an Ariègeois male, the old ghost blamed his symptoms on the smoky fire.

Midnight fast approached and with Josette heading wearily but happily to bed, Jacques decided that he too would call it a day. He was tired, head still sore, his fainting fit the other day unforgiving even to a ghost. He rubbed the lump that had formed beneath his white hair and stared out at the dark street. With everything resolved, there would be no need to keep watch tonight. *SOS Fogas* would be sleeping. Pascal would be sleeping next to her. And tomorrow morning the people of Fogas would wake up and know that their commune was safe. For now. Because Jacques was no idiot. He knew a compromise when he saw one. Which is what the préfet had offered them.

Twelve months to get their act together and make Fogas secure. Could they do it? Did Serge Papon have the stomach to see it through? Jacques wasn't sure. But time enough to start worrying tomorrow. Tonight he intended to sleep soundly.

He turned from the window just as the headlights of a car swept across the ceiling.

What now?

Through the glass he could make out a vehicle coming towards him. Small. Box shaped. And with a distinctive rattle. A Panda 4×4. It approached the bar and in the light from the street lamp he saw Christian Dupuy at the wheel, a broad smile across his face. Jacques didn't need to watch the car turn. He knew where the farmer was going. The old school.

With a satisfied sigh, Jacques crossed to the inglenook. He was already half-asleep by the time the farmer mounted the outside steps of Véronique's apartment. As Christian stepped across the threshold and lifted the postmistress into his arms, Jacques' head tipped back against the sooty stones. And when the lovers went giggling into the bedroom, the ghost fell into the deepest of sleeps, a contented smile on his face. Fogas was finally at peace.

Epilogue

Snow. High up on a mountain on the Spanish side of the Pyrenees, bright moonlight was reflecting off the white ground, holding back the darkness. Stark against the bleached scenery, the broad figure of a man could be seen, black hair and bronzed face vivid in the silvery light. Breath frosting in the night air, he stared across at the jagged edges before him.

Beyond those mountains lay France. And Fogas. And for him, revenge.

He'd known when he saw the photo. That man with the gun. That ring with the boar's head. It was the final piece of the puzzle that he'd been trying to decipher over the last five months. And as the judicial system had seen fit to drop the prosecution over the dead bear, he knew what he had to do next.

Arnaud Petit swung his rucksack onto his shoulder and turned towards the refuge where he would stay the night. Then tomorrow he would head back down to the Catalan village where he'd been living. He'd work the winter and when the worst of the snow was gone, he would return and cross the border to make his way to the small commune in the Ariège that had been the closest thing to home he'd ever known.

He had business to conclude there and until it was finished, Fogas wasn't safe.

Acknowledgements

As you will have gathered from the tale within these pages, it takes many hands to create a *Fête*. And so it was with this book. As always, I have had the benefit of sage advice — the utilisation of which is purely down to me should any faults be found — and invaluable assistance along the way. In return for their contribution to the Fogas festivities, I owe the following a slice of *croustade aux myrtilles* and a glass of Bernard's freshly pressed apple juice:

The wonderful team at Heslop & Platt, experts in French law who took my bizarre questions about divorce seriously; Catherine Leone from the *Association des Maires Ruraux de France* who knows everything there is to know about municipal councils in rural France; Saskia Bayne for giving me an insight into the life of a *collège* student in Seix; Anita Waldock, a good friend who just happens to have been hypnotised . . . ; Ashley Whaites, for not laughing at my rugby queries; Kevin Jack, a forensic expert who is now wishing he hadn't known me at school; Mike and Moira Hosking from the Auberge de l'Arac for being such generous hosts; the charming Bruno and Sylvia Lamirand from *L'Épicerie du Château* in Seix — if you want to know about saucisson, Bruno is your man!; Renée Palous, postmistress extraordinaire and a good sport to boot; my cousin, Martin Mellett, for his tireless championing of my work despite not being on commission; Ellen McMaster, whose editing of the first draft always proves fruitful; Claire Jones and Brenda Stickland for being avid first readers and lovers of Fogas; my parents, Mícheál and Ellen, for their endless enthusiasm; the team at Hodder — it's so good to have you in my corner, especially Francesca, an amazing editor and sharer of delicious recipes; my exceptional agent, Oli, for interspersing book stuff with football; and finally, always finally, Mark — thanks for making life one long *fête*.

THE FRENCH POSTMISTRESS

Julia Stagg

When her post office burns down, postmistress Veronique starts lobbying for its replacement. But her fellow residents of the small commune of Fogas in the French Pyrenees are too preoccupied to rally to her cause. Mayor Serge Papon, overwhelmed by grief at the death of his wife, has lost his *joie de vivre* and all taste for village politics (and croissants), and it seems as though deputy mayor Christian (whose *tendresse* for Veronique makes him her usual champion) will soon be saying *au revoir* to the mountain community. Add to this a controversial government initiative to reintroduce bears to the area, and soon the inhabitants are at loggerheads, threatening the progress of the sacred Tour de France and the very existence of Fogas itself.